To Claudia

Black Hole

Christian Hatton

Best wishes
Christian Hatton

Copyright © Christian Hatton 2005-2010. All rights reserved.

First published 2010.

ISBN: 978-1-4457-5616-5

PART ONE

'No Ordinary Mission'

ONE

Friday, 31st January 2048. Westminster, London. 0829 Hrs.

It was a bitterly cold winter morning and Steve Morrissey entered the Peterson building, Whitehall's newest addition which was home of the Department for Culture Media and Sport. He walked along the poorly heated corridor and entered the large lift which would take him up to the broadcasting suite. Two men stood bickering about the F.A. cup match score between Fulham and Chelsea. Simpkins, an office junior from personnel, argued that match fixing had taken place, owing to the Prime Minister's alleged shares in Fulham. With a sneer, Steve alighted and entered his office. On his modest desk lay a memo from the Media Secretary, outlining his tasks for the day. With a curse, he left his office and entered the door to the broadcasting suite.

The broadcasting suite had recently opened, relieving Television Centre of its duties a month before. The room was filled with old BBC apparatus and Steve's first task was to decide which items were worth keeping and which were destined for the garbage shoot. He picked up a dusty boom mic, which carried the BBC's logo along the side. His instructions stated that any logo in excess of five square inches rendered the object unusable. With a sigh, he tossed the microphone into the shoot, where it made a resounding echo. He caught sight of an old BBC News television camera that carried a logo far larger than the required area. A feeling of resentment at the government's avarice swept through him as he studied the state-of-the-art camera. However, his orders were clear, so he lifted it onto his shoulder and tipped it into the drafty shoot. He noticed a scrapbook on the water dispenser. He picked it up and blew the cover clear of dust. "Loving Memories of BBC2. 1964-2020." ran the title. He carefully turned the dog-eared pages, containing cut-outs from long-defunct national newspapers charting the channel's rise to glory and some of the cutting-edge documentaries which had enchanted Steve's youthful mind shortly before it went off air. Programmes about dinosaurs, ancient civilisations and coverage of the Iraq War had opened his eyes up to the rich world of television; this idealistic vision had soon been squashed during the government's rebranding campaign. News was the only mode of television that monopolised the airways now. All of the culturally rich digital television channels were either blocked from the public domain or rebranded under the Public Service Television franchise.

Suddenly a long, dark shadow was cast over him and in walked in the media secretary, Andrew Walsh. His arms were folded tightly and his long, bony face had an air of disappointment.

'Come along, Morrissey, you know better than to snoop about in here.' he joked, tossing the book down the shoot.
Steve frowned 'Is there not anyone more junior than I who could do this? I don't remember "janitor" being in my job description.'
Walsh threw his head back in laughter.
'Check your contract and you'll find listed under number 10 "any other duties."'
Steve looked at him dismissively.
'Come now, Morrissey. If you want to further yourself in this game, then you must show a little sportsmanship! I'm asking you to toss away a few pieces of bric-a-brac, not repaint the Sistine Chapel!'
He looked around.
'How are you getting on, anyhow?'
Steve shrugged 'I think it's a waste to just discard valuable pieces of equipment.'
'But you're missing the point, old bean!' exclaimed Walsh; grabbing Steve's arms 'Can't you smell that? That newly laid carpet and newly painted walls heralds the start of great things to come! Why concern yourself with the failure of past ventures like the BBC?'
Steve did not respond, but appeared unconvinced by his boss's optimism.
'What's next on your list?' asked Walsh, snatching the piece of paper.
'To liaise with the newsroom regarding the six o'clock bulletin.' breathed Steve.
'Ah yes! Your next job is to go through to the newsroom and go through step-by-step the coverage regarding the reoccupation of Basra!'
Steve took a handkerchief from his pocket and dabbed his forehead.
'Well, don't just stand there like a lemon, there's work to be done!' cheered Walsh, leaving the room.

      Steve entered the newsroom with trepidation. The room had the area of four football pitches and enough staff to man a small army. He approached Harry Scott, a semi-retired VT editor who used a walking stick, which stood at a forty-five degree angle and acted like a third leg. His brow was furrowed deeply as he studied a plasma screen which displayed a freeze-frame image of a news report.
'What seems to be the trouble here?' puffed Steve.
Scott continued to squint at the screen.
'I was just thinking, there's no way we'll convince the eggheads at the Financial Times that Basra is draining the country.'
Steve winced 'Why would you say that? We acquired the FT last month.'
'Well this particular piece of footage appears very amateurish.' Scott replied.
Steve played the footage and studied it carefully. It contained an aerial view of what purported to be Basra, but could have been Pinewood. The

ramshackle buildings appeared much the same as BBC archive footage of the Iraq War in 2003.

'Then use your initiative and get onto the MoD and ask them to provide us with adequate footage and stop wasting my time.' he raged, throwing a pile of papers in his face.

He walked around the VT area and entered the meeting room. He swiftly lowered the Venetian blinds and took his place around the table.

'What do you have for me?' he asked the network's producer.

The producer was a sensitive young woman who was always eager to please. She had a small, delicate face framed with baby-blonde hair and large blue eyes, which gave her an innocent quality.

She steeled herself.

'Well, Mr Morrissey, we have been hard at work all week, piecing together the footage…'

'You've wasted your time.' he interjected.

'Oh.' she gasped, her eyes losing their sparkle.

'I have just told Harry that his footage is inadequate.'

He looked her up and down with a frown.

'If your past ventures are anything to go by, then I'm not holding out much hope for what you were about to show me.'

'Ah.' she sighed.

'You must work quickly with Harry to obtain the updated footage from the MoD; I would set yourself no more than two hours as you are woefully behind schedule.'

He straightened his tie smugly.

'Anyway, you must listen carefully to what I have to say, as time is of the essence.'

She nodded ardently and drew her cherry red lips into a smile.

'The orders from above are that tonight's six o'clock news bulletin must point towards Iraq in explaining the hike in prices.' he explained.

'Of course, Mr Morrissey, what other possible reason could there be?' she asked, biting a pen which carried the BBC logo.

'None, of course.' he huffed.

He removed the pen from her mouth and tossed it into the waste paper basket.

'Here…'

He handed her a new pen, displaying the Public Service Television logo.

'I want you to talk with whichever anchor is due on tonight and compose an autocue which will deliver a positive spin on the government's handling of the crisis but will largely emphasise the massive impact oil incineration by insurgents is having on our economy…'

He glared at her 'Are you writing this down?'

She scrabbled around for paper and pulled out a notepad with the BBC logo on the cover. She gave an apologetic cough and tore it off.
'Begin the bulletin by highlighting the ongoing struggle between allied forces in Basra and the Ba'ath Party loyalists. When I watch the bulletin this evening, I want to see coverage of burning oilfields and hate campaigns focused on British forces. I've been onto the MoD already and we've agreed to pit the death toll of British troops at one hundred and ninety-seven, following a series of suicide bomb attacks.'
'That many? How awful!' she exclaimed, cupping her mouth in astonishment.
Steve frowned 'How long have you been in the job?'
'Almost a year now!' she beamed proudly.
'Well you've got a lot to learn about the workings of this place; it's not for the fainthearted.'
She touched her hair coyly.
He continued 'Anyway, I want to see burning oilfields, closely followed by coverage of the cash strapped NHS, making clear reference to the link between the two. Play on the heartstrings of the public and use graphic words which those in mourning can relate to; I know very few people who have neither been involved in the conflict nor known someone who is bereaved as a result.'
'But I also know a lot of people who object to the reoccupation of Basra, on the grounds that there was no evidence of any Ba'ath Party loyalists in the region. People I've spoken to say that it's just political mumbo-jumbo and a way for the government to enrich itself.' she blurted without stopping to take a breath.
Steve scowled at her.
'Have you finished?'
She nodded frantically, her bob hairdo dancing as she did so.
'Then let me tell you that you should not listen to careless, idle pub talk from your so-called friends, who will ensure that your job comes to an abrupt end if you carry on listening to them.' he yelled.
She stood like a frightened cat.
'Did you get everything down on paper?' he asked.
She swallowed 'Err...I got as far as "the ongoing struggle between Ba'ath Party loyalists and allied forces..."'

***

Steve sank a double whiskey in the bar on the ground floor and told the young man to keep them coming. He opened a copy of the Financial Times and glared at the headline: "British Forces rescue NHS".
'That's a funny headline-how can the army rescue the NHS? It just doesn't make sense to me.' smiled the bartender, polishing a pint glass.
Steve raised his bloodshot eyes up to the man.

'Look, you're paid to keep my glass full, not to pollute my airways with your inane take on things.'

He studied the young man's face more closely.

'Are you even twenty-five?' Steve asked him.

'What?' asked the man.

'You heard me.' Steve retorted.

'I'm over twenty-one; what are you getting at?'

'As of last Tuesday, anyone buying or serving alcohol must be over the age of twenty-five. Look, see for yourself…'

Steve handed the bartender the newspaper. The young man stared at the article aghast.

'How old are you anyway?' Steve asked.

'I'm twenty-two next Monday!' the man exclaimed.

Steve grinned 'Then it looks like you're going to have to find yourself a new job! It's okay, you can keep the paper.'

'Oh stop bullying the poor boy, Steve.' came a voice from behind him.

He swung around on his seat; it was Veronica Blunt from Human Resources.

'Ah, Veronica!' he exclaimed, breathing fumes into her face.

'You should have told this poor boy about the change in the law!'

Veronica gave the bartender an apologetic smile.

'Ignore Mr grumpy face here; the law makes an exception to those over twenty-one who are already employed in a licensed outlet. Here, have a drink on me.'

She handed over her multicard. Multicards were multimedia devices that resembled credit cards and were used for making calls and SMS messaging as well as a means of payment. Cash had been phased out gradually since the government came to power four years before.

'That's very kind of you. I'll just have a coke.'

Veronica peered at the lager pumps and noticed that the LCD price tags were not set at one particular price, but changed every minute or so.

'That's strange, I thought prices remained static until the close of business at six?' she asked.

'Blame the Iraq conflict.' breathed Steve.

'Keep your smelly breath to yourself, thank you very much.' snapped Veronica.

'What do you want, anyway?' Steve huffed, sinking another double.

Veronica gave him a scowl.

'What makes you think I've come all the way down here just to see *you*?' Steve turned his back to her.

'I've got a bone to pick with you.' she declared, waving her stirring rod in front of him.

'So you *have* come all the way down here to see me then?' he sneered.

'What's this I hear about you firing Trudy the network's junior producer?' she demanded.
'Huh; she was nothing but a thorn in my side from day one.' he scoffed.
Veronica got off from her stool and leered over him.
'Tell me something, do you get some sort of a sick kick from ruining people's livelihoods?'
Steve recoiled 'I can't afford to have lightweights working in such a high profile position.'
Veronica threw her head back and smirked.
'So that's what it's about? It's about you and how your boss sees you!'
'I don't know what you mean.' he muttered.
'You know full well what I mean! You bully this poor young man who struggles to provide for his family…'
'He has a family to provide for? Huh! He's barely out of short trousers!' he laughed, looking the bartender up and down.
'Well it's true, despite what the likes of you think.' she said starkly 'And there's Trudy, not the most gifted producer to have walked the earth, I grant you. But she was hardworking and eager to learn to become better and let's not forget she was a junior.'
Steve placed his glass down onto the cardboard mat gently.
'What's this really about, Steve?' she asked tentatively, leaning on the bar.
Steve shuffled away from her.
'Nothing.'
'Don't give me that Steven Geoffrey Morrissey!' she joked, taking his hand 'Seriously now, what is it?'
Steve pulled his hand free and took a deep breath and looked at the bartender.
'Do you think I could I have another, please?'
The young man nodded with a smile and refilled the glass. No sooner had the drink landed in his glass, than he polished it off.
He gave Veronica a sideward glance.
'I feel that sometimes I'm not being listened to, I guess.' he sucked in a deep breath 'I just want to get on in life. I feel like I'm stuck in limbo: not working in a lowly job, but equally not in a ministerial role.'
Veronica placed her arm around him.
'But do you think by upsetting everyone who crosses you is the correct way to show the Prime Minister what you're capable of?'
He shook his head 'Probably not.'
'I know just the thing that will cheer you up; there's a party at Chequers at eight.' she smiled.
'I'm not really in the mood, thanks all the same.' he retorted.

***

    Steve arrived fashionably late at a quarter to nine that evening. He had not been told that the party was a masquerade in honour of Harriet Dawson, the Prime Minister's wife's twenty-seventh birthday. The club had been transformed into a Hawaiian beach hut. Potted palm trees which had multicoloured lights entwined among the leaves stood here and there; Hawaiian guitars hung from the walls and Hawaiian music played through the P.A. system. Garden lamps that were placed on each of the tables lit the club, giving the place a carnival mood.
Everyone, apart from Steve, was either dressed in a grass skirt and bikini tops or in garish shirts and shorts with their faces covered by a small mask. The Prime Minister's wife approached him with a broad smile. She was a tall, slender woman with pale skin and fiery red hair. The combination of her mask's creased brow and her wide smile gave her a menacing appearance.
'Can you guess who she is?' asked another woman.
Steve rolled his eyes in boredom.
'Well the ginger hair and Cheshire cat grin kind of gives it away.'
He strode past the two women with his nose raised, leaving them aghast. He entered the bar area and sat in the gloom of the ambient lighting. He picked up a cocktail and sipped the rum and coke through the florescent pink straw. Veronica approached him, wearing a grass skirt and a coconut-cupped bra.
'You look ridiculous.' he snorted.
'Gosh, you really do know how to flatter a girl.' she snapped.
He looked at her more closely.
'The skirt makes your legs look fat, but then I suppose at least the bra hides your modest pair of spaniel's ears.'
'You're going to be wearing my pina colada in a minute.'
She glared at his tuxedo.
'Anyway, you look as if you were invited to a black tie party and that you're about to faint beneath that fourteen inch collar.'
'That's because somebody didn't tell me it was a themed evening.' he snarled into his cocktail.
'That's just as well; you would look like a dead goldfish in anything less than what you're wearing.' she laughed.
'How do you know that? You haven't seen me naked.' he remarked.
'Oh give me time.' she grinned 'A few more of those and you'll be anybody's. Besides, I've heard a lot of tales about your odd nocturnal habits.'
'Meaning?' he demanded, allowing the straw to drop from his mouth.

'Oh let's just say that you're not quite the James Bond you'd have us all believe you are. I'll leave you with that thought.' she smiled, walking in the direction of a handsome Latino man.

Steve gulped down his cocktail and was about to go after her for an explanation, when the Prime Minister's wife approached him removing her mask. Steve left his seat.
'Stay where you are.' insisted Harriet.
'But I was on my way to the loo…' said Steve.
'I want to talk with you first.' she said, taking Veronica's place at the table. Steve resumed his place.
'What's so urgent that it can't wait a minute or two?'
'I want to know why every time we meet you make it your business to act like a brat. Have I done anything that has offended you? Perhaps you think that my marriage to Geoffrey is a sham?'
'I never said that, although I'm sure he didn't marry you for your superior intellect, but then again I'm sure you didn't marry him for his dazzling looks.'
Harriet stiffened 'Look, it's obvious that you have a problem with me in some capacity, but you'd do well to remember that I have a lot of kudos by virtue of being married to the Prime Minister, in spite of what you think of me.'
Steve straightened his bowtie.
'I don't have a particular problem with you; it's more the company you keep.'
A look of puzzlement came over Harriet's face.
'You know what I think of Geoffrey; he's running this country into the ground.' Steve declared.
'My husband's policies are not my business; I'm merely something to hang off his arm at functions such as this.'
'Then where is he now?' asked Steve, looking around.
Harriet's head bowed.
'Away on some foreign summit.'
Steve's face broke into laughter.
'What?' she asked, incredulously.
'I can tell that you don't believe that yourself, so don't bother trying to convince me!'
Harriet looked away.
'Look, don't you think you owe it to yourself to claw back some self-respect? Why allow a creep like that make a fool of you.' he smiled.
'Just what are you saying?' she asked, bending her head in curiosity.
Steve took a champagne flute from the passing trolley.
'Oh, I forgot to ask if you wanted one.'
'Typical.' she huffed.

'Anyway, I propose that we have a heart-to-heart…for the good of the country. Let's call it Geoffrey's penance.' Steve announced.
'I still don't follow…forgive me for being dense.' she confessed.
Steve sipped his champagne.
'I'm sure you would like the opportunity to be more than some airhead. You strike me as being someone whose intelligence has yet to be truly discovered; I'm here to explore it.'
'Ok…' she nodded with bewilderment.
'Is there somewhere private we can go?' he asked.

They entered the suite that Harriet and the Prime Minister had under lease. They sat on the chesterfield settee, where Harriet sat awkwardly. Steve poured himself a glass of whiskey into an expensive looking crystal glass without being invited to.
'Have you not got anything with a bit less bite?' he coughed.
'I don't make a habit of allowing strange men into my room, you know.' she announced.
'That's not what I've heard.' he muttered under his breath.
'What did you want to ask me?' she breathed.
'Let's start off with a few simple questions, shall we?'
She nodded reluctantly.
'What are Geoffrey's plans for PST?' he asked.
'Like I said, my husband's policy making is none of my business.'
'I'm not asking you to divulge any state secrets; I just want to know how far he's prepared to take the network's news coverage. He's already forced ITV into administration and nationalised every other British television network and changed them exclusively into news channels.'
Harriet offered him a cigarette; he took two. He placed one in his pocket and held the other up for her to light.
'So?' he demanded, through a cloud of smoke.
She drew from her cigarette sharply.
'He mentioned something about removing Sky and Virgin packages from public viewing in the UK.'
'I bet the old fool hasn't considered the financial implications of such a reckless act.' he scoffed.
'He's certainly considered that side of things; he plans to privatise the NHS by 2057.' she disclosed.
Steve dropped his glass.
'Damn.' he cursed.
'Don't worry, the cleaners here are very good.'
'I bet they are, especially if he's using public money to pay for them.' he looked at her solemnly 'How can you be certain that's what he plans to do?'

'I may well be an airhead, but airheads have ears like the rest of you.' she said with a smile.
He managed to draw a brief smile 'Just how much do you know of Geoffrey's plans for the country?'
'Enough to know that the future isn't quite as rosy as he's telling everyone.' she gave him a sincere look 'He has big plans for you too.'
'Me? What sort of plans?' he asked, sitting up.
'Plans which will make you realise your potential.'
'How so?' he asked.
She got up 'Would you allow an airhead, such as I, to make a suggestion? Keep your enemies close by. You're interested in saving the country, aren't you?'
'In so far as I can.' he nodded.
'Then accept any offer which comes your way, in order for you to gain insight into what he has planned for the country.'
'I am just a lowly civil servant, nothing more.' he said dismissively.
'The little I know of politics tells me that there is no such thing as a lowly civil servant; just a put-upon one.'
'I thank you for your information; that will be all.' he said and walked towards the door.
'All? Is that it? Do I not at least get a nightcap?'
'I'm sure there are people downstairs wondering where I am. Happy birthday by the way.' he called back, opening the door.
'Get back here this instant! I don't think you quite realise to whom you are talking! You can't just waltz in here, extract information and waltz back out.'
He turned back at her 'What do you want me to do, break into song?'
She approached him and planted a kiss on his lips.
'No, I have something quite different in mind.'
    She led him by the hand towards the four-poster bed which was draped in satin linen and pink cushions. Harriet sat upon the bed, Steve slowly joined her. She turned her back to him and lifted her auburn hair clear off her delicate neck. She smelled of subtle perfume, which invoked feelings of arousal within him. She turned to face him and he looked into her grey eyes as she loosened his tie.
'Perhaps the rumours about you are true.' she said.
'What?' he asked, jumping from the bed.
'What's the matter? It's not your first time is it?' she laughed.
'No. Has it occurred to you I might not be excited by such an ugly woman? I think you and the Prime Minister are perfect for each other.' he exclaimed, reaching for his trousers.

TWO

Saturday, 1st February 2048. Belgravia, London. 0829 Hrs.

The heavy snowfall that had fallen the previous night covered the roads of central London, despite the best efforts of the council to clear it. Steve drove his car cautiously along the hostile roads of Belgravia, turning into the filling station at the corner of Eccleston Street. The LED digits on the price board, which were usually updated every ten seconds, remained static for the first time in five years. The digits for diesel were stuck at £8 per litre. This was an all time high; the average price at nine a.m. on a Sunday morning was £5 per litre. With a smirk, he drove to the vacant pump on the far side. He got out hurriedly and took the hose from the pump and inserted it into the filling entry. As the price digits increased on the pump, he gritted his teeth until he had filled twenty litres, costing £160 as opposed to the usual £100. As he replaced the hose, he caught sight of two youths, quite obviously not from that part of London, sitting on the grass verge at the edge of the filling station. The boy was around the age of fourteen, dressed in a tracksuit with sunken eyes that stared at Steve brazenly. The girl, who appeared slightly older, was heavily pregnant and dressed inappropriately for the harsh weather. She gave Steve a doe-eyed expression and after a brief stare, asked:
'Excuse me chap, we're cold and hungry and we don't live nowhere. Could you spare us a few quid?'
Steve gave them a disdainful look 'Have you got a card reader?'
'No sir.' replied the girl.
'Then how am I supposed to give you any money?' he snapped. 'Take a good look at that.' he demanded, pointing to the car. 'If I find so much as a fingerprint on it when I come out, I'll know who's responsible, understand?'
The youths both nodded despondently.
He turned to enter the forecourt shop. The plasma screen above the counter dominated the entire wall. As Steve reached down to the chilled cabinet to pick up a litre of milk, he noticed that the shop assistant was glued to the news programme. The news anchor, a young woman of around twenty-five, wearing a tight-fitting trouser suit and a comical grin, spoke to the viewer using an overly jubilant tone:
'This is Public Service News, broadcasting on channel 945 on the national transmitters of the Public Service Television Authority! If you've just joined us, we have been covering the story of the month! That is, the hike in oil prices across Britain. And the reason? Well, growing hostilities in the Middle East between the Ba'ath resistance and allied forces have led to widespread arson attacks on the nation's oilfields...'

The shop assistant glanced at Steve and gave him a shrug.

'I'm sorry to have to say that I really don't know *what* to think of it all really. I mean, I find it hard to work out quite how the attack on a few oilfields could lead to such price hikes.' said the man.

Steve scoffed coldly without acknowledging the man's opinion. 'Pump four.'

The assistant took his multicard and inserted it into the reader in front of the desk.

Steve walked back across to his car. He watched the two youths amble away from the grass verge looking mournful. He remembered what Veronica said to him about his rudeness and ran to catch them up to offer them a sandwich or maybe a coffee each from the shop. However, by the time the traffic had cleared for him to cross the road, they had disappeared out of sight. Without any further thought, he clambered into the car and drove slowly out of the forecourt.

Steve's New Year's resolution was to give up smoking altogether, but the last twenty-four hours had proven stressful and so he felt across to his overcoat which was sprawled out on the passenger seat and reached for the packet of cigarettes which he kept for "emergencies". He fumbled around with his free hand and snatched the crumpled packet. "UK DUTY PAID" had recently replaced the old government health warnings on the front of the packet. He took one out and wrestled with the lighter.

At thirty years of age, his handsome complexion had not yet been marred by the heavy indulgences of cigarettes and alcohol as well as other vices. He was tall, of medium build with a fresh face which held large light blue eyes and was crowned by raven hair which he wore short. His forlorn looking face told a story of a man whose life was incomplete, despite being in a reasonably paid job and living in an exclusive part of London. His face creased further as he noticed the chaos ahead:

'What the bloody hell's going on *now*?' he cursed as he joined a long queue of traffic. 'I'm not going to stand for this...'

He threw the gear stick into first and mounted the curb, driving along the edge of the empty pavement until the road forked into Belgrave Square, where he rejoined the road, turning left into Pont Street. When he reached St Martin's Avenue, he drove to his parking space and noticed it was occupied. Cursing, he swung the steering wheel quickly to the right and parked parallel to the impostor's car. He slammed the door shut and marched onto the pavement, almost losing his footing on the snow. Looking straight ahead towards his house, he spied a familiar face standing on his porch.

'Veronica. So you're the one blocking my space. Could you kindly move that old tin can so that I can park outside *my* house?' he flared.

She raised her eyebrows and folded her arms. 'Don't let's get our knickers in a twist, Steve. You know how much I hate a man who's petty over such trivial things.'

'What do you want anyway?' he snapped.

She gave him a wry glance 'You're really quite the charmer, aren't you?'

She produced a pair of underpants and held them up to the sun.

'Yours I believe?' she asked.

Steve swallowed hard and looked away.

'Kindly put those down.' he demanded.

She tossed them onto his face.

'Harriet Dawson asked me to return these to you. Good night was it?' she smirked as she descended the steps cautiously 'Really Steve-if you're to keep attending these parties, you must try to act with a bit more gratitude.' She opened her car door 'Oh and one last thing, Harriet told me to tell you that if you want to collect the rest of your belongings, they're round at her place.'

'Her place?' he exclaimed.

'Yes. And from what I gather, her husband's back this weekend. Toodle pip!'

With a wave, she edged out of the tiny gap between the cars and zoomed off down the avenue. Letting out a groan, Steve turned to go inside.

  The house was an early twenty-first century mock-Victorian three-story house, which had retained its period exterior throughout the decades. The single glazed lattice windows (although changed many times) were never replaced by double glazing and slatted wooden shutters framed them. The hallway ran for twenty meters until it met the kitchen. The chequered floor in the hallway always gave off a sweet rosy scent, which was the unique blend of cleaning mixtures, which Martha the cleaner would apply early every morning long before Steve arose. The staircase to the left was grandiose in style and generous in width. Six large oil portraits of previous occupants hung on the wall leading up to the first floor. Like Steve, all of the previous occupants (there had been far more than six) had been employed in one government capacity or other. The most famous resident and Steve's favourite, was Sir Alfred Bletchley, a womaniser who had fathered many children by three mistresses outside of his marriage. The portrait portrayed him as a goodtime man; plump faced with a large smile holding a glass of champagne.

  Steve turned right and entered the smaller sitting room. This room was no larger than 400 square feet, but because it was the warmest and most comfortable room in the house, he spent most of the time in there. There was not much inside, apart from a large fireplace with a coal fire; a black leather sofa at either end of the room and a sixty inch plasma screen mounted above the mantelpiece. He looked to his left and onto the mantelpiece which contained an old early twentieth century clock, which chimed every hour, with an envelope and a photograph of his mother tucked behind it. He reached for the old photograph and held the tiny picture fondly. It had become rare to possess pictures on photographic paper, since nowadays images were recorded either on ordinary paper or stored on multicards or plasma screens. The edges of the photograph were dog-eared and the reverse side had yellowed with age, but Steve found this to be a quaint detail. The picture showed his mother on her twenty-first birthday, it was the only visual memento he had of her. She was a tall, slender woman with Steve's bright blue eyes and dark wavy hair. Her face told a story of optimism for life ahead; not yet strained by the drudgery of married life. He placed it back behind the clock with a sigh.

There came a knock from the front door. He cursed to himself and got up from the chair and walked to the door. He opened it, allowing the cold air to rush in; there was nobody there, except for an elderly man passing by with his dog. He threw the door closed and noticed an envelope on the doormat. He took out his letter opener and removed the headed letter, which ran:

Mr Morrissey,
You are required on urgent business by the Prime Minister. Please make today (Saturday 1st February) available for a meeting that will take place at midday at Number Ten. A chauffeur will be sent for you so please ensure that you are at home.
Regards
Mrs A. Fontaine.

Steve took a deep breath, as he recalled the previous night's fracas with Harriet. He had already been stunned by Veronica's knowledge of the brief liaison. If Veronica knew of a piece of gossip, he thought, then the chances were it would be all around Westminster by now. He felt that, given the choice, he would rather people were laughing at his impotence than any speculation of an affair with the Prime Minister's wife. He felt sure that the letter was a summons to his office for an explanation; termination of his contract or perhaps worse. He lowered his trembling hand and returned to the living room to pour himself a large whiskey.

***

The car came to rest at the entrance to Downing Street. The chauffeur produced his pass to the police officer that waved them in. The car continued slowly for a few more metres until it reached the black bricked residence of the Prime Minister. The chauffeur alighted, walking around the car to open Steve's door. Getting out, he felt the bitterly cold winter wind find its way down his back.

The Prime Minister sat in the entrance hall. He sat slouched on the black hooded chair beneath the portrait of Sir George Downing. Dawson was a tall, lanky man in his early sixties. His hair was silver and arranged in a Julius Caesar style, which capped his angular face. Steve could make out a troubled look behind Dawson's rimless glasses, which made him all the more anxious.

'Morrissey?' the Prime Minister squeaked. 'I've been expecting you.' he got to his feet slowly 'Oh! And by the way, I saw the news this morning. Marvellous job, dear boy! Come, we have urgent business to discuss…'

Steve followed the Prime Minister into the Cabinet Room, where eight officials; five or six of whom were familiar to him met them. He continued behind the Prime Minister as he announced:

'We're using this room quite improperly. However, these are no ordinary circumstances!' Dawson giggled. 'This motley crew…no, no! I jest! They're quite tame really…*most* of them!' he grinned, peering down at the Foreign Secretary. 'No…these good people…whom I'm sure you recognise already…are the Joint Intelligence Committee.'

'Good morning.' they all announced.

Steve nodded politely, forcing a smile.

The Prime Minister glared at him 'I say! Do cheer up young man! I'm not exactly overly thrilled to be in here either you know. Don't you think I've other things to be getting on with on a Saturday afternoon? You're here on exciting business-you ought to be honoured, or at the very least pleased!'

'Oh…I am.' nodded Steve sheepishly.

'Good…Well I won't beat about the bush for too much longer, as we have a lot to discuss. However, I must formally introduce you to the committee members…'

He continued slowly along the long boat-shaped table.

'This is Mrs Daphne Reynolds, head of MI6…'

She smiled at Steve warmly; her smile seemed to put him at ease. Next to her sat a man of about the same age as Steve:

'This is Mr Ryan Goss, head of MI5…' continued Dawson.

He continued past the vacant chair and reached the next occupied chair.

'This is the head of the GCHQ…a fancy name for espionage…Mrs Aileen Fontaine.' Steve decided to be wary of Fontaine, because she hardly seemed to acknowledge his presence; merely raising an eyebrow. They crossed to the other side of the table-the side of the fireplace.

'Those good people are not cabinet members, but are seated strategically nonetheless. You're already familiar with the remainder, the members of my cabinet…Ken Butler, Trade and Industry…'

Butler was a comical looking man around the age of sixty. He dressed in a tweed suit and wore semicircular glasses, which rested precariously on the end of his nose. He was bald, but had grown a tuft of hair to form a comb over, which would slide out of place with each tiny movement; this perhaps explained why he preferred to keep perfectly still.

Dawson continued '...the Defence Secretary, Fred Latimer...Home Secretary, Michael Lord and of course the Foreign Secretary Bert Frost.'

The Prime Minister slowly took his place in front of the fireplace. Steve was instructed to sit opposite him. Dawson sank his head to collect his thoughts.

'You must have noticed the difficulties we are facing in the undertaking of the Enfranchise Campaign Steven?'

'Yes sir. Prices are very high.' Steve agreed.

'Correct. And the reason?' Dawson asked.

'Well of course the unofficial reason is associated with the reoccupation of Basra.' Steve shrugged.

'Indeed, but can you tell me of the *official* reason?'

'I'm afraid I couldn't sir.'

The Prime Minister leaned back on his chair and grinned.

'Neither can we, dear boy! But we have our suspicions!'

'Oh.' Steve said labouredly.

'The Bank of England has voted to increase the interest rate from ten point two-five per cent, to twelve point five. And that's only to keep inflation at a *steady* increase.' groaned Dawson.

'Ah.' Steve murmured as he considered his hefty bank loan.

'Are you sure that the Bank of England was correct in doing so?'

'Why of course it was! My dear boy! Have you bought a Mars bar recently? Eight pounds each! Good news for the obesity crisis; bad news for the economy.'

Steve briefly admired the clock, which sat on the mantelpiece behind the Prime Minister. 'What can I do about that?'

The Prime Minister held off from answering the question.

'There's hundreds of thousands...perhaps millions of pounds disappearing from our shores which is unaccounted for. We're experiencing the worst balance of payments crisis in the country's history. The first thing I want you to do when you leave here is to put out a Public Information Film, telling the people of Britain that they are only permitted to take one thousand pounds out of the country. I will be devaluing the pound directly, in order to encourage foreign investment.'

Steve breathed a sign of relief. 'So all you would like me to do is construct a P.I.F?'

'*All?* My dear boy! You make it sound as easy as changing a light bulb! It will surely require some careful planning. I'm going to give you until the end of tomorrow.'

'Right.' said Steve confidently tapping the table. 'I'll let you have the reel by five tomorrow evening. If there's nothing else, I'll take my leave.'
He got up from the table.

'Sit down man! I haven't finished.' shouted the Prime Minister.

'But I thought…'

'Do you think I would have dragged my cabinet from their families on a Saturday just so that I could tell the likes of you about some P.I.F? That's just a small screw in a very large machine!'

'So what *do* you want me to do?' Steve queried.

The Prime Minister delayed his answer to the question further.

'You're of course aware of Cliffbridge and all it stands for, aren't you?'

'Vaguely…That is, I know that it used to be a thriving residential area of City brokers until you pulled the plug on the area.' he retorted candidly.

The Prime Minister's face stretched 'I did not pull the plug on Cliffbridge! I merely sacked a few brokers from the City for moonlighting.'

'The City was a private entity, the reason it was thriving before your intervention was because it was free from the constraints of politics. Many would argue that it was a mistake to renationalise the City of London- especially given you represent a Neo-Liberal Party.'

The Prime Minister's face grew tighter '*Many* people do not have such a mammoth task on their hands!'

'Perhaps, sir. However, many more would argue that suspending Cliffbridge Borough Council from public use was perhaps…reckless.'

'I did not suspend the council! The council ceased to function because it was not levying enough council tax!'

'That's because you made the citizens unemployed!' Steve countered.

'I sacked a few people and you've got the gall to place the blame onto me…your employer?'

'A few people? You sacked no less than four thousand employees!'

'What's four thousand people in a borough that size?' the Prime Minister scolded.

'It may well be the largest borough geographically, but the majority of the area is greenbelt. In actual fact, the total population number is only in the region of nine, maybe ten thousand.'

'You've done your homework, haven't you? The question I'm inclined to ask is, why? How did you know beforehand that I was going to call a meeting about Cliffbridge? Who have you been talking to Steven?'

'I have always been fascinated by the place. Just like the public, I have always wondered how such a place can continue surviving in the face of poverty. What is more, although I am your employee, I do not align myself to a political party, I just happen to work for you, that's all.' Steve explained.

The Prime Minister's face fell into a look of fascination.

'You share my interest in the place Steven, even if that is the only thing we share. Like you, I ask myself how the place continues to survive without public amenities including the emergency services. Perhaps I'm barking up the wrong tree and Cliffbridge is acting without wrongdoing. But we both know that's not how the world works! If you put a set of disgruntled, unemployed, highly skilled economists together…add to that a playing field without interruption from the authorities and what have you got?'

'Crime, deviance…even debauchery?' Steve attempted.

'On the contrary! My boy, you've a lot to learn. No, you have a system of anarchy, sure, but not the chaotic scene that often springs to mind. Instead you have an autonomous, highly efficient black-market economy!'

'Sir, I wouldn't be the first person to question your paranoia. You have already commissioned many agents to investigate the area to little or no avail.'

'That's why I'm hiring you, dear boy!' grinned the Prime Minister.

'*Me?*' exclaimed Steve, taken aback.

'You indeed! What do you say?'

'But why me? I'm merely a lowly civil servant. I'm good at what I do, but I am not capable of anything this big.'

The Prime Minister lowered his glasses and smiled.

'You have been chewing at the bit to be placed into a role with more kudos! So I'm offering you a ticket out of your monotony and am giving you the chance to prove yourself to me and, who knows, one day you might make Chief Whip! So, Steven, what do you say?'

Steve steeled himself 'I say no thank you very much. I will not be a part of this make-believe idea.' he got to his feet 'Look, I understand that a lot of money is disappearing which is not accounted for and I do appreciate how difficult your job is, but if many others have tried and failed, then how am I an exception?'

'Wait a minute man! Let's not be hasty; we haven't discussed terms yet.' said the Prime Minister walking after him. 'Come and sit back down, there's a lad. I'm sure you'll find what I am about to tell you of interest.' Steve retook his place. 'That's better!' said the Prime Minister.

Steve remained austere.

'Now look here.' began Dawson 'The agents we sent into Cliffbridge in the past did not participate in any way in Cliffbridge's community. They were like conventional secret agents; they hid behind buildings and attended the odd public meeting, but did not fully engage in the lifestyle. I believe it is for that reason that they found nothing. I want you to be different to them; I want *you* to become a part of Cliffbridge.'

Steve flinched.

'You cannot be serious! They'd soon find me out. I'm no secret agent, just a hapless civil servant!'

'We've already thought about that.' continued the Home Secretary on Steve's right. 'My subcommittee have compiled a handbook.'

He handed Steve a heavy paperback textbook, which had a glossy cover titled: "How to be successful as a real-estate AGENT".

'Why is the word 'agent' written in uppercase?' Steve asked.

'It's merely a play on words; you will be an agent of the government, while masquerading as an estate agent.' explained Latimer.

'But I know nothing at all about real-estate. I've never even bought a house.'

Latimer leant towards him 'This book will teach you everything you need to know. Of course you won't be expected to know *everything* on the subject, but the book gives you a clear layout, together with diagrams on how to get by convincingly.'

Steve weighted the book in his right hand.

'It's awfully big. How long have I got to read it?'

The Prime Minister continued 'Your mission, should you accept, will commence eight days from now; that is Sunday 9th February.'

'A week? Is that all?' Steve exclaimed, letting the book fall to the table.

'Don't worry; you are now on leave from your work at the Department for Culture, Media and Sport. Call it a reading week.'

Steve appeared bewildered.

'The mission is codenamed: "Black Hole", owing to our economic problem.' explained Dawson. 'Clever, eh?'

'We still haven't discussed terms.' said Steve.

'Can I take that to mean that you're interested?' smiled Dawson.

'How much will you pay me?' Steve asked.

'One point six million pounds.' replied the Prime Minister quickly.

Steve nodded 'I must admit that that's more than I expected. How long will the mission last?'

'The duration of the mission is unspecified. That means that the mission will last as long as necessary for you to complete your mission objectives. You will know when your mission is complete.'

'What are the mission objectives?' Steve asked with a nervous twang.

The Prime Minister removed his glasses and pressed at his temples in concentration. 'Right, your mission objectives are as follows…Number one. Rumour has it there is a journal in the local library; you must locate it. It is titled: "The Rise of Cliffbridge". It is an unpublished article that is also handwritten. It contains vital information on the workings of Cliffbridge, which I'll need as evidence for action against the place.'

'What do I do with it once I've located it?' Steve asked.

'Guard it with your life. Failure to do so will result in the mission's failure and possibly your cover blown. The second part of your mission is to find a young woman named Thelma Harrison. She is also vital to the mission's success. Reports from previous investigators indicate that she is a well-known figure in Cliffbridge and holds a lot of information about the people of the borough, so getting to know Miss Harrison will unlock many of Cliffbridge's mysteries.'

'Any more?' asked Steve, already aghast.

'Number three. You need to get close to Neil Stubbs, the ex-mayor of Cliffbridge. He is connected with Thelma Harrison, believed to be in an on-off relationship. Little is known about what he does with himself nowadays and given his former standing in the area, makes him all the more conspicuous. As I always say: "great oaks never become shrubs". He's up to something and I want you to find out what it is.'

Steve gave him a look of unease.

'Is there anything else?'

'Yes: number four. Be vigilant; be on the lookout for *anything*. Eavesdrop on conversations; sit in on meetings; drink in the local pub…but don't make yourself appear conspicuous. We have provided you with a mundane identity for a specific purpose so as not to get caught out, so don't take too many unnecessary risks.'

He gave Steve a laboured stare.

'Look here dear boy. I have heard many tales about the place, so do be careful. We feel it will be good for you to stretch your comfort zone a bit and we think you're the man for the job, so what do you say *this* time?'

Steve caught a glimpse of the myriad faces looking back at him expectantly. Perhaps something out of the ordinary was what he needed he thought; he certainly could do with the money.

'Right…I'll do it.'

'Good boy!' beamed the Prime Minister grabbing his arm.

The other committee members patted him on the shoulder saying: 'Well done' and 'You're the man for the job'.

When the foray of cheer had died down the Prime Minister's tone deepened.

'You have a day to construct and transmit a Public Information Film to be aired on PST. In it there will be references to the link between Iraq and the recession. You also have the coming week to pack your belongings. However, you are not to breathe a word about this to *anybody*, do you understand Steven?'

'I understand.' he nodded.

'Oh! I almost forgot!' the Prime Minister exclaimed 'There's the small matter about your living arrangements.' he placed a map in front of Steve 'Okay, you'll be living in a district of Cliffbridge named Ward's End. Ward's End is somewhat more rundown than the rest of Cliffbridge; however your apartment block does not match the area. It is newly built and of exquisite quality. The building belongs to an American property developer who happens to be a great friend of mine; in fact I've just purchased an apartment on the top floor!' his face fell into a frown 'However that, of course, is strictly confidential; we wouldn't want the public drawing the wrong conclusions, would we?'

'Certainly not!' said Steve sounding half sarcastic.

'Anyway, your address for the duration will be: 26 Fox Road, London, E26 6GK. Here are your swipe cards for the main door to the building and for your own door. There is an underground car park with excellent security. But be wary some of the local 'mob', it is thought that a gang of young men work in some capacity or other for Stubbs and they happen to harbour a dislike for middleclass buildings. In spite of the good security, there are always a few vagabonds who escape the net. Other than that, I'm sure you'll find the place interesting, perhaps even fun!' his face fell again into a frown 'But don't go giving my government a bad name or you'll face criminal charges.'

Steve looked perplexed by the warning.

The Prime Minister smiled again and continued 'Well, like me you must have other things to be getting on with on a Saturday like, for example, constructing a Public Information Film! I won't keep you from your business any longer.'

PART TWO

'Chance Meetings'

THREE

Sunday 9th February 2048. Ward's End, London. 1030 Hrs.

  The snow, which had fallen during the previous week, remained as though newly fallen on the untreated roads of Cliffbridge, disguising the potholes, which littered them. Steve drove at a snail's pace since leaving the M25; the broken roads were a sight not seen by most Londoners since the government went into office. The car rose and fell as it hit another concealed hazard as he prepared to turn left into what he hoped was Fox Road. The broken thoroughfares and the cracked cul-de-sacs reflected the grey, miserable tenement flats which bordered them. Built during the 1960s as icons of urban regeneration and hope for the future, they had since attracted crime; there was not one flat which did not either have a smashed window or a damaged wall. Not a single piece of foliage was seen in the tiny gardens at the front of the ground floor flats, only dry cement or building debris. The air smelled of dust and as Steve inhaled, he began coughing violently.

There did not appear to be any former City workers living in this part of Cliffbridge, if the dress sense of the three youths on the pavement opposite were anything to go by. Three gaunt looking boys of around the age of sixteen, wearing white caps and tracksuits glared at him; the winter sun whitening their pale skin further. They gave him a look of disgust and his car a look of envy. Steve lowered the passenger window

'Oi, is this Fox Road?' he asked.

'Sod you!' the tallest youth shouted back angrily.

They cycled away, skidding on the ice. Steve began to question whether he had driven to the right place. There was no sign of anybody other than aggrieved hooligans. He continued slowly along the road, keeping his eyes peeled for the tower.

  As he passed a row of abandoned shopping trolleys, he noticed a high brick wall, which was totally covered in posters and flyers, leaving not an inch of brick exposed. One that caught his eye depicted a thickset man in his late thirties with black hair, which was swept back. In heavy type the poster read:

"Remember your leader Neil Stubbs in the election on 1st December 2047."

He stared at the garish picture puzzled by what sort of election had been staged. He did not ponder this thought for too much longer, for behind the wall a twenty storey tower stood against the grey sky like an oversized crystal. His heart settled at the sense of relief he suddenly felt. With a firm, confident grasp of the gear stick, he edged around the corner into what according to a desecrated sign was Gresham Mews. He drew up at the entrance to the pitch-black car park where an elderly man inside a kiosk met him.

'Mornin'. How can I help?' asked the man, shrivelling his face into a shy smile.

'At last someone who vaguely resembles a human being.' Steve grunted.
The man gave him a look of bewilderment.

'Look, are you new or somethin'?'

'Yes, as a matter of fact I am. This place looks like a right dump.' Steve sniffed.

'Here's my ID.' he handed the man his multicard.
The man placed the card into his reader. 'Aha, yes. Right…so you're occupying number twenty-six?'

'That's right.' nodded Steve.

'Well, you'll need this security tag. Stick it on your windscreen and make sure it stays there. The number of cars we've had broken into during January alone has been somewhere in the region of twenty.' he explained.

'I wish I could say I was surprised.' Steve scoffed, surveying his surroundings.

'So make sure it is displayed clearly or you'll find yourself braving these streets on foot…and going by your appearance, you don't wanna be doing that.' the man chuckled. 'Anyway, in you go. Find the space marked twenty-six and that'll be yours.'

The barrier lifted and Steve drove into the silent, black void. The car park extended far and wide and due to the darkness, seemed to continue forever. He continued up a ramp onto the next floor for spaces 19-30. The car park was virtually empty of cars making the engine's hum echo from wall to wall. The spaces either side of space twenty-six were occupied by more abandoned supermarket trolleys which contained aerosol tins used in the making of the graffiti above. The words "Bugger off posh snobs" added colour to the grey concrete wall above Steve's space.

  He got out and walked slowly towards the entrance door to the block. He pulled the swipe card through the reader and the door clicked open. The lobby was ill lit by a single dim orange strip light, highlighting only the staircase and the lift. He called the lift. Nothing happened, except for a mechanical, grinding sound. He pressed the button a second time; nothing happened. He gave the doors an impatient kick, causing them to part slowly. A smell akin to outdated vegetables radiated from within it. More abusive graffiti was written in purple marker pen on the mirror on the far wall. He gave the button another press to no avail; the doors remained open.

Looking towards the staircase, he noticed a family descending it. An enthusiastic little girl led a man of smart appearance down the steps, while the woman called miserably: 'Be careful on the stairs.'
The little girl reached the bottom step and glared at Steve.
'Hey Emmy, haven't I always told you that it's rude to stare?' said the man who gave Steve an apologetic smile 'Kids eh? You think you have taught them all they need to know to equip them into being good citizens but, alas…'
'Forget it, she's just a kid.' mumbled Steve, glaring down at the unusually thin girl.
'All the same…' the man countered. His face relaxed suddenly 'Anyway, tell me, are you new here?'
Steve considered his answer for a moment. He remembered what the Prime Minister had told him about being circumspect. He studied the man's appearance more carefully; his immaculate suit; his reluctant smile; his twinkling, intrigued eyes. He was indecipherable: he could have been an official like himself, in which case he would have to act with discretion. Equally, judging by his weary smile, he could have just been a consultant surgeon.
'I'm here on business.' Steve replied at last.
The man's eyes filled with more excitement 'Really? What sort of business?'
Steve immediately regretted his ambiguous explanation 'Housing. I'm in real-estate.'
'Oh I see!' exclaimed the man, while his daughter tugged at his cuff calling up to him 'Come on daddy!'
'Alright! Alright!' chuckled the man, almost losing his footing. 'Look, as you can see I'm being coerced by an infant! Best be off. The name's Maitland-Sloan. James. This is my wife Sylvia and my daughter Emma.'
'Morrissey. Steve Morrissey.'
'Well! I'll see you anon! Perhaps you'll accompany me to the local public house one evening? The Two Shillings on the corner?'
'Maybe. I live at number twenty-six on the fourth floor.' Steve muttered.
'That's settled then. Expect a knock one evening this coming week! Cheerio!'
The family exited the lobby.
'Do make sure Emmy doesn't fall over, won't you James? Her check-up is on Wednesday, remember James?' James' wife cried tenaciously.

***

Steve lifted the wooden Venetian blinds to allow the emerging sun to light the sitting room. Leaning on the sill, he grimaced at the unfamiliar view in front of him. Mile upon mile of grey buildings meandered their way towards the canals near the central area of the borough. The streets below lay silent, as though mourning their own death. His eyes were drawn to the street below, which contained the only colour for miles around. "O'Hara's", the local fish and chip shop was adorned with blue lights, which bordered the large forecourt window. The flat above it held a large neon lit sign, which flashed on and off, although this could have been a circuitry fault and not an intentional ploy. A few meters up the road in amongst the grey monotony stood another oasis of intrigue. More neon signs-this time in red. "Saunas and Massages" flashed the sign. The window to the forecourt was tinted, while what looked like a cast-iron staircase led downwards and more red lights and pink arrows descended with the steps. Steve must have forgotten to close the front door, for he was startled by the sound of a girl's voice.

'Hi! I thought I heard somebody arrive. I'm Jill; I live in the flat next door.'

She edged her way slowly and cautiously towards him. She was a petite girl in her late teens or early twenties, with a distinct air of nervousness about her which Steve found unsettling and reassuring in equal measures.

'Pleased to meet you...' said Steve only half acknowledging her.

He continued gazing out of the window. The girl's face became more relaxed as she joined him at the window. She peered out at the rolling landscape of grey.

'I expect you're new, are you not?' she asked.

Steve glanced at her for a moment.

'Why do people keep asking me that?' he demanded impatiently.

The girl stiffened at once 'Well I...Just wanted to say that I'm only next door if you need anything.'

Steve continued to glare at the bright lights as if drawn like a mouth to a flame.

'Yes, yes. Thank you very much.' he called. He looked at her 'Look, was there anything else?'

The girl smiled in spite of his rudeness, looking to see what was demanding so much of his attention.

'Ah. That's what the locals refer to as the "The Grime". Ghastly place. Brothel, you know.'

'Apart from the chip shop it's the only place for miles with colour.' Steve cited.

'I know. I'm sure that is why it's so popular with young, vulnerable men.' she sighed despairingly. 'Do you know about these things?' she asked gesturing towards the forty inch plasma screen in the corner.

Steve gave her a surprised look 'I'm no technical whiz kid, but plasma screens I can handle.'

'Yes of course, but did you know that in this area you can't pick up signals using a Microdish? That is, you can't receive the national channels on these screens, only the local channels through an old-fashioned aerial.' explained the girl enthusiastically.

Steve was unstirred by her proclamation and gazed once again at the brothel. She switched the plasma screen on. A muffled din came from the speakers, which appeared to be violin music. Steve glanced at the screen.

'What do you mean "old-fashioned aerial"?' he giggled.

'I mean that the government has no jurisdiction here and so they broadcast what they like.'

'Who's *they*?'

'Have you heard of Neil Stubbs, ex-mayor of Cliffbridge?' she asked.

'Yes, I've heard a bit about him…'

'Well let's just say that he's big round here and he likes to throw his weight around…and let me tell you, there's a lot of it!'

She let out a squeaky laugh.

He looked at the screen. It displayed a navy-blue background with white text:

60-66 MHz: Channel 3, Band I. Dominion.

Programmes start at noon, with Cliffbridge Today.

Steve stared at the screen in disbelief 'You're absolutely right-it's a VHF station!'

'That's not all…' she smiled.

Jill pressed a different channel number. A distorted and snowy picture flashed onto the screen. It appeared to be the beginning of a programme, this time the picture was, in spite of the poor quality, garish and bright. The title of the programme ran:

82-88MHz: Channel 6, Band I. Alto-Zero.

YOUR CLIFFBRIDGE, OUR STRUGGLE!!

The music for the opening sequence was altogether more subdued than that of channel three. The picture showed an old, haggard man with a snowy white beard aboard a boat on what appeared to be one of the canals. A male voice that was militaristic in tone and accent carried out the narration:

"For seventeen years, Cliffbridge has been involved in a harsh struggle; a struggle which has brought with it misery, poverty and disillusionment among us all. A struggle which was forced upon us by those who sit proudly and wealthy upon the pompous seats in the House of Commons: namely those within the government…"

The camera panned in slowly during the monologue until it concentrated on the elderly man sweeping away dead leaves from the deck. He wore a forlorn expression and shook his head as he assessed the leaky windows. The monologue continued:

"This man, a much loved figure among us all, toils through the day and into the night to bring us our staple diet of fresh fish from our waterways. Yes, citizens! One man in a desperate struggle to keep us well sustained as we continue our own struggles in maintaining our very existence!"
The scene changed to one of a restaurant full of people enjoying fish dishes, each person with a smile on their face.
"You see these good people? The object of their enjoyment was not from the decadent aisles of the bourgeois supermarket. No! We produce our own produce and that's what gives us our unique character! Neither do we have any use for money...'
The scene faded and changed to a jovial looking young woman working in a barber's shop. The camera scanned the full length of her attractive body: from her feet to her head as she styled an elderly lady's hair.
"Today, Mrs Horrocks is having her hair set by Yolanda here. See how well they look? That's because Mrs Horrocks provides our Yolanda with two pounds of fresh vegetables every Friday morning in exchange for her wash and blow-dry. And what better arrangement could any young woman such as Yolanda ask for? She hasn't the time to fuss over what to cook this evening or where to buy her food; she has two small children to care for."

The scene faded and was replaced with one containing many hundreds of male youths, each one like the two boys Steve had had the misfortune of meeting on the street earlier that morning; weather-beaten and malnourished. In this scene, they marched along what appeared to be a high street: most likely Cliffbridge High Street. They carried rifles and were dressed in plain clothes, with the majority in hooded pullovers and tracksuit trousers.
"These are our special boys. They ensure the maintenance of this intricate system of sustenance. These young men ensure that the spectre of greed, the bane of the outside world, does not engulf us. Without these men, our Cliffbridge would disintegrate like a leaf in autumn." The picture changed to show a well-dressed middle class looking man driving a newly manufactured car "Our boys are constantly on the lookout for untoward, unfamiliar outsiders. Cliffbridge has long since been cast out by the government and left to wither in the harsh cold. Therefore, what business would a man like this have in Cliffbridge? He might be on an innocent visit to see his ill brother; risking his squeaky-clean reputation in doing so by coming to Cliffbridge. Equally, he might be an agent on a covert mission to bring about the end of our triumphant story. Beware citizens! Remember to report conspicuous behaviour to Central House or call: 0120 8000 3000 anytime."
The scene changed to show a row of the people featured in the footage smiling at the camera.

"Our struggled has meant that the unfair, corrupt government of the outside has not triumphed over us! We have managed to elude them for years and we shall continue to fool them!"
Finally, the picture changed and showed a still image of the man Steve had seen on the posters on the walls in the street: the same overweight figure with the thickly greased hair and a wry grin holding a cigar.
"Remember your leader in the upcoming chairperson elections. For a fact sheet, call 0120 8000 2000 or just drop into level four, Central House. Thank you citizens!"
The programme ended; Steve switched the screen off.
Jill gave him a wry smile.
'So, *Steve*, which are you, an innocent man visiting your ill brother or an evil spy?!'
'Neither.' he retorted solemnly. 'I'm here on business. Real-estate. Anyway, who are you? I mean, what are you here for?'
'I'm a student at UCL studying psychology. I'm in my first year.' she explained.
'So what are you doing this far east?' he asked.
'My dad thinks it's out of harm's way.'
Steve gave a surprised chortle 'Well he got *that* wrong.'
Just as he spoke, the girl's face changed to one of bewilderment.
Steve became more sympathetic 'Well, I'm sure for a young girl like you it's an exciting place to live. Beats being in the middle of nowhere, like for instance Bangor.'
She gave him a small, forgiving smile. She picked up the photograph of Steve's mother which was on the windowsill.
'Who's this, your gran?'
'No, it's my mother.'
She brought the picture up closer to her eyes.
'Oh.' she paused for a moment to study the paper 'It must've been taken years ago…before they invented digital cameras!' she laughed.
Steve snatched it back.
'It was taken on my mother's twenty-first birthday. She died when I was five. This is all I have left in her memory.'
Jill lowered her head 'Oh. Look, I'm sorry. I can come across as being such a bitch at times without meaning to be.' she looked towards Steve's hand which had the photograph firmly in its grasp 'She's a fine looking woman, I can see her in you.'
Steve softened slightly 'Look, I've had a lot to take in this morning as I'm sure you understand.'
With an understanding nod, she left him alone in the living room to gaze out of the window.

***

Steve awoke several hours later on the long red chesterfield settee. He had been awoken by the darkness in the room and when he checked his multicard, he saw that it was five to five. He sat up quickly, rubbing his eyes to clear his vision. As he got to his feet, he considered taking a shower to revitalise himself. However he found that he could not advance out of the room; the bright blue and red lights from the street below demanded one more look. He rushed back to the window and looked down. The chip shop was now open and he could just make out two men sat at a table eating. This whetted his appetite and now nothing else other than food could take precedence in his mind.

The street was busier than it had been when he had arrived that morning, although only a dozen or so people lined the pavement. The wind had also got up, adding to the chill factor as well as moving the scent of vinegar towards Steve's nostrils. He had decided to change into casual clothes, wearing jeans and a sweater beneath his overcoat. This had been on the strength of the advice given to the citizens of Cliffbridge on the plasma screen, which had told them to report any conspicuous looking people. He pushed open the door to the fish and chip shop. A waft of vinegary air hit him as he jostled his way towards the counter. The small sitting area at the front, beside the entrance was now full of people enjoying their evening meals. As he stood in the short queue waiting to be served, he studied the menu on the wall behind the counter. There was just about every variety of fish imaginable. Hake, Cod, Plaice, Haddock, Trout, Salmon, every variety of Sole, Mackerel, Sprat, Pilchard, Eel, Mussel, Clam, Oyster, Crab, Lobster, Squid, Prawns of every size and much, much more. When at last it was his turn to be served, a woman of a pale complexion and red hair met him. Her delicate looking face was half obscured by a white hat that had become slightly discoloured from perpetual contact with fat. The woman, who was about forty, gave Steve a warm smile, displaying a missing front tooth.

'What can I do for you, my treasure?' she beamed. She had a strong Irish accent.
'Oh...I'll have cod and chips please.'
'Cod my love? You're gonna have to be more specific than that!' she laughed, waving a spatula in her right hand.
'Sorry, what do you mean?' Steve asked, perplexed 'How many different types of cod are there?'
'Well, let's see now...' she tapped her cheek with the spatula lightly as she collected her thoughts 'There's lemon cod, coral cod, Atlantic cod, salt cod, Pacific cod...'

Steve injected 'I'll have the lemon cod.' he gave her a raised eyebrow 'I expect you're going to tell me that you offer French fries, crinkle-cut chips…East Timorese chips?'

The woman just stared at him.

'Don't be so ridiculous.' she snapped as she scribbled down the order 'What's your exchange?' she asked.

'My *what*?' Steve asked, grimacing.

She looked him up and down.

'I can tell you're not round around here are ya?'

He did not answer, but turned round, noticing the queue that had built up behind him. The woman's attention was also drawn to the increased number of people.

'An exchange means I give you your fish and chips if you do me a favour in return.' she explained, with her arms folded defensively.

'Do you not accept money?' he laughed, producing his multicard.

'You can put *that* away! If Mr Stubbs saw that, he'd snap that right in half!' She held out a red, sweaty hand 'Cash only.'

'*Cash?* When was the last time anybody used *cash*? I was at university when cash was phased out!' he laughed.

The woman did not say a word, but looked at him sternly and placed a notepad and pencil under his nose. 'Do me an I.O.U.'

Steve suddenly remembered the plasma programme. He fumbled around his pockets and produced a packet of cigarettes. 'Will these do?'

'A done deal!' exclaimed the woman, her smile returned as she snatched the crumpled packet. 'I'll bring your meal over. Go and find a seat.'

    He turned to face the seating area. The overbearing artificial light showed a sea of tired, blemished faces with not a seat to spare. Just as he was about to turn back to the counter and change his order to a takeaway, he spotted what appeared to be a vacant seat beside the window. He ambled his way between the closely packed tables towards the table with the vacant seat, which already had three people at it. He shuffled around the table and reached the spare chair.

'Is anyone sitting here?' he asked a middle-aged woman.

'No love, sit down.' she smiled, removing her handbag and pulling the chair free of the table.

She was a plump woman of about fifty with short, tightly curled hair which contained just about every tone of grey. She had the same tired looking expression as the other customers, except her weight made her appear healthier; there were no black shadows under her eyes and her skin appeared smooth. Despite her friendly appearance, Steve wanted to avoid any verbal contact with anybody. He was not only tired, but immensely hungry by now.

His cod and chips arrived at last. The aroma which it gave off brought saliva to his mouth. Picking up the plastic knife and fork, he began gorging on the cod fillet like there was no tomorrow. He let out an intermittent blow in order to cool the morsel in his mouth before swallowing.

'Careful love, you'll give yourself a stomach ulcer at that rate!' laughed the woman.

'I'm sorry?' asked Steve with a muffled voice.

'I said slow down! You don't wanna get indigestion.' she said shaking her head. 'Honestly! You young 'uns don't know what's good for ya!'

Steve did not pay any attention to her, but persevered with his meal at the same speed, hoping to leave the shop within a few seconds.

The woman kept her eyes on him 'Hey, are you new around here?'

Steve stopped chewing and looked up and said with an exasperated tone:

'Yes I am. Next question.'

She recoiled 'Sorry love. I was just makin' conversation, you know? It's just that you don't sound local...'

'That's because I'm not.'

He took one last mouthful and got up to leave. The woman tugged his arm, telling him to sit down, which he did out of bewilderment.

'Let me tell you somethin'.' she said with little more than a whisper.

'Look, I was stood a few places in front of you in the queue just now. And I thought to myself, who's that oddball behind me? You might as well have "I'm new here!" written in pink on your top.' her voice became more sincere 'Look love. You don't strike me as the sort of bloke what goes lookin' for trouble, so I'm gonna give you a few tips.' she leaned in having checked that nobody else was listening in 'Have you been here before?'

Steve thought carefully about his answer.

'Yes...' he decided suddenly that he would have to lie further to detract any further questions '...I grew up here; I know this place like the back of my hand. I moved to Paddington, though, when I was fifteen.'

She rubbed her face thoughtfully.

'That would be about the time of The Great Change.'

'The Great Change?' he queried.

'You really do have a lot to learn, don't you?' she said shaking her head despairingly.

'I'll make just two more suggestions before I let you get on your way. Number one. Go to the library on the High Street and find a book called "The Rise of Cliffbridge". It's an unpublished manuscript which you'd find very helpful, it tells you all about what's happened in the last decade or so. My second piece of advice is to stop being so confrontational and touchy! Unless you can come across as being easygoing like the rest of us, then all you're gonna do is draw attention to yourself and once that happens that's it!'

'It?' he asked.

'Then you're a goner. In other words dead meat.' she explained, drawing a line across her neck with her finger. Her face relaxed into a smile 'The name's Mary. Mary Hamilton. I live just a couple of blocks away on Harcourt Drive.'

She paused for a moment to allow for Steve to take his turn in informing her of his details. He did not, but just gave a small nod and continued shovelling his chips into his mouth.

'What's your name?' she asked at last.

'Morrissey. Steve Morrissey.' he said with a mouthful of chips.

'And if you don't mind my asking, why are you here Steven?'

He swallowed quickly 'Why am I here?'

She grimaced 'Well yes, I'm not talking to anyone else, am I?' she chortled.

Steve thought for a moment, looking down at his plate. He remembered the textbook he had been given. "How to be a successful real-estate AGENT". That book was supposed to answer questions like the one he was being asked now. But somehow it did not feel like the right time to get into a discussion about the local properties. To begin with he had not a clue about them and on top of that he had not had a chance to even skim read the book. Therefore, the obvious thing to do at that moment was to think of something that would fend off too many questions.

'I'm visiting to look after my terminally ill uncle. We're very close.' he said at last.

'Oh I am sorry love. Does he live in Ward's End too?' she asked gently.

'Yes, on Marsh Road.'

He decided to pick a major road, one with many houses and tiny flats.

'I dare say I've heard of him...' she looked thoughtful, as she cradled her empty polystyrene cup 'Marsh Road, eh? Hmm... Full of all sorts, from squatters to scarlet women.'

'Well I'm pleased to report my uncle is neither.' he said, managing a slight smile.

She acknowledged him with a smile as she tapped her cup on the table.

'Of course, I shouldn't tar them all with the same brush. A good friend of mine lives their too. Thelma.'

As the word 'Thelma' left her mouth a shiver shot down his spine.

'Thelma Harrison?' he asked.

'Yeah that's the girl! Know her do ya?'

'Not exactly, but my uncle Les has mentioned her a few times.' he said with a casual shrug. 'A lady of the night, I hear?' he blurted, forgetting himself.

Mary's face cringed 'Are you defined as a person by what you do for a livin'?' she snapped, crushing the polystyrene cup with rage.
'No, I...' he began.
'It's not a profession she chose; she was forced into it. Long story.' she explained, sounding calmer 'Me and Thelm' go back years. I practically brought her up as my own. The government killed her mother...or so it's alleged.' she quickly added.
Steve wanted to keep on the subject of Thelma's current form in order to track her down. 'Sounds terrible.' he began. Before Mary had a chance to elaborate on the details Steve continued 'So does she work next door in that massage parlour?'
'Aha. Beautiful girl she is too. Long dark hair with a Latin complexion. God knows where she got that! Her parent's were both typically English lookin'. Everyone reckons it was a case of a visit from the milkman, if you get my drift.'
Steve made a mental note of Mary's description of Thelma.
'How old is she?' he asked trying to sound nonchalant.
'Oh, twenty-six I think...Twenty-seven in May.' she looked at him 'Why, thinkin' of payin' her a visit are we?' she giggled, giving him a wink.
'No, no; certainly not! I was just...' he began.
She interrupted him 'Don't worry my love, no one would blame you if you did; some beautiful girls in there and good natured too. See? That's what Cliffbridge is all about. Well, I'm speakin' for the Ward's End area of it anyway; easygoing and unassuming. Live and let live. Ask no questions, hear no lies!'
Steve gave her a stare.
'Blimey! I didn't realise it was that late already!' she got to her feet 'I must skedaddle, there's a film I wanna catch which starts at nine!' she wrapped her poncho around her shoulders and took her handbag.
'The book you need is in the local history section at the far end of the library. As I say, it tells you all you need to know. I work in the laundrette next door; come and find me if you have any questions or just wanna chat.' she pushed her chair under the table 'Well, it's been nice talkin' to ya and I hope to speak again soon. TTFN!'
The door flew open, letting in a torrent of ice-cold air that shot straight down his back.

    Soon after, he stood on the cold, snowy street with his back to the warm chip shop. He lifted his feet every now and then to maintain his body temperature. Gazing up at Ealing Tower, he noticed that he had accidentally left the sitting room light on; the dim, hazy yellow against the morbid black sky was enough to convince him that he was done with exploring the locality for the night and it was time to head back to what he had to call home for an undisclosed period of time.

'Are you okay there?' came a voice to his left. Standing beside him was a tall woman dressed in a full-length white fur coat. Her black eyes sparkled in the streetlight, as did her bright pink lip-gloss and her crimped pink hair. Her face was as pale as the chip shop owner's, but much more attractive and youthful.

She wore a non-assuming smile that prompted Steve not to be wary as usual, but to be settled.

'Fine, thank you.' he replied.

'Oh. It's just that you look lost.'

He looked behind where she was standing and noticed the bright pink lights that adorned the building. He was reminded at once of his mission to locate Thelma Harrison and of Mary's description of her, which did not fit this woman's. At that moment he was in two minds about whether to pursue the woman's advances. This opportunity may never again present itself, he decided.

'As a matter of fact I am. Well…not lost as such. You see, I live up there…'

He pointed up at his living room window.

'How posh!' smiled the woman, rubbing her hands to ward off the cold breeze.

'Yes, but I'm looking for somebody in particular.'

'Then I think I can help you.' grinned the woman. 'Come with me…' she said, beckoning him with her finger to follow her down the slippery steps into the basement.

***

Steve was led by the hand down the steps and through a dark doorway; he could see absolutely nothing. The closing bar of "Every Breath You Take" by "The Police" was pulsating through the ceiling from a room above. What he sensed to be the hallway smelled of perfume and he could still see nothing. He was led into a room on the right; this time he could see that it was a living room. It was illuminated only by a dim blue light; this made the leather settee, covered by a leopard skin throw, barely visible. A red lava lamp gave off some light on the sideboard, but this made little difference, only adding to the sense of mystery. The music upstairs had finished playing and there was silence, which was all the more unsettling for him.

'Sit down and wait for a moment. Who were you looking for?' asked the woman 'I'm Fay. Our policy is that we don't mess around by using silly pseudonyms, Fay's my name and lookin' after you's my game!' she smiled, bending down to kiss him on the cheek. Her body felt cold, owing to the lack of any form of heating in the room. She walked back to the door.

'Thelma. Is she free?' he asked carefully.

'Thelma? Are you free? We have a client.' she called up the stairs.
A muffled voice replied 'I'll be down in two ticks.'
Fay looked across the room at Steve, smiling 'Just a minute love, she'll be down in a minute.'
Steve nodded and scratched his neck apprehensively. Although he was pleased that he had managed to track her down in less than a day, he was not altogether comfortable with the idea of such an intimate encounter with her just yet. He would like to get to know her on a more platonic basis, before forming any kind of intimate relationship. He did not mind casual encounters with women he met at functions, but he had an inclination that this encounter may totally overwhelm him if he was not careful. He moved himself further to the edge of the seat and gazed at the plush carpet nervously.

     At that moment, a winsome woman who matched Mary's description of Thelma entered the room. She was a tall woman with bronze skin that shone in the subdued light. Without a word, she led him up the narrow bare stairs to the first floor and into a small boudoir. The room was lit dimly by pink/red light that came from a rustic lamp on the bedside table. The room was empty of any furniture, aside from a bidet in the corner and the bed, which was no higher than a foot off the ground and was without a headboard or even pillows. The room felt almost too clinical to invoke any decent level of arousal in him.
'First the money.' she said starkly.
'Of course, here.' he passed her his multicard.
She snatched it and examined both sides of the card with a frown.
'We don't accept these things. Cash only. Neither do we participate in the favour-for-a-favour scheme. No cash, no play.'
Steve lifted his coat from the chair.
'I'm sorry I wasted your time.' he said half relieved, making for the door quickly.
'Whoa! Wait a minute.' Thelma hurried over to the door to block his exit 'Let's not be too hasty…' she exhaled deeply '…Look, there's a pawnbroker on Redbridge Road.
They do cash back. Tell ya what, go there first thing tomorrow and come straight here with the money. I'm just warning you, if you don't turn up with the readies by nine a.m. tomorrow, for whatever reason, Mr Stubbs will send his boys to come and find you.'
She placed her earrings on the bedside table.
Her tone became relaxed 'You know there ain't many places in Cliffbridge what accept multicard payment. Come to think of it, you'd be hard pushed to find *any* form of money accepted in most places. But prostitution is a tricky game with no safeguards so we have to accept cash. Two hundred quid.'

She got to her feet.
 'Right...*Steve* isn't it?'
He just sat there without saying a word; his eyes staring at the wall behind her.
'Well?' she asked with an air of disappointment.
'Sorry, I've got to go. I'll see you get your money...'

FOUR

Monday 10th February 2048. Ward's End, London. 0857 Hrs.

It was just before nine the following morning and Steve was standing at the door to the brothel on Fox Road. The snow lay just as hard under foot, but had become decorated with footprints and bicycle tracks. The wind blew colder and bit at his face sharply. He held the banknotes which he had exchanged earlier that morning from the pawnbroker; a fifty, five twenties, and five tens. The notes displayed Queen Elizabeth the Second, under whose reign the last notes had been issued. They had almost disintegrated over time and felt leathery and damp. As he examined them, he could not understand why anyone would still find any use for them; even a place like this. They just seemed too inconvenient and large. He remembered taking 'dinner money' with him to school and, more often than not, either losing it or being beaten up for it. A simple multicard, he mused, was so much easier and foolproof.
He tapped the flimsy door. Thelma appeared at once, dressed in a pink bathrobe. 'Yes?' she enquired looking perplexed.
'I've brought the money. Don't worry, it's all there.' he sneered.
'Oh it's you.' she stated coldly, tying her bathrobe together.
'Yes, here...' he handed the notes over.
She held them up to the light to check the watermarks. 'Seems to be all there.'
She stepped back inside and shut the door in his face.

***

Remembering the advice given by Mary Hamilton in the chip shop the day before, Steve decided to drive into central Cliffbridge and to locate the library. He meandered his way cautiously around the one-way system until he joined the A101; the arterial road into Cliffbridge. The road rose high above the densely packed tenements of Ward's End like a large upward escalator into the sky. The grey and biscuit-coloured buildings below appeared small and simple; almost like Lego buildings. He was now cruising along the gritted A101 at just over ninety miles per hour. The highway appeared well maintained, unlike the broken roads below. Being so high up above the metropolis and so close to the teal sky, he felt like he was in control of a small aeroplane. There was hardly any traffic on the road and the car was virtually driving itself. Playing on the sound system was "The Love of Richard Nixon" by The Manic Street Preachers. Steve often played this track while driving at high speed; the heavy drumbeats and the guitar solo in the middle elevated his mood, while the controversial lyrics filled him with the reassurance that there are always two sides to every coin in a difficult set of circumstances.

Some time later, the A101 gave way to a ramp which corkscrewed down onto the Cliffbridge High Street. The road was like any other boulevard; wide with a large walkway both sides and an avenue of what appeared to be Horse Chestnut trees, although the absence of leaves made it difficult to be certain. The leafless trees, though, were the only adornment along the thoroughfare, with only the clear sky for colour. Although generally in good condition, the road was untreated and a thin layer of snow covered it. Despite the road being flanked by many parked vehicles, very few people were in sight. A skinny window cleaner with a tired complexion swept an old rag across a tinted window of an insurance broker. He wore a macabre, discontent expression.

Steve edged his way westwards along the road at about five miles per hour, on the look out for anything resembling a library. He passed a disused Tesco store which appeared to have been unoccupied to sometime; grey steel grills covered the large windows. "To Let" was written on a wooden placard; it too looked like it had been there for quite some time if the peeling lettering was anything to go by. As he passed the old shop, he saw on the opposite side of the road what appeared to be a fully functioning nightclub. "The Great Bear" flashed above the narrow entrance in blue, providing a contrast to the black façade. A large black and white poster advertising Friday night's reggae evening covered the door. Steve was not a reggae fan, although he was intrigued to see whether there was a Two Tone evening listed on the fixture list on the opposite side. He lowered the passenger window and leaned across for a closer look. A bitter breeze swept across his face, which caused the fixture list to almost detach itself from the window. He noticed a Ska night planned for the fourteenth of March, although he did not plan on staying longer than two weeks.

'You alright, gov'nor? You look lost!' came a voice.

Steve looked up and noticed a man dressed in a flat cap and grey puffer jacket.

'I'm looking for the library.' Steve explained.

The man shook his head.

'You're goin' the wrong way! And it ain't a conventional library-it's inside Central House, on the ground floor.'

Steve appeared perplexed.

'Sorry, *where?*'

'Central House! The community centre, although don't let Mr Stubbs hear you call it that! It's supposed to be a place of greatness, you know? I think it's all a load of crap myself.' he stiffened 'I didn't say that, mind...'

Steve nodded.

'Well anyway, turn round and follow the road for about half a mile and it's on your right. Can't really miss it; massive building!' he adjusted his cap 'Listen, you ain't one of them outside businessmen sorts are ya?' he asked, looking at Steve's tie.

Steve touched his tie realising that he had unwittingly dressed in one of his usual suits and had forgotten to dress down.

'No, I'm actually a dustman with a chip on my shoulder.' he said sarcastically.

'Oh…' he gave Steve a melancholy stare 'Only there have been a lot of news reports on the TV about conspicuous looking people…dressed like you. If you wanna stay out of trouble, I suggest you wear something a bit more working class.'

He touched his cap respectfully and walked away hurriedly down the adjacent road.

Steve threw the gear stick into first and turned the car to face the opposite direction and double backed along the road, passing the old Tesco store and the window cleaner. Many side roads flanked the High Street, which appeared almost as long, complete with avenues of trees and parked cars. Going along at his usual speed, he almost drove straight past Central House, noticing it just in time and swinging in to a parking space on the road. Getting out, he noticed who appeared to be the petulant boy who had sworn at him yesterday. He was dressed as a parking attendant and was only recognisable because of his beady blue eyes and skinny body.

'How long are you planning on stayin'?' the youth asked solemnly.

'You again.' remarked Steve bitterly 'I could have you for loutish behaviour.'

The boy glared at him menacingly from beneath his cap.

'Fifty quid for an hour's stay.'

'What?' exclaimed Steve 'Anyway, what about the favour-for-favour scheme?'

'Don't apply for parkin' charges. Pay up, or sod off.'

Steve glared back at the boy.

'It seems to me that you lot make up the rules as you go along.' grumbled Steve.

'This will have to do.'

He handed the boy a twenty-pound note.

'That'll buy you half an hour.' said the boy, writing out a receipt.

Steve snatched the receipt, cursed and drove into a free parking space beside the building.

He gazed at the building that he hoped was Central House. It was a vast cuboid-shaped bricked building, not dissimilar to the style of the old Television Centre in

Wood Lane. Displayed across the face of the building was a very large plasma screen, with an area of approximately eight square metres. The display ran:

82-88MHz: Channel 6, Band I. Alto-Zero. Broadcasting on Low Power. The pips used during test card transmissions came from the two large speakers below it.

Upon the roof, which was some forty feet high, stood three transmitters; one for either channel he guessed. He was unsure what the third transmitter was used for.

His eyes were suddenly drawn to the narrow multicoloured crazy paving, which led to the entrance to the building. Either side, stood sparsely arranged conifer trees, which softened the mood of the mundane building. He wandered slowly along the path until he reached the sliding doors.

He found himself inside a lobby. The air smelt of old dust, which immediately took him back to his days at Oxford. A Perspex sign that hung from above the oak reception desk read:

Ground Floor: Reception (Red Area)

Central Library   (Blue Area)

The room in which Steve was standing was indeed very red. The bricked walls, which were not covered with plasterboard, were painted in a blood-red colour.

'Yes?' enquired the receptionist bluntly.

He was a skinny man of about forty-five with a heavy grey moustache, wearing a uniform complete with a peeked cap that obscured his eyes.

'Good morning. I need to use the library.' said Steve.

The receptionist gave him a distrustful look.

'Certainly, just produce your library card.'

Steve handed the man his multicard.

'Ha! This won't get you anywhere.' the man smirked.

'Well it gets me into every other library around the country.' Steve countered.

'I dare say it does...' began the man, handing Steve his card '...but it won't get you in here.'

A wave of rage shot through Steve and he became close to giving the receptionist the reaction he was after.

'I see.' he said through clenched teeth. 'I'll just have to go to have lunch early.' he glared at the man 'Don't you get sick of eating fish and chips day in day out? I know I would.' he pulled a smug face 'I don't expect they pay you enough. Oh, my mistake, they don't pay you anything.' he laughed, flapping a ten pound note in the man's face.

'I can't be bribed.' declared the man resolutely.

'We'll see about that.' smirked Steve.

'I'm sure you could find a use for this. Something for the wife, perhaps?'

The man gave Steve another look of distrust.

'I dunno…you look awfully suspicious…They warned us about the likes of you only yesterday on the television; you fit the description of a suspicious character perfectly.'

'You don't strike me as the sort of fellow who believes everything he hears. Look, all I'm asking is that you allow me to borrow a book.' Steve said, holding the man's eye contact.

The man snatched the banknote and showed Steve to the library.

The library appeared grossly underused; there was not a book out of place in the broadly categorised "Science" section. He picked a book up from one of the shelves. It was a paperback entitled "The Heart: A Beginner's Guide". The front cover crumbled as he turned it. The page marked "Acknowledgements" crumbled in between his index finger and thumb, like a charred sheet of paper, leaving his right hand covered in dust. His eyes scanned the long parallel rows of bookcases, each with a winding handle. He recalled from his conversation with Mary Hamilton that the book he was looking for was in the local history section, towards the back. He walked quickly to the far wall. On the wall, a Perspex sign reading: "991.0-995.4 Cliffbridge History: 1950-Present" highlighted the shelves which were separate from the other books which were housed in the bookshelves. The books lay sprawled in a higgledy-piggledy fashion and in no order. There were around fifty books, each containing an account of life in Cliffbridge from the nineteen fifties onwards. He remembered that he had been told that the book was an unpublished manuscript. He felt sure that it would not take him long to find the book, however the more he searched, the less confident he became; every book in front of him was a published one. The likely possibility that the book was already on loan filled him with dread. He became more and more agitated, throwing every other book onto the floor. As he did so, the obscured wall behind the books was revealed, until at last he found what he was looking for. A thin, dog-eared piece of yellow card with the title: "The Rise of Cliffbridge" handwritten in copperplate, hit his eyes like a bolt of lightening; it had got lodged between two fallen shelves. He grasped it and pulled it free, holding it to his chest securely.

Giving a long, loud sigh of relief, he buried the manuscript under his shirt and lodged it under his belt so that it was out of sight. He made his way out of the library and back into the lobby. The receptionist stood fiddling with the ten-pound note.

Noticing Steve's presence, he lifted his cap clear of his eyes and said: 'Didn't you find what you were lookin' for?'

'I managed to read up on what I needed.' said Steve.

The man nodded 'I could get you to fill in a membership form?'

'That won't be necessary.' replied Steve and left the building.

***

Steve stood on the High Street and scanned the surrounding area in search of the launderette. He walked eastward down the road and noticed a tumbledown shop with a wooden panelled façade on the corner of Juxton Street. Rubbish, mainly discarded chip papers, tarnished the doorstep. He pushed open the door, which caused a bell to ring above it. The scent of fabric conditioner hit him, as did the stuffy air. The room was decorated with orange, yellow and brown tiling giving the place a very dated feel. The badly chipped concrete waiting bench in the middle of the room was flanked by a row of seven driers to the left and ten washing machines to the right. Although the sun by now was shining brightly in the cloudless sky, the stiflingly bright halogen bulbs splashed their brilliant white light down, flooding the room. Despite being in need of repair, the shop was managed efficiently. Laundry baskets crowned every machine and a token-operated tablet dispenser that hung on the adjacent wall to where Steve was standing contained five types of detergent and a laminated notice, which was fixed to the door, listed the services on offer, from a standard service wash to dry-cleaning.

Mary Hamilton stood at the far end, struggling to fold a double fitted sheet while removing the ash from her cigarette. Steve wondered why anyone would bring their laundry in, only to be replaced by the far more unpleasant smell of smoke. She caught sight of him as she added the sheet to the pile which was balanced on a rusty spin dryer.

'Oh! Just the man! You can help me fold these sheets!' she grinned. 'Just grab the two corners at the other end…that's it.'

She shook her head as she grappled with her corners.

'You see fitted sheets are a real bugger to handle. They're a nightmare to fold, let alone iron!'

Steve lifted the two corners of a pink floral fitted sheet, pulled tightly and walked two steps to meet Mary's corners. She peered at the manuscript, which he had left on the bottle green plastic garden chair behind them.

'So you managed to get it out okay then I see?' she said with a grin.

'It wasn't easy.' he replied.

She looked puzzled as she picked up another bed sheet.

'How d'you mean?' she asked with a frown.

'I had to bribe the fellow on the desk, because I don't carry a library card.'

'How?' she asked, handing Steve two corners.

'With a bit of money, that's all.' he said nonchalantly.

Her face seemed to drop; as did the bed sheet from her end.

'You did *what?*'

'Well, you see I had to think on my feet…' he explained.

She sat down on the plastic chair.

'You really oughtn't have done that. See, people in Cliffbridge…well, the average person at any rate, are very proud. Fish is the staple diet and the only food that's widely available. You most probably made poor old Simon feel inferior.'

'I'm sure he'll live. I haven't got the patience to walk on eggshells with people's feelings.' he said, folding his arms.

'You've probably made Simon all the more suspicious, in that you're a stranger to these parts. If you don't watch it, you'll wind up in front of the Community Panel.'

Steve looked at her, confused.

'Sit down.' she said, pulling another plastic chair free of the storeroom door. 'Tell me, have you managed to look anythin' up in the book?'

'No, I've only just got it from the library.' he said.

She offered Steve a pre-rolled Cannabis joint.

'Smoke?'

'That stuff's illegal, as is smoking in a public facility.' he said dismissively. She gave a chortle 'I can see you're gonna need some of this if you're gonna get by in *this* society!' she pushed the joint under his nose 'Take it.' He held it between his finger and thumb; it felt heavier than an ordinary cigarette. He removed the plastic casing and held it up to his nose. The pungent smell of herbs hit his nose immediately. Even during his years at Oxford he had never been tempted by Marijuana; he had been far too uppity to bother with what the government had penned as "The Poor Man's Plan".

'Why don't you? It won't kill ya.' she smiled, offering him a light.

He did not want to appear contrary and so snatched it from her confidently. He lit it, drawing deep breaths as he did so. He looked on through the plumes of white smoke that encircled. He leaned back on the chair as he felt his stress levels begin to subside.

'How is it?' Mary enquired with a smile.

'Not quite what I expected.' he said with a cough.

'I wouldn't make it into a habit. But all things in moderation don't do you no harm.' she quipped, placing a foil ashtray on the shelf behind him.

'Now to the business about this book…' she picked the manuscript up and placed it on her lap, flicking through the crinkled pages. 'Aha. Here we go… "Cliffbridge 2005-2023".' she placed a pair of rimless spectacles on her nose and began scanning the pages. After a period of approximately two minutes, she began again 'In essence, the Brown administration commissioned Salvador Dos Ramos, a Brazilian architect, to turn the greenbelt area of Havering and the western part of Essex into an urban settlement primarily for young, rich professionals. The Cliffbridge Fiscal Academy on level six in Central House, now the broadcasting suite, was where the professionals furthered their already comprehensive education in economics. Many worked in the City or in the Docklands. Mr Brown pioneered the idea in order to boost Britain's economic growth and developed the area throughout his premiership. The area was a centre for high achievers and financial masterminds. Many foreign investors brought their businesses to London, seeking a highly specialised workforce. As the economy grew, Cliffbridge expanded and expanded until in 2015 it was declared the largest London borough; both in terms of area and population. Brown, by then the former Prime Minister, was awarded the Financial Times Investor of the Year Award in 2017, but nobly forfeited the award, claiming to have "Just done his job for Britain during difficult times." The following year saw Cliffbridge being granted it's own regional assembly and so opted out of the London Assembly, however choosing to remain a part of Greater London for posterity...'

Steve blew a thick, white smoke ring into the air and then paused, attempting to collect his thoughts through a head-rush.

'So I presume something must have gone wrong at some stage?'

Mary flicked through the manuscript quickly, adjusting her glasses upon her nose.

'Yeah I was just comin' onto that...Aha! Here it is... "The Great Change 2024-2035".' She muttered the odd word as she ran her finger along the text ardently. Her finger came to a rest on a page near the back cover. Her forehead furrowed as she began to recall the past.

'Yes, you could say that.' she said, lowering her specs. 'It was the year before I lost my husband when the trouble really began around here.'

'Go on...' Steve prompted her eagerly; taking another drag.

'Well the government...then under Richards, announced in 2025 that they were going to pull out of the scheme altogether...just like that.' she said snapping her fingers. 'And why? To hide behind his own shortcomings, that's why.'

He began in a matter-of-fact tone 'So what happened then exactly?'

'In a nutshell, one minute the City was bringing lots of money to our shores and the next it was losing it like sand through their fingers.' she explained heartily.

'Something to do with the Prime Minister and, indeed the Chancellor, creaming off the profits for personal gain, resulting in a lack of foreign investment...I guess...' he said, allowing his guard to slip.

She gave him a nod 'Exactly so. Anyway Richards, under the close scrutiny of Dawson, the then Chancellor, responded in blind vindictiveness by cancelling the central funding to the academies and the elaborate health centres, affectively undoing the work of the Brown administration.'

'Hmm. So what was Richards and Dawson's excuse for their destruction of the place?'
'Well a press conference was held in Moorgate by Dawson in which he claimed to have unmasked a crime syndicate in the City and ensuring the rest of the country and the stock markets of the world that such a catastrophe would never happen again.' she explained.
'In reality though, the government was...*is* a crime syndicate all of its own.' he agreed.
Mary stubbed out her cigarette end and exhaled.
'Exactly right. It was at this time that we and the then mayor, Mr Stubbs, lost favour with the government and began to pull ranks. A secret meeting was called which was held at a disused underground station which Stubbs chaired.' she offered him the book 'The rest you can read for yourself.' she looked at him with a sideways glance 'Now you can drop the act and tell me what you're really doing here.'
Steve crossed his legs 'Sorry?'
'Don't give me that; we both know that you didn't come here to see a sick uncle.' she continued.
Steve was unable to mask his unease.
'You came all the way here to get to know Thelma, didn't you?' she said with a wry smile 'You got the word from someone that she's hot property and now that the dog's seen the rabbit, you wanna get to know her-am I right or am I right?'
'Ah.' breathed Steve with a small smile.
'I knew it, you're hooked! Sick uncle indeed!' she jeered, shaking her head 'You see, I could tell you were a man on a mission from the moment you set foot in that chippy!'
Steve felt the weight lift from his shoulders.
'Yes, you've busted me.' he smiled.
'Indeed I have! You've hardly mentioned your so-called sick uncle, you've just been rattlin' on about Thelma! I'll help you in whatever way I can, sonny Jim!'
'I was hoping you'd say that. You see, I walked away with the impression that I didn't exactly impress her last night.' he admitted.
'Aha! So you want some of the old Viagra to sort you out, right?' she grinned.
'No, don't be so utterly ridiculous.' he snapped.
'Alright, then what?' she asked, folding her arms defensively.
'I want to know how I can impress her and therefore get to know her better.'
Mary thought for a moment and brushed some washing powder from the top of the dryer.

'Take my advice, don't come across as bein' to obtainable. Thelma, just like the rest of us girls, like a man who's a bit of an enigma, get my drift?'
'Believe me, I can do standoffish.' he smiled.
'But having said that, underneath the brazen ice queen, lies a frightened little girl, so show her that you're not just another client.' she smiled.
Steve's brow sank in confusion.
'Listen, when you see her next time, play her at her own game. That is, do somethin' like invite her to see a West Ham match, complete with fish and chips and she'll be your friend forever.'
'West Ham?' he asked with disappointment.
'Look, we've all had to make sacrifices for those we're fond of; I had to become a Jew when I married. Going without my bacon sandwiches for thirty years almost done me in!'
'But I support Millwall.' he said.
'She knows that no-one's perfect! Anyhow, I've got a lot to do here and you've put me behind.'

FIVE

Monday 10th February 2048. Cliffbridge, London. 1705 Hrs.

The sun was just beginning to disappear behind the tall buildings, which stood like far-off statues against the royal blue sky. During the last few hours the snow had begun to thaw, which made a squelching sound underfoot. Rubbing his palms together, he left the laundrette behind him and rejoined the High Street. He clutched the book tightly, like his life depended on it. He walked back round to where his car was parked and there it was-unmarked and unscathed. He half expected to find at least a dent on one of the wings or a broken wing mirror where the local mob had been. But instead he found a black and yellow leaflet under one of the windscreen wipers. "Release fee: £500". He peered down at the wheels and sure enough, a red clamp covered the rear offside wheel.
'Blast!' Steve exclaimed.

He looked at his watch and then at the setting sun. He had not intended being so long in the launderette. The plan was simply to find the book and drive home in time for lunch. He remembered a Department of Health pamphlet, which a friend had worked on two years ago. He remembered reading about the effect Marijuana can have on one's perception of time; an afternoon could seem like an hour.

From the corner of his eye he caught sight of a signpost which stood at a forty-five degree angle at the mouth of an alleyway on the opposite side of Juxton Street. It read: "Ward's End 4 miles". He ambled closer to it and rested his back against a bent lamppost beside it. He scanned the area. Darkness was falling quickly and just at that moment the lamppost flashed on. The canal twisted beside him as far as the eye could see, along which a towpath stretched through an avenue of spindly trees. His vision grew clearer as he found himself trotting down the path at some speed. As his trot broke into a run, the skinny trees disappeared and the path beneath him turned from a broken stony mess to a continuous chocolate strip. The wind whistled in his ears, clearing his head of the fumes within him. If he continued at this pace, he thought, he would reach Ward's End in under an hour.

Some time later, the path bore to the right, where the trees stopped and an open field began. A lit sign read "Donkey Park". The park lay as a bottle green sheet beneath the moon's glare; dormant except for the sound of a lone owl calling and with not one donkey in sight. He could now make out the Ward's End area in the distance; the bright pink and blue lights of the adult quarter and what was probably the dazzle of Fox Road. His eyes became fixated on the far off oasis, which gave his feet more momentum, until he felt a sharp jolt on his left shoulder. He dropped the book.

'Watch it pal.' came a disgruntled elderly voice.

Steve noticed a pair of bulging eyes staring up at him. They belonged to a small elderly man holding a bottle of gin.

'I was.' Steve protested, reaching down for the book.

'You look lost to me.' said the man. 'Where're you headin'?'

Steve softened 'Ward's End.'

The man looked at Steve more closely with a squint.

'Hmm. New are ya?' the man asked, his breath smelling of gin.

'Just passing through.' Steve explained.

The man gave him a wary look.

'Visiting an uncle.'

'Well you ain't gonna reach Ward's any time soon going this way.' the man explained.

'The sign back there said four miles.' Steve pointed.

The man gave a chuckle.

'As the crow flies! But this field is littered with all sorts of obstacles like swamps filled with adders to name but one!'

Steve shrugged brazenly 'I've seen worse, but I appreciate the tip.'

The man winced 'Look here son. As luck would have it, I'm headin' that way now, I've got some fish to deliver to the chippy.'

Steve remembered the man in the newsreel and recognised him at last.

'Alright, if it isn't putting you to any trouble.'

'Nah. No trouble.' the old man breathed. The boat's a few feet upstream.'

They walked through the darkness along the dimly lit towpath. The old man's thick, white beard was just visible under the vague orange light. He maintained a frown as he staggered in front of Steve at a quick pace. He struck Steve as the sort of man whom does not interact much with other people; least of all people like Steve. After a short walk, they came to a jetty with a small fishing boat moored to it. The sulphuric smell of the canal and the darkness filled Steve with certain unease.

The old man climbed on board clumsily.

'Well on y'get then. It ain't no speedboat but it'll certainly take you to Ward's much quicker than on foot.'

The boat appeared in greater disrepair than it did on the newsreel. Rust covered the sides, while a piece of cork attempted to plug a hole on the deck, but allowed small amounts of water to trickle aboard. Steve joined the old man beside the wheel. The small motor spluttered into life. With a cautious touch of the control, the boat edged slowly away from the jetty and along the canal.

'How fast can this thing go?' asked Steve.

The old man frowned harder and groaned, pulling the control back. The motor's splutter turned into a roar as the boat began to glide above the canal like a skater on ice.

'The trouble is with you youngsters is your impatience. Now I fought in the Iraq War and we didn't win that by being hasty.' the old man exclaimed, fumbling with his snuff box.

Steve gave him a raised eyebrow 'You didn't win it at all; it's still going on.'

The man scraped a match across the box cursing.

'That's rubbish, everyone knows that. The government will have you believe anything. You must be more gullible than you look.' he said, tapping Steve on the arm with his pipe.

If only it were that simple, Steve pondered to himself. The truth was he was the one who had manufactured the propaganda telling the nation that prices had risen due to unrest in the Middle East. The news footage on the screen in the filling station the week before was convincing to the point that he had almost forgotten he had had a part in composing it. He had almost forgotten a number of things in the short space of time between leaving Belgravia and now. He looked up at the full moon, which hung low in the panther sky, trying his best not to let the noise of the motor blemish this otherwise tranquil experience. Looking past the old man on the right, Ward's End stood larger, with the neon signs becoming almost tangible.

    The boat bore left as the canal grew wider until it was almost a lake. Steve took out the photograph of his mother from his inside pocket. He gave it a wipe with his finger, revealing his mother's beauty beneath the moon's glare. The old man glanced to his left.

'Fine figure of a woman.' he coughed, as if embarrassed. 'Reminds me of a local gal.'

'Oh?' Steve queried.

'A local entertainer. Very popular with the lads…because of her natural beauty, like.'

After a moment of puzzlement, Steve realised to whom he was referring. He would never have allowed anyone to compare his mother with any prostitute; pretty or otherwise. But it was the old man's turn of phrase "fine figure of a woman" and "…because of her natural beauty" which allowed Steve for forgive him. In any case he was right; his mother did possess a natural beauty which was obvious to the most critical of eyes. Suddenly, a spray of water hit the photograph as the man steered sharply. Tiny droplets covered the picture, concealing his mother's face.

'Now look what you've done, you clumsy old fool.' Steve muttered, taking a handkerchief from his pocket and swept it across the photograph.

At first sight, it appeared that he had remedied the problem and the photograph was clear of the droplets. But no sooner had the water disappeared, than the image became hazy.

The old man's face creased.

'Who are you callin' an old fool?' he groaned.

'Look what you've done!' Steve yelled, holding the photograph to the man's face.

The image by now had completely smudged, leaving an unintelligible mess on the paper. Steve had done his best to maintain the photograph throughout his adult life by making little contact with it, except first thing in the morning and last thing at night. Not so much a spec of dust had fallen onto it in over ten years and suddenly it had disappeared; his mother had disappeared.

The old man grew more and more unsettled.

'Look, if you're gonna cause me grief then you will have to get off my boat.' he said, slowing the boat to a standstill.

Steve began to weep 'All my life I've cherished this photograph, I've never even let it out of my sight.'

The man appeared half sympathetic 'Look son, I'm sorry. I didn't mean for this to happen.'

Steve's forehead furrowed deeper 'Oh, and you think that's going to fix this picture do you?

The man looked alarmed 'Look son, it's best you get off. Ward's End ain't far now, you could walk it in ten minutes.'

He looked down to the deck where the book lay open with the leaves flicking back and forth in the strengthening wind. He glanced back at Steve with a melancholy look.

'Is this yours?'

Steve's face changed colour 'And what if it is?'

'I knew it, a government sleuth!' exclaimed the old man 'You wait 'til the Community Panel hears about this!'

Steve flexed his hands and clasped them around the old man's neck. He could feel the sinews beneath the skin become more and more tense as he strengthened his grip. The man's face reddened while his feeble hands wrestled with Steve's like a drowning puppy. The more the old man struggled, the harder Steve pressed. He could feel the jugular vein against his finger, like a steel rod. The old man's yellow tongue hung limply from his mouth. He was unable to counter the boat's turbulence as he fell to the deck with a heavy thud. A frown crinkled his forehead as he attempted to speak, but Steve could not make sense of what he was trying to say. All too suddenly, the frown left his face, followed by his last gasp.

Steve fell to his knees beside the old man. His instincts told him to check for a pulse. He placed two fingers gently on the man's neck, but there was no obvious sign of an output. He began to panic, reaching frantically for his multicard. He dialled 112.

'New Scotland Yard, which service please?' came the voice.

Steve did not speak a word.

'Hello?' the operator persisted.

Steve was crippled with fear.

'Is everything okay? With whom am I talking?'

Steve remained silent before hanging up. There was no point in asking for an ambulance to come here, he thought; they would only refuse on the account that this was Cliffbridge. He surveyed the inlet of water for any other boats; nothing. He peered at the towpath at the opposite side; nobody. His heart rate slowed in relief that no-one had witnessed the incident, but he was only too conscious of the predicament he was in.

He had not been in a predicament of any real measure since he was a boy. It was by many people's standards more of a molehill than a mountain. It was at school during a maths lesson at the age of nine when he had quite accidentally marked his neighbour's shirt with his biro. "My mum's gonna come up the school when she hears about this!" cried Marcus Cohen. He remembered the feeling of sickness in the depths of his stomach. He had sloped off home during the lunch hour to tell his foster mother about the whole thing. She pulled him up to her lap to sit on while he poured out his heart to her. She listened intently to every word, making sure her smile did not wane even on hearing about what a "bruiser" Marcus' mother was. She reminded Steve that the "best way out is always through"; something her own mother had told her as a girl. So she lifted Steve from her lap and they set off back to the school where she carefully explained the story to Mrs Fletcher in the playground. The matter was quickly resolved and there was never any sign of Mrs Cohen for the rest of his days at Oakfield Prep. Perhaps there never was a Mrs Cohen Steve had later thought.

There was no-one to turn to now though. It was now five minutes to seven on a cold, frosty night. Mary Hamilton would have been the obvious person under the circumstances, but she was a mile or two downstream and he was still unsure what she would have made of it all. He thought for a moment, looking to the neon lights in the near distance. There seemed to be no option other than to carry on as if nothing had happened and hope that the problem would just fade away like his childhood angst.

***

He knocked at the door to the brothel. His numbed hands thrashed against the brittle wooden door, causing a few flakes of paint to peel off.

'Hello?' he called 'Hello! Thelma are you in there? Thelma!' he shouted as he hit the door harder.

Between hits, he could hear the bass line of "Red Red Wine" clearly, giving him the impression that the music inside must have been almost deafening. Fearing he would not be heard, he began to kick the flimsy door.

'Thelma!' he cried at the top of his voice.

The banging was powerful enough for the single-glazed window of the upstairs bedroom to tremor slightly. After more persistent banging, the light of the room upstairs switched on, revealing a silhouette of what must have been a worker, but Steve was unable to tell if it was Thelma or not. The sash was thrown up and Thelma's head appeared between the curtains:

'Yes, yes! What d'you want?' she called down angrily.

'I just wondered if you were free?' he shouted up.

'Well you're gonna have to wait…I'm busy.' she said pulling the sash back down.

The light went off in the room.

Steve persisted with more force 'Thelma! Hurry up with whoever you have up there and open this door!'

After a minute or two the light came on once again, quickly followed by the opened sash. 'Look, I won't tell you again!' she shouted down with slit eyes. Her voice lowered 'Look, I'm with a client-come back in an hour or so.'

She drew back inside and lowered the sash.

Steve was rendered shell-shocked for a moment. A bitter cocktail of jealousy and resentment pulled at his heart. It would have been easier if he had felt possessive like any man would towards a partner. His feeling was the sort of emptiness a small boy feels when his mother shares her love with a new love interest. He did not want to share her with anybody; he needed her undivided attention.

After more kicking on the door, the door flew open suddenly, causing Steve to kick Thelma hard on the shin.

'Sorry, I wasn't expecting…' he began.

'Save it.' she interjected solemnly, rubbing her leg with a frown.

She swept her face clear of her hair and gave him a piercing stare:

'What's so urgent that you have to pull me away from a client? I'm not your possession; I have hundreds of paying clients who subscribe. What makes you so special?'

'I need your help.' he confessed.

'My help?' she asked, surprised and almost flattered. 'What with?'

Steve paused to collect his thoughts. His head was full of coherent sentences to explain in detail what had taken place earlier that night on the canal. He knew that once he had unburdened himself of his predicament, then he would feel better. Just as he was about to do so, his rational thinking side of his mind took over, realising that although he already felt a curiously strong bond to the woman stood before him, she was still a stranger.
'I thought that we might spend some time chatting.' he suggested.
'Thelma's eyebrows raised and her eyes sharpened.
'Look, I don't know what your game is, or what kind of a mug you think I am, but I'm busy. I don't have time for wet, pathetic weirdoes like you.'
She slammed the door shut in his face. A sharp feeling of rejection pierced through him like a hot knife through butter.
He eventually pulled himself together as his vulnerable side gave way to rejuvenated impatience. He began to knock at the door again; moderately at first. No answer came. He persisted with heavier knocks. The door remained closed. His heart began to beat faster, giving his mind the focus it needed. Just when he was about to retire, the door flew open with a waft of cold air. This time it was not Thelma at the door, but a large man wearing boxer shorts and a leather jacket. His eyes were unforgiving and his fists were tightly clenched.
'Didn't you get the message the first time round?' he boomed.
Before Steve could reply, everything went black.

Some minutes later he came to face down in the melting snow. He felt a tender pain across his mouth and noticed that the snow to the right of his face was pink in colour. He shimmied himself into a sitting position and touched his lips with his fingers. The congealed blood dripped onto his palm. He moved on to all fours and reached for a handkerchief. The blood quickly saturated the thin rag, which led him to realise that he could be badly hurt. Using his knuckles, he ambled onto his feet, picking up the library book as he did so. It was now badly torn and wet from the slush. He hobbled over to the nearest lamppost to shake off the dizziness and to take a breath. As his vision settled, his eyes came to rest on the small tavern a few yards away on the corner of the street.

***

The Two Shillings Tavern was a small, quaint village-like pub of medieval character. The doorway was low and wooden, with the thatched roof inches from his head. A light from a tiny lantern set into a recess in the stone wall was enough for Steve to see his way clear of hitting his head against the low wooden beam above him. He pushed open the flimsy door and immediately sought a seat to rest on, if only for a short while to gather himself in the warmth before setting off home. He found a small table with a stool and set himself down, bowing his head free of any unwanted contact with the punters.

The lounge was just as much warm and inviting as it was small and cramped. The paraffin lamps that hung from the ceiling gave off a rich peach light, which depicted the many artefacts that were displayed in the countless nook and crannies. Brass platters adorned the stone walls, while tea sets from around England sat on the bricked windowsills. The bar itself took a prominent position, stretching the full length of the lounge. The only other punters left in the lounge were two men sharing folklore tales, an elderly man playing "The Lambeth Walk." over and over on an old, slightly out of tune piano, accompanied by a young fiddler.

Suddenly a man appeared behind the bar. A tall thickset man in his forties wearing a beer stained apron began whistling to himself as he polished a pint glass. Much to Steve's disappointment, he caught his eye. Giving a suspicious frown, the man slunk over to him.

'What do you want?' asked the man bitterly.

'What do people come to a pub for, to get their nails done?' retorted Steve.

The man gazed at him.

'We have a strict policy-no under twenty-fives.' declared the man.

Steve looked to his left, and then his right 'Sorry, are you talking to me?'

'Yes, now unless you've got some I.D. you'll have to turn around and leave.'

'Are you taking the mick?' sniggered Steve 'I'm thirty years old!'

'No I.D., no sale.' the man continued 'Do you not have a driving licence or somethin'?'

Steve thought for a moment and produced his multicard.

'Here.'

The barman picked it up and examined it carefully.

'What's this, some sort of a mobile phone?' the barman frowned.

'It's a multicard.' said Steve with an air of impatience.

'I don't care what it is; if it don't have your date of birth, it might as well be a fillet of cod.'

Steve snatched it back and called up the data screen, which contained his personal information.

'There...' he said showing the man.

The man examined the screen 'Steven Morrissey...Date of birth 20-01-18...Occupation..."

Steve snatched it back.

'That's all you need to know. Anyway, most people around here aren't so hot on laws, what makes this place so special?'

The barman picked up a pint glass and began to polish it with the tea towel.
'I run a legitimate business. If others won't follow my example, that's up to them.'
He glared at Steve's wound.
'That looks nasty.' he looked closer 'That could need a stitch or two, you know.' he scratched his head looking thoughtful. 'Come through to the back.'
'I'm sure it's worse than it looks.' Steve countered with a smirk.
'Look pal, it may well look worse than it is, but I'm not havin' you drop blood all over my carpet, now come through…'
Steve was led into the living room behind the bar. The room was much larger than the lounge, which surprised him. The lighting was much more adequate and the décor was more up to the minute, with mushroom coloured walls and Egyptian vases filled with bamboo. He sat at the dining table, upon which Pete had placed newspaper.
'The wife'll kill me if she sees her precious dining table used as a first aid clinic.' muttered the barman, dousing some cotton wool into a bowel of surgical spirit.
'So what was it then? An argument over some bird or somethin'?'
'No.' Steve mumbled.
'There ain't a day what don't go by that we don't have to see to some scrap or another.' he said with despair.
He looked at Steve directly as he held the cotton wool against the wound.
'So what 'appened?'
'I paid a visit.' he said quietly.
Pete loosened the pressure on the cotton wool 'Well it's full of trouble. You want my advice? Steer well clear of that place.'
'Well I didn't ask for it.' Steve remarked bluntly.
'Your face don't look familiar…can't say I've seen you around here before. Why are you here?'
Steve paused for thought and remembered his first conversation with Mary Hamilton in the chip shop. The time had not been right then to provide her with the spiel the government had told him to give and she had seen through his story about a sick uncle; revealing himself as a pretentious estate agent would only lead to more questions, which he was sure he would be no good at answering.
'I'm just passing through.' he said quickly.
Pete nodded 'Well I mean, under normal circumstances you wouldn't be here, you'd be in A&E, although there is a resident G.P. who has still clung on, despite being offered more attractive proposals elsewhere. Her name is Doctor Smith. Her capabilities are now, of course, limited because of the lack of equipment, but she does her best nonetheless. She

lives a few blocks away at 501 Marsh Road. She might be able to take a proper look at it.'
Steve nodded. 'When exactly did the hospitals close?'
'As soon as Westminster pulled the plug on us. That is, suspended the local health authority…along with the other local authorities; schools, transport and whatnot. Idiots, the lot of 'em.' he picked up another piece of cotton wool 'Undid all the hard work Gordon Brown put in at the beginning of the century.'
He glanced down at the library book.
'What's that you got there?' he asked with a curious glare.
Steve had almost forgotten he even had the book in his possession.
'Just a library book I'm borrowing. I thought I might as well re-familiarise myself with the local history while I'm here.' he said matter-of-factly.
The barman sniggered.
'It's a bit battered ain't it? I'd like to see old Simon's face when you return it, he'll be less than pleased to say the least. It's a good read, mind; makes you proud to be a part of such a vibrant community such as this.'
He attached a small dressing to Steve's face.
'There. I think you were right, it probably won't need stitches, just keep this on for the next day or two and that should clear it up. Take the antiseptic bottle with you when you go.'

As Steve was about to get up and take his leave, the pianist walked in carrying a pint of lager. Steve froze to the chair with fear. The man he saw was none other than the old man he had just killed; or supposedly killed.
'Here you go son, me an' Liam thought you'd appreciate a pint for medicinal purposes!' smiled the old man, holding the pint out for Steve to take.
'But you…' Steve murmured. '…Aren't you from the boat? I saw…'
The old man broke into laughter, winking at Pete.
'Every time, eh Pete?! Every time! No, that's my identical twin brother Bernie-he works on the canals and on the estuary. Daft bugger! Anyone who enjoys workin' on a broken old piece of tin in all weathers and hours must want their head lookin' at! Not the life for me, although he is a miserable old so-and-so, being away from people suits him right!'
He offered his hand for Steve to shake.
'Albert Wilson. And you are…?'
'St-Steve. Steve Morrissey.' he said nervously.
'Gordon Bennett!' exclaimed Albert. 'You're face ain't half changed colour! You look like you've just seen a ghost! Here, are you alright son?'
Steve staggered to his feet 'I need to lie down.'
'No no son, have y'pint first! It'll set you right in no time. I've dropped a bit of whiskey in there for good measure too!'

'No I must take my leave now; I need my bed. You've both been very hospitable, but I feel I've taken up enough of your time already.' Steve left the two men shaking their heads in wonderment.

SIX

Tuesday 11th February 2048. Cliffbridge, London. 0720 Hrs.

Steve awoke the next morning to the sound of two elderly men chatting on the street below, managing to pre-empt the clock radio which was about to roar into life. The king-sized bed was very comfortable and above all: warm. He could already feel the cold air biting at his feet which overhung the side. The single central heating system facilitated the whole block and was set to come on between 0800 and 1000 for the morning and 1700 and 2100 for the evening; the rest of the time you either froze or spent as little time inside the block as possible. He got up, put on his bathrobe and went into the bathroom, which was en-suite. He crossed the cold, sea-blue floor tiles and faced the shaving mirror. Gazing at the lower half of his face, he gently touched the dressing near his mouth. It still felt tender, although the pain had subsided. He began to cautiously remove the tape which fastened the gauze until he revealed the wound. It had scabbed over, but was swollen.

He walked over to the shower. It was an elaborate piece of apparatus, with many settings and the cubical was a good size. He turned the dial to 'warm' and slid the lever to 'jet'. The water rushed onto his back, the pressure quickly alleviating the tension in his muscles. As the steam plumes began to envelop him, his mind became more focused on the events that took place at the pub. Having met the old fisherman's twin brother, it was clear that Bernie Wilson was no loner as he had previously thought. The feeling of sick terror scraped on his stomach as the cheerful old pianist entered the living room. First the assumption that somehow Bernie had not died, but had survived and was back to toy with his guilt, shattered his mind. Finding out that Bernie, a seemingly lonesome old man, had at least one relative whom was something of a fixture at the local pub, coiled through him like a deadly snake. The latter thought was the more troublesome of the two. He could have just about handled Bernie being alive and well and ready to expose him in front of the Community Panel, but it was more chilling to realise that when the death is discovered, a witch-hunt on a large scale would almost certainly take place.

His mind must have recorded the images at the canal, because he began to recall them vividly. The trees stood like tall, old retired wardens keeping watch over their canal. He recalled the dense dark green undergrowth and the bitterly cold wind which forced the drizzle onto it; the sulphuric smell of the canal; the turgid jugular on Bernie's neck; the sight of the gory corpse as it lay their helplessly and his vacant eyes as they stared up desperately.

The steam plumes began to disperse as he turned the water off. Reaching for a towel, he stepped onto the woolly bathmat. He pulled on his bathrobe quickly; the draft hitting him as he left the warm steam behind and entered the unheated living room. He sat down on the settee and placed his feet on the glass coffee table. He picked up the library book. One of his four missions was now accomplished, he thought with some relief and judging by its appearance, anyone would think he went to huge lengths to get at it, which he hoped would reflect well on him when he returned to Whitehall. The library book provided the basis for his knowledge about the local history, but he had discovered much more besides since arriving two days before.

Feeling in need for some light entertainment before breakfast, he decided to command the plasma screen to switch on. He selected "Dominion" from the dropdown menu. The screen switched to a grainy picture, with an intermittent burst of high-pitched noise. The following usual text was just about legible:

60-66 MHz: Channel 3, Band I. Dominion. Broadcasting on low power.
'Damn rubbish.' he cursed to himself.

He was about to command the plasma screen to change to 'Alto-Zero', when the picture quality suddenly improved. A large fluorescent yellow '3' bounced around the screen accompanied by violin music. A jubilant voice then followed:

"You're watching Dominion on Channel Three!" The '3' remained on the screen followed by "Dominion" in florescent green. Two white lines jumped on the screen while the picture changed to what looked like the outside of Central House. A large crowd were gathered outside, chanting something very loudly, causing the reporter to shout at the camera:

"This is a special news bulletin coming to you from Central House! Good morning to you! We have received news this morning that Bernard Wilson, who most of you will know as Bernie, the principal fisherman for Cliffbridge…"

Steve sat up straight suddenly. His jaw slackened as the footage unfolded before him. He knew it was only a matter of time before the corpse was discovered, but he could scarcely believe it could have been that soon. He continued viewing the malaise of people chanting angrily outside the entrance.

"We are here live outside Central House on the High Street!" continued the young woman.

The reporter fitted the government's archetypal image of how a news reporter should appear; the shoulder-length hair; the light but noticeable makeup etc. The only thing missing was the veneered teeth. She held her hand to her earpiece:

"Hold on…We are getting reports that the hearing is about to start in the Community Room on the fifth floor! Let's cross now to Theo Riddell who is inside the building…"

After a delay, the scene changed to a large hall, not too dissimilar in outlay to the Cabinet Room at Number 10. One was given the impression that a civil meeting was under way, with the power to pass legislation. Just as in Number 10, there were a large number of people congregated around a vast and elaborate table. There were officials sharply dressed and stiffly poised, with the camera crew set back behind them. A man of about forty years old sat midpoint around the table. He was heavyset, with jet-black hair greased back, and dressed in a debonair fashion. Steve recalled the election flyer and realised that the man was Neil Stubbs. Whenever the camera panned in close, his heavy brow concealed his eyes, which seemed to be staring into the eyes of another person. The camera panned amateurishly to the right, where Thelma was caught staring back at him brazenly. The reporter's commentary continued for another minute, before the dialogue between the man and Thelma began:

'Good morning everyone.' began the man in a heavy London accent. 'As you are aware, it has come to my…indeed *our* attention that Miss Harrison, sat opposite to me, stands accused of the murder of Mr Bernard Wilson on the night of the 10th February of this year. Before I continue, is there anybody present who has any additional information which may have come to light since last night?'

The camera panned left to an elderly lady.

'Nothing else sir.'

'In that case, we shall get straight down to business.' he said with a frown. He looked across the table to Thelma. Her hair was swept over her face which was slouched in her hands.

'Are you Thelma Harrison of 2B Marsh Road?' he asked.

She gave him a despondent nod.

'Oh come on Thelma! It's not like you to be so coy!' he said with a laugh. He looked around at the rest of the panel, seeking acknowledgement of his wit by his panel, but got no response.

'Yes.' Thelma said clearly.

'Aha.' he began, rubbing his chin in satisfaction. 'And you're here before the Community Panel and, indeed before Cliffbridge via our TV link, charged with the murder of Mr Bernard Wilson. Is that correct?'

'No it ain't correct!' she protested fiercely, standing suddenly.

She gave him an equally fierce stare.

'Sit down woman! Or I'll have you on remand for two months before I decide to set another date!'

She sat down grudgingly 'I ain't committed no crime. No murder, I mean.' she surveyed the onlookers. Men, women and even a few children sat in

judgement; faces full of scorn. 'I ain't!' she pleaded 'Do I look capable of murder?' she asked them.
'Then you'll find what I am about to show you, the panel and the viewers particularly maddening...'
Suddenly there stood Maitland-Sloan to the left of Steve's armchair.
'I say there old boy! You must be away with the fairies this morning! I've been knocking for a good ten minutes...I thought I heard the plasma screen, so I thought you must be in. Anyway, just doing the attentive neighbour bit and making sure you're alright for butter and milk-that sort of thing...'
Steve took no notice, but continued watching the screen. The Community Panel seemed to be viewing some footage on a large screen. The image was grainy and the sound muffled, giving it an amateurish quality. Among the grains, Steve could just about make out a figure of a woman beside what appeared to be a canal. It could have been any woman such was the clarity of the footage. However, the near perfect image of the old man, which appeared to be Bernie Wilson, made the evidence against Thelma convincing.
'Are you going to sit there and deny that the woman in this film is you?' Stubbs asked Thelma with a sneer.
'I told ya already, it ain't me. Could be anyone.' she replied resolutely.
'You must take me to Central House right away. My car is out of action.'
'My dear man! Are you quite alright? Mr Stubbs is a very dangerous man! We can't simply pull up outside before taking over the airways! Please return to your senses at once!'
Steve gave James a look of sorrow.
'I know it may sound absurd, but there has been a clear miscarriage of justice.'
James gave him a puzzled glance.
'What makes you so sure of that? In any case, this woman has something of a reputation around here. I don't think it would be unfair to assume that this is not the first time she has been in front of the panel. What's more, I doubt it will be the last.'
'Be that as it may' began Steve conscientiously 'But I have reason to believe that she couldn't have been at the canal at the said time.'
James looked at him wryly.
'Really, how so?'
'Because she was with me.' Steve lied.
'I see.' breathed James with an air of disappointment.
A minute or so passed before James added 'Well. You have your own transport, don't you?'
'I'm afraid it's a long story. Look James, I wouldn't ask unless I was in need.'

James thought for a moment, scratching his neck as he considered his response.

'I have to take my daughter to Guy's Hospital for an examination later this morning...But if we're quick...'

'Absolutely, I'll just throw some things on-I'll be two minutes.' smiled Steve.

***

The loud hum of James' car made any conversation between the two of them almost impossible. The snow had all but completely disappeared in the breaking sunlight. For a February day, it was none too cold, allowing for the driver and passenger windows to be down a few inches. Steve recalled last night's events once more; he shook his head to rid himself of them.

'I'm afraid they don't build cars like this anymore!' smiled James, attempting to lighten the atmosphere.

'What, sorry?' asked Steve, dozily.

'I said they...' he broke off noticing Steve's edginess. 'You alright my friend?'

'What, sorry?'

'You seem very anxious. Care to enlighten me?' James probed.

Steve sat up in his chair and folded his arms 'There really isn't much to tell.' he stated defensively.

He glanced again at James, who put his foot down heavier on the gas, without saying a word.

'I gather your daughter is poorly then?' Steve chanced.

James' face sank slightly as his foot came off the gas 'Yes. Suspected leukaemia.'

Steve was about to offer his commiserations, but thought better of it for fear of a backlash.

'Children are durable creatures, I'm certain she'll have you running round after her before long.'

'I'm sure.' James said quietly as he swung the wheel towards the slip road.

James wished Steve all the best before leaving him outside Central House. The two camera crews for both television channels stood scattered on the grass. The large plasma screen continued to relay footage from inside as the crew looked on. Steve seized the opportunity to enter the building unnoticed.

'Can't go up there mate, it's off-limits.' called the same youth which he had repeatedly run into before; this time dressed in security wear which was far too big for him.

Steve approached the boy, grabbing his lapels.

'Listen you little idiot. Were you the one responsible for clamping my car?' The boy recoiled fearfully.
'Yes, guv, but you were a lot longer than you said you'd be-I was just followin' orders from above, that's all.'
'Well I'm warning you-if I ever have cause to speak with you again, I'll make sure that something of yours gets clamped and it won't be your car.'
'I'll go out now and take it off.' said the boy desperately.
Steve released the boy from his grip.
'You do that. I'm just here to speak to your boss; I'll tell him just how diligent you've been.'
Steve entered the express lift that took him to the tenth floor, which was the broadcasting suite for Alto-Zero. The corridor smelled of freshly laid carpet and newly painted walls. To his left was an oak door with a brass plaque, which read: "Controller". The sunlight poured in from the large windows, throwing shadows in the form of crosses onto the carpet. He continued along the corridor until he came to the entrance of what must have been the main studio. "Quiet Please" was handwritten on the wall to the left.

He could see the events unfolding behind the many cameras and sound equipment inside. Neil Stubbs' sneering, bloated face could be seen among the many wires which hung from the cameras and boom mics.

Steve was brought face-to-face with his childhood suddenly. He was five years old again and in the hallway of the family home in Southgate. He was cowering behind the stair posts, holding back the tears. The government had just been voted in and things were already changing for the worse financially. The cost of living far exceeded his father's meagre wage as a taxi driver and so he had turned to alcohol. Young Steve had been instructed to go to his room by his mother on his father's return from work each evening, so as not to further aggravate him. Steve had grown to recognise the mood his father was in by the way he turned the key in the front door; a quick and heavy-handed turn usually meant that he had not made enough money that day. It was Steve's mother who was always in the firing line. Seven years of marriage to such a demanding man had etched creases into her face and so looked much older than her twenty-eight years. She had become skinny and had worn her clothes to threads without the chance to replace them, while his father wore a newly pressed shirt and trousers each day. These clothes barely contained his obese body and his face was always sweaty, even in the winter. Young Steve watched as his father swept back his black, greasy hair to reveal his frowning bushy eyebrows. His mother had then enquired nervously about his day, when he took a quick swig of whisky from his flask. He then grabbed her neck with his left hand, pressing her against the wall. She pleaded with him to stop, but he would not. She dropped to the ground, while Steve's father froze, staring down at the corpse like a rabbit caught in headlights. He gave Steve one last look, before he flew out of the front door; the draft causing the framed picture of his mother on the small table to smash. That was the last he ever saw of his father. Steve had run up the stairs to the old landline telephone on the first floor. He dialled for an ambulance, just like his mother had shown him earlier that month. They had arrived half an hour later. He wailed as they carted his mother away on the stretcher. He clung tightly to the corners of the walls like a limpet in a vain attempt to remain in the house. "I don't wanna go with you stupid fat people, I'm a big boy, I can stay here! My mummy said I'm a big boy now..." he had protested. Just as he was being dragged out, he managed to reach for the small photograph, cutting his hand on the broken glass and causing it to bleed. As he was driven to the local social services department, he realised that at the tender age of just five, he had to leave his childhood behind him.

  Steve entered the studio. The voices, which had been hitherto muffled, were now all too loud. He stepped over the wires and edged his way slowly around the cameras without being noticed by anybody. He came to rest at the back row of seated people, trying to blend in the best he could, until the opportunity would present itself; he did not want people to think that he had made a special trip. For an otherwise cold morning, the room was overly heated by the numerous hot air convectors. The room carried a pungent smell of perspiration, which could not escape the sealed double glazed windows behind him. He made a habit of always carrying an A6 notepad and pen wherever he went. He felt the need to begin recording evidence, especially of a 'kangaroo court' arrangement. He suddenly thought against it, so as not to risk becoming more conspicuous. Stubbs and Thelma continued to exchange grievances against one another akin to playground bickering. It struck him as odd that although Neil Stubbs was apparently trying to promote a pro-democratic atmosphere in the room, with mothers and toddlers sat behind the officials, it was the elite who seemed to carry more influence. The mother's who were dressed in jeans and baggy woollen jumpers would scoff at a scathing comment made by Thelma, or nod in agreement with what Stubbs had said, but their contributions were light and unsubstantial. The sparring between Thelma and Stubbs had quickly intensified and Thelma had got to her feet in rage.

'Are you callin' me stupid? Why would I want to hang around some dingy canal late at night anyway?' she protested.

'Probably up to something far more lewd!' jeered a mother.

  Steve got up and quite casually and strolled to the front of the room, to where Thelma was now seated. Thelma's expression remained tense as her brow began to falter.

'I have something to say which will endorse Miss Harrison's testimony.' Steve said suddenly.
Stubbs and Thelma turned with a start.
'And who the bloody hell are you?' Stubbs frowned.
'My name is of no importance, I'm merely a concerned citizen.' Steve replied.
Stubbs leaned closer to him.
'And what business have you interrupting these proceedings?' Stubbs demanded.
Steve inhaled shallowly. He could almost feel the eyes of those behind him bore a hole into the back of his head. He knew very well that he was already drawing far too much attention to himself and was about to risk being revealed.
'This woman could not have committed such an atrocity, because…' he broke off suddenly.
He was not altogether sure whether he was prepared for what might follow. But it was too late as the ball had already started to roll.
'Because..?' probed Stubbs, his eyebrows sinking further.
'…Because I was with her.'
The crowd let out a gasp, turning their heads in his direction. Stealing himself, he decided to throw caution to the wind 'I slept with her.' He continued, noticing Stubbs' brow rising slightly. '…In the brothel on Fox Road.' He turned to face Stubbs, who had broken into a sweat 'Owned by your good self.'
The crowd let out a louder gasp as they turned to Stubbs, who looked down at the table in shame.
Steve took a moment to soak up the glory, watching the sea of faces muttering to one another. He then took a moment to study the defendant's face once again. It was obvious to him that she was relieved and even grateful, in spite of the fact that she was doing her best to disguise this.
'This is nonsense!' cried Stubbs at last.
The crowd fell into silence once more.
'Then what evidence do you have against her?' Steve insisted, leaning down towards him.
Stubbs gave a technician, seated at a control table, a nod.
'Watch, if you please.' asked Stubbs, with a small smile.
The crowd's attention was drawn once again to the large plasma screen on the north wall. The picture was grainy and amateurish, with poor sound quality. Steve recalled his days as a child, when he would watch tape-recorded episodes of sitcoms on an old VHS tape, which was almost worn-out. He remembered how past episodes from the previous week were ever so slightly visible underneath in the form of bright oranges and

greens. He watched the footage with an air of scepticism. The footage contained a shot of a woman, presumed to be Thelma, in what looked like the canal in question. There were the evergreen trees and the full moon, which shone brightly onto the water. The sight of that old, bearded face which was now embossed deeply into Steve's brain, flashed onto the screen. Steve's composure began to wane slightly as he watched on. The morbidity of Bernie's face intensified, while the crowd gasped in shock as a bony and wet hand came into view.

"No! No! No!" shouted the desperate old man as he attempted to escape the stranglehold. The descent of the old man to the deck was documented in Steve's mind in slow motion. He had catalogued each stage; the bending of the legs, the wobbling of the head and the deafening loudness of the thud as the corpse landed. Steve ran his fingers through his hair, as the crowd sat transfixed to the screen, like youth during a Stalinist parade. The crowd remained stunned as the footage ended, leaving the screen to display the television station's logo and slogan.

'There you have it ladies and gentlemen. I present to you a guilty woman!' Stubbs sneered, getting to his feet to face the crowd, which began to evaluate the evidence between them loudly.

Thelma's face sank into a frown, appearing confused, upset and vexed.

'Ah told ya—I never done it. I've been fitted up.'

She gave Steve a look of perplexity. She looked keen to quiz him on his persistence, but decided to allow him to try at playing the valiant knight. Steve had kept a close eye on the footage; he had prided himself on having a keen eye for detail throughout his career. He wondered for a moment whether Stubbs had even noticed something as obvious as the fact that at no point in the footage was Thelma and Bernie in shot at the same moment. Whoever had duped her had not considered every detail. Steve felt sure that there must be more oversights besides.

Turning to Stubbs in thought, he asked: 'May we see the footage a second time?'

'What, now?' sighed Stubbs jadedly.

Steve nodded.

'Alright, but I've got another hearing in less than an hour, so make it quick.'

'May I take the controls?' Steve requested.

Stubbs turned to the crowd with a seedy sneer.

'Be my guest!' he quipped. 'Never let it be said that I am not pro-democratic!'

A few in the crowd managed a half-hearted titter in acknowledgement.

'Repeat once.' Steve commanded the screen.

The first scene commenced for the second time. About a minute or so into the action, he called out to the screen: 'Pause.' He studied a frame which included the woman alone.

'Notice how we never actually get to see the woman's face at any point.' Steve asserted confidently.

His confidence seemed to rub off onto Thelma, who sat up straighter in her chair from her slouched position.

Steve picked up on Thelma's improved mood and continued confidently.

'Resume play.' The scene changed to the old man's face. 'Pause.' he called. He turned to address the crowd 'Notice, if you will, people of Cliffbridge…' he peered at Stubbs, who glared up at him grudgingly '…Oh, I do beg your pardon. I am permitted to include these lowly people in the crowd, am I not?' Steve mocked. 'Notice how we never at any point, witness Miss Harrison here with Mr Wilson at the same time? I find that fascinating. I wonder, Mr Stubbs, what the crowd thinks?'

The crowd began to chat heartily among themselves again.

He continued, noticing Stubbs' ever tensing face.

'Notice too, if you will, the ghosting in this picture.' He raised his right arm in reference to the left side of the screen. 'See these bright greens and oranges? Notice how these are out of place in such a dark setting? Well I put it to Mr Stubbs that we have before us some none-too-clever video editing.'

Thelma bit her lower lip in measured relief, while the crowd gasped.

'Allow me to disseminate this film and demonstrate.' Steve continued. He turned to the screen 'Stop. Main menu. Show hidden files…'

The screen displayed a list of computer jargon.

'Find titles.' The screen refreshed and after a few seconds, displayed what looked like the titles of two movies: "The Buoy Setter" and "Tales From The Navy".

Steve asked the crowd 'Does anybody recognise these titles? I must confess I was nothing more than a small child when these were on our screens, but I do nonetheless recognise them as once popular movies.'

He gave Thelma a reassuring look, she looked away.

Addressing the spectators again, he continued: 'The lady from "The Buoy Setter" must be Emma Watson and the elderly gentleman in "Tales From The Navy" must be Daniel Radcliffe; legendary actors, of course. Although I am sure they would be disappointed to hear that their talents have been exploited in such a miscarriage of justice.'

Steve turned to address Stubbs.

'Look, it is obvious that you have pulled out all the stops to find the culprit. But using a defenceless single mother as a scapegoat? What motive could such a woman have for committing such a tragedy? Does she look capable of murder to you?'

Stubbs looked Thelma up and down with a sneer.

'Okay Colombo, enough's enough.' he said quietly. 'Look, no-one was pointing the finger directly at Thelma…Miss Harrison. We were merely exploring every avenue, that's all.' he pulled in a deep breath. 'Look, I don't often do this, but under the circumstances I'm prepared to make an exception. If you can prove, beyond any reasonable doubt, that it was not you who committed this, as this anonymous man so eloquently put it, dreadful tragedy, then you will be free from further investigation. As it stands, you are looking at further investigation, possibly prison. Someone's head must roll for this and at the moment it's yours.'

He rose from his chair, sucking in a lung full of air.

'You have precisely fourteen days from now. That is, if you do not deliver me with the goods by…' he checked his watch '…0945 on Tuesday 25th February, then I'm afraid it's game over.'

'Fourteen days?' exclaimed Thelma with a start.

'That's my terms.' nodded Stubbs 'Take it or leave it.'

***

'You're watching Dominion and what an eventful hour it has been inside Central House this morning!' Our leader, Mr Stubbs, has been presiding over the case following the death of Bernie Wilson yesterday. Mr Stubbs was certain he had found watertight evidence against the culprit, when an unknown stranger, believed to be not from the Cliffbridge area, stampeded his way to the front of the arena and brazenly blew the evidence against the defendant out of the water.' explained the news reporter from the plasma screen in the lobby.

'Get away from me.' demanded Thelma as she strode to outpace Steve to exit the building.

'Wait a minute!' called Steve 'Just wait.' he wheezed, grabbing her shoulder.

'Let go of me!' she raged, pulling herself free of him.

'Don't you realise what I did for you in there? I saved your bacon and I don't get as much as a thank you?'

'Ah don't need you help, got that? I would've got off without you. You're nothin' but a twisted stalker. If you don't go away I'll scream.' she cautioned, pointing at him fiercely.

'Alright, alright.' he pleaded, raising his hands in amnesty.

***

Steve walked to where his car had been stationary since it had been clamped the previous evening. There was still some unthawed snow surrounding the wheels. He gave the clamp on the rear offside wheel a hefty kick, cursing the youth for lying to him. He vowed that when he saw him next that he would make him pay for double-crossing him. He looked across to the laundrette and decided to call on Mary to see if she could influence the officials at Central House to release his car. A crisp packet had got caught in the metal latticework on the door as it flapped viciously in the wind. He gave it a pull until it was freed.

'Is anyone there?' Steve called, pushing open the flimsy door.

Mary was seated on the waiting bench near to the door. She appeared thoughtful and despondent.

'Hi Steve.' she began softly.

'Is…Everything alright?' he asked, sitting beside her.

She scoffed 'Well, you tell me. It looks like you've been busy since we last spoke.'

Steve looked up to see where the muffled sound was coming from. An old television set on the top of one of the machines displayed coverage from the hearing.

'Oh, that.' Steve breathed.

'Have you any idea of the level of speculation you have caused?' she charged, glancing at the screen.

'But I don't understand.' he protested, pulling at his collar 'I only tried to help her, that's all.'

Mary's brow softened suddenly.

'Yes, but don't you think it would have been better all round if you had just let the situation play itself out?'

'Perhaps, but I'd sooner die than allow someone to take the blame for a crime they did not commit.' he retorted with a frown.

Her forehead furrowed again.

'Look Steve. As you'd expect, people are already beginning to ask questions.'

'The evidence was circumstantial at best…and what's more, I believe her.' he rebuked.

'I wasn't talking about Thelma, I meant you.' she stated, pointing at him.

Steve gave her a look of surprise.

'What sort of questions?'

She shrugged 'Would you like a smoke?' she asked, offering him her snuffbox.

He pulled out a pre-rolled joint.

She paused for a while to consider her answer.

'The word on the street is that you're some rookie cop from the outside.'

Steve exhaled a lungful of smoke and gave a canned laugh.

'Me? A "rookie" cop? Quite apart from anything else, you make me sound like something out of Miami Vice!'

She stubbed out her joint.

'They ain't necessarily my thoughts, but you can't blame people for wonderin'.'

Steve's tone became more strained.

'I realise helping someone in need is not exactly the done thing around here, but that does not make me a common criminal.'

'But you've got to admit, it must look strange, love?' she said, softening again. 'What I mean was I can't understand why you'd go to such lengths to help someone you barely know. How do you know she didn't do it?'

'Did you not watch the whole thing? I said that I was with her last night.' he exclaimed.

'So you say, but why would you go to those lengths to exonerate her?' she questioned.

'Well what possible motive could she have anyway? Did they have a history of bad blood?' he asked.

'So you weren't with her?' Mary asked with a perplexed frown.

'That's not what I said!' he began tensely 'I'm just playing devil's advocate. Even if she wasn't with me, why would she kill him?'

Mary picked up a pair of wet socks and tossed them into the dryer.

'Old Bernie never made a secret of his opposition to prostitution and he'd often let the girls know what he thought. I dunno, maybe if push had've come to shove, she could have seen her way clear to shuttin' him up once and for all.'

Steve blew a smoke circle into the air.

'But you can't tell me that she's the only person that had an axe to grind?'

'Oh of course not love. But a lot of people will be thinkin' that there's no smoke without fire.' she gazed at him curiously 'The part I did watch, was the bit where Stubbs gave Thelma fourteen days to find the true culprit. There's somethin' that don't quite add up to me. What I don't understand is why you seem more desperate to help her than she is. I know you've told me that you don't want to let someone take the rat for somethin' they never did, but is there somethin' you ain't told me?'

Steve gazed at one of the machines, which was on the spin cycle.

'She just reminds me of someone, that's all. Someone I was close to once.' he said quietly.

'Oh love.' she said with sympathy.

'I wasn't able to help when that person needed me the most…leading to her death. There was this other man. He killed her and there was nothing I could do. Nothing.'

'And you don't want to be held responsible again, right?' she asked.

76

'I just don't want some unjust verdict ruin a poor, defenceless woman's life.' he said vivaciously.
She smiled and nodded.
'She's far from defenceless, let me tell you. Anyway, what was it you came to see me about?'
He turned in his chair to face her.
 'I need you to help me…to help Thelma.'

***

Having managed to convince the receptionist at Central House, that Steve's "unlawful" parking was just part of his desperation to ensure the course of justice for Thelma prevailed, Mary had managed to get Steve's car released. He had thanked her for her help and armed with her advice, had just arrived in Ward's End and pulled up on Marsh Road. It had started to rain heavily, appearing like transparent rice pudding as it hit the windscreen. A small row of flats, each with a tiny plot of grass, stood to the right. Although each flat was quite clearly in a bad state of repair, a new looking stained-glass windowed front door adorned them all. He got out, drawing his collar closer to his neck as the cold rain hit it. Looking towards the small patch of grass, he noticed two dustbins overflowing with rubbish. On the broken doorstep lay Yellow Pages which was torn and waterlogged. He tentatively pressed the buzzer to the left of the door. To his surprise, his call was answered in seconds. A teary, dishevelled-looking Thelma appeared, clutching a small infant.
'What do you want?' she sniffed 'I've told you I don't know how many times to sod off and leave me alone. Do I look like I've got time to mess around with you?' she said, giving him a piercing scowl.
Steve could immediately tell that beneath her sanguine exterior she harboured a deep maternal quality, which was reflected in the rosy-cheeks of her baby daughter. The little girl, aged around three, gave him a look of indifference in spite of her mother's disdain for him.
'I'm here on a serious matter. It's about a lady called Mary. Mary Hamilton.' he stated cautiously. It's awfully wet and cold. I don't suppose I could…' he pointed through to the hallway inside.
Thelma stood to one side to allow him entry.
He was led into the tiny kitchen, which was decorated with brown emulsion paint and was badly peeling. The white cupboards had mildew growing on them. The floor was tiled, with some cracked or missing here and there. The table was a nineteen eighties smoke glass table, which had greasy handprints and a hairline crack. Upon it was a full laundry basket containing wet clothes, crowned with a pair of bright red lace knickers. Thelma snatched these from the basket, noticing Steve's intrigue.

'Say what you came to say then leave.' she demanded seating herself opposite him, holding the girl on her lap.
'What's her name?' he asked, smiling at the tot.
'What's it to you?' she snapped. She immediately softened, noticing Steve's shocked recoil.
'Rebecca. Her name's Rebecca. Now what is it you're after?' she asked.
Steve rubbed his chin in thought.
'Mary was in a profound state of panic when I found her in the laundrette earlier today.'
'Hang on a minute.' she interjected 'How do you know my Mary?'
'How do I know Mary? How do I know Mary?' he asked with hesitation.
'That's what I asked.'
He hesitated further before finally answering her question.
'I saw her on the High Street earlier. We got chatting…'
'Oh no.' she gasped with shock '…don't tell me you're about to elope with her.'
'No of course not.' he affirmed.
'Good 'cos she's been out with enough losers in her time.' she looked him up and down 'Although a posh creep would be a first.'
'Seriously now…' he began solemnly '…she was all dithery and nervous. To tell the truth, I don't think she likes me anymore than you do, but she coerced me into coming to see you…'
She interrupted him 'Sorry, co what?' she asked, grimacing in confusion.
'Coerced. It means forced.' he explained.
'Alright, Wordsworth why couldn't she come here herself, instead of dragging round some low-life trash?' she asked, raising her eyebrows in contempt.
Steve gave an apologetic cough.
'Well I understand you two are not on speaking terms.'
'Yeah. We ain't been as close as we once were, no. Anyhow, what did she want?'
Steve moved his chair back instinctively, pre-empting a verbal onslaught.
'She wanted me to ensure her that I would be around to help you clear your name and find the real murderer.'
Thelma's sultry face became stretched.
'I told ya already. I don't need any help. Not from you, not from her, not from anyone. Now leave us alone - she's due her lunch anyway.' she insisted, getting to her feet and placing the infant on the floor.

   With a glance at Rebecca, Steve rose from his chair and left the flat without a word. His face was attacked once again by the viciously cold rain. To his disgust, he noticed that what looked like Thelma's dustbin had been put through the windscreen.

'Oh great; perfect. I bet it was that little bugger from Central House.' Steve shouted for Thelma's benefit, noticing she had followed him outside.
'It's probably the local mob.' called Thelma from behind him 'They see your car as an effrontery. Goes against what this place stands for.'
'An *effrontery*? My car?' he yelled through the rain 'What do you call this then?!'
'I call it getting what you deserve.' she said callously.
'Is that what you'd call it?' he asked in hysteria 'I've only just had it released from being clamped! Is nothing sacred around here?'
'Look, come inside and I'll call a mechanic.' she offered, noticing the full extent of the damage with surprise.
'Oh leave it.' he said with contempt 'You don't want me anywhere near you–you've made that crystal clear.'
'Well at least let me get you a sheet to cover the hole.' she offered again, turning to her flat.

Once inside, Steve forwent his pride and allowed Thelma to call for a mechanic. He was stunned to see that Thelma did not use a multicard to make calls, but the sort of device he had seen as a boy, it was a landline telephone. It appeared to be from around the turn of the century when they were being phased out, it was big and red and, even more unusually, it was three-dimensional.
'You don't see many of those these days.' he said with surprise.
He held the receiver to his ear. It produced a continuous tone, similar to a hum.
'It ain't no toy–put it down.' she demanded, taking it from his hand and replacing it.
Thelma glared at him with a frown.
'Who are you anyway?'
'Morrissey. Steve Morrissey. If you're about to ask me what I'm doing here, then I can answer your question…' he said.
'Go on then…' she challenged, folding her arms.
'…After I've dialled a mechanic. What's the number?'
She gave him a grudging look.
'01207 55661145. Ask for Martin Roach.'
No sooner had he made the call, than the mechanic arrived. The burly mechanic got on with the job, while Steve, Thelma and little Rebecca waited in the living room. Thelma had seemed to soften, albeit in a small way. She had allowed him as far as her living room; Steve had seldom got that far into another woman's life before. The living room was only marginally larger than the kitchen and was almost as bare. The little furniture that existed was late twentieth century black ash-effect cabinet

and table. Thelma sat opposite him on the threadbare sofa bed, watching him like a hawk.

'Do you have to stare at me like that? It's freaking me out.' Steve asked nervously.

'I'll do what I want in my own home.' she affirmed, folding her arms 'Besides, you ain't answered my question. Who are you?'

'I'm from Belgravia. I'm an estate agent, although I'm not here on business.' he explained.

'So why are you here?'

He decided that this time it would be appropriate to go along with his original story about a sick uncle. He had at last managed to soften her to the point in which she was speaking to him with some civility and so assumed that a sob story would allow her to open up to him further.

'I'm here visiting a sick uncle. In fact he's terminally ill.'

'I'm sorry.' she said softly 'Cancer is it?'

Steve nodded.

'Of the spine.'

'Sounds painful.' she acknowledged softly.

Steve did not answer her.

'Can I ask *you* a question this time?'

'Within reason.' she said half defensively.

Steve lowered his mug of tepid orange juice form his mouth.

'What happened between you and Mary? I mean, what caused you to fall out…if you don't mind my asking?'

She held her fingers against her cheeks, suggesting that the recollection was painful.

'She's got to realise that I'm a grown woman now and have a kid of my own.' she looked at him 'She just kept stickin' her oar in. It was like having a resident health visitor livin' here. I told her to give it a rest, but she kept on so I said I never want to see her again and that's how it carried on.'

'She was very concerned about you earlier on.' he assured her with a smile.

'We were very close once-she brought me up.' she hung her head low in dismay 'See, my mum and me were so close that nothin' could come between us, nothin'.' she lifted her head and gave a smile 'Except the occasional boyfriend. When I said Mary "brought me up", I meant from about when I was fourteen. Yeah, my mum was the best, I never wanted for nothin' even though we were poor. I was always dressed in the latest and I ate well. I was always told by Mary that I never looked much like my mum, but she's wrong.'

Thelma handed him a framed photograph, which was documented on old photographic paper, just like the copy of his own mother. The edges were crumpled and a crease divided it. His heart

almost leapt at the striking resemblance to his own mother. Her hair was dark, although straight, not wavy and her complexion was pale.
'You are right.' he nodded 'She does look a lot like you.'
'That's what I think.' she said with a smile 'See, I reckon it's a form of control that Mary tried to hold over me. She'd sooner have me think I look like her, a tired old bag.'
'I have a photograph of my mother with me somewhere...' he said reaching for his trouser pocket anxiously. He produced it, quickly noticing the smudging and watermarks.
'I...err...' he hesitated.
Thelma took it from his hand.
'Bloody hell, what happened? You oughta take care of your belongings, especially somethin' like this.' she gasped. She looked at him with sympathy 'Is she...'
'Dead.' Steve nodded, steeling himself.
They were interrupted by the mechanic.
'All done!' he exclaimed contently.
'Just a minute.' called Thelma.
She disappeared into the kitchen, then reappeared seconds later with a pile of potatoes which had begun to sprout; the foliage was more yellow than green. The mechanic left with a look of disappointment, but thanked her anyway. She rejoined Steve and Rebecca in the living room.
'I was just thinking how alike our mothers looked.' Steve smiled.
She returned his smile, making her appear even more attractive.
'You never said how she came to die.' she said.
She quickly realised his look of emptiness.
'Tell me to mind my own business if you want.'
Steve shrugged casually 'There's not much to tell. She died and that's it.'
She stared right through him.
'Come off it!' she exclaimed 'You carry round an old photograph of her in your back pocket. Anyone can tell that she didn't "just die".'
Steve looked on anxiously while she continued: 'Someone who dies, when everything is above board and there's nothin' anyone could've done, can be laid to rest without any worry from those who they leave behind.'
Steve grew impatient with her.
'You weren't there.'
'There's no reason to get all upset, is there?' she said softly.
Steve shook his head and began to look relieved.
'As it 'appens, I've got somethin' of my own to tell ya.' she affirmed, handing Rebecca another slice of banana.
'You know I told ya how close I was with my mum? Well it all came to a very sad end suddenly. I'd just come home from college...it was about five in the evening and I remember walking down the road and being

proper annoyed, 'cos I'd been given a bad grade for an essay, you know…' She paused to collect her thoughts.
'Anyway, in those days, I never carried a key, so I began to knock at our front door. There was no answer, so I thought to myself, this is strange. Perhaps she's got the TV up too high and can't hear me or something.' She paused, looking down onto the carpet as she recalled the event.
'So anyway, I went and knocked on the window to the livin' room. The TV *was* on as I'd suspected and sure enough, I could see her in the livin' room but…'
Her eyes began to fill with tears. Rebecca could sense her mother's unease, looking sympathetically into her mother's eyes.
'She was lying on the livin' room floor, but in a strange way, like. So I went round the side of the house and tried the kitchen door. It was open, so I ran inside and into the livin' room. My mum lay there…all limp, but still warm. I checked for a pulse and couldn't find one. She just lay there all helpless. My mum always wore a smile…even then when she lay there dead. She would always say to me "People can make you unhappy, but they can't make you frown!" even since I was a kid, she said that to me!' She reached into her skirt pocket for her handkerchief.
'So anyway, I decided to try mouth-to-mouth. With her bein' a nurse, I was brought up knowin' what to do. I kept breathing into her mouth and pushing at her chest but nothin' seemed to be happenin'. I went to the phone and dialled 112 and called for an ambulance. I got through to the operator. I told the woman on the other end of the phone that my mum was dead and she asked for her name so I told her as clearly as I could. "Janice Harrison" I said. The woman asked me to wait while she got my mum's medical history up on her screen.'
Thelma paused and smiled to herself, looking down at Rebecca.
'How awful for you.' said Steve quietly, looking into his juice.
She continued 'Well anyway, the girl eventually asked me whether I was *Thelma* Harrison. To which I replied "yes". She said: "Well you must know that you and your family were due to vacate the premises six months ago?" I said well, yeah, but we had nowhere else to go, and the woman reminded me that we had had many letters of warning, telling us that we faced eviction by force if we did not get out on time. I asked her what that had to do with my mum bein' dead on my livin' room floor and she said "Well, I'm sorry to have to be the one to tell you like this, Miss Harrison, but we cannot dispatch an ambulance to you, because of your rent arrears." The phone then went dead.'
Steve looked at her helplessly as he thought about the government's cavalier stance on council house tenants. He remembered being at a dinner at the Department for Work and Pensions and hearing numerous

stories about young children being removed from council properties and placed under the care of the social services until the rent was paid.

'What was it she died of?' he asked carefully.

'How should *I* know?' she stuttered, producing a tear '...She was refused a post-mortem.'

'I'm very sorry.' Steve said helplessly.

Thelma's face became tense.

'I think it's best you leave us now.'

Steve placed his mug onto the coffee table.

'Look, I realise you're upset, but we've got things to talk about...urgent things.'

'You weren't meant to see me in this state.' she told him, pulling at her hair in agitation. 'I've given too much away already...' she looked at him solemnly 'Don't you tell no-one about what I've told you, got that?'

'Of course not.' he replied.

'Good...Well off you go then. I've got a pile of wet washin' to sort out.'

SEVEN

Tuesday 11th February 2048. Ward's End, London. 1730 Hrs.

It was half-past five when Steve arrived at the chip shop on Fox Road. He had filled the time by thinking about Thelma while he sat in the empty shop, eating a bag of chips. He had allowed his mind to drift off into a dream, where he imagined himself, Thelma and little Rebecca playing on a deserted beach. Thelma was sketching out a portrait of him, while sitting on a deckchair and wearing a swimming costume and a large-brimmed beach hat. Little Rebecca was on his lap, reaching for his ice-cream merrily; giving into her wish of having his flake. The sun was beating down, scorching his arms, while the light breeze blew through Rebecca's short, curly hair.

The scene was placed many miles away from London and from the confines of their difficult lifestyles. Perhaps it was in another country; the sun certainly felt warmer than an average British summer and the sea was a perfect blue. Steve began to feel the moist, salty air hit his face, which eventually turned into drizzle. The sky was beginning to fill with white clouds until it was completely overcast. It began to rain, slowly at first, then becoming heavier.

Thelma's sketch began to smudge, before a gust of wind lifted the picture from the easel and into the sea. Thelma was looking towards the cliffs behind them, holding onto her hat. Her face had changed from its usual tanned complexion, to a pale one. She looked on, appearing dazed. Rebecca had started to cry, which made Steve look round behind him. A line of smartly dressed officials lined the Cliff edge.

The scene then changed to one of complete darkness. Steve was in some blackened room, with only a single chink of light. Suddenly, a spotlight came on, revealing a cage of iron bars. After this, a red light came on; revealing Thelma dressed only in her underwear. She was sprawled out on the low-level double bed, with everything she needed to survive; food, clothes and somewhere to sleep. The only thing she did not have access to was a means of escape from the cage. The cage would open every so often to allow men dressed in suits to enter. However, every time she deprived one of sex, the would-be client would eat a piece of Thelma's food, depriving her of any, until she eventually collapsed with starvation.

He was awoken by a gruff Irish voice.

'Oi, sleepyhead. We're closing. Hurry up and be on y'way.'

It was Seamus the owner. His bleached face was reminiscent of Bernie Wilson's; the smell of whiskey altered the taste of his chips, making Steve feel mildly nauseous.

'I'm actually waiting for somebody. We won't be much longer.' Steve assured him.
Seamus lifted a ginger eyebrow.
'Y'sure y'won't be? Only the wife will have our testicles f' pickled onions if you're wrong.'
Steve thought for a moment 'We *definitely* won't be long.'
Seamus retreated back behind the counter. Above the counter sat an old television set, just like the one in the launderette.
"This is Dominion!" came the ever-jubilant voice. "To help celebrate the second annual Urban Grime Awards, Dame Amy Winehouse will be performing at Central House on Wednesday 9th September! That's right citizens, for one night only, Dame Amy will wow the people of Cliffbridge with a one-off gig in recognition of local talent! Call Central House now on: 0120 55566633 to reserve your tickets. This offer runs on the favour-for-a-favour scheme, but places are limited!"
Steve recalled the aging singer from his early childhood. Her troubled past had been well documented in the national press. He did not care much for her musical style, but could empathise with her flawed character. She had been through a lot at a young age, which had manifested itself in many catastrophes.

The door flew open, throwing in a torrent of cold air. It was Thelma and little Rebecca. She made no eye contact with him, merely sitting down at his table.
'What was so important that you had to upset me like that earlier on?' she demanded.
Steve picked up the salt container and fiddled with it.
'My intention was not to upset you, I was just being the messenger boy.' he insisted. 'You see, Mary believes in you.'
Thelma's forehead furrowed 'How d'you mean?'
'Look, if I've told you once, I've told you a hundred times-you're barred!' cried Seamus' wife at Thelma.
'Look…Siobhan, isn't it? We don't want any trouble, we would just like to order.' Steve assured the woman.
The woman stared straight past him.
'We don't want your filthy sort round here. You bring nothin' but filth and squalor-drivin' away my good customers and attracting the wrong sort.' she boomed through her discoloured teeth.
Thelma handed the tot to Steve across the table and got to her feet.
'Look here, missus. I might not be catholic enough for ya, but you're no better than me. You stand there all high and mighty behind that counter, pointing at people with your spatula like it's the hand of God, when you don't know nothing.'
'How dare ya!' Siobhan protested 'Get out!'

'No, I won't.' rebuked Thelma folding her arms 'And another thing, I know what sort of relationship you had with that Bernie. Always complaining about the price of cod while he worked all them hours on that decrepit old boat. I've been in here loads of times in the past and watched you cursing as you hand him over two chip containers, before sending him away with a flea in his ear! Look, people know deep down that it wasn't me what killed Bernie that night-they're just lookin' for someone to blame. They know I ain't got no motive really.'
She gave her a steely stare.
'Each time you sent him away with his tale between his legs, you had this place full to the breeches. You think I'm the only one what noticed?'
'What are you implying?' asked Siobhan scratching her head with her spatula.
'You know full well what.' Thelma returned.
She noticed that Rebecca had begun to cry.
'C'mon. We don't have to put up with this.' she said lifting the little girl from Steve's lap.

***

Steve and Thelma sat at the dining table in Steve's living room. Rebecca sat on the carpet in front of the plasma screen, watching Terry the Train. Thelma sat with her eyes staring at the table with her coat still on.
'Can I take your coat?' Steve asked.
'We're not stayin' long.' She looked at him at last 'Will you please just say what you've got to say? I'm getting sick of these games.'
'Perhaps you'd like a cup of tea first?' he chanced.
'No.'
'Right then, I'll get to the point.' He began with a deep breath. 'Like yourself, Mary has reason to believe that you are not guilty of the murder.'
'That's big of her.' she smirked 'Is that it?'
'No, there's more. She also, like you, believes the chip shop owners had something to do with it.'
'I'm listenin'.' she said, removing her chin from her face and sitting up.
'She also thinks that Seamus and Siobhan fabricated the evidence against you to redeem themselves.'
'Why would they do that?' she asked.
'Well it's obvious you're not exactly flavour of the month around there and that there are a lot of people who don't care much about you.'
'Thanks a bunch.' she breathed.
'Yes, but Mary also suggested that we call her bluff.'
Thelma grimaced.
'You're still not making sense.'

Steve drew in a lung full of air.

'We've established the fact that a lot of people must at least suspect the chip shop owners already, so all that's needed is for us to steer people's suspicions in the right direction.'

'You mean we frame them for the murder?' she asked, her face changing colour.

'Well… *framing* is a strong word; we all know they did it. But yes, the principle is still the same, except all we're doing is letting everyone know for certain it was them.'

He gave her a contented smile.

Her face remained solemn 'What's in this for you, eh? How do I know I can trust you and that you're not workin' for the government, like everyone else around here thinks?'

Steve paused for a moment. Thelma's brow rose as if she had exposed him.

'Do you honestly think I'd use Mary to further my ends? She was genuinely concerned for you.' he said with passion.

Thelma shook her head in disbelief.

'I still don't get it. Why would you go to all this trouble? It's not as if you even *know* me.' she read his forlorn looking face 'Didn't you say you had an ill uncle?'

She got to her feet and turned to her daughter.

'You should be round his place lookin' after him, not fussin' over me.' she picked Rebecca up.

'Thanks, but we don't need your help.' she said, making for the door.

'It's not like you have any choice. From where I'm standing, I would say you're out of your depth.' Steve called hastily, running after her.

She stopped and turned on her heels, exposing a rolling tear.

'Just let me help you.' he said softly touching her shoulder.

***

Later that night, Steve Thelma and Mary stood abreast on Fox Road. Steve and Thelma, had emerged from Thelma's flat dressed in white cooking clothing, which she had kept from her days as a part-time baker at the age of seventeen. She stood dressed in a bottle green, pleated dress; a white apron and a white cap. Her hair was coloured, using an auburn spray, which she wore in a ponytail. Steve held his nose at the almost nauseating smell of fat on Thelma's apron, which she had doused in discarded cooking oil for authenticity. Steve was dressed from head to toe in white. He stood out against the night wearing bright white trousers, a white shirt and a similar hat to Thelma's. Mary came dressed in her usual clothing, which was instrumental in her role as look-out.

The three of them ran across the road and into Chamber Pot Alley, which was the backstreet of the shopping precinct. They stood just inside it, out of sight of anyone who might have been coming out of the Two Shillings pub. They stood in the cold, wet alley rigidly, like scarecrows.
'Ssh…there's definitely someone coming!' whispered Mary, sticking her head out of the alley and onto Fox Road. 'It's ten minutes to one; the pub should be emptying soon.'
Mary decided to stroll along the road, in order to see what was happening in the area surrounding the pub, leaving Thelma and Steve alone in the alley. They stood there on their guard, waiting for their catch. They could see the full moon high and bright over the Marsh Road tenements to their right. The rain hit their faces harder and harder; Steve hoped that they would not have to wait too much longer, in case Thelma's white powder on her face got washed away.
Perhaps twenty minutes passed before they heard the sound of clumsy footsteps on the road. They cautiously advanced two paces, sticking their necks beyond the gap in the brick wall and onto the road. To Thelma's relief and to Steve's disappointment, it was only Max Higgins, just another hanger-on from the pub.
'Evenin' Siobhan…Seamus!' belched the man as he staggered past them, continuing along the road.
'Eve…n.' began Thelma, forgetting herself.
Steve covered her mouth and whispered into her left ear.
'If any of us are going to attempt to impersonate an Irish accent, I don't think it should be you!'
Just for a moment, Steve turned his back to Fox Road and peered down Pot Alley. The alley was very narrow and by now, very dark. It seemed to continue forever, like a black vortex. The cold, strong wind sucked polystyrene cups and chip papers into it as if it were a giant beast. The brick wall behind which Steve and Thelma hid was plastered in old, torn posters. The posters were garish advertisements of rock bands, which were long since forgotten; one was ironically was named: 'Nothing Lasts Forever'. Another, more preserved poster, flapped spasmodically in the wind. 'Support Neil Stubbs for Leader'. This was accompanied by a stencilled mug shot of Stubbs' then slimmer face. A black cat leaped from a dustbin from the invisible section of the alley, screeching as it disappeared into a clump of tall weeds. Thelma was about to let out a scream, before Steve cupped her mouth quickly:
'Will you keep quiet?' he whispered into her left ear.
Mary poked her head into the alley:
'Get ready, Albert's will be the next voice you'll hear. I'm done here for tonight. Best of British!' she smiled.

Steve smiled and whispered 'Thank you', while Thelma gave her a brief nod of appreciation, before she disappeared into the night.

Shortly afterwards a skinny, bearded man came into view at the corner of the street beside the pub. The white beard grew larger as it approached them; it could have been none other than Albert Wilson- Bernie's twin brother. Albert whistled merrily as he passed the narrow gap in the wall. Catching sight of Thelma, the old man did a double take before stopping.

'Well well. Siobhan O'Hara.' the old man began grudgingly, folding his arms in disdain.

'Extortionist, Chip fryer, fish batterer and now...*murderer.*' he bellowed into Thelma's ear.

Steve delivered a single, but sharp blow to the back of Albert's head. He wobbled on the spot for a few seconds, before falling forward, at which time Thelma ran to catch his legs while Steve caught his shoulders. They dragged the unconscious man into the alley and away from the moon's glare. Inside the alley, Albert laid on the damp gravel among the wet dock leaves. Steve remembered how similar Bernie had looked to his identical twin brother; reduced to nothing more than a dirty heap.

'What should we do next?' asked Thelma, looking around for inspiration. Steve had planned to enter the chip shop through the door to the upstairs flat, which was on Fox Road. That was until he discovered the aroma of lavender from what must have been the laundry room below. Steve crouched beside it and sniffed. He took out his multicard and shone it at the wall and noticed a thin sheet of wood, no more than one meter in diameter. He gave it a tap.

'Looks like we may have a more inconspicuous way in; this air vent seems flimsy enough to brake and for us to gain entry.' he said, surveying it further with his multicard.

'But what's inside? We could be going headlong into their bedroom, or anywhere!' whispered Thelma, crouching beside him.

Steve ignored her. Holding the saucepan in both hands, he managed to prise the wooden plank away from its hinges, until it gave way completely.

'There!' he exclaimed, getting to his feet.

The warm air, which came from the gaping hole, smelled of newly tumble-dried clothing. Although the hole was dark, the warmth and freshness that it emitted was inviting.

'Okay, lower him down to me.' Steve instructed Thelma.

Once Albert was safely inside, Thelma reluctantly descended the steps into the dark unknown. Steve looked up and out into the alley above. The flimsy posters on the brick wall opposite continued to flap loudly, as if conveying a message of distress. Suddenly, from nowhere, a

large bird that appeared to be a tawny owl darted towards Steve, making for the warmth. He lifted the wooden plank, coving the hole just in time. The owl could be heard scratching at the wood from the other side. The large window adjacent to the steel staircase was the only source of light, now that the hole was covered up. It provided enough light to allow them to see what they were doing, without blowing their cover. Beneath the staircase, was a small steel door. Steve pulled the handle and by luck, it was unlocked.
'In here.' Steve whispered.
He dragged Albert into the cupboard, noticing a light switch on the wall. He switched the light on. The cupboard was an airing cupboard, containing what appeared to be a hot water tank, complete with a system of pipes. Thelma handed him a length of rope, which was resting on an electric meter.

In front of him, he could see the scene from his childhood, where his father had locked him in the airing cupboard for half an hour for wetting the bed. He remembered the pungent smell of old dust on the old copper pipes and the sight of the hot water tank, which was covered in a large, thick white insulation jacket. The tank had always frightened him, which is why his father had chosen to place him there. It looked to him like a fat, giant monster that liked to guzzle down hot water. His father had also told him that inside the white jacket was a dead man, who had suffered from hyperthermia and had died, despite his father's best efforts to warm the body up. Steve had been told that the ghost of the man haunted the airing cupboard and pumped the hot water around the house. It was not so much the lack of light inside the airing cupboard that frightened him, or even being trapped with a ghost; it was the ceaseless world on the outside. Steve had realised at a young age that the world continues with or without you in it. He was invisible, but could hear the squeaking sound made by his father's fork on his dinner plate as he ate downstairs in the bright living room with his unsuspecting wife.

Steve darted for Albert and quickly tied his arms to the plumbing, without having time to think about what they were doing too much.
'Right, the syringe.' said Thelma, taking it from her handbag. 'Are you absolutely sure that an identical twin would have the same DNA?'
'Of course I'm sure!' exclaimed Steve 'Anyway, did they not teach you that on your college course?'
Thelma took the old, blunt syringe, held Albert's right arm out and studied its underside. The dim light bulb depicted Albert's wrinkly arm, which shone yellow in the light, giving the impression that it was jaundiced. She spotted a varicose vein just below the elbow's crease; it hung like an old green grape. The needle punctured it slowly and the blood rushed into the syringe as Thelma pulled at the plunger. She

expected the arm to be left in a less than neat condition, given her lack of medical experience, but to her surprise the arm was left untainted.

'Good work!' exclaimed Steve, grabbing her excitedly. 'That's the hardest part over with. I've got to drench Seamus' Wellington boots in the water from the canal, so that means I'm going to have to take a chance and get onto the shop floor somehow without being seen. Have you got the beaker?'

Thelma took a small plastic beaker from her handbag. It contained cloudy water, which she had collected from the canal earlier that evening.

'Good, now I promise I won't be long.' Steve assured her, before slowly climbing the stairs to the shop floor.

    Thelma looked along the small, dark passageway and over to the back of the basement and saw the small scullery, which was where the O'Hara's washed their laundry. She slowly edged her way into it, touching the damp walls as she went. Beside the large, industrial washing machine, stood an old laundry basket that was overflowing with dirty washing. She pulled out the bottle green drench coat, which Seamus always wore during that time of the year. Taking it from the basket, she took the syringe and deposited about half of the contents onto the coat and replaced it back into the basket. A blue woman's sweater fell onto the lino floor. She picked it up and deposited the other half of Albert's blood onto the sleeves hastily. From out of the darkness, Steve remerged suddenly.

'Well done, well done!' he smiled.

'Did you do it?' whispered Thelma.

'Yes. Oh, I almost forgot...'

They walked back through the short passage and opened the tiny door under the stairs. Steve produced a vinegar-encrusted sheet of A4 paper.

'What's *that?*' asked Thelma, holding her nose.

She read it: "YOU'RE NEXT!!"

Steve had used the O'Hara's PC in the office to construct the poison-pen note.

'Nice touch.' she said with a tight smile.

Steve screwed the page up into a ball and unfolded it again. He placed it carefully into Albert's inside pocket.

'There. He should come-to shortly and will hopefully testify all.' explained Steve with some unease.

'How long do you reckon it'll be before Mary calls Central House to report it?' Thelma asked.

'That's assuming she does make the call.' he replied pessimistically.

'What makes you so unsure?' she asked, recoiling into the gloom.

'Well, I was thinking just after we said good night to her earlier, it was almost as if she might have forgotten to make the call because of the way

she said goodbye. It was as if she felt like she had done her bit for the night.'
Thelma shrugged.
'We'll see….What do we do now?'
'Do you want to come up to mine for a quick drink; I know that I could really do with one.' Steve asked with caution.
Thelma looked at him awkwardly.
 'Look, I think it's best we aren't seen together too much.' she looked away 'And besides, my babysitter will be wondering were I've got to.'
'I see.' nodded Steve sounding disappointed.
Thelma thought for a moment.
 'We'd better get out of here quick before someone sees us. I 'spose you could come round mine, but only for an hour.' she warned, wagging her finger.

***

'Thanks Shelley.' said Thelma to the babysitter, handing her a pile of potatoes as she left. The babysitter gave Thelma a look as if to say she had been short-changed.
'Do you always give people potatoes?' Steve asked.
Thelma gave him a frown as she took Rebecca to the box room.
 'I'm a single mother.'
Steve waited in the living room. It was freezing cold and the radiators were like ice.
He noticed a digital photo frame containing a picture of the mother and child. With the two of them pictured together, it was easy to make comparisons between them. Thelma's dark eyes and hair contrasted with Rebecca's paler complexion. Whoever the father was must have passed on his characteristics, he decided.
 Thelma appeared suddenly.
'Sorry about that, she always takes a while to get off to sleep…Lovely picture, ain't it?' she smiled.
'It is.' agreed Steve returning the smile.
He placed the frame back onto the sideboard and considered his words carefully. 'She…little Rebecca, I mean appears somewhat fairer than yourself…'
Thelma just nodded 'Takes after her dad in looks. Although I'd like to think she's got my ways.'
'Were you and him close?' he chanced.
She paused, her face becoming more tethered.
 'It's a long story really. He left soon after I found out I was expecting.'
'Coward.' Steve remarked.

'It was complicated. We weren't right for each other from the start and never could be. I suppose in my eyes he was this tall, handsome influential man who knew what to say and when to say it...' her face sank further '...And I 'spose he saw me as some naïve poor local girl who'd believe anythin'.'
'He wasn't from this neck of the woods then?'
Thelma stiffened more as she prepared herself for whatever reaction Steve might give. 'He was from up west somewhere...Westminster or somewhere like that. Some sort of a politician.'
'Oh...' breathed Steve.
Thelma read his face.
'I know. It shocked everyone 'round here when they found out. Ever asked yourself why I'm hated so much 'round here? It's not just because of how I make a livin'. I was hurled up as some sort of a traitor for sleepin' with the enemy and made a virtual outcast.'
Steve looked puzzled.
'But don't you work for Stubbs? I mean, the money you collect...doesn't that go into his pocket?'
Thelma sat herself down on the sofa beside him.
'That all came much later on; I was forced into it really.'
She bowed her head to disguise any emotion.
'See, it takes a certain sort of girl to get by in the game; there ain't no room for soft nuts. I realised that I had a baby on the way and the rent was due so I had no choice but to grow up.'
'I'm sorry to hear that. I would imagine that must have been a very difficult time for you.' said Steve reminiscently.
'It's not sympathy I'm after-I'm well beyond that now. I just need to know who I can trust and who I can't.' she glanced at him 'Do you still want that drink? Only it's gettin' late.'
Steve checked his multicard.
'You're right; it is getting late. I had better be off, I suppose.'
He made for the door.
Thelma called out 'I didn't mean you had to go. I mean...you can stay...so long as you promise not to run away again.'
She lifted her jumper off.
'You want your reward, don't you?' she asked seductively.
She walked over to the coal-effect fireplace and switched it on. The room seemed to warm immediately. She turned to face him. The glow of the fire lit up her body; brightening her sultry complexion.
'Come here.' she breathed, beckoning him over with her index finger.
Her dark eyes reflected the fire as they narrowed, focusing on him. Steve slowly walked towards her, becoming more exited the nearer he got.

***

Steve was the first to awake the next morning. He found himself in Thelma's bedroom, although he could not remember moving from the living room. The bedroom was very cold indeed; so much so that he had positioned himself in the foetal position to ward off the pinching draft. A gust of wind swept an origami bird from the sill, landing on the bed gracefully. Thelma opened her eyes briefly, before shutting them again in protest of the daylight. Steve arose from the bed to find that the window was open slightly. He slammed it shut, although Thelma merely turned over. Peering out onto the street below, he noticed that the snow had disappeared, revealing the first signs of spring. He reached for his trousers and threw on his shirt. Walking out into the narrow hallway, he noticed a thermostat which was pointing to 15 centigrade. He immediately turned the knob up to 25, causing the central heating to kick in. It gave a very loud rumble, followed by a resounding hum which was almost deafening. The noise had caused Rebecca to awaken with a cry for her mum. Thelma appeared briefly in the hallway, giving him a frown, before entering Rebecca's room.

'There is a reason why I don't have the heat on during the night, you know.' said Thelma, reappearing with the dazed little girl. Thelma's shocking pink bathrobe adorned with teddy bears was a contradiction to her otherwise seductive outfits she wore during the day.

A persistent knock came from the front door. Steve and Thelma looked at one another in bewilderment. Thelma drew her gown together tightly and walked to the door and opened it cautiously. To her amazement it was Neil Stubbs.

'Bad time?' he asked with a sarcastic smile.

'For you it is yes.' she snapped, attempting to close the door.

Before she could, Stubbs placed his boot in the way.

'You ain't heard what I've got to say yet.' he asserted, maintaining his grin.

He pushed his way past her, giving Steve a nod of acknowledgement, before entering the living room. He sat himself down, producing a cigar.

'I wouldn't bother with that, as you won't be stayin' long.' Thelma said.

Stubbs' brow sank as he held his novelty lighter up to the cigar.

'I wasn't planning to.' he said, exhaling a plume of smoke in her direction. 'Although what I've gotta say might be of interest to ya.' he looked around 'Perhaps a small whiskey would help me collect my thoughts?'

Thelma withdrew to the kitchen. There was a brief air of awkwardness between the two men. The events of the hearing in Central House went through Steve's mind, while he was sure the same could be said for Stubbs. Stubbs continued to draw on his cigar habitually, keeping his brow lowered.

Thelma reappeared soon after.

'Here.' she said, handing him a shot of whiskey. 'Now say your piece and be on your way; you've caused enough strain as it is.'

Stubbs' eyes were now visible. They appeared soft and thoughtful.

'Look here m'darling, I'll not beat about the proverbial, so I'll come straight to the point...' he paused to relight his cigar '...Much as it pains me to say it, it would seem that I was wrong about you.' he said with dramatic tone.

Steve and Thelma looked at each other, each looking relieved.

'How d'you mean?' Thelma questioned nonchalantly.

'An anonymous caller phoned Central House durin' the early hours of this morning and reported seein' Mr and Mrs O'Hara, the chip shop owners, attacking Albert Wilson...the brother of the late Bernard Wilson. At around seven thirty this morning, a very dazed Albert Wilson staggered up to see me at my office to confirm the caller's description. He was holdin' a poison-pen note. There seemed to be a clear motive for the murder of his brother. Mr and Mrs O'Hara have a history of grievances against the two brothers-especially Bernard.'

He softened, looking at Thelma through the smoke.

'Looks like a tidy piece of fabrication led to your wrongful arrest.' he admitted with a cough.

Thelma folded her arms.

'Well that's plain as day. Now if that's all, I need to get on.'

'There's more.' he declared, taking another cigar. 'I've got a proposition for you.' he then peered at Steve 'Well...it's a two person job really, so if you're interested, pretty boy, you're more than welcome.'

'Spit it out.' Thelma snapped.

'I want you to come work with me at Central House.' he surveyed the pokey room 'I know the money would come in handy and...'

'*Money?*' exclaimed Thelma, surprised.

'Look, you'll be workin' in the stock exchange in Central House.' he gave them a smile 'It's just my way of sayin' sorry. Take it or leave it.' he said, getting to his feet. 'I'll give you seventy-two hours to think about it. If you decide to go ahead, then I'll explain the ins and outs then. I'll be waiting for you at the reception at Central House on Friday, nine a.m. sharp.'

With that, he thanked Thelma for the drink and left through the front door in a cloud of smoke.

Thelma looked at Steve sharply.

'If you think I'm gonna agree to work with that man, you've got another think comin'.'

'Of course not; I can't stand the man any more than you can. He accuses you of murder, then when he's finally been proved wrong he comes around here and looks for cheap labour.'

Thelma continued 'And no offence, but I hardly know you. So if you don't mind, I really must get on.'

Steve's face fell.

'But what about last night?'

'Last night was a one-off. Look, I'm sure I'll see you around, but I'm not in the right head-space for a relationship at the minute.'

'I get it.' Steve nodded impatiently 'I'll just get my things and be out of your way.'

He stopped at the bedroom door.

'You were the one who asked me to stay last night. If it were up to me, I would have run a mile.'

PART THREE

'Getting Deeper'

EIGHT

Friday 14th February 2048. Cliffbridge, London. 0930 Hrs.

It had been out of sheer coincidence that Steve and Thelma had met outside Central House that morning. Neither of them had initially planned on meeting Stubbs to find out more about what he had in store for them, however soon afterward the pair had secretly harboured a nagging curiosity which had led them both to the place: unbeknownst to the other. They had exchanged looks of embarrassment and perplexity at the entrance to the building, before promptly being met by Stubbs. Steve's reasons for coming were mixed. While he was curious for what was on offer, he also felt a sense of duty to the man for buying their plan.
Stubbs presently appeared wearing a long overcoat, a trilby hat and, of course, his trademark cigar. He touched the pair on their shoulders.
'Glad you could make it; I knew you'd see sense in the end...' he peered at Thelma from under his hat '...especially you, Harrison.' he added with a sneer.
'I ain't agreed to nothin' yet.' she retorted brazenly.
'You will my girl. You will.' he smiled 'Come.'
He turned on his heels and beckoned the two of them inside. They were led to the lift beside the main staircase. Stubbs dialled a code into the keypad beside the door, causing the lift to spring into action. The carriage fell at a great speed, which cause Steve some concern.
'Isn't the basement a little far down?' he asked.
Stubbs ignored him, maintaining his melancholy stare.
No sooner had he asked the question, he noticed the LED floor number display broke into negative numbers. When the lift has ceased to stop at floor -2 which was commonly regarded as the basement, Steve became more unnerved. The lifted continued to fall at a steady pace until it came to an abrupt halt: at floor -101.
'Floor minus one hundred and one?' Thelma queried.

***

Steve and Thelma found themselves shortly afterwards in a small office, furnished with oak panelling on the walls, hanging from which were two large portraits of a more youthful and slimmer looking Stubbs. The floor was carpeted with Far Eastern tapestry, which was marred by the black stains, which coved it. The desk, at which the three of them were sat, was disproportionate to the size of the room: large and extravagant and littered with gold and silver fountain pens; a crystal ashtray; a green shaded lamp and a mini plasma screen. To their right was a heavy looking steel door, not dissimilar from a reinforced door you

would find in any bank. It was bitterly cold; far colder than at ground level. In fact, Steve compared Thelma's freezing flat more favourably to the temperature in the office. Steve's eyes surveyed the room once again and said to Stubbs:
'Isn't this all…'
'…Illegal?' Stubbs interjected. 'Well, certainly in the eyes of the government, yes we are an illegal outfit.'
He leaned back on his leather executive chair and lifted a glass of whiskey.
'I suppose you could say that what we have down here is a bit taboo.'
He pushed a cheroot into his mouth, before looking at the ceiling to consider his answer more fully.
'Having sex outside of marriage a hundred years ago was frowned upon, whereas today it happens whenever and wherever. Down here and in Cliffbridge at large, we believe that as human beings, therefore capable of rational thought, it should be up to the individual, not a government, to assess what is good or bad for them. Provided that your endeavour to satisfy your desires, whatever they might be, does not prevent another from obtaining theirs…'
Stubbs stared for what felt like too long. Stubbs' eyes eventually fell onto the desk.
'…That's when my perfect socio-economic structure becomes fragile. It's no good taking a mild approach to something that could potentially damage our utopia for everyone else. We don't have judges, juries, barristers, lawyers, courts…we instead have what I thought was enough; a community of fairness, justice and democracy. He rubbed the back of his neck almost coyly. 'You can rest assured that the O'Haras will be brought to justice and that I shall be making amendments to the legal structure to ensure that miscarriages of justice don't happen again.'
'What is this place?' asked Thelma awestruck.
'Thelma, Steven…Welcome to Subterranea!'

***

The heavy steel door at the back of the office opened slowly; the red light above it turned green. The three of them walked through and into an austere looking tunnel. The tunnel was barely six feet high and was made of brick, with wooden supports every three metres or so and was lit with the same inadequate lighting as inside the lift. Stubbs spoke as he led the way, walking at a hurried pace.
'Above, below, left, right, behind and in front of us…even out of sight of us, are rooms and offices conducting the most mind-boggling and illegal deals in the history of finance.'
He stopped to allow Thelma and Steve to catch up.

'There are two hundred and seventy-two rooms, if you count my office and the club. I'd say half of them are offices and the other half storage rooms.'

'Storing what?' Thelma asked, running to keep up.

'Ah!' cried Stubbs, who stopped sharply in his tracks, holding up his index finger.

He then turned to face another steel door to his left, typed a code into a keypad while watching Steve and Thelma with excitement.

They entered a room, which was about the size of an average gymnasium. Stubbs flicked a switch, which caused two rows of shaded lights bulbs to flash on randomly. The room was a military bunker. The large brickwork was painted bottle green and from the wooden beams on the ceiling, hung row upon row of AK47, MG42 and UZI machine guns. Cabinets containing grenades lined the room along with combat uniforms coloured in grey, white and black camouflage, perhaps for use in urban areas.

Steve caught sight of some laminated posters, each about feet square feet in area. They displayed diagrams, which were obviously designed to show how the British Army's morale might be weakened if ever a conflict broke out. One read:

"Former Soviet artillery VS a prehistoric British army: No contest!"

Stubbs grinned proudly as he admired his collection of weapons. Thelma stood looking quite uncomfortable at what she saw. A breeze swept past Steve's nose, bringing the scent of boot polish and leather.

'What's all this for?' asked Steve, his voice sounding entranced.

'This is for what we down here call "Judgement Day". We know that the government knows what goes on in Cliffbridge-we're not that naïve. They're just waiting for the right time to pounce. All we can do is to prepare for the worst.'

Steve stood looking puzzled.

'How can the government already know about this place when they've already sent...' he stopped short.

Stubbs' grin disappeared sharply.

'Already sent *what* Steven?' he paused, flicking the ash from his cigar vigorously, while keeping his brooding eyes on Steve. '...Already sent in twenty-one private investigators? Is that what you were about to say?'

Steve's voice became shaky, as it had when he had explained himself to his father for wetting the bed.

'Well...yes.'

'And how would you know about that Steven?' Stubbs asked, narrowing his eyes in anticipation.

Thelma looked at Steve, bewildered.

'Well how do you know they sent in twenty-one private investigators?' retorted Steve anxiously.
'I asked first.' Stubbs said, his grin returning to his face.
'Well…' began Steve.
'Well…?'
'Well…isn't that the word on the street?' Steve asked, excusing himself hastily.

His ears seemed at that moment to be able to pick up the faintest of sounds, as a painfully long silence followed. Suddenly, Stubbs' grin turned into laughter.

'Of course it is! You're face just then was an absolute picture!' he walked over and put an arm around Steve tightly.

Thelma's face relaxed into her usual indifferent expression.

Steve's heart rate did not decrease, however. He began to ask himself whether Stubbs might suspect him. If he had not already given himself away, the sheepish expression on his face right now might have. Before he had time to ponder these thoughts further, his intrigue was channelled into a different direction.

'Former Soviet artillery?' queried Thelma, noticing the poster.
'Yes, this is just some of the weaponry in our arsenal.' explained Stubbs, sneering at Steve through his smoke.
'What else have you got?' she asked, her intrigue returning.
'We have ten Davy Crockett equivalent Soviet nuclear warheads, but I'm afraid even *I'm* not permitted to enter *that* room, because I'm not adequately trained to handle the weaponry. A fool-hardly bugger like me shouldn't even be in *here!* Yes, we have a strong, friendly arrangement with Russian reactionaries. You see, just like them, we have the same codes of honour and like us, they were left out in the cold when their government closed its doors on the poor, so we can relate with one another. Governments, Steven, are *always* corrupt in some way, shape or form, but most irritating of all, they're greedy. If there's one thing that I cannot abide, that's greed!' he said, pointing his finger close to Steve's eyes almost knowingly.

'Nah…' breathed Stubbs, looking around and shaking his head dismissively. '…We hope the day will never dawn when we have to use any of this stuff, but one must prepare for every eventuality. Forget "He who dares wins." "Be prepared", now that's *my* motto! Come on, I'll…' he turned to exit the room.

'Wait!' called Thelma. 'How do you get all this stuff here? Ever heard of customs and excise?'

Stubbs began to laugh dismissively, as if being told by a child that he was going to beat him up after school.

'Customs and excise?!' he sniggered, studying his neatly polished black shoes.

'Of course I bloody well have my darling! As you know, Cliffbridge is conveniently located near the Thames estuary. Okay...' he paused to gather his thoughts. '...Okay, so making the pick up is relatively simple. Only a fool would accept a large shipment of weaponry, so we only accept two, possibly three creates at a time.'

'Hang on a minute.' Steve called 'Surely you must be planning an attack of some sort or at the very least demonstrating some sort of an offensive. Why else would you need nuclear weapons?'

This time Stubbs was not quite as understanding as when Thelma had stopped him.

'Well if you'd have been patient for just a little longer, then I would have told you the reason. We're stocking up because we anticipate a bombardment by the British forces sometime in the not too distant future. For now, these weapons will stay put...for as long as the British army's stay put. A fair compromise, wouldn't you say Steven?'

'Yes, yes of course.' he replied quietly.

***

The next room they were taken to appeared more like a prison than a store room, for it was dark and felt like the central heating had long since been forgotten. Even through his thick-soled shoes, Steve could feel the cold air from the black flagstones below. Thelma lifted her feet one at a time to avoid too much contact with them. By far the most chilling thing though was what Steve could see in front of him. Young female prisoners, scruffily dressed and unwashed were kept in tightly enclosed spaces, without means of escape.

'This room is known as The Holding. This is where we hold our imports while they wait to be redistributed around London. This lot....' Stubbs pointed with his cigar to the prisoners in the cell on the left. '...will go to Soho and this lot...' he pointed to the group in the middle '...Will go to Bethnal Green, while the ones on the right will go to Mile End. We contract out to local outfits, which we work closely with. Our affiliate companies have clubs and peep shows all over London. We purchase the girls at the equivalent to around...I dunno...two hundred quid each.' he smiled smugly.

'The best part is I sell each of them on for the price of a top of the range plasma screen!' he sniggered, sticking out his chin to adjust his tie proudly. Thelma looked less than impressed, looking very concerned for the young women.

'Once they're sold on, what happens then?' she asked in an exasperated manner.

'Well at the risk of sounding like I care, the vast majority of them remain in tied slavery until they pay off their debts to their owner. It's just a way of life really.'

'Debts?!' exclaimed Thelma.

'Well, yeah…' Stubbs responded, taken aback by Thelma's unexpected outburst. 'The pimps pay above the odds for their whores…and they've got businesses to run… so the girls must pay their debts to their masters. Sadly for them, they very seldom, if ever, manage to because the naughty pimps deliberately increase the value of the debts by adding extortionate levels of interest.'

Stubbs' face straightened as he noticed the other two looking solemn.

'Where are they from?' Steve asked at last.

'All of these are from various parts of China. China is our second largest partner, owing to the fact that neither Cliffbridge nor Chinese groups impose surcharges on imports.

'They look very disorientated…they all turned away from the light when it was switched on…how did they get here?' asked Steve, rubbing his chin thoughtfully.

'We had them brought over by lorry; we couldn't exactly *fly* them in!' Stubbs exclaimed.

Steve had not fully paid attention to Stubbs' explanation, noticing instead that virtually every young woman in the cells were covering their left shoulder blades with their hands, as if they causing them pain. Steve drew nearer to one girl who was wearing nothing on her top half and who had her back turned to him. He noticed a bright red symbol which was written in Chinese. About an inch lower 'LONDON' was written. Judging by the scar tissue surrounding the prints, it was as if someone had taken a red-hot branding iron and embossed the words onto their backs.

'These girls have been branded!' shouted Steve furiously. 'You just told us that they are free once they pay off their debts, but you're selling these young women with the premise that they'll remain the property of the pimps they're sold to! How do you sleep at night?'

'Careful Steven. You're takin' me for someone who cares!' Stubbs sniggered. 'But so as not to worry you too much, these lot aren't anything to do with me. That is to say that no money has changed hands over these. I just agreed to store them here for a couple of days; they're not mine.'

'So that makes it alright then, does it?' Thelma began anxiously. 'What are women to you, eh? Pieces of meat? Sex objects for dirty old men like you?'

Stubbs gave a cough, acknowledging Steve with embarrassment.

'Well that's about it for this room. You should find the next and final room of our brief excursion less fraught.

***

The room they were led into was nothing more than an average sized office; perhaps a few square metres larger than Stubbs' own office. The small area meant that the lighting was more productive, depicting about ten desks bordering the room, each with a mini plasma screen. Attached to the low ceiling, were many LED bulbs of all colours, flashing away at different speeds and sequences. A collection of wires rose up, disappearing through a recess in the ceiling.
'This, my friends, is the laundrette!' cried Stubbs enthusiastically.
'Washing clothes big business then is it? Which affiliate company do you use for that; Granny Stubbs Incorporated?' mocked Thelma.
Stubbs continued undeterred by her comment.
'This is where we collect our revenue together in one room, before it disappears up those multicoloured wires, through onto the roof, before being transmitted by the antenna to Austrian internet banks!'
'What?' exclaimed Steve, almost choking on his words.
'That's right! Those online banks are ideal for international criminal organisations, which trade with one another, because unlike conventional High Street banks, they don't require any form of identification; no names, addresses; no passports; no birth certificates. No one knows who we are! The Austrian online banks are happy because they're receiving millions in foreign currency and we're happy because we've got somewhere to store our money safely!'
'Whoa! Let me get my head around this.' began Steve, pressing at his temples despairingly. 'Whatever you export abroad, you receive foreign currency in exchange? Those countries' governments must be left scratching their heads, wondering where all their money's going, surely.'
'Indeed Steven! It's coming right here to Cliffbridge!'
'Before being transmitted through the airways to Austria.' Steve affirmed, aghast. 'I presume that most living essentials, like food and drink are imported from abroad too?'
'Yes, everything!' Stubbs enthused.
'Then not only are you draining a given country of it's currency, but also of its natural resources…things like crops and whatnot. How can a country make money for itself, when tonnes of natural resources are disappearing unaccounted for?' asked Steve in disbelief.
Stubbs folded his arms and set himself onto a table, his face becoming stern.
'You are too concerned about the welfare of national governments who are riddled with sleaze and scandal; governments who couldn't give a toss about their civil servants, let alone their citizens. Are those the governments you're worried about Steven? Put yourself in their position. You're raking in millions from aboard, through exports and millions from

cash-strapped Britain. Why then should you care about the welfare of the people, when as a president, king or Prime Minister, you're living the life of Reilly? Let me assure you Steven, it's not the already rich who benefit under the black market system, it's the impoverished; the people who *really* need it. Let me tell you both something.'

He began to survey the ceiling as he pondered.

'I wasn't always a rich man in charge of a thriving enterprise; on the contrary! My own father was a victim of the government's abandonment of Cliffbridge when I was younger. Once living in a six-bedroom house, we were cast out into the cold December winter with only the clothes we were standing up in at the time. The government had repossessed our house and had frozen our family assets. A City broker of excellent standing in the eyes of the community and, indeed the government, was swept straight into the lava pit.'

He paused to light a cigarette, struggling to strike a match.

'...And for what? So that Cliffbridge could become the government's scapegoat! Mine wasn't the only family to have suffered. Look around the place and ask anyone; you'll find many who will tell a similar story. So what do you do if you're a bright, intelligent financier with a degree in business, when you're either trying to steal your neighbour's dog to eat it, or you're begging for a job in sewer cleaning?'

'Open a place like this?' chanced Thelma.

'Well, yes. You try and survive by doing what you've trained for years to do. It wasn't long before we managed to tap into other organisations around the world that were victims of their government's incompetence or oppression and began to trade goods to maintain a certain level of survival for the impoverished. We found that large countries like China and Russia could provide us with much needed food and we provided them with medical equipment.'

Stubbs paused to study Thelma and Steve's faces as he stubbed out his cigarette, noticing that the pair appeared more sympathetic to his story.

'Crime syndicates aren't born out of greed: there's always a cause and it's rarely greed. The syndicates we deal with were or still are, a collection of families who were once wondering where their next meal was coming from. So when you talk about a government's loss of earnings, Steven, think about what those earnings are being used for.'

Stubbs' eyes lost contact with Steve's as he once again looked at the ceiling.

'Besides, it's not just the money of other government's that we're sending through the ceiling: it's that which is raked in by Subterranea! Hundred of thousands of pounds per day!'

'I'm sorry?' gasped Steve, perplexed.

Stubbs nodded almost sheepishly.

'Well we sell things to our fellow Brits as well, including prostitutes to club owners and hard to come by drugs to stressed out professionals. In fact, we collect about one sixth of our income from the UK alone. We import goods cheaply, add twenty per cent to the value and sell them on to the rich British who can afford to pay more than the Russians or Chinese, so…'

Steve interrupted him 'So British currency is being transmitted through the airways to Austria as well? Do you have any idea at all what damage you're doing? You're devaluing the Pound, while increasing demand for the Euro! Britain will be bankrupt before long and it's because of you!' Steve held his hands to his mouth in hysteria.

'I know; that's why we know that an attack on Cliffbridge is immanent.' admitted Stubbs, becoming more defensive. 'Anyway, why are you so bothered by all of this? I mean, I can quite understand your sense of civic responsibility and all the rest of it. But what I don't quite understand is why you're almost in bits over it.'

Stubbs continued to stare at him for two silent minutes; no sound came from Steve's mouth, only a nonchalant expression.

Stubbs broke the silence at last, while keeping his confused expression. 'Look, you've both had a lot to take in for one day. I suggest you both go home, get some rest and meet me at the same place, same time Monday morning.' he stood up 'And it goes without sayin' that you don't breathe a word about this place to no-one.'

Steve made for the door and stopped, turning on his heels.

'I just want to ask you one more thing before we leave.' he said.

Steve's gave him a sneer.

'Quite the little worrywart, aren't we?'

Steve walked slowly back towards him.

'Are you…and this place, involved in any way with terrorist groups?'

Stubbs flicked ash into a tray.

'Involved? I don't quite follow…'

Steve folded his arms.

'I think you know what I mean. Do you trade stock with any terrorist groups like, for example, Al-Qaeda?'

Stubbs broke into hysterics.

'Define "terrorism", Steven.'

'Now's not the time for philosophy; you know very well what I'm talking about.' insisted Steve, growing impatient.

'Al-Qaeda? Is that your definition of a terrorist group?' asked Stubbs with a stare.

'Of course it is.' nodded Steve.

Stubbs nodded and thought.

'Your government forced Al Jazeera off the air earlier this month. What would you call *that*?'
'My government?' Steve asked shakily.
'Well you're not from Cliffbridge, so you're not part of my government...' Stubbs explained.
Steve looked at the floor sheepishly.
'In answer to your question, we deal with Irish paramilitaries; it's funny how they're seldom referred to as terrorists, don't you think?' Stubbs sneered.
'You still haven't answered my question.' Steve demanded.
'We do not deal with Al-Qaeda. Is that clear enough for you?' Stubbs declared sarcastically.
'Perfectly, thank you.' whispered Steve almost apologetically.
Stubbs extinguished his cigar.
'I would think very carefully before you waltz into my quarters throwing around demands. Just you remember who you're talkin' to, sunshine.' frowned Stubbs.
'Yes, yes of course.' nodded Steve, unable to look Stubbs in the eye.
'Then I'll put your insubordination down to first day enthusiasm. Now, unless there's anything else you'd like to pull me up on, I'll bid you both good day.'

NINE

Friday 14th February 2048. Ward's End, London. 1600 Hrs.

It had started to rain heavily while they had been in Central House. Steve's saturated shirt clung to his back, while Thelma's hair had become wiry in the rain. They made a dash from the car to Thelma's front door. After struggling with her keys, Thelma threw open the door to find her less than pleased baby sitter waiting for her.
'I'll overlook the fact that you were six hours longer than you said you would be, so long as you give me anythin' other than a bunch of mouldy potatoes.' she grunted.
Thelma gave her an apologetic smile and rummaged around in her pockets and produced a chocolate bar.
'Is that it?' smirked the girl.
'That's all I've got. Sorry.' shrugged Thelma.
The girl snatched the bar before snatching her coat from the peg and flying out the door.
'Some people are never satisfied.' Thelma scoffed, shaking her head in disbelief. She glanced at him 'Listen, err…thanks for droppin' me off; saved me a wet trip home. I 'spose you oughta dry yourself off for a bit. Besides, we've got a lot to discuss. I'll stick the kettle on.'
The living room felt warmer than usual. He felt the radiator beside the settee, which was piping hot. He assumed that the childminder must have discovered how to turn the central heating on. He sat himself down beside it, holding his palms above it. Rebecca looked up at him with almost expectant eyes as he made silly faces at her. A sudden feeling of pity gripped him as he looked at the infant. He could well empathise with the girl for not having a father; although he almost envied the child for having a mother however distant she was from the child's life.
'TV! TV!' exclaimed the girl at him.
'What's that petal?' he asked with a smile.
'TV TV TV! she continued, pointing at the old television set.
'Oh, you would like me to switch on the…telly?' he asked, getting up and walking across to it.
He pressed in the square button and after several frustrating seconds, a snowy picture appeared with loud interference.
'Dominion!' cried the child enthusiastically.
'You would like to watch Dominion, would you love?' asked Steve.
'Terry Train! Terry train!' she called.
He noticed a knob above the power button that had what appeared to be random numbers printed above it. As he turned the knob, the picture grew gradually clearer.

"This is Dominion! And good afternoon to you citizens!" began the excited voice.

"Citizens, we have some breaking news to bring you. Our leader Mr Stubbs would like me to announce that he has brought justice to Cliffbridge and that the rightful culprits of the Wilson murder have been found!"

The picture faded then changed to a view of the chip shop.

"Yes citizens, Mr and Mrs O'Hara of Ward's End were found guilty of murder and are awaiting sentence! Given Mr Stubbs' track record of sentencing, it would be unlikely that the infamous pair will taste freedom for at least thirty years!" the reporter held his earpiece in place "What's this? News just in! Mr Stubbs would like to take this opportunity to thank two people for their cooperation in the case…"

Steve held his breath as he awaited his name "…Mr Albert Wilson and Mrs Mary Hamilton, both of the Ward's End area!"

Steve let out a sigh of relief that his anonymity had not been compromised.

'What's all this?' asked Thelma, handing him his tea.

Steve swiftly switched the set off.

'Nothing, just some rubbish about aliens.'

She gave him a bewildered looking frown.

'Never mind that, we've got a lot of things to talk about.'

She sat down beside him and pulled Rebecca onto her lap. After a moment's silence to consider her thoughts, Thelma continued:

'I expect that like me, you've got a lot of things flying around your head after today.'

'Not half.' Steve agreed, talking into his tea.

'Right then, so let's start with the fact that we'll be working with Neil Stubbs. Does that bother you?' she asked, reaching for a biscuit.

'Should it?' he asked cautiously.

'Well that's for you to decide. All I'm sayin' is I've worked for him for years and once he's got you on board, he's no puppy-dog.'

She placed the now restless Rebecca between them on the settee.

'People go missin'…and it's often for good.'

'What do you mean for good?'

'Put it this way, if you cross him in any way, you're as good as dead.' she handed him the plate of biscuits. 'Fortunately for me, we found a way out. Otherwise who knows what might've happened.'

Steve almost choked on his chocolate bourbon.

'Surely you're not suggesting that he would have killed you?'

'The main thing is he didn't. All I'm sayin' is, are you ready for such a commitment?'

'I think so.' he nodded.

She looked at him.

'Don't take this the wrong way, but how would you have time to take on a job *and* find time for your uncle…ain't he supposed to be on his deathbed?'

Steve's face fell.

'He's not quite that bad yet. Besides, I'd thank you not to be so facetious about such a delicate matter.'

'Town! New coat! New coat!' cried the tot.

Thelma gave Steve a warm smile, which caught him off guard.

'Damn. I knew there was somethin' I forgot.'

She picked up Rebecca's old coat; the pink outer material was badly torn.

'Fancy a trip into town before the shops shut?'

Steve was about to decline the offer, before catching sight of Rebecca's smile.

***

Steve drew up outside of the launderette. The rain continued to fall loudly as the sky darkened. The laundrette appeared like a large firefly in the gloom.

'What, may I ask, are we doin' here?' demanded Thelma.

'I thought we ought to thank Mary properly. After all, she was instrumental in our plan.' he insisted.

'You and your big words.' she scoffed, before her face helplessly rose into a smile. 'The fact is, I haven't spoken to the woman in years, what will I say?'

Steve gripped the steering wheel in thought.

'Nobody's asking you to become the best of friends, just to acknowledge her help from last night.'

Thelma gave a reluctant nod before leaving the car. She unbuckled Rebecca and the three of them entered the warm glow of the launderette. The warmth hit their faces at once and a surprised looking Mary met them, holding a bath sheet. Stubbing out her joint, she walked over to them.

'Alright?' she nodded with reservation.

Thelma looked away awkwardly.

'Yes, thank you Mary!' Steve began positively, doing his best to counteract Thelma's cold reception.

'We've come to say a big thank you to you for your part in yesterday's proceedings. We thought it proper to visit you in person to pass on our thanks.'

Mary glanced at Rebecca.

'Well you'd better come away from that door before the little one freezes.'

They sat along the back wall beside a blow-heater. Steve sat beside Mary, while Rebecca sat upon Thelma's lap on the other side of him. She busied herself observing the tares in the fabric.
'You oughta get the little one a new coat; that one's no good in this weather.' said Mary.
Thelma gave her a scowl.
'I don't need you to tell me that. You might be an expert in washing clothes, but that doesn't make you a fit mother.'
Mary appeared indifferent.
'What else brings you here? Don't tell me you've come all this way just to thank me.'
'No, I came here to buy Rebecca a new coat, actually.' Thelma asserted.
Steve turned to Mary and asked 'What do you know of a place named Subterranea?'
Thelma widened her eyes at Steve in disbelief at his lack of discretion.
'Subterranea?' Mary asked 'Why? What do you know of the place?' she asked, incredulous.
'So you have heard of it then?' asked Steve, intrigued.
His attention was immediately drawn to the youth who he was sure had vandalised his car. The boy gave him a melancholy stare from beneath his cap while he sat waiting for his load to finish. Steve rose from his chair and approached him.
'Listen to me, you anorexic little vagabond, I know it was you who trashed my car the other day. I did say that if you ever crossed me again that I would do you some serious damage.'
'Whatever.' scoffed the youth, removing his clothes from the machine.
'You're just lucky that there's a young child present, or I'd put your head through that machine.' Steve cautioned.
'You're bluffin'!' laughed the boy, taking his load to the dryer.
Steve grabbed the boy's earring and pulled it, causing the boy to wince.
'I'm warning you, don't push me.' Steve seethed.
'C'mon, let's have ya. I'm closin' up.' called Mary, pulling the boy free of Steve's clutch and showing him the door.
'But my washin'…' pointed the boy.
'You can collect it tomorrow. Come on, out you go.'
The boy glared at Steve.
'Posh git.' he grunted as he left.
Mary turned the sign on the door to "closed".
'Do you know the boy?' she asked him.
'Not really, just some kid who seems to have it in for me.'
'He's not just some kid; he works for Mr Stubbs-one of his youth community members. His name's Sam. The best way to handle him is to

111

not look rattled by him and just ignore him, that way he won't have any cause to be wary of you for bein' new 'round here.'
Steve shrugged carelessly.
'You were saying about Subterranea?'
'Ah yes.' she began cautiously 'No-one much talks of the place anymore- it's sort of forbidden by Mr Stubbs.'
'Why's that?' he asked.
'Well not many of us actually know of the place. I used to work at Central House as a janitor some years ago and I took the wrong lift which no-one other than the white-collar staff were allowed in. It kept goin' further and further down and at great speed, until it came to a sudden halt at floor number minus 101. Anyway, I don't know how much you already know, but I got lost in this strange maze of meandering corridors. I went into this room, which had been left open. All I'm gonna say is that I saw somethin' which I shouldn't have.'
'Money?' he guessed.
'By the suitcase load. Somethin' which was forbidden years ago; it goes against his model of socialism.'
She looked at Thelma, who was still studying the coat and continued:
'Here we all are strugglin' to make ends meet, while they're down there dressed to the nines and handling so much money that they don't know what to do with! Stubbs makes out to those of us in the know, that the wealth will trickle down to the people above, but nobody's seen so much as a brass farthing.'
'Yes and yet he talks about the vices associated with greed.' Steve agreed.
Mary looked at them both, reaching for another joint.
'What's this about anyway?'
Steve and Thelma looked at one another and Thelma gave a shrug.
'You're probably not going to like this...' Steve began.
'I'm listenin'.' she said quietly.
'Well Stubbs was so pleased with us for finding the so-called culprits, that he's offered us a job.' he explained quickly.
'Well that's good, ain't it?' she puffed.
'In Subterranea.' Thelma interjected.
'I see.' Mary breathed, producing a prolonged cloud of white smoke. 'I 'spose I ain't pretty enough to work down there. I'd never fit into one of them puny outfits anyway.' she caught a glimpse of the torn coat once again 'Well you can't go on livin' hand-to-mouth-not with a youngster to support.' she said to Thelma.
'We manage fine.' Thelma snapped.
'I'm sure you do love, but you can't go on livin' in that drafty old flat of yours; young Rebecca needs a future.' she softened reaching for her shoulder 'Look here, love. I know we ain't exactly been close of late, but I

feel it's high time we moved on. If I upset you before, then I'm sorry, I never meant to.'
Thelma raised her eyebrows in indifference. Mary got to her feet.
'Pretty as you are, you can't work in a well-to-do place like that in them clothes; you'll be needin' some decent clobber…'
Mary disappeared into the small store cupboard and came back with twelve fifty pound notes.
'Take this.' she insisted, pushing the money into Thelma's hand.
'Six hundred quid?' Thelma exclaimed.
'It should be enough to buy a smart outfit and a new coat for the little one. There's a "Femme" store which has just opened on the border with Havering. If you're quick, you'll just catch them before they shut.' she smiled.
'Ta, but I don't need charity.' said Thelma quietly.
'It's not a case of what you need; it's Rebecca's future I'm more worried about. Now take the money and get goin' before they shut.'
Thelma gave Mary a tearful hug, followed by a peck on the cheek.
'Thank you. Thanks for everythin'.' she said at the door.
'That's okay love. You'd best be on your way. Ta Ta Rebecca!'

***

They left behind the drudgery and gloom of Cliffbridge and entered Havering. Havering had remained largely greenbelt land, despite the upsurge in property development to the south. The air was much sweeter, although the snow still capped the hills and treetops. Rebecca imitated the sounds of the farmyard animals as they past field after field, her eyes glued to the window. She would occasionally wave her arms and kick her seat in excitement, leading Steve to wonder whether she had ever seen a real-life cow or a horse before. The sky was still laden with clouds, which lung low in the sky.
'Snowman!' exclaimed Rebecca, noticing a mound of snow beside a spade in one of the fields.

After a mile or two, the countryside gave way to suburbia, until they reached Havering High Street. They entered a small multi-storey car park beside one of the shopping centres. Steve had circled every level in search for a space until he spotted one between an MPV and a motorbike. Getting out of the MPV, he caught sight of Mr and Mrs Maitland-Sloan. Steve gave James a wave.
'Oh, hello old chap.' mumbled James with his head bowed.
'Good evening James, Sylvia.' Steve smiled. 'This is my friend Thelma and her daughter Rebecca.'
'How do you do?' James said softly with an empty smile.
'Out doing a spot of shopping?' Steve asked.

'No sir; certainly not during a recession.' he retorted half dismissively. He glanced at Steve.

'In fact we have some rather sad news. This damn recession has put me out of a job and as if that wasn't enough, our daughter's cancer has turned aggressive.'

Steve did not know what to say at that moment. Here he was, standing beside a healthy little girl and about to embark on a potentially lucrative career, while standing opposite him were two people in real need. He felt almost compelled for a moment, to mention Subterranea to James in the hope that he might find work down there before remembering the stark words of Neil Stubbs before they had left earlier that day.

'I'm terribly sorry to hear that.' Steve said sympathetically.

'That ain't half bad.' agreed Thelma with a coy smile.

Even Rebecca appeared somewhat sympathetic and in the know. She held out her toy rabbit and offered it to Sylvia.

'Oh how very kind!' she smiled, drawing away a tear 'But I think your rabbit would miss you!'

James continued 'We had to move out of Ealing Tower due to the rent costs. My sister has agreed to put us up for a while here. She lives in an apartment above the shopping complex. You see, with healthcare costs the way they are at the moment, we have had to transfer Emma to a hospital in Kent, one of the few remaining NHS hospitals in the southeast.

'I see.' Steve breathed hopelessly. 'I know it won't be of any consolation, but here's my card. Call me anytime, just in case there is anything at all I can help you with…You never know, I might win the lotto or something and might be able to help you.'

James gave a half-hearted laugh.

'Thanks old buddy. Well, it's nice to have met your friends at last.' he touched his flat cap politely and ambled into the darkness with his wife.

***

Having left the car park, they were met by the bright lights of the shopping centre. It was warm and inviting with happy looking faces everywhere they turned. Unlike the High Street in Cliffbridge, which had few remaining open shops, this shopping centre had every big-name supermarket and department store available.

They caught sight of the Femme store and entered it.

They made their way to the children's section on the first floor, in search of a new coat for Rebecca. Thelma suddenly grew very self-conscious as she noticed the middleclass children dressed in the latest clothing. As they walked passed, the heads of every staff member turned.

'What are you lookin' at?' snapped Thelma at a surly looking young shop assistant.
'Do you think we should leave?' asked Steve, noticing the gawping faces.
'Why should we? Our money is as good as theirs.' she asserted loudly, pointing at a mother.
Thelma removed the torn coat from Rebecca and picked out a silver coloured jacket, with the hood lined with faux fur. It fitted and suited Rebecca perfectly. Thelma glimpsed at the price tag.
'*How* much?' she exclaimed.
The sales assistant turned around with a smirk.
'It ain't that expensive, we'll take it anyway.' she declared, loud enough for all to hear.

Having found Rebecca a coat, they returned to the ground floor and to the ladies department. Thelma browsed the lines for what seemed to Steve to be hours, while he and Rebecca sat together on a padded bench awaiting her return from the changing room. She appeared at last dressed in black hot pants, black tights and a white crop top.
'Well?' she asked.
Steve considered his answer very carefully.
'Well it's...*happy*.'
'*Happy?*'
'What I meant was, it suits your character well...' he added.
'But it ain't the sort of gear you wear in a professional environment.' she interjected.
'Precisely!' he agreed, sounding relieved at her understanding.
Thelma disappeared behind the changing room alcove for a second time. While she was gone the same assistant asked him:
'You do intend to pay for that item, don't you?'
Steve noticed that she was referring to the new coat, which Rebecca was wearing. Rebecca looked up at the young woman and gave her a smile.
'We take a plain stance on customers who swan around in our clothing, only to leave them on the floor without buying them.' she continued.
'Swan around?' exclaimed Steve aghast 'She's only a child! What's more, I noticed a prissy looking woman upstairs fussing about some pair of jeans in the sale range for ages, before walking out empty-handed. And yes, we *do* intend to buy the coat, it's just that she happens to be cold at the moment. And no, we shan't be shopping here again!'
The woman left them looking bewildered. He had forgotten what the cut-throat world of retail was like in the ordinary world. Cliffbridge may have been a place of bric-a-brac shops and tumbledown launderettes, but at least service came with a smile-whatever the customer's status. He laughed to himself, remembering the use of the word "prissy"; that was a word often used by others to describe *him*. He looked down at Rebecca, who

gave him a smile. He felt his heart warm and a certain bond forming, how ever premature this may have seemed.

'Don't worry kid, we don't need snotty-nosed types telling us what to do, do we?' he smiled.

Shortly afterwards, Thelma reappeared and this time her choice was perfect. She had been completely transformed into a young, confident businesswoman. She wore a medium-length pencil skirt, complete with a white blouse and black shoes. She had swapped her trademark fishnet tights for more conservative hosiery.

'What do you think?' she asked nervously.

'You look…perfect. Absolutely perfect.' he replied wide-eyed.

'Do you think?' she asked.

'Without a shadow of a doubt. People won't be able to help but take you seriously from now on. You exude confidence and power.' he added.

'Don't be daft! Power? Me?' she giggled, shaking her head. 'I'll just change back…'

'No don't bother!' he exclaimed.

'Eh?'

'You'll see…'

They walked to the counter, running ahead of a customer who was about to pay. When they arrived, a sneering older woman, who appeared to be the manageress, met them.

'What on earth are you doing? You can't pay for the clothes whilst they're being worn; that's positively ludicrous!'

'Oh yes she can.' said Steve, matching the woman's smugness 'In fact, this lady will be the first person I've seen so far to actually pay for something.'

The woman frowned in disbelief.

Steve continued 'Now I know that she may not quite measure up to the rest of your clientele, but her money is as good as anyone else's. So just scan the products and let us pay.'

The woman reluctantly lifted the scanning gun while Thelma turned around for her skirt, blouse and tights to be scanned, before throwing her right foot onto the counter for her shoes to be scanned. The woman cleared her throat.

'That will be five hundred and fifty-nine pounds and ninety-nine pence.'

Thelma proudly produced the banknotes.

The woman's face grimaced 'We don't accept cash. In fact, I don't know anywhere that does.'

Thelma appeared perplexed. Steve promptly produced his multicard.

'That's more like it.' said the woman, snatching the card and inserting it into the reader.

Steve entered his pin and removed the card. 'With an attitude like yours it's no wonder this company is going into administration.'

***

Having left the shop, the three of them agreed that it was time for something to eat. Rebecca had insisted on visiting McDonald's and so they did. The restaurant was situated beside an indoor garden, with palm trees lit up in coloured lights. Rebecca sat beside Thelma, entranced by the display, while contently tucking into a Happy Meal.
'Seems all too easy.' said Thelma into her coke.
'What does?' asked Steve.
'Just inserting a bit of plastic and punchin' in a code to pay for stuff.'
'I suppose it is.' he agreed thoughtfully 'It doesn't feel like spending any money at all and that's how people get into debt, I suppose.'
'At least with cash you know exactly how much you've got.' nodded Thelma. She looked at him 'You were great in there just now.' she said warmly. 'No man's ever spoken up for me like that before. It made me feel secure. Thank you.'
'It was nothing really.' smiled Steve, revealing bits of lettuce between his teeth.
'Yes it was somethin'.' she protested. 'You really showed 'em who's boss.' Steve was about to add the episode involving the coat to his credentials, but thought better of it, fearing he would appear boastful.
Her eyes lit up suddenly.
'You know, I was a bit hasty the other mornin' when I said I wasn't interested.' she lowered her Big Mac 'The truth of the matter is, I was scared. Scared you'd leave me, just like the rest. But you've proved otherwise by stickin' up for me.'
She peered at Rebecca.
'And I know for a fact this one's taken to ya.' she smiled.
'You've also made me see things in a different light.'
'How do you mean?' he asked.
'I mean that stuff with Mary. In the end you made me realise that the problem was with me as much as her. Again, it was pride that got in the way of what might've been years of friendship and support.'
'I'm glad you see it that way now.' he nodded. 'And yes, I'd like very much to be a part of your lives.'

TEN

Monday 17th February 2048. Cliffbridge, London. 0930 Hrs.

'Sector Zee is a place of intrigue and mastery, especially to someone like yourselves who are new to the place.' cried Stubbs as he trotted ahead of them like a freight train.
They walked into a brighter section of the tunnel, where Steve could make out the faces of the other two perfectly. Stubbs' face at large appeared solemn, while his eyes revealed the suppressed melancholy from within his heart. Thelma maintained her look of uncertainty; however her posture suggested an outward confidence.
   Just as he had gathered himself, Steve found himself crossing a threshold and standing on a steel-meshed platform and looking down onto a very large warehouse about the size of two large soccer pitches. The people below were so far down, that they appeared like smartly dressed ants dressed in suits. The people below sat in rows, each to a large desk with a mini plasma screen. Some typed away frantically, while most judging by the level of noise in the room, dictated to their screens. They all faced a very large plasma screen, which displayed at the top: 'GOODS IN' and 'GOODS OUT' with a very long list of goods on each column. At the bottom, a line of large text flashed:
'RUNNING AT A MODERATE DEFICITE'
'Good morning...Welcome to Sector Zee!' said an automated voice from the large screen. Stubbs led the way down the rickety spiral staircase:
'This is Sector Zee, named thus because it was the last chamber to be completed. More importantly, though, this is the most revered chamber off all: even above the weapon stockade.'
They began to walk along the aisles between the rows of workers.
'What happens here?' asked Thelma.
'In a nutshell, this is where we buy and sell goods to and from abroad. That is, to and from groups like Cliffbridge. It's all carried out electronically, just like the Stock Exchange in the City of London. Each broker here is negotiating prices, buying and selling goods all the time. If we just...' he stooped down to one of the brokers:
'...Francine? Can I just show these good people your screen for just a minute?' he asked apologetically to a young flustered looking woman, who nodded compliantly.
Steve and Thelma leant over the young woman's shoulder to view her screen.
   The screen's display was similar in format to that of the large main screen, except the young woman's had a list of goods waiting to be bought or sold, beside which were code names including: 'Lysander 1' and

'Timothy 9'. Steve realised why the young woman looked so flustered: her list of goods to be exported was far shorter than the goods being imported. Stubbs began with an anxious tone:
'As you can see…'
He turned to the woman and gave a brief smile.
'…don't worry, I'm not picking on you especially…' he turned back to look again at Steve and Thelma. 'As you can see we're in desperate need of a turnaround. The long and the short of it is we're importing more than we're exporting.'
Steve and Thelma looked around the room to observe the men and women hard at work at their desks; most of which looked like they had not slept in days.
'It's not that they're lazy, or even incompetent; they work around the clock. Michael over there has sat there in the same clothes for nearly two days, leaving his desk only for toilet breaks and to grab a sandwich and a coffee every so often. He's married with kids who rarely see him. He is a former City high flyer…as are most of the people you see here…' He broke off, covering his lips with his index finger to collect his thoughts.
'I dunno…we need someone with an edge…confidence. Someone who can turn things around when the odds are stacked against them…someone like you two.'
Steve and Thelma looked at one another for a while.
'What is it you want us to do exactly?' Steve asked.
'What I need you both to do is to take the rudder of this ship, which is cruising headlong into a very big iceberg. I'm putting you two in charge of this stock exchange.'
Steve could tell by the strength with which he drew on cigar that even he was not altogether sure about the arrangement deep down owing to their lack of experience. Steve and Thelma surveyed their surroundings a second time. Stubbs picked up on their reticent body language:
'You'll be provided with thorough training of course. I don't expect two people who are new to this game to step in and just get on with it! It's just that sometimes you need someone who's fresh to it all to notice the obvious mistakes. I don't believe you need a degree in financial services to be able to tell whether we're buying too much wheat!' he giggled. 'As I say, I need someone who can persuade our trading partners that our goods are worth buying. The art of persuasion is an innate quality; not something you can read at university.'
He gave them a tight smile.
'I'd like to talk about this with Thelma for a few minutes if that's okay.' said Steve
'Take all the time you need.' Stubbs replied.

Steve and Thelma walked a few meters along one of the aisles, in order to be sure that they could not be overheard. They whispered to one another, exploring every angle of every possibility and the implications thereof. Thelma outlined her concerns about the possibility of the wider community finding out about their work in Subterranea, while Steve talked about the juxtaposition of socialism and capitalism. The more they talked, however, the less they concentrated on the negatives. They began to focus on what Mary had said to them in the launderette about Rebecca's future, leaving them to abandon their own apprehensions and to agree to take up the employment.

They were shown to their desks shortly afterwards. They were each given a large desk at the very front of the hall and began to explore the database with one of the supervisors. The screens at which they worked were the 'Commanding Terminals'. It was here where every order made at the other terminals was processed, before either being approved or rejected. The Commanding Terminals were connected to the 'Mother Terminal', which was a super-large screen whose sole purpose was to display the overall amount of stock entering and leaving Cliffbridge every minute. Although Steve and Thelma had only begun to familiarise themselves with the software, it seemed that Stubbs was correct in assuming that they had the Midas touch. In under an hour, the 'Goods In' column on the Mother Terminal had depleted, while the 'Goods Out' column had inflated.

After another hour had past, they were asked to attend Stubbs' office for a short meeting. Inside the office, Stubbs sat awaiting them with sunken eyebrows and his mouth pulled into a small-ridged smile, making his face difficult to read. Presently, he reached inside his pocket and pulled out a cigar.

'Right…' he began hesitantly. '…It would seem that I've wasted my time…' he lifted his eyes up to Steve and Thelma's level and continued: '…All those years. All those years and I could've just hired you two.'

Thelma's face broke into a coy smile as she touched her collar.

'How did you manage it?' asked Stubbs, looking at Steve.

'Well you see all I did was…' began Thelma

'Forgive me love, but I wasn't asking you; I was talkin' to your boyfriend here.' he said, masking his impatience with a grin.

'Perhaps I can help you with your answer.' said Stubbs, pulling out an A4 sheet of paper in front of Steve.

On it was line after line of computer jargon, which made no sense to him at all.

'I'm not sure I quite understand what you're getting at.' said Steve anxiously.

'Don't worry, I don't expect you to.'

He rocked Steve's shoulder in what Steve hoped was a friendly manner, but he could feel Stubbs' sovereign rings digging into his flesh nonetheless.
'So I'll help you shall I?' Stubbs asked.
He took a biro and drew a heavy black line beneath one of the lines on the A4:
'UKGOV: SOLD: MORRISSEY, S: 3TONNE: CORN'
'Recognise this bit?' he asked, his eyes gazing up at Steve's as his chin rested on his knuckles.
'I believe so, yes' replied Steve with an air of anxiety.
A few seconds of uncomfortable quiet hung in the air, before Stubbs broke the silence:
'Steven?'
'Yes?'
'We don't do deals with the British government.' he snapped, tearing the paper to shreds. 'Are you deliberately trying to get me into trouble?'
'No…of course not. Must have slipped my mind. I'm truly sorry.'
Stubbs' face relaxed again.
'Ah well…Listen, luckily for you…not to mention all of us down here, everything we do goes via Austria so there's no real danger of getting our fingers burnt. Just keep your wits about you, that's all I ask of you.'
'Right, of course.' Steve replied, relieved.
Stubbs sat up, tilting his chair from left to right.
'Look, I wouldn't have hired you if I didn't think you could cut the mustard. I saw somethin' in you both that suggested to me that you were special and I don't intend on lettin' you slip through my fingers.' he lit his cigar 'Besides, it's only your first day!' he pointed to the door with his cigar 'Why don't the pair of ya go home and take an early lunch? I'll see you back here in a couple of hours.'

***

Thelma, Steve and the child sat in Thelma's living room, eating lunch. Steve had asked for the fire to be lit and Thelma had grudgingly agreed. The cold draft that crept beneath the door was not countered by the heat from the fire, but shot down Steve's neck. He bit into his ham and cucumber sandwich with gusto, in spite of the bread being a bit stale. Thelma ate a more demure humus and cress roll, while Rebecca sank a plastic spoon into her fromage-frais.
'That was odd earlier.' said Thelma.
'What, you mean in the office?'
'Yeah, I mean what does he expect from us on a first day?' she continued with spirit.

'Those machines are hard. And another thing, why tell you off about sellin' somethin' to the government if he has them as a contact on the database? Somethin' ain't right there.'
Steve thought for a moment.
'Yes, it does seem rather suspect. Almost makes you wonder whether the government have some sort of a deal with Cliffbridge which he wants to keep quiet about.'
Thelma nodded in agreement 'Or somethin' the government wants to keep mum about.'
'Yes, it's all very curious.' he agreed, pondering the idea.
'Anyway, no use thinkin' about it too much. As long as we get paid on time, I'm happy.' she said switching the television set on.
Once it had warmed up, the screen displayed the transmitter information for Alto-Zero, before Stubbs' face appeared, set behind the channel's logo.
"You are watching Alto-Zero on channel six. Good afternoon citizens of Cliffbridge. There will now follow a short newsreel produced by Mr Stubbs…"
The screen then played a short tune to accompany the title, which was "The Greater Offensive." The title faded slowly and was followed by a scene which displayed the inside of the Ministry of Defence and Stuart Fielding, the Defence Secretary, reading a newspaper at his desk. A narration was played alongside this, which Steve immediately recognised as being the voice of Neil Stubbs, which ran:
"As you can tell, Mr Fielding hasn't much to get worked up about; with a well-equipped army the size of Great Britain's, which has a fruitful working relationship with MI5 and other intelligence sources, there really isn't any reason to be stirred."
The humus covered bread roll that Steve had snatched from Thelma fell onto his plate and he listened intently:
"Citizens of Cliffbridge, I expect you have seen some of the government propaganda which shows us that Britain is at the 'Driving seat of Europe' thanks to the Prime Minister's financial mind. Indeed, citizens, you have seen the magnificent skyline of Central London made up by the glass and marble government offices in Westminster as well as the HSBC tower. A clear portrayal of the sheer wealth of the nation I'm sure you would agree…"
Stubbs faded onto the right hand side of the screen, holding a cigar as he spoke.
"So, why then does Mr Dawson insist on sending agent after agent to Cliffbridge? Perhaps he has a genuine concern for the shortfall in the

national treasure for the benefit of the nation he runs; merely wishing to build better schools and hospitals…"

The scene then changed to some of the poverty-stricken streets and alleys of Cliffbridge, shown in black and white.

"…Or perhaps he wants to turn the screws even tighter on the thumbs of those people, that's *you*, whom he has already expelled from his cleansed society." he said pointing to the viewers.

Steve could almost taste his fear on his food as he watched:

"That is why we must act now! Yes now!! Before we're totally annihilated by them! Each and every one of you MUST do your bit for your community! Time is running out. To find out how you will be hired to help, call 01207 7743877, text 'HELP' to 8763452 or drop into Central House at anytime day or night. And remember, Cliffbridge doesn't need *you*; you need *Cliffbridge*!"

The picture of Stubbs faded out and was followed by canned cheering.

"That was a newsreel on behalf of the Community Panel, led by Mr Stubbs. Thank you for watching and good afternoon. Alto-Zero will resume transmission later this evening at four pm."

Thelma turned the dial to check if there was anything worth watching on Dominion, before switching the television off.

'How very odd.' said Steve quietly.

'I know. Why's he still on about the government sending agents? He seems to have a bee in his bonnet about that.' said Thelma.

'I expect he'll have us working in the munitions area this afternoon.' he said heavily.

'That's if he don't send us home after a couple of hours.' she laughed.

'Why would he do that?' he demanded defensively.

'I dunno! The same reason he sent us home this morning, I 'spose.'

She glared at him with concern.

'What's wrong?'

'Nothing, why?'

'You ain't been right since that newsreel.' she handed him a biscuit 'Look, you needn't be scared. Even Stubbs wouldn't be daft enough to think you were an agent, let alone a *government* agent. Come off it!' she laughed.

***

It was two o'clock when they arrived back at Central House. Steve had been right in guessing that the pair of them would be working outside of Sector Zee, although it was not in the munitions factory. They had been assigned to complete a manual audit of The Holding. There were only ten women present, waiting to be distributed around London. Steve was required to carryout a recommendation as to which sector of London to place each sex worker according to her appearance. A tall, slender woman would be well suited to working in the Soho area, while a fuller woman could be placed in Croydon. Steve concluded will little hesitation that four women would sell in Soho, while the other six would make it in Greater London.

Thelma's task was to give a private examination of each woman in the cubical beside the main door. She made a note of any birthmarks, tattoos or any other imperfections, which may hinder the sale of each woman. Thelma recorded one tattoo on one of the women Steve had earmarked for Soho, while those with varicose veins or birthmarks had been assigned to the less profitable areas. Thelma was examining the last woman, when the woman began to talk:

'Excuse. Excuse.' she began in broken English 'Y-You work Mr Morrissey?' she asked, pointing at Thelma's neck, just below her left ear.
'Eh?' Thelma asked, perplexed.
Thelma then noticed that she was pointing to the tattoo she had been given when she had started working as a prostitute. "09088" was her personal ID number.
'As a worker? No...Not anymore.' said Thelma sternly.
'Then you happy, yes?' the woman asked with a smile, revealing a missing incisor tooth, which Thelma promptly made a note of, cursing herself.
'Yes...I mean no...Sort of.' Thelma considered herself 'I miss parts of it. You meet a lot of interesting people and it pays well.'
The woman appeared glum.
'We no keep money. We work alone without friend.'
Thelma paused, placing her equipment on the floor and felt sorry for the woman.
'Think of it this way; it's better than being hungry and living on the streets.' Thelma smiled.
The woman began to weep into her hands.
'I-I have daughter in China. She very young and I not see her for long time.'
Thelma remembered being virtually forced into prostitution and the uncertainty that came with it and being separated from her child for long periods of time. A forty-eight our shift was quite enough for her; she dare not think what being separated from her child for weeks on end felt like.
'The other women.' the woman continued 'They are same. I not know them well, but one woman sold her kidney for little money to feed her family. Then horrible man say kidney no good and must work for him to pay him back. She end up here.'

Thelma struggled to keep her composure. She could not believe how she had let herself be taken in by Stubbs' ruthless scheme, especially knowing what it was like being a prostitute. Thelma looked once more at the poor, defenceless woman.

'Look, wait here, I'll be back soon.'

Thelma exited the cubical and rejoined Steve. Steve sat on a wooden chair, awaiting her impatiently. He appeared almost blind to what was in front of his eyes, apparently not sharing Thelma's newly acquired passion for justice.

'Steve, we have to get them out of here.' she declared.

Steve's face became alert.

'Don't be so absurd. We've done our job, so let's go and report back to Neil.'

Thelma drew nearer to him, shaking her head in disbelief.

'Don't you get it? These are real women with real lives! They ain't just some herd of animals: they're real people, with real feelings.'

'How do you suggest we get them out?' he asked, softening.

'I've hatched a plan. It ain't much, so there's no guarantee it'll work-we'll just have to play it by ear…' she drew in a deep breath 'You report back to Stubbs with our findings and I'll take this lot out of here.'

'Where are you going to take them?' asked Steve, frowning.

Thelma braced herself.

'I'm gonna take them to the brothel on Fox Road.'

Steve gave out a laugh.

'And have them work there?'

'Well it's better than workin' under some slave driver. It ain't perfect, but the girls more or less choose their hours and there's no boss breathin' down their neck.'

'What will we tell Stubbs?' he asked.

Thelma appeared slightly shaken.

'Err…We'll think of somethin'.'

'What about the guy on reception? You'll have a tough time getting them out without him suspecting anything.' he said.

'Like I said, we'll just have to play it by ear, we don't have any choice.' she gave him a look of unease 'Well…Are you with me on this, or what?'

'Do I have a choice?' he asked with a small smile.

'No.' she replied strictly.

***

After a brief explanation to the women, Thelma collected them together and led them to the express lift, which took them to ground level. In the full glare of the sunlight, the women appeared much paler. It was obvious to Thelma that they had not seen sunlight for quite some time as the light caused them to wince. The elderly gentleman on reception had become well acquainted with Thelma since working for Stubbs, although previously he had little to say to her other than the odd negative comment.

'Ah hello there Miss Harrison! What's this then, a break for freedom?' he asked, lowering his glasses.
'I should be so blooming' lucky!' she said with dramatic expression.
'Mr Stubbs has given me the none-too-pleasant task of takin' these out to stretch their legs!'
'Oh.' he breathed 'Then you'll not mind me checking then?' he asked, reaching for his telephone.
'You could do, although Mr Stubbs don't like bein' disturbed while in meetings; especially when a fuss is bein' made over nothing.' she said, doing her best to mask her anger behind a tight smile.
'Tosser.' she said quietly as she exited the building with the women.

   They arrived at High Cliffbridge tube station. This stretch of the East London line had been put on a part-time service since the 2012 Olympics, although the service had been greatly reduced since the government took office. The strong wind almost swept the eleven from their feet and into the vortex below, where polystyrene cups and chip bags circled. The gates were open and with no ticket officer present, the eleven took their chances and hopped on the train bound for Ward's End. The other three passengers in the carriage stared at the ten Chinese women. The passengers appeared to be from the other side of London and therefore easily distracted by the avant-gardes dressed in provocative clothing.
'Seen enough, have ya?' hissed Thelma at one la-di-dah woman.
The woman pulled her handbag nearer and looked away, shocked.

   Thelma and the ten women alighted at the tube station on the corner of Marsh Road. This time a stationmaster stopped the small party and asked them to present their tickets. Thelma screamed "pervert!" at the top of her voice, prompting a youth to appear, grasping the obese stationmaster by the tie. Thelma saw her chance and instructed the women to make a break for it and jump the wheelchair barrier. Outside, they ran as fast as they could until they reached the entrance to the brothel on Fox Road. Before Thelma had time to knock, the youth which had been helpful just a couple of minutes before, reappeared.
'So ladies, what am I gonna get in return?' he chanced with a seedy grin.
'Nothin', you anorexic twat.' retorted Thelma.
The grin fell from they boy's face.
'Look, we live in a favour-for-favour society, don't we? All I'm askin' for is my due.'
'This place is for men, not little boys who *think* they're men. Now why don't you run along back to your master like a good boy?'
The youth became agitated.
'I wouldn't touch any of you lot with a bargepole. God knows what I'd catch.' he blurted, running back the way he came.

Thelma smiled at the women confidently.

'Now that's how you deal with a toe rag!'

The woman who Thelma had spoken to in Subterranea declared 'You very good, Miss Harrison!'

With a nod of appreciation, Thelma took a deep breath and gave the door a loud knock. After a short wait the door flew open, releasing a torrent of warm air onto their faces. Pamela the coordinator stood at the door, puffing on a joint. She was dressed in a red satin dressing gown and appeared both surprised and disappointed at seeing Thelma.

'What do *you* want?' she asked dismissively.

'Pamela, hi.' Thelma began heavy-heartedly 'I know I haven't been in for ages, but things have happened. I work for Stubbs more closely now and so I've moved on.'

Pamela gazed at Thelma's attire.

'I can see that. You always were too big for your boots. While the rest of us make do with what we've got, you always wanted more.' she breathed out a thick cloud of smoke onto Thelma's face 'And what's more, since hearin' about what goes on down there, we've turned our backs on Stubbs and want nothin' more to do with him.'

'Down where?' asked Thelma nervously.

'You know very bloody well where I mean. Subterranea, ain't it? Stupid name as well. Not as stupid as what it stands for though; prospering on the backs of the likes of us. We all thought Stubbs was one of us-tryin' to revive Cliffbridge in the face of the government.'

Thelma looked dismayed.

'He still is! It's just that what he's doin' is more complicated than everyone thought.'

'Don't give me that bullshit. He's lining his own pockets. He's a politician at heart and always will be. And you're just some fancy-piece for him to look at while he works.'

Thelma looked thoughtful for a moment.

'Look, much as I'd like to talk about this more, I've a few presents. Call them consolation prizes.'

'Don't patronise me. I don't want nothin' from ya.' scowled Pamela, closing the door.

'Wait a minute.' called Thelma, holding the door open ' Just for the record, I don't like Stubbs any more than you do; if you knew *half* of what goes on down there, you'd have a fit.' she turned to the women and then back at Pamela, who had softened 'These women are from all over China. They were brought all the way over in a lorry and straight down to Subterranea. They are all slaves and at the moment, belong to Stubbs before being sold on for a profit.'

The joint fell out of Pamela's mouth in shock.

'My God.' she said quietly, picking up the joint 'That's sad, but what do you want me to do about it?'
'Take them in.' Thelma pleaded 'Take them in and they can work for you. At least they won't be slaves and will be well looked after.'
Pamela scratched her head and thought for a moment.
'You're askin' a lot of me, Thelm.'
'I know.' Thelma nodded with a sincere smile 'But would you? As you can see, they're a good lookin' bunch and I'm sure they'll work hard.'
Pamela nodded reluctantly.
'Alright.' she conceded 'But I ain't doin' this for you-especially not for Stubbs, okay?'
Thelma looked at the floor 'I ain't exactly told him yet.'
'He ain't half gonna have a surprise when he finds out!' laughed Pamela. She stood aside 'Come on, let's have ya ladies…'
The women looked at each other and shrugged fatalistically, before entering the brothel.
'Look after them Pam.' said Thelma sincerely.
'I will.'
The door closed without any further discussion.

***

Meanwhile, Steve sat at his terminal in Sector Zee. He searched the catalogue until he found the prostitutes listed. He selected the ten women and placed them under the "sold" category.
"IncomeNET:£25,000" flashed onto the screen; Steve hoped that nobody was paying attention to the Mother Terminal while this was displayed. He suddenly recalled the whole idea of moving the prostitutes being Thelma's. He also remembered only too vividly, the verbal onslaught inflicted upon him by Stubbs earlier that day. He looked around him, noticing the sea of harassed faces working busily on their screens. He then considered Thelma's joyous face when she heard him agreeing to help in her emancipation plan. This thought was quickly followed by his belief that Thelma would not much care if he were to insert her details beside the sale audit. She would understand, he thought, provided he explained his already fraught position with her. He flexed his fingers, before hastily inserting: "Prostitute: Sale: Harrison,T." His finger hovered over the 'submit' button. He had not altogether thought this through; although on balance he knew that under the circumstances it was necessary and would be able to cope with the consequences should any arise. He pressed the button.
'Ah Steven! How's it going?' came Stubbs' voice from behind him.
Steve pressed the 'minimise' button in alarm, hiding the data.
'Not bad, thank you Mr Stubbs.' said Steve nervously.

'Good!' Stubbs looked over to Thelma's desk 'Where's Thelma?'
'She's gone to complete a spot of market research.' Steve lied, quickly realising that he had opened a can of worms.
'Market research? Where?' Stubbs asked with a curious frown.
'Oh…She astutely thought that having swiftly completed the audit in The Holding, that it would be a good use of time to undertake a survey on people's attitudes to the favour-for-favour scheme.'
Stubbs drew on his cigar rapidly.
'Yes, but I pay her to be here! No-one cares what the ungrateful buggers above think-Cliffbridge would be little more than a farm without this place!'
Steve coughed nervously.
'Ah well, you know what the fairer sex can be like. Once they have an idea, how ever silly, they run with it!'
'Quite, quite.' Stubbs nodded 'How did the audit in The Holding go?'
'Very well indeed. I'm pleased to announce that you have a very healthy and profitable stock down there.'
'That's music to my ears!' Stubbs' eyes grew rounder with excitement 'Were there any abnormalities I should know about?'
'No, not really. Although one woman had a missing tooth; an incisor I think.'
'I'll have the orthodontist see to that I the morning.' he sat himself down on Thelma's desk 'On a more sombre note, can I ask you a question?' he asked, stubbing out his cigar onto the foil ashtray.
'Of course you may.' Steve gulped, feeling the butterflies in his stomach awakening.
'How do you think people see me?' asked Stubbs.
'Oh, I'd say you have the full respect of the borough.' replied Steve with a smile.
Stubbs appeared somewhat disappointed.
'I see. Are there any particular words you would use to sum up people's opinion of me?'
Steve's eyes narrowed in thought.
'Strong, a shrewd leader, confident, unshakable…'
Stubbs smiled half-heartedly.
'More importantly, Steven, how do *you* regard me?'
Steve appeared incredulous.
'*Me*? Well…I would definitely say you are a strong character, with Cliffbridge's welfare at your heart.'
Stubbs nodded and gave him a half-hearted smile.
'I'm flattered. The thing is, those are the words often used to about me.' he stood up and giggled coyly 'You see, the interesting thing is, people

seldom use words like "caring" or "loving".' he faced Steve 'Do you have any children of your own?'

'No...' Steve replied, looking perplexed.

'No neither do I, although I would have liked a boy; someone to give this place to one day.' said Stubbs thoughtfully.

'Never say never.' Steve smiled, wagging his finger.

'Huh! At my age? All I can really hope for after a long shift is my hot water bottle to cuddle up to! And even that's going cold on me.'

He peered at Steve, revealing his large black eyes.

'Look son, you've got a good 'un there in Thelma-hang on to her or you'll find life passes you by.'

Steve looked around 'But isn't this your passion? You've built it up from nothing to something quite magnificent.'

Stubbs let out a loud laugh.

'This place? No, if I could put my pride aside for one minute, I'd sooner sell up and settle in the country and get married.'

He noticed Steve appeared tired and harassed.

'Look son, why not logoff and go home? You can call the missus and tell her to call it a day too.'

'No, it's quite alright!' smiled Steve, trying to look more alert.

'Ignore me, I was just getting a bit self-indulgent…Must be getting soft in my old age.' admitted Stubbs with a frown 'Off you go, get off home. See you in the mornin' bright and early.'

ELEVEN

Tuesday 18th February 2048. Ward's End, London. 0730 Hrs.

Steve and Thelma awoke to a glorious sunny morning. Steve had virtually moved in with Thelma and Rebecca and was enjoying the family lifestyle; far more than he had envisioned. Having thought on what Stubbs had revealed to him the previous evening, he was willing to put aside his independence and bachelorhood in favour of an existence whereby his presence counted for something. He gazed out of the bedroom window and noticed that the chip shop was closed for business and had been boarded up. Chip papers and polystyrene cups circled in the wind outside it, as if in mourning for their old home. This bleak picture contrasted with the colourful blooms that adorned the roadside. Daffodils, crocuses and snowdrops brought colour to the lingering grey that had become a dominant feature in Steve's mind.
With a sense of zeal, he awoke Thelma who lay sleeping like a baby all night. He gave her a shake on the shoulder until her eyes opened. Once they had stopped flickering, they rested on Steve's. They appeared forlorn and reticent, unlike the bright, spirited eyes that he had come to admire.
'Is it mornin' already?' she yawned.
'I'm afraid so!' he cheered.
She raised her head and grimaced.
'Why are you so perky this mornin'?'
'Oh you know! Spring's just around the corner and there's a real sense of renaissance in the air!'
She smirked 'Am I goin' out with a walkin' dictionary? I can barely manage slang at this time of the bloody mornin'!'
'Get up and let's have breakfast.' he asserted, pulling the duvet from her. She tried to pull it back, but Steve was stronger.
They sat with Rebecca in the tiny kitchen. The central heating rattled into action, much to Steve's relief. Thelma had pushed him aside from the stove when attempting to prepare scrambled egg. He had somehow managed to spill half of the ingredients onto the floor and down his dressing gown, while Rebecca had sat in her highchair laughing away at him. Having retired to the stool around the table, Thelma continued. Her agitation had continued into the morning, prompting Steve to question whether something was on her mind. She bashed away at the eggs with the fork with a stern face.
'Is something the matter?' he asked at last.
'No, why should there be?'
'No, of course not...' he paused '...Won't you come and sit down for a minute? I have something I'd like to tell you.'

'Can't you see I'm busy?' she snapped, throwing the fork onto the worktop.
Steve looked shocked.
      No sooner had he begun contemplating Thelma's outburst, when a knock was made at the front door. Steve walked slowly and cautiously to the door, with his head bowed forlornly.
'Hello love, I'm sorry to disturb the both of you so early but there's somethin' I'd like to say.'
It was Mary. She looked as dismal as he now felt.
'Join the queue.' Steve breathed.
'Oh? What's wrong love?' she asked, touching his face sympathetically.
'Oh nothing.' he sighed 'Come through to the kitchen.'
Inside the kitchen, Mary sat on the stool, where Steve had been sitting and looked at Thelma apprehensively. Thelma appeared indifferent to her presence, continuing with the breakfast preparation.
'This ain't a good time Mary.' she stated starkly, slicing a loaf of bread.
'I can see that love, but I've got somethin' important to tell the both of ya. It's about what's 'appened.'
'What do you mean?' asked Thelma impatiently.
Mary folded her arms.
'It's about Subterranea.'
'What about it?'
'People have become very…militant about the place.' explained Mary, picking up a Clementine from the bowl.
'People feel cheated by the ruling system: almost betrayed. They don't feel that Neil has been honest enough, hiding behind socialism while he lines his own pockets with real money.'
Thelma put the bread knife down and turned to face her.
'People manage, it's not like anyone starves around here.'
Mary shrugged.
'Shops everywhere are closing.' she looked right into Thelma's eyes 'I've decided to close the launderette.'
Steve's eyes widened with shock.
'The launderette? Why?'
'I don't see why I should live on fish from the canal and mouldy produce any longer, while Neil plays the champagne socialist; it just ain't right.' Mary insisted.
'Where will you work?' Steve asked, still in shock.
'A distant relative has offered me a room at her place in Havering; near the shoppin' complex. I dare say I'll find some work in one of the shops.'
Thelma looked disappointed, removing her apron.
'But you've worked in that launderette years, you built it up from nothin'. You're the backbone of this place.'

Mary shook her head.

'Yeah, but *whose* backbone love?'

Thelma looked thoughtful. Her face then creased into rage while tears began to form in her eyes.

'You're just jealous!' she yelled.

Mary's forehead furrowed in disbelief.

'Jealous of what love?'

'Me and Steve! You can't handle the idea of me bein' happy for the first time in ages. It's still about having control over me, ain't it? You've lost your control and my life's moved on and you can't stand it.'

'Hey, don't you think you're being unfair to Mary? She's only letting us know what her plans are.' said Steve diplomatically.

'Don't you dare tell me what to think!' she told him sourly 'You might be my boyfriend but you ain't the boss of me.'

Mary appeared awkward.

'I think it's time I was on my way. I've obviously spoken out of turn.'

Thelma stopped weeping suddenly and gazed through the tears at Mary, who had made for the door.

'Wait a minute. How come everyone suddenly knows about Subterranea? I thought you said you were the only person to know of the place?'

Mary wagged her finger at her.

'I said that a few others knew too.'

'Yeah, but why is it that after we told you the other day about it in more depth that everyone's suddenly becomin' militant?' asked Thelma curiously 'I took ten prozzies from The Holding to the brothel and I was told by Pam that her and the others had turned their back on Stubbs once and for all. Pam never said nothin' about the place before.'

'Like I said, it's time I was leaving.' Mary declared.

'You're a flamin' bitch!' Thelma screamed, hurling a cup at the door as it closed.

  Steve stood beside the door stunned, quite unable to believe that he had narrowly escaped being hit by the cup. After he had recovered, he walked around the table to where Thelma sat crying into her hands. He touched her back gently, feeling her breathing. Rebecca gave her a concerned look.

'Mummy will be alright petal.' he assured the tot.

'No, mummy won't be fine.' she sobbed, lowering her hands.

She glanced at him.

'Do you think she realises what she's done? She could've single-handedly brought Cliffbridge to its knees-just for the sake of pride!'

Steve rubbed her back affectionately.

'We don't know that for sure dear.'

'Why are you defendin' her? I know her better than you. She puts on this front of being this helpful, harmless old woman, but she's out for what she can get.' she countered.
Steve looked anxious.
'There's no way she could have told anybody, is there?'
Thelma nodded 'There's no other explanation.' she walked over to the worktop to pour a mug of orange juice 'When I arrived at the brothel yesterday, Pam had a face like thunder. She told me straight away that I had no business being there, now that I work in Subterranea. It'd be a hell of a coincidence if she'd found out from someone else-she never mentioned it even *once* before.'
Steve's look of concern intensified.
'If Stubbs learns of this, it could lead back to us.'
'Of course he's gonna get wind of it! The brothel's about to close and it sounds like the launderette already has.' she exclaimed.
Steve thought for a moment.
'Is Stubbs aware of our friendship with Mary?'
'*Friendship*? What friendship? As far as I'm concerned, that woman's dead.' she said bitterly, finishing her juice. She looked at him 'Anyway, what was it you wanted to speak to me about so urgent?'
Steve maintained his thoughtful stare through Thelma.
'It doesn't matter now.'

***

Later that morning, the two of them sat at their terminals. Steve was doing his best to conceal his fear from her by burying himself in work and leaving everything else, including that morning's events to one side. The problem was that he could not completely focus on what he was doing, which manifested itself in serious errors and he had therefore lost some potentially lucrative deals.

Thelma sat straight in her executive chair, as confidently as she ever had, dictating frantically at her plasma screen without pausing to take a breath. Steve wondered how she could possibly concentrate on her work and put on a brave face. Thelma's eyes were glued to her screen.
'Moscow, will you buy four metric tonnes of coal at five thousand British pounds? Thank you…deal confirmed. Red Panther, will you buy ten thousand times one packet of thirty codeine tablets at two thousand British pounds? Thank you…deal confirmed…' she said to her terminal with haste.
A memo flashed onto their screens, which ran:
"Please attend my office ASAP. Regards, Neil."

Steve and Thelma made their way nervously to the office. Stubbs' met them with a face that gave nothing away; his eyes buried deeply beneath his brow and his mouth drawn up in a tiny smile.

'Good morning Steven, good morning Thelma.' said Stubbs nonchalantly, resting his chin on his hands. 'Take a seat.'

Nobody spoke a word for thirty seconds, until Stubbs noticed that Steve's brow was becoming covered in sweat:

'Thelma, you might find this interesting-take a look.' He produced a sheet of A4 like the one Steve had been shown the day before. It read:

'UKGOV: SOLD: HARRISON,T: QTY10: SEXWORKER.'

'Does this mean anything to you, Thelma?' he asked.

Thelma peered down at the paper, sweeping her hair free from her face and revealing a confused expression.

'But I don't get it, I never approved, let alone actually *sold* anything to the government. That's strange...' she muttered, studying the paper further.

'Strange indeed!' agreed Stubbs with a nod. 'Shall I tell you something else that's strange?' he asked.

'What's also strange is how you've sold each prostitute for the full askin' price and the books don't balance...ergo: there ain't one brass farthing to show for it.'

Thelma looked at Steve in bewilderment and back at Stubbs.

'I never sold no prostitutes to the government.' Thelma declared quickly. She looked at him 'You know how I feel about those women who work in that brothel: they're like sisters to me and when I went down to The Holding I could see they looked frightened and needed protection...'

Stubbs lit a cigar.

'I'm listenin'.'

Thelma continued '...Well I took it upon myself to save them from a miserable life, under some demon's control.'

'My girl, they're not like you or I; they're mere commodities to be sold.' he stated, grinning through the smoke.

Thelma's face became red with rage.

'I ain't no politician, but even *I* know that don't sound like a true socialist talkin'.'

Stubbs' face dropped, while Thelma continued:

'I took them down to Ward's End and asked Pamela to take them in. She agreed and as far as I know, they're workin' for her. But I swear I never said nothin' to the government-cross my heart.' she said desperately.

Stubbs' face became more relaxed.

'I see. Good old Pamela.' he said wryly. 'But I still take issue with you goin' behind my back. How do I know I can trust you again?'

'You just can, alright?' she said impatiently.

Steve, meanwhile, sat there while his breathing became more laboured. His heart compelled him to defend Thelma, while his brain told him that such an action would almost certainly bring him punishment of some kind, notwithstanding the fact that Stubbs had opened up to him the day before. The more he studied Stubbs' face, the more there was an apparent likeness to his father. His father's quick temper had been all the more difficult to predict because of his low-hung brow, which cut off any clues to his mood. Up to the point of his mother's death, Steve had harboured such a great deal of respect for him that nothing he said or did threw up any questions in Steve's mind. He was beginning to build up a similar sort of bond with Stubbs, although unlike his father, Stubbs regarded respect as being a two-way street.

Stubbs regarded Thelma, breaking the silence.

'Look, I won't pretend to be too disappointed in you, because I'm not. Sales figures for this quarter are better than ever and I am pleased with my decision to give you both a free reign. Just be careful with taking too much initiative at the expense of the welfare of Cliffbridge; it's a fragile society at the best of times.'

***

It was later that evening and Steve and Thelma were nearing the end of their shifts. Having considered the narrow reprieve from Stubbs, Steve made a few adjustments to his trading schedule. He attempted to reopen the sex worker deals that he had cancelled the day before. It was only when he noticed a sharp reduction in weaponry and artillery sales that he realised that prostitutes, artillery and weaponry came as a package, which was indivisible; so a cancellation of a prostitution deal meant a cancellation of arms and artillery.

The Mother Terminal was just as healthy as ever and was becoming healthier still. Thelma was glued to her screen as always closing deals that without her could have gone either way. She had done little, though, to change things unlike Steve. She had not cancelled any deals, nor had she opened new ones. She had instead traded-off Cliffbridge's aging wheat stockpile for a large shipment of Irish whiskey, which she knew Stubbs loved so much.

'Thelma?' Steve called.

'What?' she answered, sounding harassed.

'You asked me earlier what it was I wanted to say.'

'Did I? I don't remember.' she said indifferently.

'Well, what I was trying try say was that…and I realise that this morning was not the right time to say it, given the circumstances and…'

Thelma turned from her terminal and peered at him.

'Look, can you just say whatever it is you've got to say, because I'm busy.'

Steve became more nervous.

'Yes, of course. Well, as I was saying a moment ago, that although we have only been together a short time, I feel that we have developed a mutual feeling of trust. I also feel that I have grown accustomed to your company in a way which makes me feel able to face whatever may come my way.'

Thelma looked confused.

'Is this your way of asking me to marry ya?'

'No no! Of course not! No!' he caught sight of her looking a touch disappointed '...Unless you were considering marriage?'

She raised an eyebrow 'Do I look like the sort of girl who gets married?'

'Oh well...' he began, considering Thelma's question.

'Don't answer that.' she said quickly.

Steve continued 'What I was building up to say, was that I feel that our relationship has already moved on a stage and that I love you and although I might not be quite what you had in mind originally, I...'

Thelma interrupted him 'What did you say just then?'

'Just that I might not have been quite what you had in mind before, but...'

Thelma shook her head.

'No no-before that.'

Steve looked momentarily confused.

'Oh...the bit where I said I...'

'I love you?' she asked with a smile.

'It might have been that part, yes.' he nodded with a bashful smile.

'If that's how you feel, then so do I.' she said with a warm smile.

***

Later that evening, Steve, Thelma and Rebecca sat in Donkey Park. The large recreational ground was awash with colourful flowerbeds while the low angle sun provided them with a red tint. Rebecca chased the seagulls from their resting place upon the overflowing litterbins. Thelma sat upon the damp grass in thought, while Steve sat on a bench, which was covered in the same abusive graffiti as in the lift at Ealing Tower. Thelma had returned to her troubled mood since Steve had emptied his heart out to her earlier that day. Steve was unsure whether given time to reflect, Thelma no longer shared his love for her. Her moods were becoming more unpredictable and could change in an instant, making her all the more difficult to approach. He had offered her a place beside him on the bench, but she had refused on the grounds of the litterbins being too close. The bitter wind bit at his neck, causing him to turn his collar up.

'Steve, I've got somethin' to tell ya.' she declared, joining him at last on the bench. Her voice sounded quaky 'It's sort of to do with what you told me earlier.'

'If it's about the 'L' word, then I quite understand if it's too soon.' he said.

'No it ain't that.' she began softly 'I just thought that since we're in the business of makin' grand declarations, I might as well say my piece.'

She touched him on the arm.

'You mentioned you love me earlier, right?'

Steve nodded nervously.

'Well it's because of your openness that I'm able to be honest with *you*.' she said, her face growing more desperate.

Steve chewed the inside of his mouth nervously.

'The relationship isn't working out? If that's the case then at least that would explain why you've been blowing hot and cold on me all day.'

Thelma looked puzzled as she lowered her arm.

'There ain't nothin' wrong with our relationship...is there?'

'I'd like to think not, but I would like an explanation for your recent behaviour.' he said desperately.

She looked over to Rebecca who was dancing in the sunset's glare in front of them.

'God, I wish there was some easy way of sayin' this.' she whispered glumly.

'I'm pregnant.'

Steve cleaned his right ear hole with his little finger.

'What?'

'You heard me.' she snapped.

'*Pregnant?*' he asked again.

'Yes, as in up the duff; bun in the oven. Now do you get it?' she called impatiently.

'Yes, but how?'

Thelma looked at him with narrowed eyes 'Do you want me to draw you a picture? Didn't your mum tell you about the birds and the bees properly?'

'She never had the chance, but that's another story.' he said tensely 'What I mean is, you told me you had a diaphragm fitted. I don't understand.'

Steve looked on thoughtfully.

'But I've always been so careful; I made absolutely sure that this wouldn't happen.'

'Oh thanks a bunch! Am I really that repulsive?'

Steve did not answer her, but continued in thought.

'Are you absolutely sure?'

'I've taken two pregnancy tests and I'm never normally late.' she confirmed.

'But perhaps they were faulty. You must take another test, just to be totally sure. Better still; go to your GP to have a more thorough test.'
Thelma got to her feet and glared down at him.
'Two things. One: I've taken two tests, both of which have come up positive. Two: in case you hadn't noticed Cliffbridge don't have GPs!'
He too stood up and looked at her directly.
'Is this some kind of scheme to manipulate me into staying with you for good?'
Thelma's face paled in dismay.
'I thought you were different to all them other losers, but you're just out for what you can get.' she wiped a tear from her eye 'Well sod you Steve. Sod you.'
She took Rebecca's hand and ran along the path as fast as her legs could carry her.

TWELVE

Wednesday, 19th February 2048. Ward's End, London. 0700 Hrs.

    The next morning, Steve awoke in his apartment for the first time in several days. He had only just become accustomed to the cold drafts, which haunted Thelma's flat and the slamming of doors from her neighbours. The twenty-one degrees centigrade temperature in the apartment now, seemed too hot and the silence all around too eerie. He flung his thick duvet off and sat up. He would normally have reached for his slippers, but even his thin pyjamas were too cumbersome. He entered the shower, setting the temperature to 'tepid' and the speed to 'slow'. When he had finished and got dressed, he quickly set about looking for the thermostat, which he found in the kitchen and turned the setting down to ten degrees.

    Having taken a seat at the plush breakfast bar, he suddenly felt a sense of emptiness. The chrome refrigerator and the espresso machine no longer seemed important to him; he longed instead for the dingy kitchen with the temperamental washing machine at Thelma's. He reflected on the previous day's events as he bit into his burnt toast. He meditated on the way Thelma had regarded him as he told her of his love; her eyes seemed to dance and her lips reddened as his loving words entered her ears. Her newly found happiness had persisted into the evening, until the setting sun cast a shadow over her brow and ebbed away her euphoria as she prepared to tell him the news. Steve had been like a grown-up steeling candy from a small child; robbing her of her little piece of joy. His mother had told him that to be a man was not to be selfish and greedy, but to be kind and generous-especially with people's feelings. He felt disheartened at the notion that he was beginning to forget his mother's appearance in absence of the photograph and had already forgotten her wisdom.

***

    Steve arrived at Sector Zee to find Thelma's terminal vacant. Her usual messy desk, complete with discarded tissues and rubber bands, was now tidier than his. He called across to Michelle who informed him that she had been temporarily repositioned to the broadcasting suite above ground. When he had asked why she had left, the woman could not give him a definite answer, although she told him that it was something to do with not being able to concentrate fully on the job in hand. He too had found it difficult to concentrate and had let seven deals slip through his fingers until it was lunchtime. He decided that it was high time he confronted Thelma about the previous evening, so he logged off at his terminal and left Sector Zee. He entered the express lift to the ground floor and took the stairs up to the broadcasting suite.

The suite was much quieter than his last visit, where Thelma was under cross-examination. There appeared to be no-one inside, except the handwritten note which read "On Air" meant that there must have been some sort of activity in progress. He cautiously opened the door and crept inside. The stifling hot air hit his face as he entered and sat himself down on a single chair beside the door. The hum of the fan heaters pulsated across the large room, interrupted by no other sound. He began to wonder whether Thelma had already gone to lunch ahead of some busy schedule. Before he could move, the large plasma screen above the platform at the north side of the room flashed into action.
"This is Alto-Zero, broadcasting on VHF channel three."
The volume that the screen emitted was extremely loud, prompting whoever was in the controlling room to reduce it to a more comfortable pitch. Steve waited anxiously for the figure '3' to disappear from the screen. After a few seconds of muffled interference, Stubbs appeared holding his trademark cigar.
"Good afternoon Cliffbridge." began Stubbs solemnly.
The picture changed to an aerial view of Cliffbridge. Stubbs continued to talk over the footage.
"Citizens, it is with regret that I am the one who must tell you of the spectre of greed which has taken a stranglehold on our community. A tiny minority of people…some I am sorry to say are…or rather *were* the backbone of our unique civilisation, have brought about a terrible plague of greed seen only before outside Cliffbridge…"
The VT changed to show a macro shot of an early twenty-first century ten pound note.
"Capitalism, citizens, led to the largest recession at the beginning of the century, hitherto unseen since the Great Depression. Many of you will not remember this time of grave misery and discontent, but it was through ill management of credit through loans and borrowing that led to job losses and dispossession…"
The scene changed to an aerial view of Westminster.
"…And if that were not enough to convince people of the torment which capital brings, we were faced with the abandonment of Cliffbridge by Westminster some twelve years later! Once again, many job losses and dispossession. It was this act of contempt for our hard work in the City of London that led us having to fend for ourselves in the cold, harsh winter of 2020…"
The screen changed to the degradation of properties in the Ward's End area.

"…I am confident that every single one of you will recall the years which followed; the poverty, the hunger and perhaps most maddening: the humiliation inflicted upon us. Thousands of highly skilled men and women were reduced to little more than down-and-outs, while the rest of London flourished under the IMF bailout. .."

Stubbs returned to the screen.

"…So it's with puzzlement that I am faced with the betrayal of so-called loyal citizens: citizens who were at the forefront of this borough's return to glory! Citizens whom I'm sure you would trust not to betray you by inflicting more misery and hardship onto us…"

The camera panned closer towards Stubbs' face.

"…These citizens have operated in connection with the national government!"

His face grew redder as he stubbed out his cigar slowly.

"Dissidents will be brought to justice for the good of our community."

The screen returned to the figure '3' as the announcer advertised upcoming programmes on both channels. The screen then switched itself off.

Steve exhaled heavily; the sound of which was audible above the humming of the heaters.

'Steven!' called Stubbs, emerging from the control room with Thelma. Thelma appeared nonplussed at the sight of Steve and it was fairly clear that she had made herself at home in her new surroundings, judging by her air of confidence.

Stubbs gave him a broad smile.

'What did you think?'

'Oh it was certainly… *direct*.' said Steve dreamily.

'Good!' Stubbs cheered 'I hope it had the desired effect I was aiming for.'

'Oh it did.' Steve nodded with a wry smile.

Stubbs nodded 'Needs a bit more editing and tweaking here and there, but…'

He noticed Steve and Thelma looking at one another anxiously.

'…You two have obviously got lots to discuss, so I'll leave you.' he said, leaving the room.

'What have you told him?' Steve asked Thelma cautiously.

'If it's my pregnancy you're talkin' about, then I ain't said nothin'.' she smirked and folded her arms.

'If that's the case, then how did he know we had something to discuss?'

Thelma's face softened suddenly.

'I just told him things we a bit difficult between us at the moment and I needed some space.'

'Oh marvellous, so now he thinks there's a chink in our armour.' he said impatiently through clenched teeth.

'Well what would you call it?' she demanded, placing her clenched fists onto her hips.
'You announce you don't want our baby and you can't find a problem? Now do you see why I prefer to keep men at arm's length?'
'Which brings me onto my next point. How do I know it's mine?' he asked.
A long silence followed during which time Thelma pierced a hole through Steve's head with her eyes. As with the previous night, Steve regretted uttering those hurtful words the split second they left his tongue. If there was any chance of reconciliation before, there was virtually no chance now. He contemplated softening the blow with an excuse that he was not thinking straight, but that was the best he could come up with and so he allowed his horrified expression do the talking.
'You arsehole.' she said shakily as tears formed in the corners of her eyes.
'What are you sayin'? Once a prostitute, always a prostitute-is that it?' she shouted.
'No, I…'
Thelma interjected 'If you took an ounce of interest you'd know I've left that place for good. My life's moved on, and to a much better place; or at least I thought it had.'
Steve looked almost as upset as Thelma 'All I meant was…'
'Get out and leave me alone. I don't want you nowhere near me.' she shouted.
'But I…' he tried.
'Get out!' she cried.

***

    After making more mistakes in Sector Zee, Steve left the place with a heavy heart. Outside, the weather reflected his sombre mood; the rain fell like spears, while the harsh wind persistently struck him. His head was full of things to say to Thelma, but as he opened his lips the appropriate words mutated into hurtful words. He had spent the entire morning gearing himself up for talking to her and had prepared a heart-warming speech which had included his desire to father a child, how ever soon in their relationship. It was not so much out of spite, which had driven his mouth to twist this speech into something dreadful, but more a feeling of insecurity. That is, he had longed to be part of a loving family all of his life and the tiniest possibility that this privilege would desert him would have been too much to bear. He had hoped that perhaps Thelma would have been a little more forgiving and provided him with the answer he was looking for. However, the excruciating silence which had followed his words of destruction had been filled with the notion that it was irrelevant whether the child was his or not; the fact that she had chosen him to be the father was good enough. As with any difficult time he had faced in the recent past, he decided to pay Mary a visit. He left his car in the car park and took the short walk to the launderette. From a distance, it appeared darker than usual, as if redecorated in black paint, or perhaps it was a reflection of the overcast sky above. He drew nearer through the haze and found the door open, allowing the torrential rain to pour in. The door was covered in black graffiti, which had not had a chance to dry in the rain. The word "Bitch" was scrawled across the glass, disappearing into black water before his eyes. The windows on the left and right had been smashed, allowing the wind to rattle the broken Venetian blinds. He stepped inside slowly for fear of what further damage he might find. He breathed a sigh of relief when he found the lights were off, which meant that at least there was hope that perhaps Mary had not been present during the break-in. He looked all around. The same black spray paint had dried onto the stainless steel washing machines. "Meglamaniac", which had been misspelled, was written beneath the drum. Steve wondered whether the vandal even knew what the word meant.

He explored the back end of the shop. The green plastic garden chairs lay in a higgledy-piggledy fashion and the ashtrays lay upturned on the floor. Picking them up, he wondered whether Mary had already sought assistance for the damage, or whether she had not come in at all that day. He remembered how on a Wednesday she liked to close up early and attend bingo in Havering. If that had been the case, then she would have been unaware of the break-in and if he worked quickly enough, he could remedy the problem without her noticing. He was ready to make enquiries for a window repairer to come, when he noticed Mary's purse on top of the spin dryer. He picked it up and opened it. To his astonishment, he found that it was completely empty of cash. She usually used cash sparingly for herself and when she did, she would always take her belongs with her when out. He caught sight of a pound coin, which was on its side on the floor. The head of Queen Elizabeth II had almost worn down to blend in with the rest of the metal. He noticed that the year it had been made was nineteen eighty-eight: the year of his mother's birth. He picked it up and placed it into the pocket, which had housed the photograph of his mother.

He grew more and more anxious and perplexed. He checked the small office and, although more abusive graffiti covered the walls, she was not in there. He began to search the premises for clues as to where she could be. It was possible that she had collected some cash from her purse to pay for the damage, because no burglar he had heard of would have left an expensive-looking purse behind, let alone bothered to close it. This assumption was marred by what he noticed on the white lino floor. Green scuffmarks ran in broken lines from the back of the shop to the front door. Mary always wore the same shoes in all weathers: bottle green sandals. It seemed to him that there was a possibility of some sort of altercation involving Mary; he could think of no other reason for what he saw. A lump formed in his throat as he recalled the scene from his childhood when his mother had been killed.

He dashed outside into the gloom and ran across to Central House in search of Thelma. He ran up the stairs to the broadcasting suite and threw the door open. Thelma stood in the middle of the room, embracing Stubbs.
'What's going on?' Steve gasped.
Thelma quickly broke away from Stubbs.
'I thought I told you to leave me alone?'
'Now I can see why.' Steve said bitterly.
'It ain't what it looks like.' she rebuked.
'I don't care. You've got to come quickly, the launderette's been broken into and there's no sign of Mary.' he declared desperately.
'Hold your horses a minute pal, slow down.' began Stubbs 'What did you actually see?'
'The launderette smashed up, graffiti everywhere, stolen money...'
'*Money*? What, up there? In Cliffbridge?' asked Stubbs incredulous.
'Yes, that's right.' nodded Steve 'That wicked capitalist commodity which you want to protect us all from. Have you seen Mary?'
Stubbs' face fell.
'Not personally, no.' he turned to Thelma 'You'd better go with him and find her before it's too late.'
'Too late? Why would it be too late? So you know something?' asked Steve panicky.
'Not personally, no.' Stubbs repeated with a sneer. 'Go on, off you go. Take all the time you need.'
Steve and Thelma edged towards the door. Steve took a last look at Stubbs whose face quickly became encircled in smoke; concealing any expression that might have given him away.

***

Steve and Thelma left the building and ran across to the launderette. Thelma, in spite of Steve's assurance that Mary was not there, insisted on taking one final look. When they arrived, the level of vandalism astonished Thelma; her lip faltered as she entered. Steve felt some sympathy for her, knowing that how ever great his friendship was to Mary, this could not be matched by the years of bonding which joined Thelma to Mary; notwithstanding the unspent years of reconciliation.
'I told you love, there's no-one here.' said Steve gently.
'This ain't about you this time Steve.' she blurted 'Have you checked the backyard?'

'Yes, everywhere.'
'And you've checked the office?' she asked.
'Yes, everywhere.' he insisted.
Thelma's anxiety grew as she peered down at the green scuff marks.
'Oh my God.' she exclaimed, cupping her mouth 'What's 'appened?'
Steve looked more desperate.
 'Look, you know Mary better than I do. Where do you think the most likely place is which she could have gone to?'
Thelma grimaced, kneeling down beside the marks as her tears hit them.
'How the bloody hell should I know? She's most probably been dragged out of here, literally kickin' and screamin'.'
Steve glanced at the marks, agreeing to himself that that was the most likely explanation.
'Well ok…Is there any particular place where people tend to be found after they've been reported missing?' he asked.
Thelma's weeping ceased for a moment as she collected her thoughts.
'Oh I dunno! Although thinkin' about it, there is one place where people have been found quite a lot.' she said, looking up at him.
'Good…I mean that's something to go on.' smiled Steve sounding more hopeful.
'Where is this place?'
'Donkey Park.' she replied.
Steve frowned as the name entered his ears. In just two weeks Donkey Park had become a place of ill fate for him. On the one hand, he hoped that Thelma was inaccurate in her assumption, while on the other; he just wanted to find her, wherever she was. He drew in a deep breath.
'Donkey Park? Why there?'
'Look, think about it. It's a large, desolate field most of the time, hardly anyone goes there. Shallow graves have been discovered there over the years and it wasn't so long ago they found Bernie's body.' she explained.
'Yes, but don't you think it would be a sick act for them to dump her there, especially after what happened to Bernie?' he asked tentatively.
'Who's *them*?' asked Thelma, perplexed.
'Sorry, I wasn't thinking.' he said, excusing himself with a cough.
'No, come on. Are you sayin' what I think you're sayin'?' she demanded, prodding him with her finger.
'Are you suggesting that Stubbs had somethin' to do with her disappearance?' she persisted, becoming more hysterical.
'Do you honestly think he'd be stupid enough to kidnap her, let alone dump her *there*?'
Steve bit his lip anxiously.
 'It would be a sort of payback… perhaps.'
Thelma frowned deeper.

'What are you sayin'?'
Steve remained dazed for a while longer, staring into space. He broke his silence before Thelma could probe him further.
'You're probably right. If Stubbs had taken Mary, it would be more likely to have been to somewhere further a field like, say, Epping Forest.'
'No, you still don't get it, do you? Stubbs couldn't have had anythin' to do with it: he's been with me all day.'
'I bet he has.' Steve muttered 'I'm not suggesting that Stubbs was in any way directly involved, but you heard what he said. When I asked him whether he knew anything about her disappearance, all he said was "Not personally."'
'Exactly!' she exclaimed, pointing at him fiercely 'He wasn't involved.'
'Not personally, no!' he quoted.
Thelma shook her head dismissively.
'You might have time to joke about it, but I have to find my friend.'
'No-one's joking!' he shouted in protest 'I'm telling you he had something to do with it, however indirect.'
Thelma exhaled, rolling her eyes to the heavens.
'Look, I'm off to the park.'
Steve looked deep in thought.
'Hang on a sec, what makes you think she would be there of all places?'
'What are you on about now?' she sighed, turning back.
'I'm not sure I fully understand. Why look there? How do you know she hasn't been bundled into some van, or taken hostage in a disused warehouse?'
Thelma's face paled.
'What? I just meant that we'd be savin' time by goin' to the place where a lot of people are found after they've gone missin'.'
Steve's eyes narrowed.
'You and Neil haven't got some scheme going, have you?'
'What did you mean?' she asked.
'You tell me.' he said, folding his arms.
She glared at him.
'Oh I get it, you're sayin' *I'm* to blame for this. It wasn't enough for you just to blame Neil?'
'No, I...'
'Save it!' she shouted 'Why not make it a hat-trick? You've already accused me of deliberately gettin' pregnant and sleepin' around; why not add kidnapper to your list?'
With a whimper, she flew out of the door.

***

They arrived at Donkey Park having run all the way from the launderette. Steve trailed behind Thelma, panting heavily as they arrived. The sun was setting behind the far off high-rise buildings, leaving just enough light with which to make out nearby objects. They began to search around the perimeter of the park for signs of Mary, finding nothing other an old pair of headphones. Thelma decided it was time to start exploring the copse of trees that bordered the canal to the east. Steve trembled slightly as he cast his face eastward as the memory of Bernie Wilson began flooding his mind. A flock of pigeons darted from the copse suddenly with what sounded like a call of distress, causing Steve to jump.
'What's the matter with you?' asked Thelma impatiently 'Come on, let's get goin' or it'll be too dark. If you wanna get back into my good books, you'd better pray we find Mary.'

They reached the copse shortly afterwards, on Thelma's insistence that they run. The canal's pungent smell of sulphur hit Steve like a bullet to his nostrils, while the fierce wind slapped his face, as if chastising him. The slippery undergrowth sent him careering down a slope of wood chippings, landing in a shallow bog beside the towpath. Thelma gave a laugh from above, while Steve cursed wretchedly. The sudden change in mood seemed to lift his spirits slightly, causing him to crack a smile. The smile left Thelma's face as she too came hurtling down the small ravine, landing in a heap beside him.
'Touché!' sniggered Steve.

Steve was taken by surprise at Thelma's reticence when she did not acknowledge the humour. There was something, which had caught her attention on the slope, causing her to stare up. She promptly staggered to her feet, brushing off the dry mud from her knees.
'What is it?' asked Steve.
Thelma did not answer him, but dug her feet into the chippings and slowly began to scale the slope. Steve followed quickly behind her in earnest, asking her all the while what was so urgent that she had to climb the steep slope. It was when they were about halfway up that Steve noticed a mound of earth with something sticking out of it. On closer inspection, that something was a dog-eared shoe, which smelt as sulphuric as the canal itself.
'Look!' cried Thelma.
She pointed to what appeared to be a newly inserted wooden cross, with a plastic memorial poppy attached to it. A short epitaph read:
"Bernard Anthony Wilson 1988-2048. Iraq War veteran and much loved local."

Steve stepped back anxiously. What was before him was nothing more than a shallow grave in a neglected part of the park. A thin, two-dimensional cross was the only feature which marked the grave at all. Steve was brought face-to-face with the realisation that although much loved by the community and a war veteran, Bernie Wilson would merely become the subject of tittle-tattle in the Four Shillings and before long the wooden cross would wither away.

'A wooden cross, in a shallow grave and in a shitty East-London park. Is that all this man is worth?' Steve asked Thelma, impassioned.

'Forget about *him*, we've got to look for Mary.' she asserted.

'Forget about him? How can I?' he demanded, producing tears 'Don't you think he deserves more than this?'

Thelma looked at him sympathetically.

'Look.' she whispered, taking his hand 'You're right, it is bad. But this ain't your fault; it's to do with having no consecrated land for burial, that's all.'

Steve nodded in agreement and smiled up at her.

'Don't you think they could have at least buried him the standard six feet?'

'I dunno.' she shrugged 'I 'spose there must've been some reason why they never. Come on, let's try and find our Mary before it's proper dark.'

They climbed the remainder of the slope and back into the copse. They ventured towards the centre of the wood and began checking behind thickets of leaves and under fallen branches for any signs of Mary. There appeared to be nothing which gave any clues as to her whereabouts. Thelma gave him the occasional look of dismay, as if she was beginning to doubt her earlier assertion that Mary had to be somewhere in Donkey Park and perhaps was beginning to buy into Steve's theory that she could be elsewhere: perhaps Epping Forest. Steve's ears pricked at the most beautiful birdsong. A robin danced in the fallen leaves while looking at them, unabashed by their presence. Steve gave the bird a whistle, to which the robin replied with a chorus. It began to bob up and down gleefully on the dead leaves and started to walk around an oak tree, prompting Steve and Thelma to follow it out of adoration. The bird came to a halt beside a tangled web of brambles.

'Bless it. Must've wanted us to see its nest or somethin'.' said Thelma.

'No, there's something else, I'm sure...' said Steve almost to himself.

'How d'you mean?' she asked, gazing at the bramble heap.

Steve did not answer, but advanced slowly towards it where the robin continued to sing beautifully. The bird disappeared into the brambles as Steve edged closer, coming to a stop at the other side of the heap.

When no sound came from Steve for half a minute, Thelma joined him at the other side.

'We ain't got time to mess around! Mary could be lying dead somewhere and it'll be too dark to find her soon.' called Thelma, sweeping her hair clear of her face.

It seemed to him that the more they hopped, the more the birds revealed something to him. Perhaps it was the true beauty of their song, or the daintiness in which they hopped about the leaves; whatever it was, Steve could not quite put his finger on it. Thelma, meanwhile, stood tapping her feet impatiently.

Steve did not have to ponder his curiosity for much longer, for what was revealed was only too stark. As each robin hopped, a leave was swept away to reveal a piece of the riddle, until the puzzle was completely uncovered. There, lying beneath the rancid-smelling leaves, a helpless, innocent old woman stared up at them.

It was Mary Hamilton.

'Oh my God, no!' screamed Thelma, kneeling.

'Surely there must be a pulse. Check!' he demanded.

Thelma wailed inconsolably.

By now the sunlight had given way to moonshine, depicting Mary's lifeless eyes. Steve knelt down and pressed against her neck but could feel no pulse. He tried her chest, but it neither rose nor fell.

'Can't you try CPR?' cried Steve into the drizzle 'I've never been shown how.'

'What's the point? Go ahead and feel her.' she sobbed.

Steve produced his hand slowly and touched her arm. It was turgid, suggesting that Rigor mortis had begun to set in. He kissed her cold hand before letting her arm fall from his grasp onto the leaves.

The images from his childhood where his mother lay dead on the hallway floor came back with a vengeance. He had tried to hold them off for as long as he could, but the pictures were too powerful and vivid to avoid. Mary now gave him that all too familiar empty, lifeless stare which stood along side the image of his dead mother. He reached for Mary's hand and held it once again. It looked like the hand of a porcelain doll's; white and lifeless. He leant onto her bosom and allowed himself to let go of his pride, weeping like a child on his mother's corpse. The tears soaked into her maroon cardigan while the smell of soap powder shot up his nose with every sob he made. His crying was made worse by the thought that once again, he was unable to prevent the death of his mother at the hands of his father. Two robins landed on her feet.

'Get off her!' he shouted, throwing his arms around violently.

'She's gone, Steve.' wept Thelma.

Steve cleared his tears with his sleeve.

'How did you know she would be here? Eh? What made you so sure?' he demanded.

'Oh please Steve, don't start that again!' she sobbed.

'Of all the places we could have searched, you picked this one! You brought me here, you made me see my mother dead! Why did you do that to me, why?' he cried through the wind.
'I told ya already!' she yelled.

Through his tears and the trees, Steve caught sight of a figure dressed in white, some fifty yards away in the murky open field. The figure appeared to be one of Stubbs' youthful henchmen and as Steve peered through the gap in the undergrowth, he recognised the boy as the youth who had caused him so much trouble many times before.
'Where're you goin'?' yelled Thelma 'We can't just leave her!'
'Ssh...' insisted Steve, keeping his teary eyes primed on his suspect.
'Don't you shush me, especially at a time like this!' she warned, pointing at him threateningly.
Steve edged back towards her, avoiding the dry sticks that might have given them away. He bent down at her ear and shared his suspicions with a careful whisper.
'You what?!' she yelled, getting to her feet at once 'You mean *him? That* skinny little runt?'
Steve restrained her with one arm and covered her mouth with the other.
'Let go of me!' she seethed through Steve's fingers.
Steve grabbed her neck tightly, tilting her head towards his mouth.
'Don't you think I want the same, huh?' he said through gritted teeth.
'Ouch, you're hurtin' me!' she protested, wriggling.
'Now you listen to me very carefully.' he continued 'We'll go through to the field *quietly*, do you understand?'
Thelma did not respond, but continued to wriggle under his tightening grip.
'I asked you a question!' he shouted.
Thelma at last gave him a nod.

No sooner had Steve released her than Thelma herself made a break for it, running through the gap in the bushes and into the open field. Steve promptly gave chase but could not match her determination. She slipped and fell on a patch of remaining snow, but quickly got to her feet and continued running, leaving Steve in her wake.
'Come here you little idiot!' she shouted at the youth.
The boy turned and, noticing Thelma's anger began sprinting at great pace. Steve made the split-second decision not to give up, but to draw on all he had and increase his speed; running through the pain in his calves. As he passed Thelma, he could smell the perspiration on her skin. The boy's white hooded top became more visible as Steve advanced on him and the moon's glare intensified through the clearing clouds. It was not long before Steve caught up with him, pulling him to the ground by the hood.

'You hooligans still haven't learnt after forty years that hoods make for perfect handles!' laughed Steve hysterically, holding the boy's bony wrists behind his back.
'Get off me you posh pillock!' cried the boy.
'So it *is* you.' said Steve. You can't hide from me like a coward beneath that ridiculous top!'
'What's your problem? I ain't done nothin.'
Steve picked the trowel and a penknife from the youth's baggy tracksuit bottoms.
'What's this then? Don't tell me, you were out doing a spot of night time tree planting?'
Just then Thelma caught up and, grasping the trowel, struck the boy with it.
'Who's the coward now, eh?' she seethed, holding his head against the ground under her boot.
It was Steve's turn to tear a strip off the boy.
'Now listen, you worthless piece of scum. Do you have any idea what you have done?'
The youth did not reply, but gave Steve an indignant look.
'Do you?!' demanded Steve shouting into the boy's ear.
'Yeah.' murmured the boy.
'Do you know who that woman was?' Steve asked him.
The boy shook his head, and in doing so, rubbed his face in the mud.
'I can't hear you! Speak up!'
'No. I don't.' admitted the boy.
'Then I'll tell you!' Steve exclaimed, pulling the boy to his feet.
The moon's light depicted the fear in the boy's eyes.
'That lady, Mary Hamilton, was the making of this place, long before you were even born.' Steve turned the boy in the direction of the grave 'What you don't realise, is that by murdering her, you have just ensured that your life will become even more meaningless and miserable than it already is.' he held the penknife against the youth's neck and moved in close to his face 'Do you honestly think that nobody's going to care about Mary? Eh?'
'I don't know what you mean.' gulped the boy.
'Then you're even more gullible than you look!'
Steve twisted the boy's head around to face the illuminated buildings beyond the park.
'Take a look around you. Out of all of those flats and houses, how many friends and allies do you think Mary had? Go on, take a wild guess.'
'I dunno.' mumbled the boy.
'We've got to be talking hundreds. In any case, every drinker in The Four Shillings, every customer in the launderette…bar you, of course…I could go on. Do you think they are going to take kindly to the idea of some low-

life scum like you having taken the life of such a well-loved woman like her?'

The boy hung his head and said quietly: 'She was just some capitalistic reactionary.'

'Just some *what?*' questioned Thelma.

'Just some capitalistic…' Steve relayed.

Thelma raised her eyes to the heavens.

'I heard what he said. What I'm gettin' at is, that sort of talk doesn't sound like a scank.'

Thelma drew closer to the boy and held the trowel beneath his chin.

'Who put you up to this? Who sent you?' she asked with narrowed eyes.

Before the boy could answer, a silhouette appeared, growing larger as it approached. When at last it reached them, there were still no clues as to whom it was; the dark clothing and top hat cast a large shadow onto the moon-drenched grass.

'Is somethin' the matter?' asked the figure, removing his brimmed hat.

It was Neil Stubbs.

Thelma lowered the trowel and Steve removed the penknife. A few seconds of silence passed, while Steve and Thelma glared at each other.

'I'm not interruptin' some sort of initiation ceremony or nothin' like that, am I?' Stubbs sniggered, producing a cigar and lighter.

'What are you doin' here?' asked Thelma.

'Fancied a bit of an evenin' constitutional! The night air's good for the old ladders and rungs, so they tell me!' he giggled, lighting the cigar.

'Don't insult me.' sneered Thelma, edging closer to him 'It's you, ain't it? You put this little brat up to it.'

Suddenly two other skinny youths appeared, this time armed with a pistol. Stubbs beckoned them to lower their weapons.

Stubbs gave a chortle.

'Sorry love, you're gonna have to be a bit more specific than that!'

'You murdered the closest thing I had to a mother!' shouted Steve, planting the penknife against his neck.

'Ain't that sweet!' mocked Stubbs, breathing smoke into Steve's face 'Cos you ain't got a mother no more, have ya? Nah, she was murdered by your dad when you were five, ain't that right Stevie-boy?'

Steve lowered the penknife, becoming sorrowful.

'You ain't half made a big mistake this time.' said Thelma to Stubbs.

'Ooh! Let's not go tellin' porkies out of school! Them are big accusations, my girl. *Very* big.' said Stubbs with a straight face. 'I think all that work in my gaff has messed with your heads. I reckon what you both need is a holiday. I'll tell ya what, why not take a sabbatical? A very *long* sabbatical.' he sniggered.

'You're sacking us?' asked Steve, bewildered.

'There ain't no room for sentimental lightweights in my firm. I'll make sure your severance pay is included in your wages.' Stubbs announced, dropping his cigar butt on the grass.
'We don't want your filthy money!' shouted Thelma.
Stubbs shrugged indifferently.
'Why did you kill her? Just answer me that. Was it because she was a threat to Cliffbridge?' asked Steve, becoming more composed.
'So you saw my clever little announcement on the news, then!' he sniggered.
His face quickly grew solemn.
'I did warn people not to cross me, and what do they do? They do just that.' he looked at the pair sternly 'But I'm tellin' ya, I might be many things, but a murderer I am not.'
He turned to his compatriots.
'Come on boys, there's an awful smell in the air...'
With that, he straightened his hat and disappeared into the darkness, leaving Steve and Thelma reeling from shock.

THIRTEEN

Saturday, 29th February 2048. Havering, London. 1300.

The days that followed Mary's death, had been plagued by heavy rain. The grim task of collecting what was left of her belongings from the launderette the previous Tuesday, brought Mary's death home further for them; the green scuff marks on the floor became etched on Steve's mind. There was not much to collect there, except for some paperwork, some soap powder and that old pound coin. The day after, they visited Mary's flat in Ward's End to completely clear the place out ready for the new tenants to move in the following day. Steve felt shocked at the urgency imposed upon them to clear the flat when they were still reeling from the murder which had taken place only a few days before. Although the process took a few hours more than clearing the launderette, in the end all there was, was an old vacuum cleaner and a collection of old brass figurines and other bits of tat. Both Steve and Thelma were taken aback by how the sum of Mary's life was contained in just one small bin liner.

The task of arranging the funeral was more complex. There had been some difference of opinion between Thelma and Mary's close friends about whether she wished to be buried or cremated. Thelma remembered Mary joking about how she would take hours to 'cook' and would hold everyone up at the ceremony and so had opted to be buried instead. However, Chelsea and Candice were adamant that Mary had talked about cremation. In the end Thelma insisted that given the fact that Mary had once been her legal guardian, that she alone should have the last say and so it was finally agreed that Mary would be buried. The decision for where she would be buried was eased by Mary's sister Stacey getting in touch. In all of the turmoil, Thelma had completely forgotten to inform her about the death. Stacey had telephoned Thelma enquiring about Mary's wellbeing after not receiving a reply to her calls. Stacey had been a welcomed tower of strength and insisted that her sister be buried in the ground of SS Mary and John church in Havering, not far from where they had both grown up. She looked markedly different to how Mary had looked. She had a willowy body and a daintier face, with a pretty complexion for a woman in her late sixties. The arrangements had, in the main, gone according to plan except for the time at which the service would take place. Stacey had wanted the service to commence at two o'clock to allow for the weather to brighten up, but the rector was forced to bring the service forward an hour in favour for a funeral service for a child.

Thelma, Steve and Stacey stood at the entrance to the nineteen-fifties C of E church. The building was prefabricated and should have been dismantled years before, but had come to be regarded as part of the area's character and so the local council had agreed to keep it as it was. It had an unassuming quality about it, standing no taller than twenty feet and in need on a new coat of paint and the bright sun glistened on the peeling patches of the iron.

Steve felt his stomach begin to churn as he contemplated giving Mary's eulogy. It was merely through lack of paper that he had decided to write the eulogy on the reverse of his mother's photograph, although once written had become symbolic in some way. He cradled the photograph in his hands and began to murmur the words to himself in preparation; he was eager not to spoil his chance to say goodbye. Presently, the precession of the one o'clock funeral came through the entrance. A tiny magnolia coffin, no longer than three feet, past Steve. A feeling of numbness ricocheted through his body, finishing up in his legs. He made the sign of the cross, bowing his head. He returned to his standing position and saw a familiar face pass him.

It was James Maitland-Sloan.

The numbness grew more potent within his veins as his old acquaintance looked at him woefully.

'James?' whispered Steve, covering his mouth with a handkerchief in shock.

James whispered in his tearful wife's ear and left the procession.

'Steve.' began James in a forlorn whisper.

'Please don't tell me that is...' Steve croaked.

James sealed his eyes and nodded.

'Last Friday.'

'But when we last met you, you mentioned an NHS hospital in Kent. How did it come to this?'

James' eyes creased tighter.

'The cancer became more virulent. The hospital did not have the adequate resources to fund her treatment.'

Steve looked at his feet at a loss for what to say.

'I hear that you and your lady friend have not let the recession get the better of you.'

'I'm sorry?' asked Steve.

'Some cushy job in an illegal financial outfit, thousands of feet below Cliffbridge.' James continued.

'I'm afraid I don't...'

'Please don't be condescending. I've heard everything. And what's more, I'm not one to judge; especially when things are so desperate. I just wonder how much economic knowledge you possess and what you could have offered the company. Ten years training at Canary Wharf among the world's greatest financial minds, all for nothing.'

'I'm terribly sorry…'
'No, it's just a pity really.' James said reflectively 'If I was as fortunate as you, my daughter might still be with us. Pity…'
Steve's face paled.
'Shame, looks like those clouds are thickening.' said James rejoining the procession.
Thelma and Stacey looked up at the greying sky with a frown before entering the church.

***

The church's interior did not reflect the exterior in any way. It was like a T.A.R.D.I.S; small and unassuming on the outside, but large and awesome on the inside. The walls, although whitewashed concrete, had the most exquisite tapestries handing on them. The church was renowned for its short aisle, causing a bride to walk it three times before the organist could complete the wedding march. Varnished pine pews that shone beneath the bright down lights flanked the aisle. The pews stood largely empty with fifteen mourners sat sparsely on either side. When Steve had enquired about the poor turn out, Stacey assured him that those who really mattered to Mary were present. The three of them shuffled their way to the front row on the left, closest to the lectern where Steve would shortly deliver Mary's eulogy. Steve felt some sort of obligation to be strong in the face of adversary from the two grief-stricken women either side of him. Thelma's face was scarlet and her eyes puffy under the weight of her tears. Stacey, who sat to Steve's left, remained composed, although her solemn face perhaps masked her inward emotion.
The casket was a wickerwork eco pod fastened with palm leaves. A digital picture frame containing Mary's happiest moments in her life sat on the casket, each displayed for twenty seconds. Steve had not been allowed to attend his mother's funeral service. His foster mother believed that he was too young to be faced with an upsetting ceremony. He had been taken to Alton Towers for the day, but had been too short for most of the rides and, to add insult to injury, the day was much the same as it was today; overcast and miserable. From that day forward he had grown evermore curious about funerals and what they consisted of and when he had reached adulthood, had regretted his foster mother's decision.
At last the rector took to the lectern and addressed his meagre audience. He was a man of about fifty with heavy features and rosy cheeks. His eyes remained firmly on the lectern as he spoke:
'It is a sad day that draws us together to mourn the passing of our sister Mary. Some of the more senior among you will recall Mary as a young child attending this very church building most Sundays…'

The rector's words meandered in and out of Steve's ears as he failed to remain focused. Although he knew little of Mary's early years and was keen to learn more, he had too many difficult thoughts shooting through in his mind. The news of James' daughter's death had placed a chill in his heart. On that first day in Cliffbridge, she appeared spunky and full of life, free of any concerns for what the future might have in store. Her father also seemed carefree on the surface, with no inclination of any future financial hardship. It was Sylvia, his wife, who made no secret of her concerns for her child as they left the car park. Steve had always harboured a respect for women, especially mothers, who shouldered the burdens of family life, carrying more than their fair share. Steve was aware that he had changed somewhat since he had moved to Cliffbridge, but it was James who had brought this home to him. He had always been ambitious at any cost and could have been accused of being self-centred, but now he was caught up in the system he swore to bring down; a system where money prevails at the hands of the corrupt few. This time the cost was high and could not be recouped. His action or inaction had lead to the death of a child; how ever indirectly.

The rector had long since finished talking and "Let It Be" by the Beatles played through the tinny sound system. Thelma and Stacey knew that Mary did not much care for traditional hymns like "All Things Bright And Beautiful" and so had decided to fragment the service with tracks that carried some meaning.

It was now the point of the service where the eulogy would be delivered. As the final bar of the song faded, Steve shakily got to his feet, clutching the photograph tightly. Stacey gave Steve an ambiguous stare, one that could have been a look of encouragement or a scowl given to an impostor. He had not the time to ponder this further and so took to the lectern and placed the paper before him, clearing his throat.

'Good afternoon friends.' he began.
'Good afternoon.' echoed the congregation.
Steve took his handkerchief and swept the sweat from his brow anxiously. He continued nervously.
'I took the liberty of delivering this concise account of Mary's life from the point of view of a short-term friend, so you'll forgive my ignorance.' He scanned the faces of the congregation for votes of confidence; Thelma was the only one to manage a forced smile.
'I saw Mary for the first time a matter of weeks ago. Some of you may be sitting there wondering what right I have getting up here and talking as if she were an old friend. Well that was Mary all over.' he began with a coy smile. 'It didn't matter to her that I was unknown by the community or didn't know who I was: she took care of me; nurtured me; gave me all the things I needed to get by in an unknown environment. Many people

questioned my motives and me. Not Mary. She just helped me when I needed it and steered me in the direction of my gorgeous girlfriend and her wonderful daughter. When people slung mud at the innocent, Mary was there working out a way of how to exonerate them. Although those around her were precious with their possessions, Mary was the first to put her hand into her pocket.'

Steve raised his head and looked at the congregation.

'It may not surprise you to hear that Cliffbridge does not have coroners and so the cause of death will remain unknown. However, I am confident that if an autopsy was carried out, that true justice would prevail on those guilty and, more importantly, a heart so massive would be found that it would provide enough compassion to right the wrongs of the world a hundred times over.'

He suddenly remembered the pound coin that he had recovered from the launderette. He took it from his pocket and held it up to the light.

'Before I leave you, I would just like to draw your attention to something which many of you will not have seen in a long while…'

He began rotating the coin between his finger and thumb.

'…I recovered this coin from Mary's launderette and believe that it portrays Mary very well indeed. That is, it is small; has very little purchasing power and has begun to wear away at the edges. However, unlike multicards which have limitless spending power, this coin has been treasured, looked after and above all, well loved; something which in a capitalist world we are loosing sight of.'

He walked over to the casket and placed the coin on it and returned to his seat.

***

An hour and a half later the wake took place in the church hall. The room was completely unfurnished, except for the many steel chairs, tables and the long wooden table containing bland, colourless food. It appeared all the larger because of the small number of people; only six people (which included Steve, Thelma and Stacey) were able to stay for the wake. Steve sat at one of the tables with a plate containing two cold sausage rolls and a heap of cold pasta shells. The burial had caused Steve to cry wildly for the first time since he was five. Indeed, it was the first time in his life he had attended a funeral. It had been raining heavily and people were dressed in black overcoats and sunglasses, holding oversized black umbrellas. They appeared like ravens crowding one of their dead, preventing any stranger from having the privilege to gloat on their weakened song. Steve had been excluded from the fold, perhaps unintentionally, because he had had to nip to the toilet. He was unable to access the grave through lack of room. He had politely asked people to move around the grave to allow him space, but all he got was narrowed eyes or no acknowledgement at all. He had been filled with the same level of resentment as at the time during his childhood when his foster parents had taken him to Richmond Park for his eighth birthday. He had invited some of his classmates along with him and each had taken a seat on the roundabout while Steve had gone to the toilet. He had returned to find the children merrily travelling faster and faster without a care for him. His foster mother had asked them to slow down to allow him to get on, but the children just shook their heads dismissively. Steve had been filled with anger and had charged at the roundabout, grabbing a girl by the pigtails, pulling her off. Without being reprimanded, he had been escorted by one of the mums to the café for an ice cream to cool off.

  Being a fully-grown man of thirty, he knew that now was not the time for such juvenile antics, but the incessant rage had already taken a stranglehold on him. He knocked an elderly woman from her feet and ran at the open grave, landing inside. The rector removed his glasses to check that he had not just imaged what he thought he saw. Steve lay facedown on the casket, hugging it and wailing inconsolably. It was all too final for him. He knew that once the body was interned, that there was no way back. The onlookers gave him looks of disgust and began throwing handfuls of earth at him scornfully. A little girl, perhaps a relative, began to cry as she witnessed Steve hugging the casket. The church grounds man came and coaxed him out and took him to the church hall.

  Steve had come to realise that it was more than likely out of disgust towards him that the other nine people had left early. The water level in his polystyrene cup had risen a few millilitres as his tears fell in. Thelma came to join him at the table.

'Honestly Steve. What were you thinkin'? Today of all days.'

Steve creased his face, allowed more tears to fall.

'Never mind that now anyway. What's done is done. I think it's high time we talked.' she said, sipping at her grape juice.

'Not now.' he croaked.

'About what you saw in Central House between me and Neil.' she said quickly.

'It's not an issue. I couldn't care less what you two get up to.' he looked away 'Nothing matters anymore.'

She took his hand.

'It was just a hug of sympathy. I had to confide in him about us and he was just showing some concern, that's all.'

'Like I say, I'm not fussed.'

She slid his paper plate to one side.

'Okay. Well, I'd like to talk about the baby then.' she said looking him in the eye.

'What's there to talk about? I opened my big mouth, a load of rubbish came out and he presto, I've lost out on an opportunity of a lifetime.' She cradled his hand again.

'No you ain't. I want this baby and I want you as its dad.'

'Me? A messed up cry baby with unresolved psychological issues? What kind of a father would that make me?'

'The kind of father who's understandin' and is there for his kid. The kind of father who's in touch with his feelings.' she left her seat and leant down beside him 'There's none like you Steven Morrissey and that's why I want this baby to have you to look up to.'

A tear ran down his cheek.

'Do you really mean that?' he asked tentatively.

'I've never been more serious in my life.' she beamed.

Steve felt the cockles of his heart warm and tears of happiness replaced the tears of despair.

'Can we go home now?' he asked.

Thelma nodded 'I expect the babysitter's wonderin' where I've got to.'

'I think she deserves at least a bar of chocolate for her efforts today.' Steve smiled, wiping a tear away.

FOURTEEN

Sunday, 1st March 2048. Ward's End, London. 0930.

It was a warm, sunny morning when Steve awoke in Thelma's bed. It was the best night's sleep he had had since he was last there. He had released his pent-up angst through a marathon lovemaking session the previous night. It had been the first time he had climaxed since the beginning of their relationship. He had attributed this to the comforting surroundings of Thelma's flat. The constant murmur of the refrigerator had sent him soundly to sleep and he had awoken at peace with the world. He had had a long conversation with Thelma about Mary's past life and how he had been the missing link between the loss of a premature baby and the prospect of a happier future. This had provided him with closure he needed and although he knew that the coming day and weeks would inevitably be difficult, he also knew that Mary belonged in his past.

He made his way into the kitchen and took a wet cereal bowl and spoon from the draining board and wiped them dry with the sleeve of his bathrobe. He gave the milk bottle a sniff and found that the milk was turning. He would have usually cursed at such an inconvenience, but today would mark the beginning of the rest of his life and so poured the half-rancid milk onto the stale cornflakes and took this breakfast into the living room. He switched the television set on and twiddled his thumbs, waiting for the screen to warm up. The transmitter details for Alto-Zero indicated that programmes were not due to commence until ten; it was ten to. As he sat, almost mesmerised by the garish colours, there seemed to be something trying to get through; something discrete but there nonetheless. Faint, sparse black and white pixels lay behind the data, appearing just as the badly edited footage had at Thelma's hearing. The pixels became more potent and then almost disappeared. Just as he was trying to make some sense of it, the programme began:

"Good morning! You are watching Alto-Zero, broadcasting on VHF channel six. Today's programmes will begin with an address by Mr Stubbs…"

Steve turned the dial gingerly to make the picture of Stubbs sharper.

"Mornin' citizens. I regret to say that I have some news, which saddens me. In spite of my best efforts to secure our anonymity and wellbeing, people are seeing fit to betray me further."

Stubbs' face reddened as he pointed to the camera.

"People are leaving in their droves and drawin' attention to Cliffbridge and all it stands for. Beyond our fifteen square miles, there lay government agents all over the place offering large sums of money in exchange for intelligence. What's more, I am well aware that these excitizens, whom I once counted as loyal friends, are selling themselves to the unscrupulous regime, like prostitutes. I have a duty of care to every man, woman and child in my jurisdiction. Some of my strong, loyal stalwarts have taken offence to such treachery and have taken it upon themselves to hit back. They, like me, want to protect themselves from the grabbing hand of capitalism…"

The picture changed and children playing happily in Donkey Park were shown.

"Here is our natural gem, an emerald in amongst the grey buildings. As you can see, people enjoy the vast expanse and clean air this area provides…"

The scene changed to show the park by night.

"However, naturally such a place is perfect for exacting revenge on those guilty of crimes far beyond even the most hardened of criminals. Criminals, citizens, like the late Mary Hamilton. Now, I don't condone violence of any description, nor on anyone. But I feel for those people who feel threatened by careless acts of treachery. I can see why someone would want to halt the proceedings of a capitalist windbag."

The picture returned to show Neil's face.

"There ain't much I can do about those who have already cried off to the government, but if my attention is brought to anyone makin' a mockery of our way of life, through acts of betrayal or otherwise, I will see to it that those responsible will pay with their lives…"

The Holding in Subterranea was displayed.

"And finally citizens. We are mobilising troops around Cliffbridge who have orders to fire at will on those seen leaving or entering Cliffbridge without authorisation from myself. Be warned, citizens, be warned."

The programme ended there, followed by a musical interlude.

Steve's feeling of wellbeing had deserted him. He dashed into the bedroom and awoke Thelma.

'Get up! Get up!' he cried anxiously.

Thelma opened one eye.

'What is it? Get back into bed, we don't have to go to work anymore, remember?'

'No no! You don't understand! I just saw on the television that Stubbs was guilty of Mary's murder, he said so himself!'

Thelma sat up in bed.

'What?' she asked with a drowsy frown.

'Didn't you hear me? Neil Stubbs said himself that he had something to do with the murder.' he affirmed, pulling the duvet from her face.

'Wait a minute. You just said that he was actually guilty of the murder.' Thelma said, grimacing with confusion.

'So?'

'So now you're sayin' he just had somethin' to do with it.'
'What's the difference?' he shrugged with a desperate smile.
'Well it's the difference between the right word in the right ear and actually stickin' the knife in.'
'So what? Are you saying we don't have anything to go on?' he asked through gritted teeth.
'Even if we did, what good would it do? He's pretty much the judge and the jury himself. He's like the king: immune from prosecution.'
'But we could tell the national government.' he said in earnest.
Thelma laughed mockingly.
'Ain't you seen the news lately? This place will be crawlin' with soldiers before long.'
'So let's get out while the going's good.' he said punching the air.
Thelma scoffed 'Ain't you forgettin' somethin'? I've got a young daughter to protect! I ain't riskin' her gettin' shot by no renegade soldier thank you very much!' she folded her arms defensively and turned away.
Steve grabbed his hair with rage.
'Am I the only one around here who cares? I mean to say, the culprit as good as confesses on live television and you lie there without a care in the world!'
Thelma stroked his face reassuringly as he sat beside her, weeping.
'Look love, Mary's gone.' she said softly 'No amount of blame will ever bring her back. There's bound to be little reminders of her now and again.'
Steve nodded 'I'd only just put her behind me and was ready to move on. Now I'm not so sure.'
'There are gonna be times when you have a mini setback, that don't mean you're goin' backwards.' she smiled.
Steve giggled 'Since when were you the shrink?'
'I learned from the best!'
She gave him a look of sincerity.
'Look, would it help if you spent some time with Mary alone; at her grave I mean?'

***

It was ten minutes past five and the sun was beginning to set behind the church, providing a mahogany light across the yard and a supernatural mood. The grass parted in the strong wind like long, shaggy hair. He decided to ignore the warning given by Neil Stubbs on the television. If he was shot dead, at least that would eradicate the tearing pain in his heart, he thought.

The newly laid earth supported one bunch of white lilies that Stacey had provided. Steve placed down a collection of wild flowers taken from Thelma's backyard beside them with a simple note:
"To mummy. Love Steve."

He began to arrange and then rearrange the two bunches of flowers compulsively around the grave. Each time the setting sun hit one bunch, the other bunch would be in the shade. After ten minutes he discovered that it was impossible for the two bunches to share the dwindling sunlight and so allowed Stacey's bunch to bask in the glory. He took a deep breath and looked to the heavens, knowing that Mary was not present on Earth.

'Mummy. Is it alright if I can call you that?'
He waited as thought expecting a response.
'I'm sure you don't mind. Anyway, I would just like to say that I am so sorry for my behaviour on your special day, yesterday. I took the spotlight from you and made the whole thing into a circus act, completely discrediting you and all you stood for. I hate funerals, you see. Well…I'd never been to one before. I'd always wondered what happened during them. Of course, I knew that there were priests and coffins involved, but the rest remained a mystery. I hope you didn't mind us choosing an eco pod; it's just that Thelma remembered how you liked to be demonstrative. Anyway, what was I saying? Oh yes. I never went to a funeral. You see, I was kept away from my other mother's funeral by my foster mother-not her fault, I was quite young, you know. Five. Spent a rainy day at Alton Towers instead and as if that weren't bad enough, I couldn't go on most of the decent rides. Too short! So I really wanted to make a good impression at your funeral. I dressed well…I think. I spent days convincing your sister to allow me to write your eulogy and some more days writing it. I read it well…I think, although I got some odd looks from some of your friends. I can't blame them really; I was an unknown telling them about someone they'd known for a lot longer. Still, the day was panning out ok, all things considered. But then, I made a cods of it. I showed myself up. I never meant to, it just happened. I felt excluded. I almost got the impression that the rest of them were trying to punish me for just being there. I don't know. Anyway, I just came by to clear a few things up and to say goodbye. Rest in peace…Mummy.'

He blew a kiss skyward. The wind deflected the kiss onto his left cheek, which he covered with his hand and smiled. He turned back to face the grave. Standing there was an elderly man whom he recognised from the funeral. The man was very slim with deep-set wrinkles in his face, appearing like a vulture; bald and hungry looking. His sinister appearance was softened by his large light blue eyes, which seemed to be smiling at him.

'It wasn't your fault.' said the elderly man.
'Sorry, I should introduce myself. Harry. Harry Maitland-Sloan.' he smiled, producing a gloved hand.
'I mean, the girl with the pigtails. She's my step-granddaughter Harriet. She's easily frightened, I'm afraid. I guess it was the fact that she had to suffer two funerals in one day. Harsh, I know, but I was left to look after her after my niece's funeral and I was close to Mary once-long story…'
Steve gazed into his large eyes.
 'Sorry, you said your name was Maitland-Sloan?'
'That's right.' Harry smiled 'I gather you were acquainted with my nephew James?'
'Yes.' Steve nodded despondently 'Only for a short while.'
Harry padded Steve on the shoulder reassuringly.
'Neither was that your fault.'
'I'm sorry, I don't follow…' Steve confessed, frowning.
'My niece's death, Emily.' said Harry softly.
'How do you know James blamed me?'
'Oh, he blamed everyone he cared about - me included. Even his beautiful wife Sylvia.'
He placed a basket of flowers on the grave and made the sign of the cross and placed a woollen hat on.
'What's more, everyone I spoke to thought your eulogy to Mary was beautiful. You were the talk of the pub last night; for all the right reasons.' he added.
'Are you sure?' asked Steve, aghast.
'Quite sure. You summed up Mary quite well in only a few, well-chosen words. Well done.'
He gave Steve a firm grip on his shoulder and left him.
The faltering light from the setting sun had passed from Mary's grave and onto the grave to his right. With an intrigued smile, Steve sidestepped a pace to the right and read the inscription on the grave. This grave was comparatively nondescript, with no flowers, just a lichen –covered tombstone. He felt a sense of pity for whoever lay there, there seemed to be a lack of love from those they left behind.
Just at that moment, his eyes widened and his mouth became dry as he read the short epitaph:
"May God keep you, Elspeth Jane Morrissey. b. 27th October 1988 d. 2nd October 2023."
He wiped away the lichen to check that he had not just imagined what he saw. He wondered for a moment whether there was a possibility that there could have been another Elspeth Jane Morrissey. He wiped away more lichen and revealed more:
"Devoted mother to Steven Morrissey, for five treasured years."

A tear left his eye as he embraced the headstone tightly as he wept loudly to the teak sky.

***

Steve arrived back at Ward's End just after sunset. He unlocked Thelma's front door in anticipation and made straight for the living room. He called out for her but no reply came. The television set was left on with no one watching it. It was a programme about how to gain a good carrot yield on Dominion. It looked rather boring, so Steve turned the dial to Alto-Zero as he often would before switching the set off. Alto-Zero played a recording on that year's Grammy Awards. The black and white grainy picture beneath the programme had intensified and was now accompanied with a muffled sound. He turned the dial gingerly to the left and back to the right in order to try and eliminate it, but no matter how slowly he turned the dial, the background picture remained. In fact, it was growing in intensity by the second; only by a few hundred pixels, but becoming clearer. Soon the black and white pixels became colour ones and the sound became less muffled. Whatever transmission was trying to get through, it was certainly strong enough to override Alto-Zero. Steve sat transfixed by the technological battle until Alto-Zero faded away completely.

"This is Public Service News. The Prime Minister would like to address Cliffbridge..."

The Prime Minister was shown outside Number Ten looking rather smug. "People of Cliffbridge. You are probably sitting at home baffled by what you are witnessing! You are witnessing the tightening grip that my government is taking over the country as a whole. That is to say that there is no longer room for municipal towns in my vision for our nation's future; especially corrupt and greedy ones like Cliffbridge. I expect you thought that we would never cotton on to your elicit way of life, not to mention the money laundering which has caused the death of innocent Britons through an inadequate NHS. Every single one of you whether a man, a woman or a child, are guilty of a crime most grotesque. By merely being present there, you have ensured that this country plummets towards the standards of a second world nation...'

The Prime Minister paused for effect and provided the viewer with a melancholy grin.

'I must congratulate you on your stringent effort to escape the long arm of the law. I am aware of your capacity for war and your steadfast determination to see my government and I perish. What you are perhaps not aware of is our limitless intelligence resources. What we may lack in terms of our armed forces, we more than make up for in our intellectual

fortitude. I am a firm believer that the brain is mightier than the fist…although I am not afraid to flex my muscles when necessary…'
The picture changed to show Central House as a blazing inferno, reminiscent of 9/11.
'We have already destroyed your administrative base. Your two VHF television channels have gone off-air, so at least you can be sure that you are no longer being fed lies for breakfast, lunch and dinner…'
A picture of Neil Stubbs was then displayed at the top right-hand side of the screen.
'…We are still on the lookout for Neil Stubbs, your formidable leader. We will find him and when we do, he will be dealt with using a suitable form of punishment. His propaganda drive has failed you! While you were on meagre diets of vegetables and boiled fish, your humble leader was lining his pockets with our taxpayers' money. I expect this loss to be recouped and now that I know who is responsible, I will make certain that every last penny is shaken out of you.'
The screen went blank and was replaced by an old BBC test card. Steve felt himself becoming flustered quickly. His jellylike legs barely supported his body as he slowly walked over to switch the set off. He called for Thelma, this time with an air of despondence. When no reply came, he walked into the bedroom to find Rebecca playing with her dolls on the bed.
'Where's mummy?' he asked her.
Rebecca pointed and said 'Bathroom.'
'Right. You be a good girl and carry on playing nicely with your dolls.'
He ran his hands through his hair in panic and walked across to the bathroom. Inside, he found Thelma sitting on the toilet with her hand covering her face. Clotted blood lay in pools all over the lino, giving off a pungent, unpleasant odour. He clasped her forearm in order to uncover her face, but she held it firmly in place.
'What is it love?' he asked her softly.
'Nothing, just leave me alone.' she said in distress.
'Is it the baby?' he asked tentatively.
She gave a nod from beneath her tense arms.
'I've lost it. I've lost our baby!' she yelled, before covering her face again.
'Oh love.' he croaked, cradling her head.
'I started getting these stomach cramps about an hour ago and before long, I started losing blood.' she wept into her sleeve.
Steve creased his eyes in sorrow.
'You poor thing. Are you still in pain?'
'Not so much now. It's starting to go away.' she puffed, clenching her middle.
Steve sucked in a lungful of air.

'Look love, there's something I need to bring to your attention.'
'If it's to do with Mary I'll hear about it later. Now really ain't the time!' she affirmed with a tense face.
'No love, it isn't that. Have you seen the news?'
'The news? I'm losin' our baby and you're askin' me if I've seen the news?' she exclaimed in disbelief.
'No, but I mean…'
'I don't care how excitin' the headlines are, I just ain't interested right now!' she interjected.
'Love, you're not listening.' he looked at the pools of blood 'I realise you are in pain and that you are, as I am, extremely upset…'
'Well that's putting it mildly!' she shouted.
'…But there's something else. I walked in and the television was on, it was some boring programme about carrots, so I changed channel. Anyway, as I was watching the re-run of the Grammy Awards and something strange happened…'
'Strange? How d'you mean?' she asked, cringing at another attack of pain.
'Well another television channel…PST…hijacked Alto-Zero's signal and the Prime Minister addressed Cliffbridge. It was a special message to us.'
'Sorry, you're not makin' sense. If that's meant to be a joke to cheer me up, it's gonna have to wait, I'm afraid.'
'No I'm deadly serious! Geoffrey Dawson said that he was wise to Cliffbridge's functioning and how every man, woman and child here is responsible for the diminishing National Health Service.'
His face fell further.
'That would include me. I had a part to play in James' daughter's death.' he breathed.
Thelma held her hips and writhed in pain.
'Maybe it's just some counterpropaganda put together by Neil Stubbs. He's probably just tryin' to scare us all into obeying him.'
Steve thought for a moment.
'No, it couldn't be that.'
'Well I ain't in no fit state to go anywhere at the moment. I'll need to get to a hospital before long.' she puffed.
There was a loud knock at the front door.
'Are you expecting visitors?' he asked.
'What do you think?!' she blurted.
'Well I don't know, it's not as if you planned a miscarriage, is it?' he said desperately.
He gasped as the penny dropped.
'It must be them!'
'Who?' she asked.
'The government. Quick, we must hide. I'll get Rebecca.' he said calmly.

'Where shall we hide? Look Steve, I'm really not well.' she confessed with a look of desperation.

The knocking grew louder and more persistent.

'Hello? Police. Open this door…' came a deep voice.

'We'll hide in the airing cupboard. They won't find us there, if they do, it'll be the last place they'll look.' Steve instructed.

'I thought you had a phobia of airing cupboards? Something to do with the noises they make?' Thelma quizzed.

'If there was ever a time to face phobias, it's now.' he said nervously.

He made for the bedroom to collect Rebecca, while Thelma entered the airing cupboard.

'Police! You are outnumbered! Come quietly or we'll be forced to break down the door!'

Steve grabbed Rebecca and joined Thelma in the tiny airing cupboard, leaving the door open an inch.

'Look my precious little darlin'! We're gonna play a game! It's called "hide from the policeman." You must keep very very quiet, or we'll be found by the nasty policeman and lose the game! Do you think you can be very quiet for mummy?' Thelma asked her daughter desperately.

The little girl looked confused, but nodded nonetheless.

'That's my girl! If you can keep quiet, mummy will get you an early Easter egg!' she whispered 'Now keep very, very quiet, that's a good girl!'

'Easter egg! Easter egg!' cheered Rebecca loudly.

'Ssh! What did I tell you? You must keep very quiet!' Thelma reiterated desperately.

'This is the police and MI5. Your home is surrounded! I'm going to give you to the count of ten to open this door or we'll smash it down!' shouted the deep voice.

Steve, Thelma and Rebecca stood as still as they could in the stifling heat of the airing cupboard. They had forgotten to turn the heating off from the hallway. Rebecca held her doll tightly and looked bewildered. The countdown had commenced. Thelma looked at Steve with wide eyes as she kept her hand over Rebecca's mouth. As the seconds dwindled, so Thelma's clutch on Steve's hand tightened.

'That it, we're coming in!' shouted the voice.

    Rebecca gave a muffled yelp as they heard the door fly open. The sound of heavy boots hastily walking along the short hallway was heard. There was also the sound of dog paws trip trapping along the tiles. The noises dissipated momentarily as the search party searched the living room, then the master bedroom. Suddenly the sound grew in volume as they returned to the hallway.

The footsteps halted at last.

Steve and Thelma looked at each other. Steve wondered whether because they had found nothing, that perhaps they we're going to call off the search. They waited in earnest for the word to be given.

The sound of a dog sniffing came from beneath the door. Thelma's grip on Rebecca's mouth tightened; she knew how excited Rebecca got when she was near any furry animal. The sniffing intensified as the wet nose swept ever faster from left to right. Suddenly the dog let out a loud bark to alert the police. The thin door flew open and the three of them squinted at the bright touch lights. Rebecca was grabbed by one armed officer and carried off screaming for her mother. Another officer lifted Thelma from her feet in a fireman's lift and carried her away, reading her rights.

'Steven Morrissey?' asked the Detective Inspector.

Steve nodded.

'I'm arresting you in accordance with the Terrorism Act as amended 2017.'

His feet and wrists were cuffed, before he was lifted off of the ground by two large police officers and carried away.

PART FOUR

'Trial and Terror'

FIFTEEN

Monday, 2nd March 2048. Location Unknown. Approx. 1200 Hrs.

Steve awoke in some large whitewashed hexagonal room topped by a glass ceiling some twenty feet above. Bright sunlight poured in, drenching the walls and the white tiled floor. His clothes had been removed and replaced by white overalls with a roll number on the right of his chest. His movement was not restricted in any way and so was free to roam the large, empty room. A plasma screen was fixed on one of the walls but remained off and so he was left with nothing to demand his attention, aside from the endless questions which scrolled though his mind. Why was there no obvious sign of a way in or out? Where were Thelma and Rebecca? Were they okay? Where was he? What time was it? He knew that it must have been close to noon, because the persistent sun hung directly above the glass roof.

As he pondered these thoughts, a rectangular section of the opposite wall began to darken and a figure appeared. As it approached, he could see that it was a man in his early thirties, carrying a clipboard beneath his right arm. He approached Steve with confident strides, but was not too gracious to join Steve on the cold floor.

'Good afternoon, 65475. My name is Agent 060 and I'll be looking after you during your stay here with us.' said the man with a casual expression.

Steve grabbed the man's lapels desperately.

'Please, where are my partner and her daughter? You must tell me where they are!'

The man smirked 'I am not obliged to do anything.'

Steve loosened his grip.

'I just need to know. Are they safe?'

'Yes, 65475, your partner and her daughter are quite safe. Your partner's daughter has been placed in foster care, while your partner is being questioned.'

'Being questioned where?' Steve demanded.

The agent paused.

'You will see her soon enough, 65475.'

Steve gave him a curious stare.

'Why do you call me that? My name is Steve Morrissey.'

'We like to ensure that each detainee is given the same level of status. That is, a name like, for example, Montgomery suggests superiority, whereas a name like Gary may be associated with the hoi polloi. I may be inclined, if prejudiced, to give preferential treatment to one and not the other. A number removes embarrassment for us and the detainee alike.'

Steve looked puzzled by this philosophy.

'How long am I being detained for, and for what reason?' he asked.
The agent looked away in thought.
'You are deemed by the government to be an enemy of the state and therefore a terrorist. Because of the aforementioned, you are not privy to the directives of the Geneva Convention.'
'You mean I could be held here indefinitely?' asked Steve anxiously.
The agent smiled 'Your partner is co-operating with us and providing you do the same, there is no reason why the pair of you shouldn't be released.'
Steve nodded compliantly.
'When will I face questioning?'
'All in good time. You need to undergo a series of tests and rehabilitation programmes before you reach that stage.'
'Tests? What sort of tests?' asked Steve, doing his best to disguise the hysteria in his voice.
'Nothing to worry about, I can assure you. You will view a series of programmes on the plasma screen which will allow us to determine how soon we will move on to formal questioning.'
'It feels hot for the time of year. Where are we?' Steve asked, looking around.
'We're somewhere in Southern Spain; the exact location is classified knowledge.'
'What is this place? Somewhere like Guantanamo Bay?'
The agent laughed.
'No, we're far more sophisticated than that place ever was!'
Steve looked up at the glass ceiling.
'What time is it?'
'It's seven minutes past noon.'
The agent placed his multicard back into his pocket.
'Time becomes an unimportant commodity here, the days seem to merge into one another and before you realise it, a year has past.'
'A *year*?' gasped Steve.
The agent continued 'It's like I say, providing you co-operate with us, then there's no reason why you should stay any longer than necessary.'
Steve paused for thought.
'So when does the programme commence?'
The plasma screen flashed on. A blank orange screen appeared, followed by a test card accompanied by a high-pitched note. The screen turned black.
'Induction program: phase one. Please standby...' came the vocal narration.
Slowly, a window blind covered the glass above until the room was in complete darkness, aside from the screen. Steve drew his knees up under his chin in apprehension. He instinctively shimmied closer to the agent as

the footage began. The Prime Minister was shown on location in an exotic setting, leering at the camera:
"Good afternoon Steven...Or should I say prisoner number 65475! I hope you are finding your quarters comfortable; or at least bearable! Of course, you know that your world and my world are markedly dissimilar. You are hundreds of miles away from Britain, languishing in some cell, while I'm on holiday in the Caribbean with my gorgeous wife and children..." He lifted is hand to his mouth and whispered "Oh and just between you and I, a rather dishy local girl who visits when the wife and children are collecting seashells! In fact, that reminds me, I must remember to put in a claim form for her expenses. Anyway, I digress; this is just a message to wish you well during your stay in Spain, although unfortunately you won't get to see the Costa Brava where you are! Take care Steven and all the best from me, my wife and the two boys and...you know who!"

The screen flashed off and Steve was left feeling slightly riled by what he saw, but had risen above the reaction that the Prime Minister was looking for. He was already privy to the floundering nature of the Prime Minister and the goings on in Chequers and elsewhere. The thing that annoyed him was the mentioning of taxpayers money being misused.

'How did that clip make you feel, 65475?' asked the agent carefully.

Steve outstretched his legs.

'I'm not sure really. There wasn't anything in it which really surprised me; the PM is well known for keeping mistresses in various publicly funded locations.'

The agent gave him a frown.

'Judging by your exasperated tone, I would say that the film did have some effect on your temperament.'

'I just think that it was contrived. I suspect that the film was concocted for my benefit and that not every detail was correct.'

The agent smiled.

'Yes, I was told you worked at the DCM&S...' he paused '...Perhaps you need to be convinced further.'

The agent instructed the screen to move onto Phase Two. The screen displayed a chess piece pawn with Steve's head superimposed onto the top of it. The chequered squares carried titles, which included "NHS Faux-Pas", "Economic Meltdown" and "Cliffbridge". The only other piece on the chessboard was an oversized king, which had the Prime Minister's face and was far away from the pawn. The king was confined to the back row of squares, which were the only ones to include titles such as: "Absolute Power", "Tax-Funded Holidays" and "Scapegoat Herder". Each time the king moved to the square titled "Absolute Power", the pawn would be forced to move to the nearest square with the title "NHS Faux-Pas".

When the king moved to "Tax-Funded Holidays", the pawn was forced to "Economic Meltdown" and when the king moved to "Scapegoat Herder", the pawn moved to "Cliffbridge". As the footage unfolded, the irritating musical interlude increased in tempo. Soon, the pawn was put into a checkmate position before being devoured by the king. The screen then clicked off.
'How did that make you feel, 65475?' enquired the agent.
Steve sat grinding his teeth.
'What else would you expect? He's exactly like that; a tyrannical bully who apportions blame onto others.'
'Yes, but how did that footage make you feel?' persisted the agent.
'Frustrated, mocked...I suppose annoyed.' Steve admitted.
'Good.' smiled the agent.
'Good? How is that good?' asked Steve, sitting up.
'It means that we're making sufficient progress.'
'And what does that mean?' Steve persisted.
'That provided you maintain this level of cooperation, it won't be long until you're ready to stand trial.'
'But I'm ready now!' exclaimed Steve jumping to his feet.
The agent rubbed his chin in thought.
'I'm afraid you are not. We have a way to go yet. Sit yourself down and watch the last clip of the segment.'
'The segment? How many segments are there?' Steve demanded.

Once again, the screen clicked on. This time, it looked as if Steve was no longer the focus of attention. Public Service News's familiar title music rang on to display the headlines. These were solely in connection with Cliffbridge, but neither Steve nor Thelma was featured in them. Steve sat in a confident posture as he contemplated respite from ridicule. The news anchor began with the degradation involving the brothels of Cliffbridge and the backward thinking favour-for-favour scheme. The prostitutes were branded as lowlifes and scum, while the other citizens were named as idealistic layabouts. The two television stations' ill thought-out propaganda campaign was deemed laughable and incoherent. The greatest blame for the recession was placed on Subterranea. The money from the national health budget was seen as being stolen and laundered in Sector Zee, portrayed by a cartoon of a shady-looking man stealing medicine from a crying baby. The final feature of the bulletin was in reference to Neil Stubbs. The anchor made no secret of the fact that Stubbs was still at large, but reassured the country that it was only a matter of time before the secret services caught up with him. A reward for any information was pitted at one million pounds.

It was to great surprise and horror that Steve learned that there was more. The anchor continued:

"…And just before we go, we feel that is only right that we tell you who is culpable for such mistrust and treason…"

Steve's mug shot was shown behind the anchor's right shoulder.

"…This man, Steven Morrissey, an ex-civil servant, is being held largely responsible for this catastrophe. He was entrusted by the government's top agencies to investigate the London Borough of Cliffbridge on the Thames Estuary. The area, once a heaven of financial masterminds, was drawn into corruption and quickly became a leech biting on the ankle of the nation's infrastructure. Mr Morrissey of Belgravia, London, expedited the development of the area through working in the zone of the secret society set aside for financial abuse known as Sector Zee. He is currently languishing in an undisclosed detention centre, awaiting trial. More on this story and other news on our nine o'clock bulletin…"

The screen clicked off. Steve rocked back and forth, with his knees drawn up to his chin. The agent tentatively placed a firm hand on his shoulder.

'You want to know what I'm feeling, do you?' shouted Steve.

The agent nodded with an apprehensive smile.

'The government stinks! I hate the Prime Minister and his ridiculous government! You and I have both seen what a corrupt man he is and where the bulk of the money has really gone! I can't believe the public aren't cottoning on to it! Why are they so blind?' Steve yelled, frisking his fair.

'Having said all that, we both know that's not about to be aired in the public domain. Dawson is embarrassed by Cliffbridge and would never dream of allowing the public to find out about it-it would ruin him!'

The agent rested his index finger above his lip as he collected his thoughts.

'Perhaps. What strikes me as perplexing is the fact that your partner, Thelma Harrison, has not been mentioned in any of the footage. What do you make of that 65475?'

Steve ceased pacing the floor.

'What do you mean?' he frowned.

'Perhaps your lady friend was somewhat preoccupied during our investigation and kept below the radar.'

'I don't follow…' Steve murmured.

The agent produced a pink cardboard packet of pills.

'These were recovered from your girlfriend's bathroom.' said the agent, handing the packet to Steve.

He read the details on the label: "For foetal termination."

He could feel his mouth becoming drier as the fiery rage collected in his stomach. He threw the box at the plasma screen.

'Is this some kind of sick joke?' he yelled.

The agent attempted an explanation but was thwarted.

'Is this your way of trying to make me as angry as possible? Is this part of the process?' Steve seethed, leering at the agent.

'I can assure you it is not.' the agent protested solemnly.

'Then why would you tell me? What's it got to do with you?'

The agent got to his feet.

'So you believe me then? You believe that your so-called partner is capable of such an act?'

'Of course I bloody well don't! She lost the baby through miscarriage. *That's* how she lost it.' Steve insisted.

The agent took a deep breath.

'Did she give you any indication that she was unhappy with the pregnancy? Did she have any reason to believe that perhaps *you* were at all unhappy?'

'No...' replied Steve, doubtfully.

The agent gave him a puzzled look.

'You don't sound too sure.'

'Of course I'm sure!' Steve shouted, turning his back to the agent.

'...It's just that your partner told us that she had reason to believe that you did not share her enthusiasm for the pregnancy; saying that it did not fit in with your plans for the future.'

Steve turned to face the agent with a face of fury.

'How dare you come in here with such a far-fetched, appalling fabrication!'

He lunged at the agent, tackling him to the floor, before striking him repeatedly on the face, until he drew blood.

'Are you sorry yet? Eh? Answer me you swine! Say you're sorry!'

Two heavyset prison wardens entered, lifting Steve from the agent, carrying him to one of the walls, placing his wrists in shackles.

SIXTEEN

Tuesday, 3rd March 2048. Somewhere in Southern Spain. Approx. 0700 Hrs.

Steve had had the whole night to think through the previous day's fracas. He had been tormented by nightmares involving dead babies and pregnant women. They reminded him of yet another child's life that his actions had ended. He hated Thelma like he had never hated anyone before; the mere thought of her made him retch. The way he viewed it, Thelma had denied him the chance of fatherhood and when he was released, he would track her down and make her see what she had done; there was simply no way he was about to forgive her for such a punishing blow. His dreams had not explained why the agent had been so callous as to show him the pills. He wondered whether he was an embittered man who took joy in rubbing people's faces in their misfortune, or whether it was simply part of the mysterious process.

The low-angle sun told him it must have been early morning. He had not eaten in nearly twenty-four hours; this did nothing to improve his feeling of inertia. He desperately needed the lavatory and he could feel his gut aching; he now had some idea of the purpose of the tiled floor. Suddenly the agent entered the cell at a quick pace, finishing at Steve's feet. He wore a dressing over his nose and a bitter expression. He stooped down and said:

'Punching people on the nose will not get you out of here.' he began sternly 'You've just put yourself behind by one day.'

Steve pulled at the shackles.

'I need the lavatory.' he snapped.

The agent threw up his hands dismissively.

'You may have access to our facilities as soon as the process if over.'

Steve rolled his eyes.

'You just said I've delayed the process by one day.'

'It all depends on how today goes.' said the agent 'An apology would not be a bad start.'

'I'd rather shit myself thanks.' Steve snarled.

'Then that is your choice.'

The agent turned on his heels and began to walk away.

'Hang on.' called Steve.

The agent looked over his shoulder.

Steve continued 'Perhaps I was a little quick to place the full blame onto you. I feel that maybe I would have been less savage had I'd eaten.'

'You haven't earned the right to eat, drink, use the lavatory or even sleep soundly yet. Let's see what today brings.'

The agent released Steve from the shackles.
'Are you ready to continue the process?' he asked tentatively.
Steve gave him a jaded nod. The cover enveloped the glass ceiling and the room was thrown into darkness. The plasma screen clicked on and displayed a test card. Before the agent commanded the next phase of the process to commence, Steve said:
'You seem to know a lot about me. Will you tell me who you are?'
The light of the screen depicted the agent's fatalistic expression.
'I suppose I could make an exception for a fellow civil servant.' he breathed.
'My name is Gerald Redgrave. I am thirty years old and am married with two children: a boy and a girl. There. Can we proceed with the process now?'
'Where did you complete your degree?' Steve persisted.
'Balliol, Oxford. I studied PPE between twenty thirty-six and twenty forty.' sighed the agent impatiently.
'Then you'll remember me then. I was in that cohort at Balliol, but I studied straight economics.'
The agent glanced at him perplexed.
'I don't think so.'
Steve did not letup. 'I remember you! You used to have a thing for that blonde piece who sat in the front row of the theatre during the morning session on Wednesdays. Mandy, wasn't it? Anyway, it was common knowledge that she did not share your passion!'
The agent turned to face him.
'Morrissey?'
'Yes, that's me! I'm afraid she regarded you as a bit of a swot.'
The agent looked away.
'She was nothing more than a common whore.'
'I'm sorry if I touched a nerve, but it seems like she slept with everyone on the course apart from you!' Steve chuckled.
The agent grew short tempered.
'And you would know all about two-bit whores yourself, wouldn't you 65475?'
Steve grimaced 'I don't know what you mean.'
'I hear your girlfriend was once one of those.' sneered the agent.
Steve looked at the floor.
'It's a long story, although you have no business bringing that up.'
The agent persisted, undeterred 'Well since we're in the business of getting to know one another, I only thought it fitting to find out more about you.' he turned Steve's head to face him 'Talk to me.'
Steve resisted the strain of the agent's hand.

'Prostitution was not her chosen career. She was more or less forced into it.'

'I'm listening…'

Steve swallowed hard 'Well she told me that some MP got her pregnant and that's what soured her relationship with the rest of Cliffbridge…I don't know much more beyond that.'

The agent's eyes narrowed in intrigue.

'Did she ever mention this MP's name at all?'

'No, not that I can recall.' Steve looked into the agent's eyes brazenly 'Why, how is this relevant to the process?'

The agent grinned 'Don't you get it? It was I who got her pregnant! Me, the college loser who could never find anyone to sleep with! Although I am no MP.'

'How much did you have to pay her?' Steve scowled.

The agent maintained his melancholy stare.

'What is it 65475, are you upset that I was the first to break her in?'

Steve could feel the sweat seep through his pores.

'You mean…she was a virgin?'

'Yes 65475! A virgin!'

Steve's brow relaxed 'Now I understand. You showed me those abortion tablets as a way of maintaining some sort of hold over her.' Steve's face broke into a sarcastic smile 'I get it! You couldn't stand the thought of someone else, least of all me, giving her a child that was not yours!'

The agent's smile diminished.

Steve continued 'You're nothing but a sad, pathetic man who uses his so-called power to take advantage of dispossessed young women. You shirked your responsibilities as a so-called father and forced her to go into prostitution.'

The agent's face fell.

'You're hardly a paragon of virtue yourself, *Steve*, are you? I've heard what a scoundrel you are around Westminster; the parties at Chequers and the illustrious affairs with Ladies and baronesses.'

'I've never made a secret of the fact I like to play the field a bit.' Steve asserted 'It is well publicised that I am a home-wrecker and a spineless gigolo, but never would I take advantage of a poor, bereaved young woman and force her into prostitution!'

'I'm sure that was nothing more than an unfortunate coincidence.' said the agent indignantly.

'I no longer believe in coincidences.' Steve said, softening 'I made a shocking discovery just the other day.'

The agent raised his bow, intrigued.

'I had just attended the funeral of a much-loved, dear friend of mine; in fact she was far more than a mere friend. She was the mother I never had.'

The agent's face stretched in sympathy.

'And do you know what I found?' asked Steve, wide-eyed with anticipation 'As I was paying my last respects, alone, I happened to see my own, real mother's tomb beside hers.'

'That's fascinating, but why are you telling *me* all this?' asked the agent.

Steve's head cowered beneath his shoulder.

'You are the first person I have told. My intention was to tell my partner the night we were arrested.'

'You mean they arrested you both on the same day that your partner lost the baby, on the day that you paid your last respects to your surrogate mother *and* on the day you discovered your mother's tomb?' asked the agent, incredulous.

Steve nodded 'But the point I'm trying to make is, that I believe things happen to us for a reason. That is, sometimes even the most painful of events can lead to a tonic.' he glanced at the agent 'And I suppose, using that logic, if Thelma had not been a prostitute, I may never have met her.'

The agent hung his head sheepishly 'Shall we get on?' he asked softly.

The plasma screen clicked on for the next phase of the process. It displayed a shot of a dilapidated hospital bed. The text "NHS In Crisis" scrolled across the screen slowly. Steve watched with wide eyes as the Prime Minister appeared at the bottom left-hand side of the screen. "Steven, I would like to take the time to show you what the taxpayer's money buys for the National Health Service. You may be sitting there thinking that my government has closed many NHS hospitals and you'd be correct. That is not because of the government's neglect for the needs of the country: quite the opposite. The rise in NHS expenditure was becoming unsustainable. So we decided to channel all of our money into fewer hospitals that were already in the top fifty in Britain for performance. These hospitals are for those people who truly need a service which is free at the point of use. By *need* I mean those whose household income falls below the £60,000 threshold. I am a realist, Steven. We are in the grip of a recession and my treasury cannot afford to bolster up the middleclass while those on low incomes suffer through overcrowded wards and overstretched doctors…"

The scene changed to show a paediatric ward in an NHS hospital.

"This, Steven, is the children's ward at The Royal Kent hospital. This was once the nation's leading cancer specialist children's hospitals in the southeast. Sadly though, this hospital, like many others, can no longer afford the life saving equipment needed to keep the children from succumbing to cancer; particularly leukaemia. Here is one girl: to protect her identity, we have called her 'Child E'. Child E was admitted to this NHS hospital a while ago when her parents could no longer afford private care. But they fell on harder times when they discovered that this hospital had a shortage of chemotherapy. Their daughter was somewhere way down on the hospital waiting list for the treatment.

Sadly, Child E died of the MRSA virus the day before she was due to receive potentially lifesaving treatment for her cancer. It really saddens me when I think of my predecessors and how proud they were of the NHS. I too was once very proud of the fifty outstanding, world-class hospitals. But since I discovered who was responsible, I have become infuriated with rage! You, Steven, killed this girl! Some poor sod's daughter, denied her right for life!"

'No!' cried Steve, gripping the agent's arm in terror.

'Please, switch it off. Don't make me watch any more of this!'

The agent pulled himself free of his grip.

'Do you recognise the girl in the footage, Steve?'

'I don't know her. Now please, switch the screen off, I beg of you!'

'No, I don't expect you do; not with all those wires and her fragile state.' said the agent.

'Yes, I'm afraid I do recognise her. Now please, switch it off!'

The Prime Minister continued to talk from the screen.

"Would you like to know what became of Mr and Mrs Maitland-Sloan?"

Steve covered his ears. The agent forced them clear.

"They were found floating in the Serpentine in Hyde Park last week. I've lost count of all of the deaths, suicides and murders which you caused, Steven."

'Switch it off, please!' screamed Steve.

"This catalogue of homicide began when you were just five years old, Steven. Social Service archives from the year 2023 tell us that your father was of a fragile state of mind; dependant on alcohol. He was a well-meaning man who, like any other parent, found life a little difficult at times. These archives also tell us that you have mild autism, which over the years you have learnt to control. This condition would occasionally manifest itself with collecting things; old photographs; old television sets; even early twenty-first century cars. But perhaps most fascinating of all, were you're your violent outbursts; often inflicted onto your mother. You see, Steven, the coroner's report highlighted trauma to her neck, thought to be as a result of repeated striking. Social Services also have documentation which tells us that you would occasionally strike your foster carers until the age of thirteen. The conclusion of all this documentation cites that although your father placed his hands around your mother's throat, it was not that which killed her. The coroner ruled out asphyxiation and concluded that she suffered a stroke…"

'You lying fool!' screamed Steve at the screen.
'I'm warning you, 65475, keep watching!' exclaimed the agent.
The footage continued.
"…as a result of repeated trauma. Now, your father was duly released from custody when the report was published and to protect your fragile mind, you grew up assuming your father was to blame. You were to blame, Steven. I have the documents to prove it!"
The screen clicked off and the blind uncovered the ceiling.
 Steve got to his feet.
'He's lying! How dare he? I did not kill my mother!'
The agent offered a tissue.
'I'm afraid it is true.'
'But it isn't!' protested Steve, leering at the agent 'I watched my father kill her with his bare hands!'
The agent stood up and cupped his mouth.
 'Listen, Steve; let me put it to you in another way. Have you ever heard of those people who are involved in an accident and lose their sight; often when no damage has been inflicted onto the eyes?'
Steve looked puzzled.
The agent continued nonetheless 'Well, doctors say it's nature's way of protecting the mind from a traumatic incident.'
'I'm sorry, if you must speak in riddles then at least slow down!' said Steve, pacing the floor hysterically.
'Perhaps that wasn't such a good example.' admitted the agent with an apologetic look. 'What I'm trying to say is that for such a young child such as you were, perhaps your eyes were closed to the truth?' cautioned the agent.
Steve grabbed the agent's neck.
 'What? You're not suggesting I swallow all of that drivel, are you?!'
The agent began to cough underneath Steve's tight grip. Steve eyeballed him for as long as it took for the agent to change colour, before coming to a devastating realisation. He loosened his grip and sank slowly to the floor.
'It *is* true.' Steve whispered to himself as the penny dropped in his mind 'Look at what I'm capable of.'
The agent sucked in air frantically, looking dazed.
'You see, it's been part of who I am for all of my life.' Steve continued, glancing up at the agent 'It's part of my instinct; if I feel threatened I literally go for the jugular.'
Steve's face paled around his bloodshot eyes.
'That's how I killed Bernie Wilson!' he gasped.
The agent touched Steve's back sympathetically.
A tear ran down Steve's snow-coloured cheek.

'I killed my mother!' he breathed.
The agent sat beside him.
'I think you're ready to stand trial.'

SEVENTEEN

Wednesday, 4th March 2048. Somewhere in Southern Spain. 0900 Hrs.

It was the next morning and Steve stood tensely in a stiff suit, flanked by the same two prison wardens that had apprehended him two days before. The stockier of the two had a face that resembled a boxer dog held Steve firmly beneath his left arm. Steve winced at the sunlight that poured in through the window to his right as he waited with baited breath for the oak door in front of him to open. He looked more like his old self; he was smartly dressed; had taken a shower and had shaved. While he looked good on the outside, he struggled to control his faltering lip which had not stopped trembling since being made aware of his past. Suddenly the door opened. The conference room's layout was markedly similar to the cabinet room at Number Ten. Around the large mahogany table sat the Prime Minister (tanned from his sabbatical) and the Joint Intelligence Committee. Where the Committee had expressed glee upon meeting him just a month before at Number Ten, they now appeared disdainful at Steve's presence in the room. The Prime Minister got to his feet and removed his spectacles.
'Why the long faces? You were all happy enough when you packed me off on your Mickey Mouse mission.' Steve scoffed as he scanned the glum faces.
The Prime Minister frowned.
'Sit down man; we don't have time to play about.'
Steve rebuked the hypocrisy with a sneer and sat down opposite the Prime Minister.
The Prime Minister settled himself into his chair with a woeful expression.
'We had so much hope for you, my boy.' he breathed.
The chair of the GCHQ interjected 'With respect sir, we ought to keep to the matter in hand.'
'Yes, yes of course we must. Please begin.'
'Thank you sir.' smiled Fontaine.
She turned to address Steve 'We will be exploring the charges over the coming days. The purpose of this meeting is to determine if it would be sensible and in the best interest of national security to send you back to Britain, or whether in fact you should serve your sentence here. The hearing will last a maximum of three days, at the end of which you will know the outcome.'
Steve grimaced 'So whatever the outcome, I will be detained?'
Fontaine pressed her index fingers into her temples and looked at him impatiently.

'May I remind you that subject to your status as a terrorist, you do not have the privileges as outlined in the Geneva Convention?'

'Yes of course, but for how long?' he asked.

Fontaine dismissed this question with a raised eyebrow and placed her glassed on and referred to a pile of papers.

'You were commissioned to the mission codenamed: "Black Hole" in February of this year, is that correct?'

'That is correct.' nodded Steve ardently.

Fontaine continued 'A civil servant working in the Department for Culture, Media and Sport, you started in your role as a covert agent working under the guise of an estate agent; am I right?'

'You are right.' nodded Steve, placing his clasped hands on the table.

Fontaine adjusted her hairclip and winced.

'Quite a difficult persona to portray, given your limited knowledge of real-estate, I'm sure you would agree Mr Morrissey?'

Steve swept his hand across his forehead in protest to the heat.

'Hmm…My degree touched upon contemporary housing and trends in the market, but nothing that would qualify me to pass myself off as a competent or a convincing estate agent.'

The Prime Minister's ears pricked up at Steve's statement.

'Your new identity was prepared with meticulous and diligent thought by the Home Office's subcommittee. We even drafted in professionals from London's top businesses to compile your handbook on good practice in real-estate, am I wrong, Secretary of State?' he asked the minister.

'No, you are absolutely right.' the Home Secretary agreed. 'Many evenings and weekends were spent compiling the handbook.'

Steve frowned 'I dare say that is true, but it's one thing to read a book, how ever comprehensive it may be, but it's quite a different thing to put into practice…'

He adjusted himself in his seat, now slightly riled.

'…especially when undertaking an espionage mission for the government at the same time.'

Fontaine gave him a smile, which this time showed some empathy for him.

The head of MI5, Ryan Goss, who sat to the left of the Home Secretary, was the next to speak. The large skin tags on his eyelids flapped as he collected his thoughts.

'Hmm. One of your main mission objectives was of course to locate the book of Cliffbridge's heritage from the main library. It is our belief that you did indeed manage to get the book from the library without causing too much of a stir. However, I understand you got into some deep water…if you'd excuse the pun…later that night, is that so?'

'You might say that, yes.' agreed Steve quietly.

'Perhaps you'd like to speak up and elaborate on that Mr Morrissey?' Goss requested.
'Of course I shall.' Steve asserted, folding his arms 'An elderly man ran into me as I was leaving the High Street along the canal, which runs through Donkey Park in the recreational ground. It was getting dark rapidly and my car had been clamped and the elderly man took pity on me and offered me a lift back to Ward's End on his boat.'
'To which you agreed, I take it?' asked Goss.
'Well naturally; I was in a strange part of town and was still getting my bearings.' Steve asserted.
'I see, so what happened then?'
'I boarded the boat with the man and we began our trip upstream.' said Steve nonchalantly.
'Aha. So how did a peaceful, evening boat trip turn into a murder case?' asked Goss with a glazed, perplexed look.
'It wasn't murder!' exclaimed Steve, getting to his feet suddenly 'You have prejudged the situation without further questioning!'
'Sit down Mr Morrissey, or I'll send you back to the cells!' ordered Goss. Steve eyeballed Goss for long enough for him to look away. Steve slowly resumed his place.
'Would you say you have a short fuse, Mr Morrissey?' asked Goss with impatience.
Steve's heavy breathing returned to normal as he considered the question.
'Yes, at times, but nothing that would lead me to commit murder.'
'Then would you care to explain what happened during the boat trip?'
Steve exhaled heavily and glanced at the Prime Minister.
'I kept a photograph of my late mother; it was the only one I had...'
Steve broke down in tears. Goss bowed his head and shrugged in the direction of the Prime Minister.
'It's okay Steven.' said the Prime Minister softly 'We're not going to make this any more uncomfortable than it needs to be. Just recount the events on the boat and we'll put aside any prejudices.'
Steve gave a nod as he blew into his handkerchief.
'It all happened rather quickly.' began Steve, wiping his face clear of tears 'I was admiring the photograph of my mother in order to pass the time. I realise the man may have just been trying to be friendly, but I didn't care much for his conversation. Anyway, I was looking at the picture and he made some throwaway comment about my mother's resemblance to another woman, which I took offence to.'
'Sorry, resemblance to whom?' Goss interjected.
'A prostitute.' Steve confessed quietly.

'A prostitute? Naturally that you have got your back up; nobody wants to hear their mother being compared to a prostitute.' Goss's eyes widened 'This prostitute. Was she Thelma Harrison?'
Before Steve could answer Fontaine interjected 'Please keep all segments of the inquiry discrete from one another, Mr Goss.'
'I was merely exploring a line of enquiry.' Goss stated with exasperation. 'It is vital that the respondent is able to recount events in a systematic fashion, or else it is difficult for us to gain maximum awareness of each event.' insisted Fontaine sharply.
'Your assertion is sustained, Mrs Fontaine.' concurred the Prime Minister. Goss looked on indifferently.
'You mentioned you had a disagreement involving the photograph. Did the argument escalate?' asked Goss, as he reached for a glass of water.
'No, that was soon over; it's what happened next that is significant. You see, quite by accident, a spray of water came up from the side of the boat as we turned around a bend and landed on the photograph. I may have muttered a curse, but like I say, it was an accident; no one's fault.'
'So?' asked Goss.
'So the old man, instead of offering his assistance, proceeded to wipe the picture with an old, dirty rag, causing it to smudge.'
'So what did you do then, kill him for ruining an old photograph?' asked Goss.
'No, although I admit I felt provoked by this time.' Steve took a sip of water 'You see, he caught site of the manuscript, the one which you asked me to recover from the library.'
Goss spluttered as he drank from his glass.
'I'm sorry?' he probed.
'You heard me.' Steve rebuked.
'I see. So what lengths did you go to in order to protect the manuscript?'
'I strangled him.' Steve confessed with little emotion.
'You strangled him?' asked Goss, looking alarmed.
'I find it hard to believe that surprises you, given the fact that you are part of the intelligence services and that you have eyes and ears everywhere.' Goss acknowledged him with a wry smile.
'Did you feel any sort of guilt or remorse? I mean, I applaud your diligence with regard to the manuscript, but did the man's actions warrant a killing in such a gruesome way?'
'It's the only way I know. Apparently, I killed my mother using that method; ask the Prime Minster.'
Goss gave Steve a prolonged stare, conveying his disbelief at Steve's brazenness.
'No further questions.'

It was the Defence Secretary, Fred Latimer's turn to cross-question Steve. He adjusted his comb-over delicately, before taking a sip of what looked like red wine.

'Good for the heart, you know.' he smiled.

Steve's face remained blank 'What makes you think your time is any more precious than mine?'

'Indeed. Get on with it, Secretary of State.' called Fontaine from across the table. The other committee members began to heckle the overweight man, until Fontaine signalled for quiet. He seemed undeterred by his lack of popularity as he began:

'Mr Morrissey, we unearthed two bodies from the Ward's End district of Cliffbridge, the area in which you were residing. They were that of Mr and Mrs O'Hara of the chip shop on Fox Road. It was initially assumed by the locals that it was these people who were to blame for the murder of Mr Bernard Wilson.'

He looked into Steve's eyes, leaning over towards him.

'Could you explain to us why they were led to believe this?'

The whole room looked on intently. Steve's forehead became clammy.

'I suppose it was as a result of some misguided witch-hunt. You see, in Cliffbridge things are decided and action plans are implemented at a community level and so naturally the criminal justice system is...sorry, *was* somewhat draconian.'

The Secretary of State continued: 'I see, so rather than own up to killing Mr Wilson, albeit in self-defence, you were prepared to lay the blame at the door of two completely innocent members of the community?'

Steve shuffled in his chair.

'It wasn't as cut-and-dried as you're trying to make out. We're not talking out a legitimate town where everything runs according to the constitution. This is a place where people have to do what they can to get from one day to the next.'

'Quite, but you weren't a part of that society, you were a civil servant acting in the best interests of the people of Great Britain.' stated Latimer.

'I realise I may have been in some way responsible for the deaths of Mr and Mrs O'Hara, but ultimately it was Neil Stubbs, the former Mayor of Cliffbridge, who saw to the killings.' Steve insisted.

Latimer sipped his wine slowly.

'I do sympathise, however you're actions led to no less than three deaths. Two of which were totally unnecessary and with a small piece of foresight, could have been prevented.'

He sank into his chair and signalled to Fontaine that he had finished with a jaded nod.

Daphne Reynolds, the head of MI6, turned to her right to address Steve.

'You had some contact with a Mrs Mary Hamilton, is that correct?' she asked, peering under her long raven fringe.
'Yes, that's correct.' nodded Steve.
'I see.' she said, studying her notes. 'Our sources described your friendship as, and I quote: "A mother-son relationship".'
Steve drew a deep breath.
'I suppose you might call it that, yes.'
'Could you tell me a bit about how you came to meet her and more about the nature of your friendship?'
'It would seem that your sources have already informed you.' Steve said sounding half surprised at the question.
'I should like to hear your version.' she scowled.
Steve rolled his eyes impatiently.
'Well we met in the chip shop on Fox Road. I sat down at her table and we struck up a conversation; we appeared to have something in common. We exchanged stories of our past and I quickly developed a sort of bond with her, it was like talking to my late mother again. She made the whole experience in Cliffbridge feel almost bearable.'
'I see.' she smiled. 'Would you describe your friendship as being a balanced one, or would you say it was perhaps more one-sided?'
'What are you getting at?' Steve asked suspiciously.
'Please answer the questions put to you to the best of your ability.' retorted Reynolds.
Steve considered his answer for a moment.
'Yes, I would describe our friendship as being mutual. She was like a second mother and I suppose I was the son she never had.'
'Then it must have come as quite a shock to have seen your second mother lying dead in front of you in the local park?' she probed with a dramatic stare.
'Of course.' nodded Steve.
'Forgive me, but if it was such a surprise to you, then maybe you can explain why she was attacked by one of the local mob?' she glanced down at her notes 'One of Neil Stubbs' henchmen testified openly that Mr Stubbs gave the order for her killing.'
'Surely you cannot be holding *me* responsible for that? She was everything to me!' he protested, slamming his fist on the table and getting to his feet.
'Sit down mister Morrissey! Either remain calm or you'll be escorted back to your cell. I will not tolerate aggressive behaviour during this session.' called Fontaine.
Steve slowly sat back down, cursing as he did so.
Reynolds continued 'Look, I'm not suggesting that you were in any way directly responsible for Mrs Hamilton's murder, but it is understood that she was murdered because she was suspected to have killed Mr Wilson. So

whether you accept responsibility or not, your lack of positive action at the beginning led to yet another death.'

'That's tantamount to blame in my book.' said Steve defiantly 'Besides your sources, wherever they came from, leave a lot to be desired.'

'Please explain.' asked Reynolds, sweeping her fringe clear of her eyes.

'Gladly.' said Steve confidently 'I had it on good authority that Neil Stubbs learned of Mary Hamilton's desire to close the launderette and to encourage others to close their retail units too.'

Reynolds looked perplexed 'So you're saying that Neil Stubbs ordered the killing of Mary Hamilton on the grounds that she was a threat to the status quo?'

'That's what I believe, based on what Mary told me and also on a local television broadcast.' Steve confirmed.

'I see.' Reynolds conceded 'But do you not think that your lack of judgement in connection to the death of Mr Wilson played a part in Mrs Hamilton's murder?'

'Now you're twisting things.' Steve cautioned, pointing at her threateningly.

'Oh come on Mr Morrissey! Who are we to believe, our reliable sources or your sketchy account of events?'

'You are free to believe whatever you choose. I am fascinated by your need to cross-question me, given that you already have what you deem to be reliable sources.' Steve mocked with tightly folded arms.

'I have no further questions.' concluded Reynolds with a stern face.

   Ken Butler, the Secretary of State for Trade and Industry sat to Steve's right.

'The final topic of the day will explore the damage to Britain's economic progress and the associated effects. Mr Morrissey, could you begin by describing Subterranea; what took place there and your involvement?'

'Yes, Subterranea, as the name suggests, was an underground trading facility below Central House. It comprised of three main rooms and several admin offices. The main rooms were The Holding, where prostitutes were kept while they waited to be distributed around London. The Arsenal was where weaponry was kept and Sector Zee was the trading facility.'

'And what was your involvement in the place?' asked Butler, his eyes broadening.

Steve exhaled heavily.

'Well Neil Stubbs offered Thelma and I a job down there once he had learned of that we were not to blame for the death of Mr Wilson.'

Butler scratched his head, perplexed.

'Sorry, I don't quiet understand. Why would he offer you both a job? Are you saying he suspected you of the murder?'

'He suspected Thelma at first and so he offered us jobs by way of an apology.' explained Steve, sitting up in his chair.
'Aha.' nodded Butler with a small smile 'We'll come onto your relationship with Miss Harrison in our opening session tomorrow. So you agreed to work with him. Why?'
'For the simple reason that I wanted to gain a closer insight into the workings of the place for the benefit of the mission.' Steve stated confidently.
'Very gracious, I'm sure.' said Butler, scratching his beard and peering down at his notes.
'So why was it that we decrypted some files from Sector Zee which pointed towards your involvement in the sale of our natural resources to other criminal outfits around the world?'
Steve gulped down a mouthful of water.
'My intention was to keep my head down and not draw any attention to myself and to find out about the idiosyncrasies of the place.'
Butler gave him a prolonged stare.
'Mr Morrissey, do you know the number of women trafficked into Britain for prostitution a year?'
Steve shook his head.
'Then let me tell you. Around two million and now we know where they were housed.'
Steve's face paled.
Butler continued 'I could rattle on about the affects your part had on our education system; our growing crime rate but I won't. Instead, I would like to draw your attention to the affects to our National Health Service.'
'I've already been dragged through that alley while being held in the cells.' said Steve.
'Then you'll be well prepared for what I am about to tell you, won't you?' sneered Butler.
Steve's face paled further.
'Let me put it to you in lemans terms.' began Butler, pressing his knuckles onto the table 'Your work in Subterranea led to the biggest increase in infant mortality since the nineteen sixties.'
Steve coughed into his drink.
'Surely that's an exaggeration at best!'
'I can tell you, it is not.' he glanced at his notes 'An acquaintance of yours, a Mr Maitland-Sloan had an ill child, who I am sorry to say, died as a direct result of Cliffbridge. As you may already know, Cliffbridge is situated right by the east coast where Britain's docks for the import of goods are. It might fascinate you to hear that we do not manufacture the essential cleaning fluids needed to keep our hospitals free from viruses; we

have to import them. Neither do we manufacture the pharmaceuticals needed to cure certain cancers; we have to import them.'

Steve slouched in his chair, while his lip began to tremble.

'Mr Morrissey, my desire is not to upset you, but to draw your attention to the facts.' he indicated a smile and continued 'We apprehended a young thug, believed to have been employed by Neil Stubbs. He was seen negotiating with haulage firms, while freight lorries were seen entering Cliffbridge. You can probably guess what we found in those lorries when we inspected them.'

'Cleaning fluids and pharmaceuticals.' sighed Steve.

'That's correct Mr Morrissey.' nodded Butler with a disappointed look.

'I had no idea.' whispered Steve.

'Mr Morrissey' Butler continued 'Did you or do you have reason to suspect that any of the illegal dealings which Mr Stubbs had with other outfits included any terrorist groups?'

'I too suspected that Mr Stubbs may have had such dealings, but he assured me that my fears were unnecessary. May I also add that had I had known categorically that there were such dealings, I would not have taken up employment in the place.'

Butler nodded in acknowledgement.

'Could you describe to us your relationship with Mr Stubbs?'

Steve sat up in his chair.

'He was a resourceful man who must have seen something useful in me.'

Butler smiled 'You say that with a degree of pride.'

Steve shrugged 'I suppose he made me feel useful.'

Butler nodded 'Did it not bother you that you were associating with a criminal capable of murder?'

'To begin with I wasn't aware of his full capabilities.' Steve answered.

Butler narrowed his eyes.

'Would you go as far to say that you regarded him as a father figure?'

'I hated my father for killing my mother and I still hate him even now that I know better. He never praised me; he was always bad-tempered and never brought home enough money.' Steve's face brightened 'Whereas Neil recognised my potential and credited me with respect. I also felt safe in the knowledge that he didn't know who I really was.'

Butler grinned 'You see, while all of this is very touching, the mission was not some journey of self-discovery or to make friends, it was a high-octane mission, carefully designed and planned to bring down a ring of crime. Do you not see that?'

'Yes, I do now.' Steve agreed.

Butler sat down 'I have no further questions.'

Fontaine looked at her multicard.

'We'll end proceedings there for today. Mr Morrissey, you will be escorted back to your cell and will be brought back here at nine a.m. to resume proceedings.'

The two wardens were summoned and escorted Steve out of the room.

EIGHTEEN

Thursday, 5th March 2048. Somewhere in Southern Spain. 0900 Hrs.

Steve had not slept a wink and had refused breakfast. His hair hung lankly over his forehead, while his jacket hung on him as if on a clotheshorse. He had little energy and the prospect of another day of taxing questions left his stomach churning, as if calling out for mercy. With a nod from Fontaine, the wardens left the committee room. The committee looked less than pleased with Steve as he sat himself down at his place. Fontaine remained standing, her face soured as soon as Steve entered the room. The other committee members ranged from appearing just as unwelcoming, to looks of indifference.
'Good morning Mr Morrissey, we shall get straight on with today's proceedings, which will focus on your relationship with Miss Thelma Harrison. Prime Minister, please begin.'
'Thank you, Mrs Fontaine.' he turned to Steve 'My first question to you is regarding how you came to meet Miss Harrison.'
Steve inhaled labouredly and exhaled with force as he ordered his thoughts.
'My first real encounter with her was on my first day in Cliffbridge. I had decided to pop out for supper and went to the fish and chip shop on Fox Road' he thought for a moment. 'I had engaged in conversation with Mary Hamilton and somehow Thelma was mentioned. As I recollect, Mary had been Thelma's guardian since her teens. Anyway, Mary assumed I had come to pay her a visit and suggested I did so. As you all know, one of the mission objectives was to befriend Thelma in order to secure as much knowledge about Cliffbridge as possible.'
'Tell me more...' the Prime Minister asked, now intrigued.
'I decided, against my better judgement, to go to the brothel on Fox Road. I was standing outside, deliberating, when one of the workers came out. I told her that I was after Thelma and she made some joke about how Thelma was the most sought-after one. Anyway, we went inside and a little while later, Thelma met me and we went upstairs.'
The Prime Minister frowned.
'Did you engage in a indecent act?'
Steve became agitated 'No! We went upstairs and I found the whole place too much to deal with, the cinnamon sticks and the red light; it was far too clinical.'
The Prime Minister lowered his glasses.
'Am I to assume that had you met her in a place without cinnamon sticks and red lights that something would have happened?'
Steve paused, twiddling his thumbs.

'There was something about her that seemed all too familiar. I couldn't put my finger on it at the time, but something told me that it would have been inappropriate.'

'Inappropriate?' the Prime Minister questioned.

'I don't know... she already felt closer than a stranger, that's all.'

The Prime Minister smiled.

'Come now, Steven. You can tell me what ever it is you need to say.'

Steve drew in a deep breath.

'I suppose it would have felt incestuous.'

The Prime Minister nodded intently.

'Drawing on what you told Mr Butler in yesterday's session, I am getting the feeling that perhaps you likened Thelma to a family member?'

Steve nodded slowly with his eyes closed.

'My mother.'

'I think I can see a theme developing here.' nodded the Prime Minister. 'So how did you get from regarding her as a mother figure to girlfriend material?'

Steve took a sip of water.

'I ran out of the brothel and the next day I returned to seek help.'

'Wait a minute, you ran out of the brothel without explanation and the following day you ask her for help?' sniggered the Prime Minister.

'I had just killed Mr Wilson and the launderette would have been closed, so I couldn't have called on Mary for help, so I ran the rest of the way back to Ward's End.'

'I see, so at least we should commend you for going to seek help. So what did you tell Miss Harrison?'

Steve swept his hand through his greasy hair.

'I needed to be comforted.'

'So you told her what had happened at the canal and that you killed Mr Wilson?'

'No, I never got that far. You see, I was refused entry into the brothel. She thought I was some sort of a weirdo and didn't want anything to do with me.'

The Prime Minister sipped from his glass.

'So you decided to keep the killing a secret?'

'At that point she was a stranger; I had no business telling her.' Steve protested.

The Prime Minister leant forward.

'Did you ever tell her the truth?'

'Well I alluded to it on occasion...' Steve stammered.

'Yes or no, Steven?' demanded the Prime Minister.

'Well, perhaps I did once when...'

'Yes or no!' insisted the Prime Minister.

Steve shook his head 'No sir.'
The Prime Minister smiled 'So tell me how your relationship developed.'
Steve paused and studied the elaborate woodcarvings on the ceiling.
'I was watching the plasma screen in my flat, which was able to receive VHF signals. The local station was streaming footage of Thelma's capture by Neil Stubbs in Central House. Stubbs and his committee had reason to believe that she was responsible for the murder of Mr Wilson.'
'Now we're getting somewhere.' breathed the Prime Minister in the direction of Fontaine.
'Okay, so then what happened?' he asked.
'In the interest of the mission, I took it upon myself to get a lift to Central House and testify against the claims made against her.' Steve explained passionately.
'A lift from whom?'
'From James Maitland-Sloan - a friend.' Steve said with a nervous cough.
The Prime Minister tapped his pen on the table in thought.
'You certainly put him through his paces; it's a wonder he wasn't driven to a nervous breakdown by the end of it all. Why did you ask him?'
'My car had been clamped, like I said.'
The Prime Minister nodded.
'So you went down there and presumably got her off?'
'Yes, it was difficult, but I managed to convince the panel that she was innocent.' Steve explained falteringly.
'I see, so could you tell us what your masterful emancipation plan consisted of?'
Steve pulled at his collar sheepishly.
'Some local, who doubtlessly had it in for Thelma, put forward a DVD displaying what looked like Thelma at the scene of the killing.'
The Prime Minister's brow furrowed.
'Sorry, what do you mean when you say, "What looked like Thelma"?'
'I could tell that the DVD was a hybrid of two films which had been badly edited to make it appear to the panel that Thelma must have been to blame.'
The Prime Minister maintained his confused expression.
'How could you tell it was an edit?' he asked.
'The picture was grainy and I recognised some of the footage from two movies. I requested the use of the plasma screen control and managed to decrypt the files, which backed up my suspicions.' Steve explained confidently.
'Very noble. Not many people would have gone to so much trouble for someone else; particularly a stranger.' sneered the Prime Minister, placing his glasses on.

'Like I said, I had a mission objective to complete and without Thelma, there would not have been an objective to complete.'
'Indeed.' agreed the Prime Minister 'So what happened then? Presumably you swept her off her feet and she was indebted to you for being so brave, is that it?'
'No, I didn't want her to feel beholden to me. In fact, she remained wary of me for a while after. In time we began to chat and she discovered we had something in common.' Steve smiled wistfully.
'Let me guess, she lost her mother too?'
'As a matter of fact, yes. She was denied urgent medical attention by the local authority because the rent was six months in arrears. It's thanks to your government she is dead and thousands of others too, I shouldn't wonder.' Steve exclaimed bitterly.
The Prime Minister stiffened.
'You had a mission objective to consider, which for most people would have occupied a hundred per cent of their thought processes. Did you not think a relationship would complicate things further?'
A wave of anger in the form of adrenalin passed across Steve's body, causing him to sit higher on his chair.
'It just happened. Nobody's ever too preoccupied to notice a good catch when they see one. If everyone focused one hundred per cent on their work at the expense of falling in love, then there would be a hell of a lot of single people walking this planet!' said Steve, shaking his head in disdain.
'Quite.' the Prime Minister conceded. 'What I meant was your investigation involved deep and tricky espionage. Did it not occur to you that you might run the risk of letting your guard slip at any point?'
'Of course it did, but naturally I was extremely professional and maintained a large degree of discretion.'
The Prime Minister smiled and looked down at the desk in front of him.
 'You were close to Miss Harrison's daughter, Rebecca Harrison.' he looked back in Steve's direction 'I think I know you pretty well...or at least enough to know that Steve "the heartbreaker" Morrissey, Whitehall's very own Casanova, would never dream of getting involved with someone else's child.'
'We were in love...*are* in love. It seemed like a sensible thing to do.' Steve shrugged.
The Prime Minister smiled 'As I've mentioned already, this was a high-risk mission with a lot a steak, not some lovey-dovey quest for love.'
Steve lowered his fist from his chin.
 'Can I ask who or where your sources have come from?'
The Prime Minister appeared shocked at the request.
'Sent in the agent.' he instructed Fontaine.

***

Steve grew tense as he anticipated the entrance of Agent 060. He had taken advantage of Thelma and already had some sort of a hold over him. It was not Agent 060, but a tall, delicately-built woman, whom had a look of determination and an eagerness for him to perish, like a lion stalking its victim.

'Special Agent Fifteen!' exclaimed the Prime Minister with a joyous grin. The Agent removed her leather gloves, keeping her stare on Steve. She removed her red beret and dropped it onto the table. The warden who escorted her in took her overcoat and placed in around Fontaine's chair. Keeping her eyes on Steve's, she walked over to him confidently with a hand placed on her hip and in his left ear whispered:

'What a surprise, eh Mr Morrissey?' she giggled.

She continued to stare at Steve while holding out her filtered cigarette for the warden to light. Steve was in complete awe of her, but in a way perhaps less than even the Prime Minister. It was as if that every single person, including the Prime Minister, was doing her a disservice by being in the presence of such a revered lady. Steve waited for her and the committee to drop whatever charade she was playing, but it continued. Steve broke the eerie ambience.

'I thought you were…'

'What, in some prison such as this?' she laughed violently, taking a long deep drag from her filter.

She turned to the Prime Minister.

'Go on; put the helpless little boy out of his misery.'

The chairman gave her a smile and turned to Steve.

'Steven, meet Special Agent Fifteen, MI6.'

She widened her grin and her eyes.

'How very pleased I am to meet you, *Steven*!'

'I still don't understand what's going on!' Steve protested.

It was the Prime Minister's turn to speak:

'You see, Steven, the mission was just as much a test for your loyalty to my government as it was to bring Cliffbridge down. Special Agent Fifteen has been working on the Cliffbridge case for some four years. Her research into the place and its illicit way of life has been, to put it modestly, tireless. She has raked the area with a fine-tooth comb and studied each and every significant figure in the area, until she became competent enough to fill the shoes of Thelma Harrison.'

Steve's lip trembled as he heard the revelation.

'But surely this can't be true?' he asked weakly.

'Ah yes, Thelma. It's a pity you couldn't have met poor Thelma Harrison; if you liked me you would have liked her. Although I couldn't quite adapt to her overly sensitive disposition…' she pondered, puffing smoke-circles towards the ceiling.

'I'm not sure I quite understand you.' Steve admitted as his breathing relaxed briefly.

She gave him a condescending smile.

'I wouldn't expect you to darling!' she took another drag as ordering her thoughts.

'Mr Dawson was correct when he described my research as tireless; although pedantic would have been my chosen word. That is, I never slept during my research…I almost became neurotic as a result of the severe pressure I was under… my hair even started to fall out. But that didn't stop me.' she warned with a wagging finger 'Never once did I consider pulling out of such a great opportunity to bring a criminal municipality to its knees.' she placed her cigarette on the glass ashtray in front of her and put on a more solemn face.

'I naturally paid very close attention to Thelma Harrison. I shared many of her physical characteristics…her bra size, dress size, hair texture, height, weight…even our inverted nipples! Everything was the same, except for my nose and teeth which had surgical attention.'

Steve was struck by the way that her demure, Home Counties accent completely transformed her into a well-educated woman of the world. When she stood, she stood with grace, with her nose in the air. When she sat, she sat regally like a princess. He could see glimmers of his girlfriend behind the stranger's eyes. He continued to believe that Thelma was being held captive, perhaps inside this stranger's body. Soon, he believed, she would leap out and tell him he needed to awaken from this nightmare and to get Rebecca's things ready for nursery.

'What became of the real Thelma?' he asked humouring her.

'She was brought here. The rest is classified information.' she snapped.

'And Rebecca?'

'I adopted her, raising her as my own daughter.' her voice became more subtle, her face more vulnerable-looking.

'I've grown to love her very much and I make sure that she is well looked after.'

Steve shook his head in disbelief.

'I'm sorry, but I refuse to believe all this.'

'Believe it, Steven; this is as real as it gets.' she grinned, blowing a smoke circle in his face.

Steve thought for a moment.

'Hang on a minute. Agent 060, the agent who mentored me, said that he is Rebecca's father.'

She gave him a raised eyebrow.

'That pathetic excuse for a man has a lot of unresolved psychological issues; I think you'd make a great couple!'

'Don't sit there and mock me!' Steve seethed, leaning towards her with his hands outstretched.

'Temper temper!' she scoffed.

'Remain seated Mr Morrissey, or I'll have you removed!' shouted Fontaine from across the table.

'It's okay Aileen, I can handle him!' grinned Special Agent Fifteen, leering at him.

She got off the table and paced the squeaky floor.

'You know, there is one thing Thelma and I have in common; our difficulty with men.'

She lit another cigarette.

'My father was very controlling. I grew up resenting him. I was always told to stop dressing like a boy and to play with dolls instead of action figures. Of course, all that did was cement my resentment towards him and men in general. I became inwardly stronger, I fell in love with my wife and that made me stronger still. When I was offered the chance to screw over a man like you, I jumped at the chance.' she said as her eyes locked onto his.

'Right...' nodded Steve with a sneer.

She looked away at last.

'And just to prove what a coward this man really is, I would like to show him and the rest of you what a twisted, calculating mind he has. Perhaps this will satisfy some of your questions, Prime Minister...'

Special Agent Fifteen produced a multicard and connected it to the plasma screen behind where Steve was sitting. The screen flashed on and displayed a list of computer jargon; the same jargon as displayed in front of Stubbs and the Community Panel.

'This was recovered from Mr Morrissey's plasma screen at his residence in Cliffbridge.

As you can see, the file was created at eleven p.m. on the night Mr Wilson was killed. In essence, the DVD tried to portray me as the murderer.'

The committee gasped and began to speculate between themselves.

'I must say that that's news to me, I...' he lied, trying to sound astonished.

'Oh really?' Well you can imagine how surprised *I* was when I learned that the whole community suspect me!' she exclaimed, furiously.

'Were you ever going to own up?' she asked, stubbing her cigarette out in front of him.

'Of course I was!' he pleaded.

'Liar.' she countered.

'Okay, enough.' called Fontaine 'Please resume your line of questioning, Agent.'

Special Agent Fifteen continued 'I have to say Steven, as a girlfriend I would have been shell-shocked at what you did.' she turned again to address the committee 'I think you would all agree that what we have here is a worm who'd sell his own mother to further his own ends.' the committee said nothing, but looked disdainfully at Steve.

'So we can add perverting the course of justice to the list of charges.' she concluded.

She placed he coat back on, noticing the coldness of the room. She sat on the table, resting her feet on a chair.

'Do you remember that infamous ultimatum that Neil Stubbs gave us?' she asked him.

Steve nodded with closed eyes.

She continued 'We were given forty-eight hours to find the real culprit. Not one to concede that enough was enough and admit the truth, Steven here, decided to go for gold and keep up the pretence by hatching a plan to frame two innocent local chip shop owners. With the help of Mary Hamilton as our lookout, we lay waiting for Albert Wilson, Bernie's twin brother in Chamber Pot Alley, which is the link way between Marsh Road and Donkey Park. We stood dressed as chip shop workers, wearing white aprons and hats. After the tip-off by Mary and having made sure that Albert had fully acknowledged us as Siobhan and Seamus, we pulled the drunken Albert Wilson into the alley and Steven knocked him out using an ordinary household frying pan. We managed to get him inside the premises via an opening which led into the laundry room. Having got him inside the airing cupboard, Steve tied him to the piping. The arrangement was for Steven to climb the staircase into the shop and dowse the O'Hara's boots in the water collected from the canal, while I siphoned off some blood from Albert's arm, which I spread over the laundry beside the washing machine. You see, as Steven kept reiterating at the time, the DNA from one identical twin carries the same makeup as from another. So the idea was, Albert would eventually come-to and testify that Siobhan and Seamus O'Hara were guilty for the murder of Bernie Wilson, having seen the bloodstained clothing and being kidnapped by the two chip shop owners.' she exclaimed, throwing the multicard on the table.

The Prime Minister held his hands together, as if praying for inspiration. He shook his head in disbelief and threw down his glasses. Two committee members offered him words of encouragement and a glass of water. He glared at Steve:

'So you lied to the committee and I. Do you know how serious a-crime that is?'

Steve bowed his head.

'I'm afraid there's more.' announced Special Agent Fifteen.

'Oh please, no more.' begged the Prime Minister, picking up his notes and fanning himself.
'I would like to conclude by pointing out that in order to avert blame on his part, Mr Morrissey gained access to my terminal in Sector Zee and input data which suggested that I sold ten prostitutes to the government.'
The Prime Minister looked at Steve incredulously.
'You led Mr Stubbs, and God only knows who else, to believe that we bought ten prostitutes?'
Steve leaned forward.
'I did that with the best of intentions, I can assure you.'
'Then I should like to hear you try to explain yourself, boy!'
Steve took a sip from his glass.
'Firstly, Mr Stubbs was beginning to suspect me of who I really was and he would have wanted to know where the prostitutes had disappeared to. You see, it was Special Agent Fifteen's idea to free the prostitutes from Mr Stubbs' control and to take them to the brothel in Ward's End. All I did was to balance the books so that Mr Stubbs wouldn't ask questions.'
'What do you mean that's *all* you did?' exclaimed the Prime Minister 'Don't you think that was some undertaking? The last thing I want is for the public to suspect I'm taking backhanders from criminal outfits!'
The Prime Minister maintained his look of disgust in Steve's direction, before his eyes fell back onto Special Agent Fifteen.
'Was there anything else?'
'I have no further evidence to add.' she shrugged.
'Thank you Special Agent Fifteen for your input, your contribution has been most enlightening.' he smiled wearily.
'Steven, is there anything you would like to say before we draw a close to this session?'
Steve nodded.
'Yes there is something I'd like to say.' he folded his arms defensively and addressed the committee.
'I'm sure you all regard me as a criminal, with no regard for the law. I'm sure you all see me as a political dissident, with no respect for the government.'
He looked at the faces around him, noticing their nonplussed expressions.
'I'm sure that you see me as a serial killer, with no regard for human life.'
He paused again, noticing the sea of raised eyebrows. He continued regardless and with emotion:
'You have heard the evidence against me and I'm sure that your minds are already made up. But consider the strength of the evidence presented to you and ask yourselves how reliable it is. Special Agent Fifteen professes to know everything about me and what went on in Cliffbridge

but perhaps there are things which she still doesn't understand about my mission.'

He got to his feet.

'Please hold firmly in your hearts and minds while reaching your decision that the mission assigned to me was no easy one, especially to an inexperienced civil servant such as I. Consider the others before me who have tried and failed to bring down Cliffbridge and remember it was I who delivered.' his voice softened into a tearful plea 'But above all this, remember that whatever you may think of my actions, I carried them out without malice of forethought, but as a necessity; the mission would not have been a success otherwise.'

The Prime Minister looked at him, appearing thoughtful.

'I see. Thank you Steven. If there is nothing else anybody would like to add, I'd like to declare this session over. Steven, we shall be considering your evidence and that of Special Agent Fifteen very carefully indeed.' He looked at his multicard.

'The final session will commence tomorrow afternoon at one o'clock prompt. During the brief session, the decision will be read to you by Mrs Fontaine and one way or another, the case will be closed. So, I shall look forward to seeing you in here at one p.m. tomorrow.'

NINETEEN

Friday, 6th March 2048. Somewhere in Southern Spain. 1100 Hrs.

Steve sat in his cell, awaiting the two wardens. He had been summoned to meet Special Agent Fifteen, but the location had remained a guarded secret. As he sat, still exhausted from the previous day's proceedings, he tried to guess at the outcome. He felt safe in the knowledge that he had provided the committee with a good, strong account of what he had been through and the difficulty of the mission. He had also explained how although the evidence against him was factual, there were reasons for his actions and they were in the interest of the mission. Perhaps, he thought, he should have mentioned Special Agent Fifteen's involvement a little more. If he had not been quite so panic-stricken during yesterday's session, he might have discussed her role in Subterranea; he had at least cancelled deals with other criminal outfits, while she had bought and sold thousands of commodities. In a calmer state of mind, he could have testified against her, even though it is unlikely it would have made any difference. He decided as he paced the floor, that there was just as much reason to be confident about the outcome of the trial. He was not about to cower behind a verdict that was still unknown; he was going to show the Prime Minister and the committee that whatever the verdict, that he was no shrinking violet.

The door flew open and the usual two wardens appeared. They took an arm each and escorted Steve along the corridor and down a flight of steel stairs. As they passed a window on the landing, Steve noticed that the sky was overcast and a strong wind battled the acacia trees. He also managed to catch a glimpse of his reflection in the glass; his face appeared more angular beneath the thickening ginger beard. As they descended the stairwells, the corridors grew colder, while the walls grew thicker with copper piping, pressure gages and storage systems. Finally they reached what must have been the lowest floor, owing to the fact that there were no more stairwells. Steve was swept along the long, narrow corridor as the bitter draft hit his face. The sound of leaky pipes intensified until they reached a steel door with a keypad beside it. One warden typed a four-digit code and the heavy door slid open with ease.

Behind the door was a large dark blue metallic room, lit by row upon row of dim white lights. These shone down the hard floor that contained row upon row of what looked like upward-facing steel cupboards. On the far side Special Agent Fifteen stood inside one of the cupboards, while Rebecca looked down at her from the side. The wardens let go of him and left the room. Steve slowly walked towards The Agent and her daughter. He peered down into the cupboard, where The Agent looked up at him.

'Ah Steven, I was hoping you would come.' she smiled.

'It wasn't as if I had a choice.' Steve rebuked.

The Agent shrugged.

'Would you be so kind as to help me up?'

Steve reluctantly outstretched his hand; she clenched it with force, causing him to nearly topple in.

'Are you alright Steven? You seem very edgy.' she asked jadedly.

He peered down into the pit and then at Rebecca.

'It's very cold in here; it's no place for a young child.'

The Agent began to fasten Rebecca's coat. She swung her head back in his direction.

'I'm on inspection duty. My task is to assess the place to determine whether the cases should be scrapped or used for another purpose.'

Steve looked puzzled.

'What are they?'

'This place as a whole is known as The Crypt. These things are encasement tombs, no longer used as they are considered inhumane.' she explained with an air of disappointment.

'Why did you ask me to come?' he asked, stepping back from the edge.

She took Rebecca's hand.

'She's been asking after you ever since you went away.'

Steve eyes filled will tears and he leant down to Rebecca's level. The little girl gave him a warm smile, which was surrounded by chocolate ice cream. She held a rag doll firmly against her chest.

'Who's that you've got there, eh?' smiled Steve touching the doll.

Rebecca recoiled, holding the doll ever tighter.

Steve gave her a perplexed smile.

'Does it have a name?'

She loosened her grip 'Uncle Steve!'

Steve peered at Special Agent Fifteen who looked away awkwardly.

He looked back at the child.

'Well, love. When I get out of here you can show me all the places Uncle Steve likes to go!' he stooped beside her left ear 'I'll let you into a little secret; I think you'll find Uncle Steve likes to visit the London Eye and likes to go on picnics!'

The little girl let out a coy giggle.

He stood up straight and gave the agent an intense look.

'Do you not have *any* empathy for this poor little soul? Its one thing to use her as a tool as part of your mission to masquerade as Thelma Harrison, but taking her from her real mother just so you could take her place, that's quite another.'

Special Agent Fifteen looked thoughtful.

'Look...I know it seems like such a cruel, barbaric thing to do to a child, but I can assure you that a lot of good's come out of it.'

'*Good?*' he gasped. 'Do you know what it's like to lose your mother; moreover, to be a young *child* and to lose your mother? I'll tell you what, when she's of an age where she's in the position to find out the truth, she won't thank you for it.'

She frowned 'She won't ever be in the position to find out, the intelligence services have made sure of it.'

'But there'll come a day when this government will be voted out of office, and there will come a time when the state will not have the monopoly over the media. When that day comes, all of their sick and twisted deeds will be the fuel for the newly-independent media.'

The Agent turned away sharply.

'Such a day will never come to pass.'

Steve grew agitated 'So all of those times together as a family meant nothing?'

'We were never a family.' she announced lighting a cigarette.

Steve snatched it from her mouth.

'You always told me you hated those things!' he exclaimed.

'You're wrong. Thelma hated them, not me.' she snapped, snatching the cigarette back.

He gave her a sharp look.

'I still don't believe this is happening.'

He edged nearer to her.

'They've got to you, haven't they?' he asked, gazing into her smoky eyes despairingly.

'Do you know what? I'm finding it hard to imagine how any of this could make sense.' he continued breathily 'I say that none of what you or the Prime Minister said in that boardroom was true.'

Special Agent Fifteen winced dismissively.

Steve continued 'I say that you Thelma Harrison of Fox Road, Cliffbridge was corrupted by the Prime Minister or one of his agents in one of the cells.'

'That's ludicrous.' she said sternly.

'Then look me in the eye and tell me I'm wrong. Tell me that they did not take you straight here and feed you with lies, blackmail or whatever else to get you to turn against me.' he challenged, keeping his eyes fixed on hers.

'You're wrong.' she stated, maintaining eye contact.

Steve appeared a touch disappointed 'Alright, then tell me that all those times together meant absolutely nothing. Look at me and say that you weren't genuinely annoyed when we went to that shopping complex in Havering and made to feel worthless by that obnoxious woman.'

She blew out a puff of smoke heavily.
'Of course I was angry; I had a child to think of.'
Steve instinctively reached for her neck, before taking her shoulders.
'Come on, come on! I know you're in there somewhere, Thelma; I know you are!'
She stood there like a manikin.
'You're wasting your time, Mr Morrissey.'
Steve began to cry.
She looked sorrowful suddenly.
'I too had a mission, remember? We were playing ourselves off against one another; you had your mission to see through and so did I. You pulled me into your schemes and you were pulled into mine. And you know what?' she gave a small laugh 'In the end we were both pawns in the government's campaign. Dawson didn't stop to think about my feelings during my mission.' she looked at him 'Tell me, were you kept from contacting the outside world during your mission?'
'Yes...' he replied with confusion.
'As was I. Not once was I allowed to make any contact with my family in Chelsea. And like you, I didn't know how long the mission would last. "As long as it takes" was the words used by Dawson.'
'But you had Rebecca. She's your family now. I had no family with me.' he sniffed, turning back round to face her.
'Yes, but my mother's lying in the Royal London with terminal cancer. She was ill when my mission began in February, but she's in a coma now.' she announced mournfully.
'Oh.' breathed Steve sympathetically 'The Royal London. Isn't that an NHS hospital?'
'Yes, I'm afraid it is.' she admitted.
Steve gave her a look of curiosity.
'She didn't tell me she had an unpaid gas bill. Had I known, I would have paid it and ensured she was placed in private care.'
Steve ceased his weeping.
The Agent glanced at him.
'Perhaps I haven't been completely honest with you, Steven.'
'What ever gave you that impression?' said Steve sarcastically.
She drew a smile 'I'm referring to what I said in the boardroom about my childhood. My father wasn't all bad, but I secretly harboured a need to have a child of my own.'
'You have Rebecca...' Steve pointed out.
'Yes, but I mean a child which I gave birth to myself!' she exclaimed.
Steve brow relaxed as he listened.
'So you see, I suppose what I'm saying is, that our time together, though it was under false pretences, did mean something to me.' she admitted.

'How do you mean?' he asked.

She cursed to herself.

'I hate it when people see this side to me.'

'That's something you and Thelma have in common.' said Steve wryly.

She continued 'I was pregnant with your child.'

'Yes, "was" being the operative word.' shouted Steve.

'I also lost it through miscarriage; that scenario, I can assure you, was not a fabrication.' she announced delicately.

Steve frowned 'But those pills…'

'Pills?' she asked curiously.

'Don't you dare pretend that you don't know what I'm talking about.' he warned.

Her look of shock did not falter.

'You really don't have any idea what I'm talking about, do you?' he breathed.

Special Agent Fifteen shook her head frantically.

'When I was held in the cells I was shown a packet of tablets; pregnancy termination tablets.'

The Agent bowed her head.

'I had no idea they were going to use that against you. No, it was a bona fide miscarriage; no amount of acting could emulate that level of agony.'

'And when… or rather *were* you going to tell me?' he quizzed.

'Yes, of course. I was waiting for the right time.' she said, averting her eyes again.

'When was that going be, as they sentenced me to life in this place? You really are full of surprises, aren't you?' he snapped.

She peered at him through the smoke.

'Working for MI6 has brought me status and exhilaration; it offers me espionage missions in far away places and every day is new and exciting…'

Her face became troubled.

'But what it cannot offer me is a stable life and the opportunity to mother a large family; something I've dreamed of since I was a little girl.'

   Steve studied her face. She revealed a sensitive side to herself, which he had not seen since Cliffbridge. He remained unsure whether all of what she had said was altogether true, but he was satisfied with the brief display of affection. The Agent had climbed back into the pit and was struggling to remove a dark stain from the base. He steeled himself:

'There was something I was about to tell you, or rather Thelma, the day I was taken away.' he mumbled.

She looked up at him with a wince.

'Sorry, what is it?'

Steve drew in a deep breath.

'I wandered back to the cemetery to pay my last respects to Mary and I made a shocking discovery.'
She persevered with her scrubbing without a response.
Steve's spirits sank at her apparent lack of care.
'Well, anyway, I discovered the grave belonging to my real mother, right beside Mary's.'
She ceased scrubbing and looked up at him open-mouthed. She stood up in the pit.
'Your own mother's grave is next to Mrs Hamilton's?' she asked aghast.
Steve was put off by her formal reference to Mary.
'Yes.' he replied softly.
'That must have come as something of a shock to you.'
Steve looked away in an effort to withhold his tears.
'I was longing to find you and tell you, only…'
'…Only you didn't think I was who I am.' she nodded.
'It just doesn't feel the same anymore…' he confessed.
The agent sighed 'You must think I'm a real piece of work.'
Steve smiled diplomatically.
'Perhaps I am.' she looked up again 'That was a touching eulogy which you read at the funeral. I researched Mrs Hamilton's lifestyle and her history thoroughly enough to get by, but it would seem that you truly knew her.'
Steve shrugged.
'It doesn't matter anymore.'
The agent picked up her brush and resumed cleaning.
'Would you like me to help you with that?' he asked.
She glared up at him.
'Yes, it's just a patch of stubborn grease. The Prime Minister wants it spic and span before inspection.'
'Don't they have cleaners for that?' he asked as he lifted himself in.
'Of course, but the Prime Minister wanted me to see to it that they are up to standard.'
Steve picked up a cloth and began scrubbing the other side of the greasy patch. It spelled rancid, like the tomb of a newly discovered mummy.
'How do these contraptions work exactly?' he asked as he scrubbed away.
The agent stopped and surveyed the contraption.
'Well, it's quite simple really. The convict would lay face up, while one of the wardens locked the top.'
'Then what?' asked Steve naively.
The Agent looked at him with unease.
'Well that's it. The convict will either die through asphyxiation or thirst. The encasement effectively becomes the grave in which the prisoner remains.'

'So why are they all open?'
'Like I said, they're largely considered an inhumane method of capital punishment and they're no longer used.' she replied.
'What's your opinion?' he asked her.
She peered all around the pit for a while.
'I suppose it must be a rather nasty way to go, but no method of execution is pleasant.' she said matter-of-factly.
She picked up on his sense of awe.
'Would you like to have a go at seeing what it might be like?'
'I'm sorry?'
She gave him a friendly smile.
'I think I know you well enough to tell when you want to try something out.'
'No, it's ok thanks.' he replied, shocked.
'Alright, then how about I lay down in here and you cover me over? I'll then tell you what it feels like.' she suggested.
She got into a lying position.
'Okay, you get out and cover me over.' she instructed.
Steve glared at her with bewilderment.
'It's alright, just do it.' she assured him.
He lifted himself out and peered down.
'Are you quite sure?' he asked.
'Quite sure.' she confirmed.
He reluctantly lifted one door over; it was heavy and required both hands. He paused again.
'I'm about to pull over the other door. Are you certain you want to go ahead?'
'Yes, but be quick!' she called up with an echo.'
Steve quickly lifted the other door over, sealing the pit shut. A muffled voice came from inside. He pulled at one of the doors, but was unable to manoeuvre it because of his tired arms. The mumble was repeated, this time sounding more desperate. Steve heaved at the handle, working through the tearing pain in his left arm. After a few more heaves, he pulled it clear.
'I'm sorry; I had trouble releasing the doors. Are you alright?' he called down anxiously.
'Yes, I'm fine. I was just trying to tell you that there's an easier way of opening the doors.'
'Oh?' he asked, searching the doors.
'Yes, there's a little button on the outer-side of the left door.'
Steve found the tiny red button and looked sheepish.
'I beg your pardon, I should have said. It's actually surprisingly warm in here.' she smiled.

Steve rubbed his arms to fend of the chill. He scratched his greasy head and thought for a moment.
'Do you think I might have a go?' he asked carefully.
The Agent got to her feet.
'Well of course...if you're quite sure.' she agreed, looking surprised.
She outstretched her right hand for Steve to pull her out. Once she was out, she joined Rebecca at the edge. She gave him a smile of encouragement and he turned to lower himself in. The small wet patch where they had removed the grease had already dried in the humidity. He took a deep breath and lied down and looked up at Special Agent Fifteen.
'That's it Steven, just lie still and soak up the atmosphere.'
She gave him a reassuring smile.
'Are you ready?'
'Yes, but please be quick. I'll shout twice when I'm ready to come out.' he called.
The Agent nodded and pressed the button. Steve braced himself as the doors slowly came over, gradually blocking out the light until he was in total darkness. He could see nothing, not even his hand as he held it in front of him. He had to rely on his other four senses to guide him to an insight into the final hours of a condemned man.

The most vivid sense was his hearing. The sound from the water pipes was now a rushing torrent of water. The fumes from the bleach beneath him were engulfing him by the second, while the comfortable warmth was becoming stifling heat. He challenged himself to lay there for as long as he could stand it. He was able to suppress the vomit-inducing stench of the bleach by holding his nose. He was able to withstand the cumbersome heat by blowing cool air onto his hands as they covered his nose. It was the intensifying sound of the water as it rushed through the system that he could not control. He was able to cover his left ear with his free hand, but that made the sound all the more poignant. Scenes of his childhood came flooding back.
'I'm ready! I'm ready!' he called.
No response came from above.
'Hey!' he shouted 'I'm ready to be let out!'
Steve grew agitated when he could hear nothing above the rushing water.
'Let me out! Let me out!' he wailed.
Gradually, a crack of light appeared above, slowly becoming wider. Steve got to his feet and began hyperventilating as the cool air entered the chamber. When at last there was enough space to climb out, he did so in earnest.
'Where were you? I almost suffocated in there!' he gasped.
'You were in there fifteen seconds.' declared The Agent.
He sat there in disbelief, trying to get his breath back.

'Fifteen seconds?' he wheezed.

'Yes, you're not claustrophobic, are you?' she asked anxiously.

He nodded frantically.

'Then why didn't you say so? I would never have allowed you in!' she protested.

'I needed to do that.' he insisted, his breathing returning to normal 'I needed to face my fear.'

The Agent looked at him dumbfounded.

'Look you had better get ready for the hearing; you haven't got long.'

'Okay.' he nodded with a small smile.

She placed an unsteady hand on his shoulder.

'You have every reason to be optimistic about this afternoon's outcome.' she said, doing her best to sound warm.

'What makes you say that?' asked Steve, sounding unconvinced.

'There's a lot of added value which they are going to have to consider carefully. I have witnessed people being granted extradition on lesser charges.' she explained.

'I'm sure.' he nodded with a troubled expression.

'What do you think they're going to say in today's session?' he asked, turning to her.

She pulled a tight smile.

'Do you know what? I believe that having decided to take the plunge by stating your case boldly, they will have realised your hidden depths and you will escape this place.'

'Do you really think so?' he asked with a sanguine smile.

'It's as likely.' she nodded 'Go and wait by the entrance and I'll call for the wardens.'

TWENTY

Friday, 6th March 2048. Somewhere in Southern Spain. 1300 Hrs.

The afternoon brought with it hazy sunshine, following the downpour that morning; this filled Steve with a sense of ease, together with Special Agent Fifteen's encouraging words. It was not like him to be early, but today was unlike any other and he had spent the time since The Crypt rehearsing his confidence and strengthening his resolve. He was given a smarter looking suit to wear for the hearing; this one was far more flattering than any other he had worn, for it seemed tailor-made to divert attention away from his lanky frame. The door to the conference room stood ajar and he could hear the Prime Minister muttering to Fontaine, although Steve could not strain his ears hard enough to hear the muffled words. The Prime Minister met him at the door:

'Ah Steven, you are perfectly on time. Please come inside and we'll get straight down to business.'

Steve could glean from the Prime Minister's upbeat tone that his difficult job was almost at an end and this complex case was about to be closed. Steve walked inside where he noticed the tables and chairs had been rearranged with a single table facing another, behind which the rest were organised in rows of three. The Prime Minister sat himself down at the single table at the front of the room, while Steve was led to the table facing it. The rest of the committee found their places and settled down for the hearing.

Special Agent Fifteen sat immediately behind him, preventing him to read her face of any emotion. He felt like a naughty schoolboy who had been summoned to the front of the class; his heart quickened as he awaited direction from the Prime Minister.

'Welcome back Steven.' smiled the Prime Minister warmly.

'Thank you, sir.' Steve responded confidently.

'As I'm sure you can appreciate, we have all been working into the night, weighing up your version of events against those of our esteemed colleague, Special Agent Fifteen.'

'Yes.' nodded Steve.

The Prime Minister took a sip of water.

'After much discussion and drawing on lots of evidence, we have reached a unanimous verdict pertaining to your future; more on that a little later. How would you describe the proceedings thus far? That is, would you say that given the circumstances, you have had a fair opportunity to put forward your case?'

'Under the unusual circumstances, I would say so, yes.' agreed Steve.

The Prime Minister peered at him above his glasses.

'I'm detecting a rather optimistic vibe from you, Steven. Would I be correct in that assumption?'

'I'm keeping an open mind at this stage.' declared Steve, placing his hands on the table.

'I see; very wise.' smiled the Prime Minister.

He looked past Steve and at Special Agent Fifteen.

'Would you like to add anything in summary to the process?'

Steve twisted his neck slightly to the left.

'My involvement in the hearing has been limited, as you are aware. However, I have maintained a close eye on Mr Morrissey over the past month or so and overall I would say that he has displayed a level of commitment to the task and loyalty to the government that falls far below the expected standard. He has feathered his own nest by using the mission as an opportunity to ingratiate himself with Neil Stubbs, our nemesis. We have heard of the killings and deaths which have been as a result of Mr Morrissey's lack of judgement.'

She broke off to take a sip of water.

'That said, there are more pieces of evidence which I believe are pertinent to the case. That is, you have not discussed Mr Morrissey's positive attributes that include his hard work in achieving all of the mission objectives. He accepted a lofty mission without any prior training. He also tracked down Thelma Harrison; he located the manuscript and he found Neil Stubbs. I would say that none of the aforementioned should go unnoticed.'

The Prime Minister nodded.

'Duly noted, although of course you're speaking off the record now.'

'Yes, of course.' she agreed.

'Is there any member of the JIC who would like to comment on the events leading up to the inquiry?' asked the Prime Minister.

Fontaine, who was sitting on the far right and in Steve's peripheral vision, got up and spoke:

'I would just like to say that I feel that Mr Morrissey has made a substantial number of fatal errors and these will undoubtedly pass without retribution. However, it is also fair to say that Mr Morrissey, I'm sure, was acting in a way that only a novice would and therefore perhaps should be judged in accordingly.'

The Prime Minister smiled in appreciation.

'Right, well that leaves me to sum up the proceedings, before I can reveal the outcome.'

He peered down at his notes and back at Steve.

'Taking everything into consideration, I would conclude that the basis for the mission was sound, in that we had reason to suspect that your loyalty to the nation fell short of the minimum level of commitment expected, notwithstanding the fact that we entrusted you to undertake a challenging mission to assist in the downfall of an illegal municipality. In short, you were a capable, but a faithless member of Westminster. That leads me to your charges. Mr Morrissey, please stand.'

Steve rose clumsily, while the Prime Minister placed his glasses on to read his notes.

'Mr Morrissey, the committee and I have ruled that for the death of Mr Wilson, you are found not guilty of murder, but on the count of manslaughter; guilty. For your part in perverting the course of justice, leading to the deaths of Mr and Mrs O'Hara, the committee and I have found you guilty. For the drain on Britain's National Health Service, leading to the deaths of a nominal number of sick patients, the committee and I find you guilty on the count of serial manslaughter.'

Steve's legs collapsed beneath him, falling onto his chair. He turned to face Special Agent Fifteen and gazed at her helplessly through his teary eyes; she sat emotionless. The Prime Minister removed his glasses and peered at him.

'Mr Morrissey, will you please be upstanding!'

Steve clenched the arms of his chair and pulled himself up.

'Therefore, given the value-added accounts of your character and the difficulties which faced you, I am going to issue you with a jail sentence, suspended for eighteen years.'

Steve could hardly believe his ears.

'Did you say *suspended?*'

'Yes, Steven. That would mean you are free to leave this place and return to Britain as a free man.' smiled the Prime Minister, warmly.

Steve cupped his mouth, aghast.

'You mean I can leave today?'

'Yes, if it wasn't for the final charge of treason.' announced the Prime Minister solemnly.

Steve's smile slowly left his face.

'What?'

The Prime Minister peered down at his notes.

'The panel and I deliberated for many hours on the subject of your betrayal of the mission, owing to your co-operation with Mr Stubbs. This compromised not only the mission's success, but the future of our country. We concluded that you did not display due diligence in ensuring the mission was a success and left the future of our economy open to failure.'

Steve fell onto his chair. The Prime Minister continued:

'On the charge of treason, the panel and I have therefore found you guilty.'

He looked down at Steve.

'This means you are not at liberty to return to the United Kingdom neither as a free man, nor a detainee.'
'I don't understand.' said Steve.
The Prime Minister removed his glasses slowly.
'You are to remain here. You will shortly leave this room and be taken down to The Crypt and be secured within one of the encasement tombs.'
Steve staggered to his feet.
'Hang on; there is clearly some sort of mistake. Special Agent Fifteen told me that those morbid things aren't used anymore, because they are considered inhumane!'
He turned to face The Agent.
'Come on, tell him! Tell him what you told me earlier!'
Special Agent Fifteen shrugged helplessly.
'Tell him!' he demanded.
'I'm sorry.' she whispered.
The Prime Minister continued 'Special Agent Fifteen is correct when she says that they are now considered inhumane. However, they are reserved for people who should never see the light of day again; for people who are a large threat to the dominant ideology of Great Britain; for evil, underhanded criminals and traitors.'
'This is insane!' Steve hurled 'This is nothing more than an illegitimate kangaroo court with no place in the judicial system! I am not a criminal; I am a victim!'
'Take him down.' instructed the Prime Minister.
The two wardens swooped in and took an arm each.
'Let go of me!' shouted Steve, resisting their hold.
'Please! I beg you sir, please reconsider your verdict!' Steve pleaded.
He became more measured as he smiled at the Prime Minister in desperation.
'I beg of you, sir, please don't allow me to face such a horrific fate. I am not that much of a threat to you, I promise you!'
'I said take him down!' shouted the Prime Minister, throwing his wooden hammer at one of the wardens.

***

Soon after, Steve was brought face-to-face with his lifelong nightmare. He had many nightmares of being buried alive during his life; it was as if the government had got inside his mind and had taken total control. His five senses were on high alert as he soaked up his bleak surroundings. The freezing cold, musty air slapped his cheeks as if chastising him further, while the deafening sound of the water pipes tore at his eardrums like a screaming toddler. It was the sight beneath him, however, which was most profound. The very pit he had helped to clean earlier that day was the one in which he was about to meet his end. He shuddered as the thought crossed his mind that perhaps Special Agent Fifteen was toying with his emotions while knowing that he would be reunited with the chlorine-smelling tomb. He stood with a warden clutching each arm, while Special Agent Fifteen stood with Rebecca at the opposite side. Rebecca wore a perplexed expression, clutching to her stuffed toy. Special Agent Fifteen held her hand, staring across as Steve mournfully; her eyes appeared like those of a rabbit caught in a car's headlights-wide and urgent. As Steve gazed at them, her face became more intense and desperate.

Steve twisted his neck to face the two wardens.

'Do you think you could ask everyone to leave except Special Agent Fifteen and her daughter? I should like to say goodbye to them properly.'

The warden on Steve's right nodded.

'Under the circumstances, I don't see why not.' he turned to look across at the committee behind him 'Everyone apart from Special Agent Fifteen and her daughter are to leave now.' he turned to his colleague 'Could you take them back up?' With a nod, the second warden walked around the pit and led the way out of the room.

When all but the three of them and the remaining warden were left in the room, Special Agent Fifteen looked over at the warden.

'You must leave us as well.' she said.

With that, the soldier bowed and left them alone.

'You sure have a lot of clout around here, don't you?' said Steve with a despondent titter.

'Yes, well I couldn't let you go without you saying goodbye to Rebecca' she smiled.

Steve gave her a forced smile. He looked at Rebecca and gave her a more genuine smile and patted her gently on the head. He stooped down to her height and held her toy bear.

'Can I hold Uncle Steve?' he asked with a smile.

Rebecca nodded.

'I think he's got something he'd like to say to you, listen...'

He held the bear's mouth against her left ear, which brought a smile to her face.

He put on a lisp and a squeaky voice, moving the toy's head up and down as he spoke. 'You have to promise Uncle Steve that you're going to look after mummy.'

His voice returned to normal as broke.

'Uncle Steve wants you to be a good girl for mummy.'

He handed back the bear and pointed up to the ceiling.

'I'm going to live in heaven and meet God and all the angels!' he said, trying to sound excited.

He got to his feet and turned to Special Agent Fifteen.

'We had some good times together, didn't we?' he asked tentatively.

She said nothing and just smiled.

'Yes, well, of course you had a mission to see through…as did I.' he murmured.

She gave him a concerned look.

'Are you scared?'

Steve paused as the smile left his face.

'Scared?' he asked.

The question had for the first time made him consider how he should be feeling; he had not yet been made to do so. He wanted to break down in tears; to be held by her and told that he had just awoken from a long, bad dream and that everything was going to be alright. However, he caught sight of Rebecca's smile that had remained since talking to her through her teddy bear and decided that he did not want to be remembered by her as a nervous wreck.

'Scared? No…Well…Perhaps a bit. But I dare say they've made some allowances for…' he peered down into the hole '…well, you know.' he looked at her again 'If I'm feeling any sort of emotion right now, it's anger, bewilderment and a sense of injustice!' he exclaimed, stamping his foot. 'When I think of how many others have fallen victim to this so-called government's actions. To give but one example, poor little Rebecca's mother! She will grow up never knowing her real mother's love!'

His face softened as the little girl's face fell.

'Just ensure that you give this child all the love and stability she deserves.'

'You can be certain of that.' she smiled, reaching for his cuffed hands. 'Is there anything else you'd like to talk about?'

'No…I don't think so.' he replied, uncertain.

His face unfolded suddenly.

'Wait a minute. There is something. Were you aware all along that this would be my fate? Did you ask me here this morning just so that I might be unnerved before the hearing?'

She looked him in the eye.

'No.'

Steve relaxed slightly 'Ah.'

Suddenly, Rebecca held up the teddy bear to Steve.

'Take Uncle Steve with you to heaven.' she smiled.

Steve stooped down to take the bear.

'Th-thank you sweetheart.' he stammered, forcing back the tears.

'Baby Jesus look after you!' she said with a smile.

'Yes…I'm sure he will.' he replied, clutching the bear.

Special Agent Fifteen gave him a prolonged smile, before giving him a tight hug. Steve could feel his legs being squeezed as Rebecca hugged them tightly.

'You are the bravest man I have met in all my years as an agent.' she whispered.

She gave him another tight squeeze and asked:

'Shall I ask the warden to come in now?'

Steve nodded with closed eyes.

She walked over to the door and nodded to the warden, who marched back inside; this time holding a rifle. She turned back to Steve.

'I'm going to go now Steve-it's not really something a young child should see. You understand, don't you?'

'Of course I do.' he said, clearing a tear from his cheek with his left shoulder 'Just make sure you don't let her forget about me.'

With a nod and a smile, she left the room with Rebecca.

The warden locked the door and walked over to where Steve stood gazing down at the hole.

'Are you ready?' asked the warden.

Steve did not answer him straight away, feeling a surge of adrenalin rush through his veins. He peered at the door to the room and then back at the warden as he considered making a break for it, how ever futile the attempt may prove. In a split second, the images from earlier that day when he was last confronted with the tomb flashed before him; the nauseating smell; the deafening sounds and the lack of light. Among this, he envisioned his escape and how far he would get. If he did manage to somehow leave the compound, he told himself that there would be little point in living a life without the woman he loved and being apart from the little girl he had come to think of as he daughter. He drew in a deep breath:

'I'm ready.' he nodded, trying to sound matter-of-fact.

The warden managed a softer expression.

'Some prisoners prefer to lay face down as the door closes. It doesn't make any difference of course, but I'm told it saves any panicking.'

Steve nodded.

'It's up to you how we do this, but it's best if you get in without any assistance and just lie down-as if getting into bed to go to sleep for the night.' the warden added with a reassuring smile.

'Could you remove the handcuffs? Only I need to lower myself in.' asked Steve with trepidation.

The warden obliged, placing his weapon on the floor. Steve's wrists immediately caught the cold draught. He sat down at the edge and lowered his legs into the pit. The cold air ran straight up his trouser cuffs and pinched at his shins, causing him to shudder.

'Awful draughty this time of the year.' smiled the warden.
Steve put his weight onto his two hands, which caught hold of the rope ladder that had been placed there and lowered himself in slowly. When he reached the bottom, he laid down on his side, clasping at Rebecca's teddy bear. The soldier came to the edge and called down:
'You alright? Make yourself comfortable.' he said with an apologetic chuckle.
'Feel free to say a few words…or to pray if that's what you're into.' he added.
Steve shook his head, gripping the bear tighter.
'The cover will come across quickly and once it's across that's it, okay?'
'Okay.' Steve confirmed nervously.

   The steel doors began to close slowly. He glared up at the ever-diminishing light and tried to fight off the rising panic within him. His fingers began to tap the steel base in an attempt to appease the growing potency of his senses. The pit became totally lightproof, leaving his ears wide open to the rushing water. His fingers sped up as the smell of the bleach hit his nostrils. Suddenly, he was unable to control his panic any longer and, coupled by the smell of the bleach, he retched until he was sick. He soon decided that the best way to spend his last moments was to pretend to be laying beside Special Agent Fifteen in their bed in Cliffbridge. It was difficult to imagine given the cold, steel base of the pit, but the teddy bear contained the scent of her perfume which brought fond memories of happier times together. Although it was bitterly cold, he took some comfort in remembering that he always slept best during the winter months. He heard the door to the room slam shut. Instead of trying to picture Special Agent Fifteen outside questioning the soldier on how things went; he imagined her warm, curvaceous
form huddled against him; her soft breath on his face; the gentle touch of her fingertips on his neck.

***

   Special Agent Fifteen sat with Rebecca inside the Prime Minister's suite, watching the news on the plasma screen:
"This is a Public Service News special report from Cliffbridge! News just in!' began the news anchor 'Steven Morrissey has been found dead in Richmond Park! This news has baffled officials and locals alike…"
The screen showed an aerial view of the park, before the camera panned in on the cordoned area which was full of forensic scientists and photographers.
 "…As you can see, officials are working closely with forensic teams and locals in trying to piece together what actually took place. Scotland Yard is due to hold a press conference tomorrow morning, which will be shown

right here on PSN. However, early indications show that this is an act of suicide. Mr Morrissey of Belgravia had spoken out strongly against the British reoccupation of Basra and had built up a large degree of animosity between himself and his superiors in Whitehall. Mr Morrissey appeared before the Home Office select committee last month over claims that he was cooperating with combatants in the region. Growing speculation followed surrounding his reclusion from public appearances and faltering mental health..."

The Prime Minister entered the room and paced his glasses on slowly to view the screen.

'Did everything go okay with our wonder boy?' he asked.

Special Agent Fifteen placed Rebecca onto the carpet.

'If you're asking me whether Mr Morrissey felt as free from pain as he should have been, then the answer is…I hope so.' she replied, giving him a frosty reception.

The Prime Minister removed his glasses and glanced in her direction.

'Is there something I should know about the two of you?' he asked curiously.

Special Agent Fifteen glanced at Rebecca and then at the Prime Minister.

'All you need to know is that Steve was a good man with good intentions. The only entity that I shall hold dearly in my heart, aside from my daughter, is my loyalty.'

ACKNOWLEDGEMENTS

I would like to thank the following and those too many to mention, for their love, support and strength without which such an intense novel could never have been possible. I hope that this book goes some way to rewarding you and that you find it a thought provoking and enjoyable read.

Sue for her strength and undying love.
Daniel and Jamie for their love and belief.
Mum for her tireless editing, support and love.
Robin for his technical prowess.
Martin for his faith in me and the novel.
Robert for his interest and moral support.
Dad for his wisdom and car rides.